# NOT AS IT SEEMS

## A GOTHIC ANTHOLOGY

# &You Anthologies

*Another Chance to Get It Right: A New Year's Eve Anthology*

*As the Snow Drifts: A Cozy Winter Anthology*

*Craving You: A Spicy Valentine's Day Anthology*

*Recipes for Romance: A Sweet Valentine's Day Anthology*

*Just One . . .: A Summer Romance Anthology*

*Not As It Seems: A Gothic Anthology*

# Not As It Seems

## A Gothic Anthology

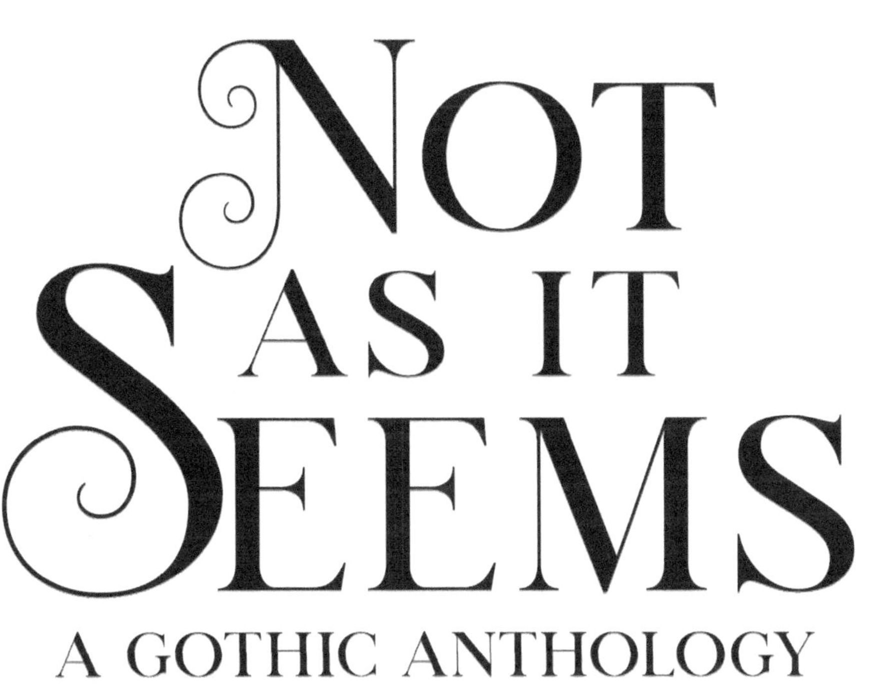

Edited & Arranged by
Courtney Umphress

And You Press
an imprint of Nicole Frail Books, LLC
www.andyoupress.com

# Contents

When Louise, a forensic pathologist, realizes the same dead body keeps reappearing in her morgue, she starts to question if she's losing her mind or if something more sinister is taking place. She is driven to desperate measures in her search for the truth.



In Victorian London, a woman settles into a new home with her family, looking for a fresh start. But when she starts planning her young son's birthday party, strange events occur, and she finds that the past will not be so easily buried.



A journalist visits a tech mogul's oceanfront mansion under the guise of interviewing him while secretly investigating his sister Marin's disappearance. Her exploration of the property, and all she finds along the way, leaves her questioning whether Marin's death was a tragic accident, or a murder.



A vampire awakens into a city where prosperous glass towers shadow the poverty that rules the streets. Used to terrorizing those streets, he is forced to face a supernatural presence that is even more dangerous than he is.



A young man catches sight of a beautiful young woman watching him from a cottage by the woods. Convinced the woman wishes to meet with him, he enters, only to be haunted by the mistakes of his past.

# Introduction

## Courtney Umphress, Editor

GOTHIC FICTION EVOKES A MOOD no other literary genre can accomplish. Its shadowy, foreboding worlds cultivate a sense of unease and tension while drawing readers in with an irresistible blend of mystery and intrigue. The authors in this anthology draw from that tradition, tapping into our fascination with the darker facets of life. The characters within invite you into gothic worlds that will play with your emotions and challenge your perception of reality.

Merging the gothic aesthetic with the thriller, fantasy, and horror genres, this collection takes you to different but equally chilling locations, from seaside manors to grand homes to even isolated neighborhoods. You'll wander through graveyards and explore houses that seem to watch your every move. You'll hear the faint ringing of a bell you can't see and feel the oppressive heat of a land you just want to escape. You'll travel through past lives and try to solve long-forgotten murders. You'll question why people are suddenly dying with their chests sunken in and why all the creatures in a nearby swamp are horrifically disfigured. Most importantly, you'll do this all knowing that everything is *not as it seems*.

Though these stories incorporate the classic elements of gothic literature, what distinguishes them is a narrator who might lead you astray. Maybe you're being deliberately deceived, or perhaps a person cannot truly know everything about themselves and the world they live in. Regardless of what the narrator wants you to believe, some things can't be denied: The mind can be deceptive, revenge is a powerful motivator, and family secrets can't always stay buried.

As you read this collection, we hope your journey into the dark and dreary world of gothic fiction leaves a lasting impression.

# The Owl and the Shrew

# The Owl and the Shrew

## Sarah Bjork



### Part One: The Hollow

The windows of Bellamare Hollow still watched like frowning eyes. That was what Margot used to say when they were little, convinced the great manor by the sea was alive. Breathing, watching. Knowing their secrets, their dreams.

Now, even as an adult, Nell Lancaster felt the same breathless prickling as she followed the cracked steps toward the weatherworn stone facade. It felt anything but enchanting to Nell. Not now, not ever. It stood as it always had, a postcard of the past.

Too big to feel cozy.

Too cold to feel warm.

Tendrils of ivy clung to the portico, coiled around the columns like leafy snakes. The brisk sea breeze curled through the trees, briny and sharp, carrying the scent of damp stone and salt. Goosebumps climbed up her arms, and she pulled her sweater tighter around her shoulders, trying to find warmth within its thin fabric.

Nell tried to think of why she'd let so much time pass between her and this grand house. It all seemed so illogical now. And as she stood beneath it, the weight of those lost years felt profound. Her regret, unendurable. Tess Lancaster—her grandmother, her compass, the woman who had raised her and Margot after the accident—was gone. And now, the house waited in silence, holding in all the words that would go unspoken.

Nell shook off the tightness clenching her limbs, drank in a deep breath, and grasped the doorknob. The ornately carved door groaned as she pushed it open, its hinges tinged with coarse sea rust. As the door latched into place behind her, the present seemed to melt away. Inside was still and strange, almost expectant, like stepping between pages of an old story where she was the main character, and she'd only just arrived.

The house was frightfully cold and teeming with dust and cobwebs. It felt familiar, like home, but also different somehow. Lonelier. Vacant of life, like an empty seashell after the tide had gone out. It reminded her of *Jane Eyre*, her favorite novel, when Jane described Thornfield Hall as "a shell, a tomb, a sepulcher."

Had Bellamare Hollow suffered the same fate?

Nell's boots clapped against the weathered wooden floorboards of the foyer, echoing against the vaulted ceiling and down the hollow corridors. A crack of amber sunlight stretched through the windows, illuminating the floating dust motes like tiny fireflies and painting the mahogany staircase in a blood-warm bronze.

The parlor lay dimly on her left, with two slouching armchairs in front of the cold, stone hearth. Across the hall, through a stone archway, her grandmother's study waited in stillness, suspended in time. A tower of loose papers leaned precariously on the edge of the writing desk as though the woman who once sat there might return at any moment.

Above the desk hung a framed cover of *The Owl and the Shrew*. It was faded now, the colors dulled by time. Her grandmother's first poetry book for children, written for and inspired by Nell and Margot. It marked the beginning of her grandmother's long career as a children's author, the thing that introduced her words to the world.

But she had always belonged to her granddaughters first.

Nell caressed the dust-covered glass, her lips curving into a soft, faraway smile. She could still see her so vividly—her grandmother, in a thick cardigan no matter what time of year it was, hair pinned back neatly, wearing a tint of rose lipstick and watching from the shadows of the veranda as Nell and Margot played beneath the crooked trees. She'd sit quietly, sipping tea and absorbing the nuances of their personalities, capturing their spirits and stitching them into stories, the words strange, lyrical, breathing with their essence.

Nell wrapped her arms around herself and squeezed her eyes shut. She missed her so much that it nearly knocked the breath out of her.

"Her pride and joy," a voice murmured behind her, soft and close. "After us, of course."

Nell spun, her breath hitching. But even before her vision adjusted, she knew. *Margot.* A laugh escaped her as relief swelled. She wrapped her arms around her sister. Margot's sea-green eyes still gleamed with the buoyant glow of a dreamer, her caramel hair with fringed bangs tied back in the same messy bun she'd worn through her late teens and early twenties.

"I haven't even taken my shoes off and I'm already halfway to cardiac arrest," Nell said with a laugh, the tension easing from her shoulders. "You and your dramatic entrances."

"Didn't mean to scare you . . . or *did* I?" Margot grinned. Her voice was still airy, delicate as lace. "I'm glad you're here, Nell. I missed you."

"Me too," Nell said, her smile faltering. "I'm sorry I didn't make it sooner." The words stung, and a tight ache throbbed in the void in her chest meticulously carved away by guilt and regret.

"You're here now, and that matters," Margot said, looping her arm through Nell's. "Now let's get you settled in."

With flutes of Prosecco in hand, the sisters lingered in the kitchen, stories spilling out like music, the years between them slipping quietly away. Eventually, Margot disappeared into her room—a ground-floor suite tucked in the back corner of Bellamare, where the ancient forest met the sea. It sat at the cusp of both worlds, nestled in the very heart of the Hollow.

Nell's childhood room was far more solitary, more suited to her need for quiet. Perched high above the manor in the old tower, it rose above the cliffs and sea, where the ocean swelled below and the sky stretched endlessly above. The horizon, just the tip of her thoughts, her wonderings. She felt at peace there, more so than anywhere else on the grounds.

As she ascended the grand staircase, her fingertips traced the banister's curve—smoothed by generations of hands that came before. The sensation of it was carved into the folds of her memory. The wood creaked beneath her boots in all the familiar places. For a moment, she felt like a child again.

☽ 4 ☾

Then, a draft floated past her, as if someone had just passed by. Nell's brows furrowed as the chill crept across her skin. The house had always been drafty. She wrapped her sweater more snugly around her shoulders and pressed on.

The third floor had a single long hallway with narrow corridors branching like veins. She turned right, then left—the path, second nature. She finally reached the archway to the stairwell that spiraled loosely up to her old tower room. A strange sensation lingered there, something hollow and somber, and she felt her throat tighten.

Then, somewhere beyond the roofline of the manor, the sun slipped behind a mass of gray clouds, casting the hall and stairwell in a shroud of gloom. A gloom deeper and darker than she remembered. The air shifted, followed by a feeling in the pit of her stomach, like an elevator dropping. Her mouth went dry, and a thrum of adrenaline pulsed through her nerves. A feeling of wrongness. An unmistakable urge to scream, to run.

Nell bristled. It was one thing to be tired, but something else entirely to feel this silly about a shadowy stairwell. She swallowed down the inexplicable feelings like a rigid pill. This had been her sanctuary. Her perch. Her corner of the sky. So, she straightened her spine and traversed the curl of the stairs up to her room.

At the top, the tower door hung slightly ajar, spilling a band of dim, gray light across the landing. She took a step forward—

And the door slammed shut, hard and fast, right in her face.

# Part Two: Whispers in the Gloom

Nell froze, her breath quaking against the thick, wooden door that stood mere centimeters from her face. The echo of the impact rang down the stairwell and reverberated through her bones. She blinked hard, swallowed, and then mentally filed the nearly nose-breaking door slam into a neat little box labeled: *Drafts . . . Probably.*

She rolled her shoulders back, stretched her neck to the right and left, and then turned the doorknob. The tower room was exactly as she remembered— remnants of her younger self, fully preserved and intact. Gray light filtered through the salt-fogged windowpanes. The air smelled faintly of old books, dust, something musty and unpleasant, and a faint hint of something herbal and spicy, like rosemary or cinnamon.

To the right, the armoire loomed, quiet and tall. It held the clothes of her youth, timeless and understated. On the left, her four-poster bed stood draped in pale linens. She had always preferred neutral tones over color. The cheerful chaos was too loud, too boisterous. She preferred the ones that whispered—dusty grays, sea-worn whites, and blacks deep enough to drown in.

The velvet cushions of the window bench in the alcove were still curled in their corner, worn soft by quiet moments of serenity and reflection. Nell's Corner, her grandmother used to call it. A place where she'd spent hours curled with a book or sketchpad, drawing the sea, the cliffs, and the ever-shifting horizon through the tall, three-paneled windows.

As she regarded the space that had once meant so much to her, something stood out that didn't belong. A glint of pink and gold on the windowsill. Still half-filled with tea.

Her grandmother's porcelain teacup.

Nell frowned. It was an odd thing to be sitting so casually in her room.

She reached for the cup and lifted it gently. Still warm. A faint mark of lipstick curved along the rim—the same soft rose color her grandmother used to wear.

The hair on the nape of Nell's neck prickled. Her eyes flashed back to the ledge where it had rested. Perhaps she'd missed something. Something that might explain its presence there.

Because it certainly wasn't her dead grandmother leaving her things about.

A layer of dust coated everything around where the cup sat. Everything except the circle it left behind. A perfect little hollow, a shape so impossibly precise it felt like a lie.

Grief rose in her throat, heavy and unmoving. Her grandmother's presence would haunt her; she knew that much. But not in the way of dark shadows and cold drafts. No, it would live in the mundane: in every piece of unopened mail, every folded cardigan, every carefully placed teacup.

These were the ghosts that lingered.

She lifted her chin and pressed her mouth into something straighter. This was something Margot had left. That was all. It was the only possible explanation. She turned toward the door, the teacup cradled carefully in her hands.

Then she heard it.

Not so much a sound as a sensation, like breath brushing against the inside of her ear, cold and fragile. A voice, or perhaps two, murmuring somewhere unseen. Words she couldn't quite reach, as if spoken into water. Or time.

She went still, scarcely breathing. For a moment, the only sensation that existed inside her was fear. Stiff and irrational, it swelled inside her like something poisonous and festering.

The house was empty. She was certain of that. And yet, from just beyond the silence, a whisper rose, hushed and breath-thin:

*"Are you here?"*

The cup quivered in Nell's hand, the porcelain chiming like pebbles skittering across a frozen pond. The voice was familiar in a strange sort of way, like something that existed on the periphery of memory. Something too close to be imagined, yet too distant to be tangible.

She turned her head slowly, her gaze landing on the tall windows in the alcove. Its panes, blurred with sea mist, glistened. Then, something moved in the glass. A flash of shadow, the suggestion of an outline moving past the edge of vision.

A reflection of someone moving right behind where she stood.

A flutter of panic stirred beneath her ribs. She spun, heart hammering, scanning the space where the presence would have been.

It was empty.

"Margot?" she called, her voice faltering against the sinking feeling that Margot was not the presence she felt.

Silence surrounded her.

Not silence in the way of absence, but the pinprick stillness of something waiting.

Nell retreated slowly back down the stairs, each step stiff with unease, her mind struggling to rationalize what she'd heard. Seen. *Felt.*

Her boots landed on the crimson rug of the third floor, and a shaky exhale escaped her lips. But the moment brought no reprieve. Whispered hums slipped through the hallway from behind her, ahead of her, all around her.

Her entire body stilled.

Then, in the mirrors lining the wall, something flitted across the glass: a shadow, a smear of gloom floating from frame to frame, vanishing at the bend in the hall.

Nell hesitated, barely a breath of thought. She should have turned away. Told herself it was a trick of the light. But this felt different—important, somehow, like a thread tugging tight beneath her skin. She set the teacup on a side table and hurried after the shadow into the dusky corridor.

She turned, then turned again, finding herself deeper in the unused wings of the manor. The air grew stiller, the forgotten halls narrowing like a funnel. Still, something thrummed inside her, a frantic compulsion pressing her forward.

A wisp of darkness danced across the lone mirror at the end of the last corridor, then vanished to the right. When she reached the corner, Nell stopped cold. There was no hallway—just a wall. A wall hung with a large, framed painting.

*The Owl and Shrew.*

She didn't remember this one. It was different. Pale, almost sickly, as if the colors had been drained away. On one side, the Owl perched on a spindly branch, eyes fixed on the viewer, its inky feathers dissolving into the bruised gray sky. Opposite, the Shrew stood frozen, mid-step, at the edge of a stone bridge, its center collapsed into a chasm of fog and emptiness. Behind them, the woods split—one side sharp and jagged, the other softened by haze. The only color that bloomed from the canvas was the white petals of hemlock curling along the bottom edge.

There was something forlorn in the Owl's expression, while the Shrew looked urgent—desperate.

A chill tingled against her neck. She paused, brow furrowed, her lip pulled tight between her teeth.

*No, that wasn't right.* The chill wasn't *high.*

It curled around her ankles, a whisper of air too cold for a sealed corridor.

She crouched low and drew in a sharp breath.

An edge. A nearly imperceptible sliver of space traced up the wall, across, and back down again. A rectangle, hidden behind the painting.

The air inside her lungs vanished.

A door.

# Part Three: Light and Gray

Nell's thoughts raced as she eased the painting from its mount and propped it gently against the wall. Behind it was a narrow latch, flush with the woodwork, almost invisible. She stared at it for a moment, then pressed it, barely aware she'd been holding her breath.

The door clicked open with a sound that felt strangely intimate. Dim light spilled into the room. Some part of her recognized the space before her mind could pull its name from the clutches of her memory.

The air felt different. Dense and hopeless.

Like grief.

In the room's center was an old hospital bed, its middle sunken from years of use. Dust coated the table and IV pole beside it. Wan, silvery light stole through the velvet curtains in waves, brushing the windows that watched the sea beyond. The scent in the room was faint but jarring—old lavender, antiseptic, something sour beneath it.

Photographs lined the shelves and walls. Her mother, mid-laugh, eyes vibrant. Her father, arm draped around her grandmother and mother, in the garden. Young Margot and Nell in matching sweaters, their hair pulled back into pigtails, their mother in a flowy spring dress between them. In another, their grandmother cradling their mother as a child, wrapped in smiles and summer sun.

Every wall held a piece of *her*. A swell of sorrow rose through her, leaving her knees hollow and unsteady. This was her mother's room. The place where she had lived—if you could call it that—after the accident.

Something inside Nell buckled. There were parts of her past she couldn't quite grasp, stretches of time blurred like a photograph left out in the rain.

But maybe that was what grief did. It turned solid things into smoke.

And now, the memories came rushing in, sudden and unrelenting.

The fall.

The coma.

The grief that followed, seeping not just into her blood, but into the bones of the house itself. It lived here. Breathed here.

It never left.

Nell traced her fingers across the antique armchair that sat next to the bed. She could see herself, smaller then, sitting in that chair with a crayon-smudged drawing or a well-loved picture book in hand. Reading to the still form beneath the blankets. Hoping her voice could reach somewhere deep inside.

Her grandmother had always said that even though her mother could no longer speak or move, her heart still heard them. That she still loved them, in the only way she could. That stories and dreams could still find her, even in the dark.

Hot tears pricked behind Nell's eyes as guilt tore through her. How could she have buried this room so deeply?

She sat heavily on the bed and let the grief spill free. When the storm inside her ebbed, she wiped her cheeks with her palms and forced herself to stand. She'd let herself have this release, but it was time to get back to reality. Margot was going to send a search party if she didn't reappear soon.

Nell turned back toward the door, then stopped, her body going rigid, the air around her suddenly too thick, too still.

The feeling rose in her throat, ghostly and dry, like ash. But this wasn't grief. This was something else. Something nearer. Watching.

Her gaze drifted toward the mirror opposite the bed. She gasped.

Her grandmother's face stared back at her, sunken and pale, dull eyes boring into hers with a ferocity as sharp as ice.

She staggered back, heart hammering, stumbling into the chair. She hit the floor hard, elbows jarring, head spinning with sudden vertigo.

*What the hell?*

Nell rubbed her elbows, scowling hard enough it hurt. But the shock wore thin, and her gaze snapped back toward the mirror, to the eyes that had held hers, steady and unblinking.

It was empty.

A clammy chill gripped Nell's body, and she trembled. Her grandmother had been there—but she hadn't. Her face tangible, yet a terrible delusion.

Nell swallowed against the lump rising in her throat. *I'm turning into Poe*, she thought. First, the whispers. Now, visions.

Before long, she'd be raving in verses of madness.

Pulling herself up from the floor, Nell reached instinctively for the side table—and halted. Something jutted from the half-open drawer, barely visible. She frowned. She was sure the drawer hadn't been open moments before.

Carefully, she drew out a few brittle sheets yellowed with age. "Light and Gray," the title read, the words penned in a wavering hand.

Nell stared at the pages for a long moment, the paper tingling against her palm like a secret aching to be told. She began to read.

### "Light and Gray"
*The Owl observes through fractured glass.*
*The Shrew still knows what came to pass.*

Nell's mouth dried. *Owl and Shrew?* Was it possible that her grandmother had drafted another poem? She read on.

*The mirror knows, the window shows,*
*But neither tells the truth it owes.*

The hair rose across the back of her neck. This poem was strange, unlike any of the poems she'd written before.

Still, it felt familiar somehow.

*A whisper stirs the dust and gloom.*
*A secret in a forgotten room.*

Nell blinked, realization crashing through her like a bolt of lightning.
This wasn't a poem about their beloved characters or the past.
It was breathing. It was *now*.

The blurred shadows in the mirror. The whispered voices. The hidden door. And now—this poem.

A line from Poe drifted up unbidden through the haze of her thoughts.

*"The house and the domain of the family had, at length, found a voice."*

Perhaps Bellamare Hollow had found its voice, too.

# Part Four: The Disturbed Night

Nell folded the pages carefully and slid them into her pocket. She descended the stairs in a daze, caught somewhere between reason and the swell of something stranger. What she needed in this moment, more than anything, was normalcy.

What she needed was Margot.

Nell wound her way through the ground-level corridors, cold air biting at her skin. At Margot's door, she knocked once, then twice, and eased it open. Her room was empty, but strangely, it looked almost untouched.

If Margot hadn't returned there to settle in, where had she gone?

A soft humming drifted down from the kitchen. With it, the sweet scent of chamomile.

Nell followed the sound to find Margot perched on a barstool, paper and pencil in hand, softly singing their grandmother's favorite song, "Yesterday" by the Beatles. Nell smiled, stiffer than she'd intended, and quietly joined in, the gentle melody drawing her back toward solid ground. As the last notes faded, Margot rested her head lightly on Nell's shoulder.

"There's so much to be done," Margot said, tapping her pencil against the paper. "It's a little overwhelming." She flipped the paper around, which appeared to be more doodle than to-do list. "The angst, it really pulls you under when you least expect it."

*And flat-out dread*, Nell thought to herself.

She wanted to ask Margot if she'd experienced anything strange since arriving back at the house, too. But as the question formed on her lips, her mouth snapped shut.

She could almost hear Margot's voice in her head:

*Please don't lose your grip on reality right now, Nell.*

*Do I need to worry about you throwing yourself off the cliff, too, Nell?*

The thought pulled her under, steady and soundless as an anchor drifting through the depths of the sea.

No. She wasn't like their father—consumed by grief, blaming himself for their mother's fall, moving through life with all the vibrance of a sunken stone. Until one crisp autumn day, he stepped off the cliff and left them orphaned.

No.

She was not *broken*.

"Are you hungry?" Margot's voice cut through her reverie. "I left some chicken soup in the fridge."

Nell managed a small smile and shook her head. Her eyes crinkled as a memory formed. "You remember Mom's Special Soup?" she said, chuckling.

Margot snorted. "Oh my gosh! I haven't thought of that in *years*!" She hopped off the stool and poured another mug of tea, yawning. "You'd read in one of your books that this soup had healing properties, so we made a gigantic pot and then spilled half of it all over her room. The nurse was furious!"

Nell laughed. "And Grandma *still* didn't kill us for it. She loved that we were always trying to save Mom." But as the laughter faded, Nell's stomach tightened, and she suddenly felt pale. Almost as if the void in her chest had stretched, contorted.

"Keeping Mom safe was always our most important job. Grandma let us feel like little nurses. How proud we were." Margot's eyes softened, and she placed her hand atop Nell's. "I still am, you know, Nell. It hasn't been easy for either of us. Yet here we are, together, getting through this life. There's nothing we can't do when we're together."

Margot pulled Nell into a warm, familiar hug—one that held years of sisterly love, shared grief, and burdens.

Yet why did guilt coil so sharply in Nell's chest?

She slipped free, smoothed her sweater, and poured a mug of tea for herself. Maybe tea would help her sleep. Maybe it would help dull her racing thoughts.

"I'm glad to be here, too, Margot. But I—" Nell's voice cracked.

She turned to continue, and . . .

Margot was gone.

She stood, stupefied. Perhaps Margot's hug had been to say goodnight?

Nell finished her tea and set the mug in the empty sink. She didn't see Margot's cup. Her sister must've taken it with her.

Nell climbed the stairs to her room, each step echoing as though the house itself was watching. The landing felt off—tilted, uncanny.

Distorted.

Sleep came at last, but with it a nightmarish parade of images and sounds intent on unmooring her mind. A beeping so shrill it felt like daggers in her skull. White flowers—luminous, beautiful, and horribly out of place. Fractured voices locked in a furious, broken argument. A dark staircase, with a single, red petal on a cracked step. A teacup tumbling from trembling fingers. A single, bloodcurdling scream. Fists rapping heavily against a door.

Nell snapped awake.

*Bang. Bang. Bang.*

"Nell!" Margot's voice thundered from the other side. "Open the door—right now!"

*Bang. Bang. Bang. Bang.*

She rubbed the sleep from her eyes. The dark room felt cavernous and cold, the mist of each breath floating from her lips.

*Bang. Bang. Bang.*

"Nell!" Margot shrieked, panic and anger lacing every syllable.

A jolt of fear shot through Nell's chest. She swung her legs out of bed, perched on the edge for a moment, heart racing.

She crossed to the door, hand trembling as she gripped the handle and yanked it open.

No one was there.

# Part Five: A Petal Red

Murky morning light seeped into the bedroom. Nell felt miserable, depleted—bordering on unhinged. Stress did that, right? Brighter light did nothing to warm the room; if anything, the walls seemed to crawl closer, tightening around her like a clenching hand.

She threw on the warmest sweater she could find—simple, white cashmere—and wandered downstairs into the kitchen. The coffee machine gurgled, but Margot was nowhere to be found.

Nell poured herself a mug of coffee and drifted into her grandmother's study. She settled into the burgundy herringbone-wool chair and rested her feet on the matching ottoman. From her pocket, she withdrew the folded pages of "Light and Gray." She didn't know what truths she sought, only that something vital was hidden in its lines. So, she read on.

*A banging that disturbed the night,*
*Strife about what's wrong and right.*

Nell, again, found herself rooted in place. *Banging*. But hadn't that just been a dream?

# Not As It Seems



*The Shrew ran fast; the Owl stood tall.*
*But neither saw the coming fall.*

A fall? Her mind leapt to her mother's accident on the stairs so many years ago. But no, that didn't fit. This was *now*. Unless . . .

Nell sprang up from the chair and darted for the staircase. "Margot? Margot, where are you?" Urgency tore through her as she swept through rooms, peered down corridors, and checked the balconies overlooking the cliff. No sign of her sister, and Nell didn't know whether to feel relieved or terrified.

The last place she thought to check was their mother's room. No obvious precipice inside, yet something tugged at her, coaxing her in that direction.

She stopped short at the heavy painting of the Owl and Shrew propped against the wall.

Had it *changed*?

No, it *couldn't* have.

But she hadn't remembered the tiny fleck of red on the shattered bridge—a lone flower petal staining the canvas.

Nell's pulse thundered as she manipulated the latch and slipped into the room. A cutting, icy wind brushed through her hair and all around her. The curtains swirled as brisk sea air rushed through them. She hurried over to the windows and peeked her head out. Far below, waves battered the cliff side. There was no trace of Margot, though she wasn't sure there would be if she'd fallen here.

She slammed the windows closed.

Nell sank into the armchair, bewildered. Exhausted. As far as she could tell, Margot *hadn't* fallen. Why had she conjured such things in her head?

The *poem*.

She tugged it from her pocket and unfurled it. Read.

*One drop of bloom, a petal red,*
*A stain upon the path she fled.*

Her brow furrowed. The meaning escaped her, yet it struck a chord she couldn't name.

Suddenly, the phonograph in the corner sputtered on. A cacophony of music, drippy and muddled, resounded against the four walls that surrounded her.

*"The song is ended, but the melody lingers on.*
*You and the song are gone.*
*But the melody lingers on."*

All sensations but panic were eviscerated. A miasma of terror, grief, guilt, and absurdity began to swallow her whole.

She was mad. Utterly unraveling.

This was clear now.

Nell slowly approached the phonograph and turned off Ruth Etting's dismal ditty. Silence flooded the room once more. Her muscles clenched; a clammy chill raced across her skin. Shaking, she did what any girl might do when she felt lost, scared, and alone.

She crawled into her mother's bed.

The sheets were stiff and cool. She sank into the depression that had once held her mother, her cheek pressed into the pillow as though she could feel her mother's heartbeat beneath it. Her heart ached; her eyes burned with exhaustion.

As sleep's edge claimed her, faint voices drifted in from somewhere distant—familiar, distraught.

*No. I can't. I'm not ready yet.*

*This would be a huge mistake.*

*I need more time.*

Nell's mind swirled in a fog. She was there, but also not there. A whisper of existence hiding in the opacity of a dream.

Then one voice cut through the mist—warm, insistent, impossibly real.

It belonged to her mother.

*Nell . . . it's okay. It's time.*

A breathless pause. A tether, broken.

Then a long, shrill beep.

Nell jolted awake, gasping, fingers digging into the sheets. Her throat tightened as the truth coiled within her.

*I killed our mother.*


# Part Six: The Echo


Darkness undulated around her as she crept up the staircase toward her tower room.

Or perhaps the darkness *was* her.

Her hand gripped the banister, its solid form a weak tether to reality. She barely noticed the landing falling into view—until something caught her eye.

A gleam of red.

Nell stopped mid-step, her fingers tightening around the banister. A flower petal?

*No.*

A single bead of red, deep and glistening, clinging to the wooden step ahead. Fresh. Viscous.

Nell stooped, struggling to pull air into her lungs. The space around her twisted and swirled, folding in and then out, like a living thing breathing in the dark.

The past came crashing back—violent, merciless, inevitable.

*Bang. Bang. Bang.*

Margot's fists pounding against her door. Her voice raw. Furious.

Betrayed.

*Nell, open the door!*

*How could you?*

*Why didn't you wait for me?*

A blur of palpable fury and devastation.

Margot fleeing, her hand missing the banister . . .

A slip.

A scream—cut off, swallowed by silence.

The sickening, unforgettable thud at the bottom of the stairs.

Nell staggered back, her heart pounding so hard it seemed to drown out the entire house. "No," she said, whispering against the silence. "No, no, no . . ."

But the blood was still there. A stain now, years in the making. A splotch of red, oddly reminiscent of a flower petal.

And she remembered it all.

Nell sat on the stairs, her thumb sliding over the lone petal.

The choice had been hers. Not Margot's. Not her grandmother's. Hers alone.

She hadn't meant to steal anything.

She just couldn't bear to watch her mother suffer another day. She deserved peace, not a living tomb, not the slow, cruel suffocation of life. She deserved finality, a chance at whatever came next.

She had believed—God help her, she had believed—that it was an act of mercy.

*She wanted this*, Nell had told herself. Margot was too emotional to let go.

*Someone needed to be strong.*

But the truth was far harsher than the memories she'd buried. And when Margot found out, when she had pounded against Nell's locked door, pleading, raging, it was too late.

Nell had stolen not just their mother's last breath, but Margot's chance to be there, to say goodbye, to make peace.

And Margot had fled.

And she had fallen.

Never to rise again.

And it was all because of her.

"Margot? Are you here?" Nell's voice called out, barely above a whisper.

She waited for a long while, suspended in silence and desolation, cursing the black wretchedness that was her soul. The wretchedness that had poisoned everything she loved, leaving her utterly and irrevocably alone.

The world fogged around her, stone and wood and salt and sky all blurring into one colorless haze.

*Finality.*

That was what she had wanted for her mother. It was what her father had so desperately sought. It had already claimed her grandmother—and taken Margot from her, too.

*Perhaps it was time for her, as well.*

Her grief wasn't loud—it hummed, low and endless, beneath her skin.

She followed the stairs down, the air swollen with the weight of her guilt. In the kitchen, her hands moved without thought. Muscle memory. Or fate.

She pulled a dust-covered tin from the highest shelf of her grandmother's apothecary cupboard. The label was faded, nearly unreadable.

*Hemlock.*

Hesitation stirred at the edges of her mind, but she pushed it away. There was no fixing what was already so very broken. She filled the kettle, lit the burner, and waited for the water to wail.

Outside, the sea sighed against the cliffs, a sound she had known and loved all her life.

When the tea was ready, she poured it into a delicate porcelain cup—her grandmother's favorite. A fragile thing. Beautiful, even cracked. Stained.

She stared at the cup for several moments until a thought slipped in, quiet and insistent. Slowly, she reached into her pocket and drew out the brittle pages of "Light and Gray" and read.

*One fought to live. One longed to stay.*
*The truth was lost in light and gray.*

Nell pressed the paper against her chest, tears spilling down her cheeks.

Margot had loved too fiercely, hoped too blindly. She had placed her faith in Nell—when perhaps none had been owed.

> *One lives the past; one lives the pain—*
> *Yet both are bound to what remains.*
> *One is the echo, one is the scream,*
> *One holds the truth; one holds the dream.*

Nell's fingers curled tighter around the porcelain, allowing herself to feel the pain she could no longer outrun. It was raw. Heavy. And hers to bear.

She had taken the vitality, the very light, from someone she loved so dearly—and left behind nothing more than an echo. The shadow of a scream.

Her hands trembling, she lifted the cup.

"I'm sorry," she whispered to the empty kitchen. "I'm so, so sorry."

And she drank.

The tea was bitter, sharp and wrong, but she welcomed it. She let it settle into her, seep into her blood, her bones, her very soul.

As she set down the cup, the edges of the room started to sway. The world tilted as the house groaned—a low, mournful sound. And from somewhere, faint and urgent, a voice called through the fog. . . .

"Nell . . . please come back."


# Part Seven: The Scream

The room spun as Nell staggered to her feet. Voices murmured from somewhere unseen, threading through the walls, calling her name.

She stumbled through the foyer, the corridors stretching long and hollow, doorways bleeding into one another, swallowed by a salty, gray fog.

Somewhere ahead, a flicker of light. A wisp of music. A voice, familiar and warm, calling out to her.

She pressed forward, her steps slow and unsteady, the walls rippling at the edges of her vision. Each step was heavier, her feet drawn forward by a hypnotizing pull.

The door to her mother's hospital room stood ajar, a strand of candlelight leaking into the dark hall. Inside, the air shimmered, thick with salt, smoke, and the weight of something ancient.

The phonograph spun in the corner, crackling softly—

*"The song is ended . . . but the melody lingers on."*

Margot sat on one side of a table, her head bowed in a silent prayer, a circle of melted candles flickering around her.

Opposite her sat their grandmother, still and watchful, her hands curled around a photograph.

A deep, marrow-aching chill clenched her bones. The room breathed, inhaling her confusion and desperation. Exhaling her fear.

Margot lifted her head, her eyes locking on to Nell's across the flickering candlelight. A threshold between worlds, opaline—close enough to touch.

Nell opened her mouth to speak, but no sound came. She followed Margot's gaze as it dropped to the photo resting softly in her grandmother's palm.

A young woman, maybe twenty-five, smiling gently, her dark hair wind-tossed, a book clutched under one arm.

*It was her.*

No.

*It couldn't be . . .*

Nell's gaze jerked back to them. Margot's hair, streaked now with gray, glowed in the candlelight. Her grandmother's face was thinner than she remembered, lined and hollowed by the seasons Nell had not been there to share.

Time had passed. *Too much time.*

Her breath hitched. How could she have missed it? How could she have been gone for so long?

And then—

The memories tore through her, sharp and sudden, the truth snapping into place.

The hemlock-laced teacup falling from her grasp . . .

Her body wilting beside Margot at the bottom of the stairs. Two halves of a goodbye, slowly falling into silence together.

Then, a slow, broken gasp. Margot's green eyes fluttering open, soft as butterfly wings.

And Nell, already slipping away.

Their eyes met, and in that breathless moment, everything was both too late and not enough.

Nell's fingers had twitched, reaching for her sister—for a second chance—but her body had already started to give way.

The last thing she saw was Margot's face twisted with grief and disbelief before she was swallowed by the dark.

Nell stumbled back, reaching for the old hospital bed, but it was dust and air now, no more real than the fragments of memory swirling around her.

The quiet roared in her ears. Her hands shook.

It wasn't *Margot* who died that day.

It was *her*.

And somehow, she'd never left.

*Why?*

The answer struck hard and late, like a blow she should've seen coming. She'd always said her father was broken. But she was just the same—cracked, fractured. In all the same places.

And now she understood.

How grief scrapes you hollow. How guilt settles in your bones like rot.

He had leapt. She had lingered.

Guilt was a ghost, and it had clung to her even in death.

Margot's voice reached her again, quivering but sure. "You're forgiven, Nell. You always were. And you are so loved. It's okay. You can let go now."

A hush fell within her, as if the grief had grown tired of holding on. The ache inside her eased, her soul loosening with a final quiet breath.

The candles flared, bright and golden, filling the room with a sudden impossible warmth, like an embrace.

Nell felt herself drifting. Weightless, unmoored, untethered from the sorrow that had bound her. Then, a release—like wings batting upward through the breeze.

The candles flickered out.

# Part Eight: The Truth and the Dream

*Margot*

Darkness fell across the room, but a lingering warmth curled close around her. The only sound filling the space between them was the low rumble of the sea.

Margot lowered her hands, blinking against the sting of tears. She knew it had been Nell. Deep down, she'd always known.

The creaks on the stairs, the sounds in the halls.

The windows slamming closed.

The slow shift of the old armchair.

The phonograph abruptly halting at twilight.

Part of her had wanted to keep Nell—any scraps and fragments she could. But it was wrong. She deserved finality.

*Peace.*

Margot reached across the table and held her grandmother's hands in her own.

"Even broken wings can find their way home," Margot whispered. "I knew she would."

The sea sighed against the cliffs of Bellamare Hollow, carrying away the last of the night.

*Truth, once named, won't stay confined—*
*For love endures through death and time.*
*In light and gray, we fade, we gleam.*
*Bound forever by truth and dream.*

# About the Author

**Sarah Bjork** is a writer, mom, and professional overthinker with a love for creepy manors, unreliable narrators, and poetic dread. These days, she haunts the Pacific Northwest with her family, laptop, and far too many half-finished ideas. If you like lyrical prose, emotionally damaged houses, and stories that pulse beneath the floorboards, you're in the right place.

You can find Sarah on Instagram at:
@sarah_bjork_author

To learn more about Sarah, visit her website at:
www.sarahbjorkauthor.com

# The Stroke of a Pen

# The Stroke of a Pen

## Roxanne Werner

DETERMINED TO CONQUER THE MOUNTAIN of paperwork on my desk, I flexed my cramped fingers, dipped my pen in the inkwell, and was about to put pen to paper when the bell on my shop's door jangled.

A tall man wearing formal clothes and a top hat stood in the front room. It was an unusual sight, as most of my customers sent junior clerks or paid street urchins a few pence to drop off the work they needed copied. I hurried to wipe the ink from my hands, roll down my sleeves, and don my coat, hoping to appear respectable to a new client.

I emerged from the back expecting a brusque reprimand for making him wait, but he seemed in no hurry. Although he must have heard me, he continued to prowl about, poking his walking stick into corners and flipping through the sample pages of my penmanship on the counter.

Attempting to attract his attention, I cleared my throat. "May I be of service, sir?"

He turned slowly.

I stifled a gasp. Though I earned my living as a simple scrivener, I was at heart an artist. Roaming London's streets whenever I had a free moment, I collected all manner of faces for future paintings. My sketchbook contained the rich and poor, healthy and sick, joyful and melancholy. But I had never seen a face like his.

His visage had a profound effect on me, and I doubted I could capture its aura by putting oil to canvas. It was not that his features were unnatural or malformed. Indeed, if anything, he appeared too perfect to be a living, breathing being, with a long, tapered face, prominent cheekbones, an aquiline nose, and large, dark eyes that stood out against his alabaster skin.

"I was told you were an artist, but perhaps I misheard?"

His voice was soft, almost hypnotic.

The door's bell jangled, and Elizabeth entered the shop. "Bill, the mistress asked me to fetch her new hat from the milliner, and I thought I'd nip in for a moment before the girls' lessons. I have tomorrow off, and if you have time, we might go for a picnic in the park."

She looked past my visitor as if he weren't there.

"I'm sure William will be pleased to join you, and if he accepts my commission, he'll have more money and time to spend with you. He might even take you to the new Aquatic Vivarium at the zoo." The stranger tipped his hat and smiled at her. "After all, we have so little time in this world. It's best to enjoy it while we can."

"Oh, beg pardon, sir." Elizabeth blushed. "I don't know how I could have missed you standing there as big as the Tower of London. And here I am putting my foot in it when Bill, I mean William, and you were discussing important business. I'll take myself off and let you get on with things."

"No trouble, miss. You are a pleasant break from a dreary world."

Elizabeth flushed even redder, nodded, and hurried out the door.

"Now, William, if I may have your undivided attention, I have a proposition for you."

"Please, sir. I have little in the way of comfort here. May I suggest we take a short stroll down the street? There is an excellent coffee shop where we might discuss your proposal." I reached for my hat.

He held up his hand. At the sight of his long, tapered fingers, graceful and elegant, I whisked my ink-stained stubs behind my back. "There is nothing to discuss." He tapped his cane on the floor, then pointed it at me. "Either accept my offer or not. I will not haggle."

I blinked under his stare. "But sir, you have not made your offer."

He paused, as if considering the merits of my statement, then went on as if nothing were amiss. "As I said, word of your artistic talents reached me, and I hate to see them wasted on mere copy work. From time to time, I need invitations made. I will provide you with a list of names and dates. All you have to do is allow your creativity to flow into your penmanship.

"*Calligraphy*, I believe, is the word. I want borders drawn around the edges—scrollwork, floral designs, whatever strikes your fancy. You might choose a flowered one for the female guests. I leave that up to you. I will supply pens, ink, and paper, and pay you a salary of fifteen pounds per week. The rate will remain the same no matter the number of invitations. You must complete them within the week. No excuses. If you fail, I will terminate your contract." He paused, waiting for my answer.

Fifteen pounds a week! It was a princely sum, enough for me to ask Elizabeth for her hand.

"Do you accept my terms or not?"

I stood there, open-mouthed. It was a dream come true. "I-I accept." I extended my ink-stained hand to seal the deal and instantly regretted it.

He looked down his long, patrician nose. "Your word will suffice." He removed a sealed envelope from his inside pocket. "Here is your first assignment. Whatever materials you need are available at the store listed at the top. The owner will bill my account."

I took the envelope with trembling fingers, afraid of staining the smooth linen stationery.

He counted out fifteen pound notes. "Here is a week's payment in advance. Enjoy your day with Elizabeth." His lips twitched into the semblance of a smile.

I thought he meant to be kind, but perhaps his facial muscles were not used to the expression.

"I will return in one week. Make sure you are done."

I stood there staring for some time. He didn't disappear in a puff of smoke, but I had no recollection of him walking out the shop door. I broke the seal on the envelope.

Fifteen names and dates. It was but an hour's work, even with embellishments. Was I dreaming? But I held the pound notes in my hand. Noting the store's name and address, I locked the list and money in my safe.

After scrubbing the ink from my hands, I donned my coat and hat and headed for the shop. I had a week to complete my task, but I wouldn't wait until the last minute. I would prove I was a good investment.

Widow's Cauldron was an overcrowded warren of narrow, winding alleys whose wooden, thatched-roof buildings went up like a tinderbox during the Great Fire of 1666. According to legend, its perpetual fog and rain were not due to being built on a low-lying fen, but to the weeping of the widows after the conflagration. They were in full voice today. Having neglected to bring an umbrella, I turned up my collar and pulled my coat closer as I searched for Scribner Lane.

"Buy a flower, sir?" asked a young girl with a tray of wilted violets.

I removed thruppence from my pocket. "I'll take a bunch."

"They're only a penny," she said, holding out the violets and refusing the extra coins.

"I thought you might do me a favor."

Her smile dimmed, and she backed away. "I ain't that kind of girl, sir."

"What? Oh, no, no," I stammered. "You misunderstand. I only wondered if you could direct me to Scribner Lane."

She looked sidelong at me. "I aren't goin' down no alley with you." She pointed. "Turn left at the third street. You'll find it."

I tipped my soggy hat and, clutching the pitiful violets, followed her directions. The turn took me into a maze of alleys with rickety wooden shops crammed together as if leaning on each other for support; the streets were paved with more mud and puddles than cobblestones.

I was about to give up, thinking the girl had misdirected me, when I came to a dead end with a lopsided sign saying Scribner Lane. *Lane* was an overstatement. It was a short stub boasting only one shop set back from the main roadway. Twin stone spires from a nearby church towered behind it, blessing it with the disquieting look of having horns.

I climbed the steps, stopping to scrape my shoes and shake off the rain, like a wet, muddy hound smelling of damp wool. So much for making a good impression.

As I entered the building, a loud whoosh made me duck. An enormous raven took off from the lintel, flew over me, and landed on the shop's counter. Grasping a brass handbell in its beak, the bird rang it until a jovial voice answered, "Coming, Quilliam."

A man emerged from the back room, wiping his hands on a cloth. My artist's eye summed him up with a single word—round; from his shiny, bald dome to his expansive paunch, over which stretched an apron splotched with so much paint and ink that its original hue was indeterminate.

"Mortimer Ravenscroft." He offered his hand. "And you must be the scribe Mr. Décès hired for his invitations. I didn't expect to see you so soon."

The raven cawed and snapped its beak.

"Yes, yes, don't get your feathers ruffled. I haven't forgotten you." He waved his hand with a flourish. "And this is my assistant, Quilliam."

I raised my eyebrows as the raven bobbed its head at me, taking a bow. Without thinking, I tipped my hat in acknowledgment and offered him the violets.

The bird strutted across the counter, puffing its chest feathers.

"Tsk, tsk. You're spoiling him, but you've made a friend, Mr. . . ."

"Westcott. Call me Bill."

He smiled. "Well, Bill, you needn't have come all the way out here in the rain. I planned to have everything delivered to your shop Monday morning. It's too much for you to carry."

"I thought it was a box of paper, envelopes, and ink. It can't be so heavy."

"Paper can be heavy in large quantities, and then there are the inks, pens, spare nibs . . ." He ticked the items off on his fingers. "Not to mention the easel, canvases, paints, and brushes."

"What! I understood my assignment to be fifteen invitations this week."

He shook his head. "This week. But you will need supplies for the weeks ahead."

"Well, I suppose stocking up makes sense, but I won't need canvases and paints to make invitations."

"Mr. Décès considers himself your patron. He wants you to pursue your artistic career, as well. Don't you want to?"

"Of course, but . . . I didn't expect my employer to . . ."

He waved his hand. "You should think of Mr. Décès as your patron. In the old days, artists, musicians, poets . . . all the arts were appreciated. It's nothing for him to buy you a few supplies. He's rich. Just look at what he's done with the Church of the Holy Martyr."

"The what?" My brow furrowed.

"Didn't you see the spires behind our shop? The Church of the Holy Martyr was destroyed in the Great Fire, but Mr. Décès bought the property and restored it to preserve the Gothic architecture."

"He owns a church? Is that allowed?"

"It's no longer a church. He converted it into a mansion where he holds his parties. But the churchyard behind it remains sacred land; the graves are from two hundred years ago, before the fire."

My face must have betrayed my confusion, for he put his arm around my shoulder and walked me out to the porch. "Excuse the familiarity, my boy. You are young, with a full life ahead of you. Take my advice and seize the opportunity. Leslie Décès may be eccentric, but his patronage is priceless."

The rain turned into a light mist. I strode in an erratic line, dodging puddles that seemed big enough to drown in. At the end of the lane, I glanced back. The proprietor must have lit the lamps because the two front windows blazed like eyes under the horned spires of Leslie Décès's mansion.

Determined to shake off my misgivings, I made my way back to the main street and proceeded until it dead-ended. The lonely mansion looming before me took my breath away. The spires belonged here. No longer hornlike, their slender fingers stretched heavenward, flanking a large rosette stained-glass window over the pointed arch of the front entryway. Birdlike gargoyles perched along the roof's edge.

I gasped as one came to life and swooped over the graveyard. It was Quilliam, carrying the violets in his beak. He dropped them on a grave, cawed, and flew off. An ornate wrought iron fence enclosed the graveyard. The gate was locked, but I peered through the rails. A chill ran up my spine. The carving on the marker Quilliam's violets graced read—*Leslie Décès, September 4, 1666.*

"My great, great, great grandfather. He died in the fire."

I jumped as the low, melodious voice of Leslie Décès spoke in my ear.

"What brings you here, William? It is a damp evening to be poking about ancient graveyards. You might catch a chill."

"I-I . . . went to Mr. Ravenscroft's shop to get the supplies for the invitations."

"I see. And while you were so close, you decided to pay me a visit? Very amicable of you, however, you have not been invited to my home. Ours is a business arrangement, William, and unless you receive an invitation, you will find no welcome here." He pointed at the heavy doors of his castle. "I advise you to hurry home. It is a long walk, and night is coming. You wouldn't want to disappoint Elizabeth tomorrow."

He strolled away without another word and disappeared into the deep shadows beneath the archway.

I leapt out of bed, heart pounding, and my nightshirt drenched in sweat. I'd been trapped in the maze of Widow's Cauldron as flames roared through the streets. The nightmare was so vivid, people's screams and the smell of charred flesh lingered even on waking. I crossed to the window and leaned out, only then becoming aware that the screams were the cries of the local costermongers and the burnt flesh, the aroma of fried sausages.

Dismissing the dream, I dressed and set out to meet Elizabeth for our picnic. With her best bonnet framing her face, a light shawl covering her shoulders, and a cheerful berry-print dress accentuating her slim waist, her appearance convinced me the funds that would allow me to marry her were worth a few nightmares. We strolled along the cobblestone street, stopping to supplement the basket she'd packed with a few fruit pastries and a jar of hot tea from the local street vendors.

When we reached Kensington Gardens, the sun was high and Elizabeth's face flushed with color. We spread the old blanket I brought for our comfort in a quiet spot beneath a London plane tree.

Elizabeth removed her bonnet and shook out her chestnut curls. "So, did you gain a new client? I hope I didn't disrupt your meeting by barging in yesterday."

I bit into a roast beef sandwich and washed it down with a sip of tea. "You didn't disturb us. I believe he found you charming. I should be jealous."

"Bill, stop teasing. Did he hire you?"

"He offered me fifteen pounds a week."

"Fifteen pounds!" Her eyes widened. "What does he expect for such a sum?"

"Nothing illegal." I stood and paced the length of our blanket. "He wants me to make invitations for him using calligraphy and fancy borders."

"Invitations? To what?" She plucked a daisy from the grass and spun it between her fingers.

"Look, Elizabeth!" I pointed to a bird in a nearby tree. "Doesn't a thrush mean new beginnings and happiness?"

She shaded her eyes. "I don't see anything."

"I must have scared it away."

"Still, you saw it. It must mean you will take this job. A new beginning . . ." She blushed and looked at me from under her lashes. "And happiness." She chewed on the daisy stem. "But you didn't answer my question."

"What?"

"What are the invitations for?"

"Oh . . ." I waved my hand. "What invitations are usually for . . . parties, dinners, you know."

I sat down next to her and took her hand in mine. "Elizabeth, I know how much this money would mean to us, but . . ." I searched for the right words. "If—if I take this job . . ."

"If? You mean you might not?"

"No, no, of course I did. He already paid me a week in advance. Let me tell you about the rest of my day." I gave her a factual, although somewhat edited, account of my afternoon's adventure.

"Oh, what a clever bird." She laughed and clapped at Quilliam's antics. "And such a curious shop owner. Are you really to pursue your painting?"

When I described the mansion, her eyes lit. "Oh, Bill, imagine going to a ball or dinner at such a place, the ladies in gowns, the men in all their finery. Do you think he will ever invite us?"

"Perhaps."

The last thing I wanted was for either of us to be invited to Leslie Décès's mansion, but she'd looked so excited that I allowed her to keep her dream. The next day, I let my misgivings drift away with the morning fog and, taking up pen and ink, I embarked on my new career.

Within three months, I'd saved enough to propose, and Elizabeth and I were married. I refurbished the apartment above the shop. The two of us lived there comfortably but discussed buying a small cottage for when we had a family.

Life settled into a routine. Leslie Décès picked up the finished invitations and delivered a new list every Friday. At first, he inspected each one, praising my artwork and reminding me how important it was that there were no errors in the names or dates, but in a few weeks, satisfied with my accuracy, he stopped checking. Although Elizabeth often asked me to take her to see his mansion, I always made an excuse, and in time, she gave up. I had no desire to press my luck with another excursion to Widow's Cauldron.

Mr. Ravenscroft's driver delivered supplies once a month, and to Elizabeth's great surprise and joy, Quilliam came along for the ride. She fussed over the vain raven and gave him treats like a favorite child. I thought his fearsome beak and talons would frighten her, but he behaved quite gently. We thrived; I even sold a few of my paintings. But as months passed with no sign of children, lines of sadness gathered around Elizabeth's eyes.

Elizabeth took an interest in my work and began to help me. She filled the ink-wells, replaced the worn pen nibs, and, showing a flair for design, helped me come up with new patterns for the invitations. When they were completed, she checked for inkblots and errors, guaranteeing that whatever we handed in was perfect.

"Bill, I was thinking. Mr. Décès must know a lot of people." Elizabeth blotted a freshly inked design.

"I'm sure he does. But what makes you say that?"

She dipped her pen and began another pattern. "He never invites anyone to his parties more than once."

My hand jumped, leaving a large splotch of ink on the page.

"Why Bill, it's not like you to be so clumsy. You'll have to get a fresh sheet and do that one over again."

I laughed and selected a new sheet of paper. "Maybe the affairs are so boring that no one wants to go more than once."

She made a face. "I don't believe that."

"Well, you have only been helping me for two months. Rich people often visit the country or travel abroad during the summer. Perhaps when they return, their names will reappear."

"Maybe." She chewed the end of her pen. "I still think it's odd."

"I never noticed. I use the list and don't pay attention to the names."

"But I have an excellent memory for names, and I'm sure none have been repeated."

"Whatever the reason, it's not our affair. As long as he keeps inviting people, we have an income."

Late in the summer of 1854, the volume of invitations increased. When my employer brought another list of over forty names, Elizabeth questioned him. "Mr. Décès, do you think it wise to have such large gatherings with cholera sweeping through parts of the city? Aren't you concerned people will get sick?"

He folded his hands over the top of his cane. "When death is near, people need a distraction, something to keep their fear at bay. I'm performing a service by having more parties. Don't you agree, William?"

"It is not my position to question my employer."

Elizabeth raised an eyebrow at me and wiped the ink from her hands. "You may have a point, Mr. Décès, but only if you're certain your parties do not spread the contagion."

He nodded. "Of course, madam. I would never want to inflict more damage. I will take your warning to heart."

She took him at his word, but it was many weeks before the size of his parties decreased, and only after the epidemic ended.

While taking a stroll one afternoon, Elizabeth and I passed a churchyard where a new grave marker was being set. Elizabeth stopped to watch. "Bill, come here. A stone mason has copied one of our designs. We should demand payment from him."

"Elizabeth, many designs are similar. I'm sure it wasn't stolen from our work."

"And I'm sure, it was." Her face reddened. "That—" She stabbed her finger at the stone. "—is one of my floral designs. I copied the petals from a flower in a bouquet you gave me. No one could randomly create the same rose."

I patted her hand. "Well, even if they did, we don't have a copyright on the designs. We're doing well. I don't begrudge someone else making a profit. We have even saved enough to buy the cottage we used to talk about."

Her expression changed in an instant. I should not have brought up the cottage. Her eyes glistened with unshed tears, and her words were brittle as ice when she spoke. "The two of us have no need for a cottage."

"Elizabeth, I'm sorry. . . . I didn't mean to upset you."

She brushed by me. "I'm tired, William. I'd like to go home now."

That cursed stone. If only we hadn't walked past it. The men finished setting it and left. With them out of the way, there was no mistaking the design was ours. At least Elizabeth hadn't noticed the name and date. Like the design, they matched an invitation I wrote last week. I hurried after her.

Elizabeth barely spoke at supper, and I, lost in my own thoughts, paid no attention.

When she stayed in bed for the next two days, I called in a doctor, although she insisted she was fine. I paced downstairs while he examined her. He assured me it was not cholera, but she was run-down and melancholy. He prescribed a tonic and suggested, "Some fresh air and a change of scene can work wonders in cases like this."

Mr. Décès arrived late in the afternoon. "Where is Elizabeth, William? The shop seems dimmer without her."

"She is resting upstairs."

"I hope it is nothing serious." His normally dour face grew pensive.

I took the envelope with the new list and handed him the completed invitations. "The doctor recommends a trip."

He nodded. "London's smoke and fog can take a toll. I'm sure a few days away will be beneficial. If you send word where you'll be, I can pick up the invitations and deliver the next list there. It's no trouble. Give Elizabeth my best wishes for a speedy recovery."

"Thank you."

I brought Elizabeth's meal upstairs and settled down to polish off the new list as quickly as I could. I didn't want it hanging over us while we were away. I broke the crimson wax seal with the mirrored *D* and removed the paper. There were fifteen names, but my eyes refused to see anything but the name about halfway down—*Elizabeth Westcott, September 20, 1854.*

To my great relief, Elizabeth had long since stopped hoping to be invited to one of Les Décès's affairs. Yet in just eight days, her wish to attend one would be granted. No! I would not let her.

I struck the desk with my fist. I'd lied to her and myself all this time, but I had to face the truth. Ever since the first day, I'd suspected who my employer was and what his invitations meant. When Quilliam dropped the violets on Leslie Décès's grave, it confirmed my fears, but I'd told myself it was none of my business. I wasn't hurting anyone. I didn't make the lists. We needed the money, and Décès would only hire someone else to create the invitations if I didn't. But until now, none of the names had been someone I knew.

Elizabeth! I buried my head in my hands. She was too young, only twenty-seven. I would not let him take her. But how could I stop him? I was a mere mortal, and he was—

But even he must follow the rules, or why the invitations? Why did he stress the importance of not making any errors? Did the invitations possess a power even he could not defy?

I picked up my pen and prayed the saying *the pen is mightier than the sword* would prove true. Picturing Elizabeth's face framed by soft, chestnut curls, I let the design flow from my heart onto the page. When I finished, I blotted the paper and picked up a finer nib to write. My hand shook, and I would have splattered the page with ink, but I stopped and drew in several deep breaths. I must do this right. No mistakes. Nothing that would void the invitation. *Elizabeth Westcott, September 20, 1904.* It was done. I folded it, placed it in an envelope, and wrote her name across the front.

I pulled out a new sheet, added a basic geometric edging, and wrote *William Westcott, September 20, 1904.* If Elizabeth must attend the ball, she would not go alone. I would escort her.

I completed the rest of the list and prayed my ruse would work.

A week went by before we were ready for our trip. Elizabeth fussed over everything with a kind of nervous energy. Leslie Décès arrived. He gave a genuine smile when he saw Elizabeth, bent over her hand, and kissed it. "I am glad to see you up and about again, madam."

"Thank you, Mr. Décès. I'm sure our trip will help me achieve a complete recovery."

"I will not delay your departure." He turned to me. "You have the invitations, William? Here is your new list."

He handed me a thick, sealed envelope, and I gave him the box of finished invitations.

"Perhaps I should check them over. I know you have been worried about your wife, and you may have made an error."

"There are no errors, Mr. Décès. Everything is as it should be."

He flipped through the stack and froze at the sight of Elizabeth's name. Didn't he know who was on the lists? I'd swear his horrified look was real when he read my name on the next envelope. His hand shook as he looked at me. "You're sure these are correct?"

I met his gaze. "Yes."

"Once sealed and sent, they cannot be changed. You know what they mean?" Again, he searched my face.

"Yes, and they are correct."

"How long have you known?"

"From the first day. I know a bit of French. Enough to translate the word *décès*."

"And yet you took the assignments?"

"Without your funds, I would never have been able to marry Elizabeth."

He shook his head. "You understand, you can no longer work for me."

I nodded.

"I will continue to pay your salary until you attend the ball. You are a brave man, William, worthy of Elizabeth. I will miss you both."

He took the box of invitations and strode away.

Unsure if my alteration of the invitation had worked, I hovered over Elizabeth the entire day of September 20, 1854. She appeared well, but what if she choked on a bit of food or tripped going down the stairs? The invitations only fixed a date, not the manner of death. There were so many ways death could claim her.

"William, whatever is the matter with you today? You're following me around like a lost puppy. I can't breathe without you counting my breaths."

"I'm sorry, Elizabeth. I'm a bit on edge today. Pay me no mind."

"That's hard to do with you glued to my side."

It wasn't until the clock struck midnight that I breathed freely. The modification I'd made to Elizabeth's invitation had worked.

Our trip to Bath offered everything the doctor could have wanted. Fresh air, the distractions available, and a change of scenery worked wonders on both of us. We danced in the ballroom, attended the theater, and enjoyed strolling through the town.

Bathing in the famous hot spring waters not only rejuvenated our bodies but washed away the guilt I felt from trafficking with Death. I'd hidden my actions from Elizabeth, thinking to protect her, never realizing the wall my deception built between us. Knowing that our new invitations would arrive eventually no longer concerned me. If anything, it made me savor the time we had together even more.

Once we were refreshed in body and mind, our love blossomed anew. Nine months after our trip, Elizabeth gave birth to our son William, followed two years later by our daughter Margaret. We bought a cottage on the outskirts of London as we'd always dreamed of doing and raised our family. I pursued my painting, and we lived a comfortable life, never discussing the money that was anonymously deposited in our account every month. Whatever else Leslie Décès might be, he was a man of his word.

Our house was rarely quiet. Our children blessed us with five grandchildren and countless pets. The wrinkles at the corners of Elizabeth's eyes deepened, but this time they were from smiles and only made her more beautiful.

Today, September 20, 1904, our altered invitations arrived. Having expected them, I'd made all my preparations. I left my will with a letter addressed to my son explaining everything. Whether he believed it or thought it the product of an old man's overactive imagination was up to him.

"This came in the mail." I handed Elizabeth the fine linen envelope, wondering if she would recognize my handwriting.

She glanced at it. "It's about time," she complained. "He waited until I was too old to enjoy a fancy ball, but I'll prove him wrong."

That evening, dressed in our best finery, we hired a carriage to drop us off at the front gate of Les Décès's mansion. I took Elizabeth's hand, and we walked together to the door.

"Elizabeth, I have to explain—"

She patted my arm. "No, you don't, William. I know you too well for you to be able to hide things from me, and I, too, know a few French words."

I stared at her. "How long . . ."

She rapped my knuckles with her fan. "Don't dawdle, William. It's one thing to be fashionably late, but one shouldn't overdo it."

The door swung open. Leslie Décès motioned us inside. He looked the same as he had fifty years ago, but I was not surprised. What did surprise me was that he wore a servant's livery.

"Welcome, William and Elizabeth. It has been a long time." He winked at me, acknowledging our shared secret.

"Isn't this your house?" I asked, looking around.

A loud "caw" was followed by a blur of black feathers that flew straight to Elizabeth.

"Quilliam! I didn't know you would be here, or I would have brought treats. Oh, how I've missed you. My children and grandchildren never tire of hearing stories about you."

Mortimer Ravenscroft, dressed in formal attire, descended the main staircase.

"You?"

"Yes, William, me. I know I don't look the part. That's why I let my emaciated, dour-faced servant handle all the interactions with humans."

He approached Elizabeth and kissed her hand. "I am happy to meet the woman who beguiled my two most trusted servants." He nodded at Leslie Décès and Quilliam. "I congratulate you and your bold husband. You are the only two who have ever rewritten their fates. I trust you made good use of the time."

The doors to the ballroom opened. Music, laughter, and light spilled into the foyer. Mortimer looked at me. "Will you escort your wife to the ball, or shall I? She is only fifty years late."

I took Elizabeth's hand, and we walked together into the ballroom. "May I have this dance?"

"Indeed, you may."

I took her in my arms, and as we waltzed around the room, the years fell away. Elizabeth looked as young and radiant as the day we first met.

She laughed. "All these years, I told you there was nothing to fear in Les Décès's mansion."

And I had to admit, she was right.

# About the Author

**Roxanne Werner** was born in New Jersey where she haunted libraries and bookstores. Every year Santa left one eagerly awaited present—a book, which she devoured before New Year's. A lifelong bookworm who learned to write in Elvish from reading Tolkien, she was not surprised when a fantasy about calligraphy crossed her mind. One awesome critique group, a patient partner, and two nagging cats helped chase the idea from her head onto the page where it became "The Stroke of a Pen."

You can find Roxanne on Instagram and Bluesky at: @roxannemwerner

To learn more about Roxanne, visit her website at: www.roxannewerner.com

# Wretched Children

# Wretched Children

## L.M. Copeland

IT'S THE SMELL I NOTICE first, sickly sweet and cloying as I pick my way down the strip of earth that runs alongside the Chérie's slimy banks. Behind me, Miss Viola's voice is whip-sharp, and each time she calls my name, it's in a higher octave than the last.

As if that will draw me back to the house. I'm already due a lashing, and I've no intention of facing it anytime soon. The thought of Charlotte's smirk as she watches Miss Viola bring the willow switch against the backs of my legs sends the world pinching inward, until all I can see is the river ahead.

Miss Viola refused to hear my side of the story, like always. Just drew her lips together as Charlotte howled at her side, one side of her face still painted red from the slap I'd delivered to it just after breakfast. Wouldn't listen when I told her Charlotte snuck into my room the night before and left a razor blade beneath my pillow.

I could explain as much as I wanted, but the result would remain the same.

The river runs high and muddy today, gurgling like so many drowning voices. Like the noises I wish I could squeeze out of Charlotte, though I banish that thought before it can hang too sweet on my tongue.

Like Reverend Redwine says during his Tuesday visits to the Chérie Parish Girls' House, the notion of a sin is just as bad as the sin itself, and I'm not keen on sullying my soul any more than necessary.

*But still.* The thought curls my lips like a cat's whiskers. *It would be so lovely.*

Overhead, the sun beats down as if it, too, wants to punish me. I swat at the gnats fluttering at the back of my neck, where sweat beads down my back and pools in the waist of my workday skirt. The mosquitoes hover closer, aiming to add to the collection of bites that dot my arms and legs like constellations.

The smell grows stronger the closer I get to the river. I recognize it, of course—any girl who spends more than a few months at the house knows the scent of the creatures spat up from the river's depths. Even Charlotte, who tries her best to be different from the rest of us, with her petticoats and kid gloves and gifts from parents who never visit or write.

It doesn't work, of course. We all know she's just like us—a girl deemed burdensome and tucked away in the armpit hollow of Chérie, Louisiana.

In one way or another, the Girls' House has always been a place for unwanted women. Once, Dr. Elohim Beaumont called this house his namesake sanitorium. He made his fortune peddling a permanent solution to wealthy families fed up with their opinionated wives and daughters. Drugs and shocks and so-called treatments that left the women quiet and mild-mannered, their minds as empty as the skies overhead.

For decades they lived like that, the women wandering the grounds in a stupor, fenced in by the trees and the river and the thick iron gate that sits at the forest's edge. If the treatments didn't work, if the women stayed loud or unruly or confident . . . Well, there was always the Chérie River, happy to gulp down the limp and lifeless bodies Elohim fed into its waves.

And when arsenic took the good doctor—hidden, as the rumor goes, in Elohim's nightly brandy—the hospital went with him, leaving the place empty and dark until Miss Viola saw her own future in its bones.

Today, girls sleep in rooms that once held manacled beds and still bear the half-moon grooves of fingernails. We practice French in the windowless study where women lay helpless at the hands of a man wielding a sharp stick and a hunger for poisonous power. Make daisy chains in the grass where they wept for hours without wondering why.

And while Elohim is long dead and all but forgotten, I sometimes wonder if those women still wander the halls when no one else is looking.

Now, the flies lead the way as I gingerly approach the gurgling river. They trail toward the source of the smell like moons drawn into orbit, their needling buzz low and loud enough to feel in the back of my teeth. I pull my shirt above my nose, squinting through tears up and down the banks until I spy a river-brown shape pressed into the mud.

A catfish, I realize. All whiskers and wide, gasping mouth and ink-black eyes fixed on the storm building in the distance. The fins on each of its sides smear uselessly against the mud as if trying to propel itself back into the water.

I crouch beside it, ignoring the bile that burns at the back of my throat and the shivering curtain of insects that hang in the air around us.

Every so often, the Chérie belches up one of her wretched children to shrivel and die in the unforgiving Louisiana sun. Things with too many eyes or not enough limbs—creatures not found in our lesson books or the Admiral's war stories or the rambling sermons of Reverend Redwine.

"I'm sorry," I say, and its pinprick eyes roll to meet mine.

Just beyond the fins, the fish's body splits into twin tails that smack at the bank, one after the other. They end in finger-fine claws, each tipped with a nail so clean and neat it could belong to any proper lady. As I watch, a dragonfly hovers above it, eventually descending to rest on the fish-thing's mud-streaked side.

Its mouth works once, twice, as if gasping on the air that poisons it. The tails thrash in unison now, scattering the flies and leaving them humming in irritation. The dragonfly, however, remains. Wings twitching and iridescent, oblivious to the throes of the dying thing beneath it.

In the distance, thunder clears its throat. I open my satchel and remove the wooden box that once held candles in the girls' home cellar.

"It is beginning," the fish-thing says in a voice like a child's whisper.

Then, the creature gives a hard, gurgling shudder and goes still.

To my relief, Miss Viola's office door is shut when I slink downstairs just in time for dinner. My legs burn like fire, but I refuse to give Charlotte the satisfaction of tears at the table. Instead, I stare down at my lap in silence, letting the chatter of my girls' house sisters draw my thoughts away from the slender welts that paper the backs of my thighs.

Charlotte watches me with hawk eyes from her perch beside Miss Viola's chair. Next to Charlotte's napkin sits the dainty handkerchief her parents sent her last Christmas. For days, she'd crowed over the slip of lavender silk, blissfully rubbing it against her rosy cheek whenever she thought someone might be looking.

Ruby nudges me with an elbow. In the gray, stormy light, her floral dress shines almost ivory against her dark-brown skin. I lean close to her, and the coconut smell of her lotion is like a warm hug.

"I bribed the Johnston boy for rolling papers when he delivered the flour this morning," she whispers. "Care for a smoke after lights-out?"

I squeeze her arm in return.

"That sounds lovely."

"Good." She flashes a smile. "The attic. Half an hour after lights-out."

Smiling, I pull my eyes back to my plate, where a heap of fried catfish sits alongside potatoes and collard greens straight from Miss Emmi's garden out back. Just picking up my fork sends a ripple of pain across the welts, and I try not to flinch as I bring a lump of fish to my mouth. It tastes like the mud that runs along the Chérie's banks.

Through the dining room's enormous windows, past the covered porch with peeling paint and termite-ravaged columns, a thunderhead envelopes the horizon. Lightning crawls along its black belly, and even from miles away we can hear the murmured rumblings of its thunder.

"Monster of a storm, that is," the Admiral says from his seat, punctuating the words with a wince. The cane at his side glints dully in the jaundiced light. "Hope none of y'all ladies was expectin' to go to town in the next few days. Liable to be a hell of a flood."

"Will we be safe, Admiral?" Lucy, the youngest of my girls' house sisters, flinches at the latest peal of thunder. Her knuckles blink white between the folds of her skirt.

The old man's craggy face softens. "Now don't you worry, little miss. We're up high on this hill, like a bird in a nest. It'd take all the water in the Chérie and then some to reach us."

That seems to calm her, though the other girls trade glances around the table. Concern, curiosity, annoyance conveyed in a raised eyebrow or a slight purse of the lips. The secret language we've created during our years at the Girls' House to skirt Miss Viola's wrath.

The Admiral drains the rest of his sweet tea in one gulp and pushes back his chair.

"Miss Emmi, if you don't mind tellin' Miss Viola I'm out tendin' to the porch." The Admiral winces as he braces his weight against the cane and stands. "That last step just about gave way earlier. Damn thing—sorry, ladies—the darn thing's right near rotted through."

Miss Emmi responds with a stiff nod. She's already on her feet, gathering the bowl that holds the last of the mashed potatoes. A moment later they're both gone, and the conversation shifts back to the clinking of cutlery and murmur of my house sisters' conversations.

*"C'est une belle journée."* Charlotte's singsong voice rises above the others. *"Une belle journée pour une promenade parmi les fleurs."*

"What're you doing?" asks Teddy, a pretty girl with red hair kept in two long plaits.

"Practicing my French," Charlotte replies airily. "Mama and Papa just purchased a chateau in Paris."

I snort into my plate, and Charlotte's face goes sour.

"Do you have something to say, Madeline?"

Before I can respond, Ruby elbows me in the ribs.

*"Maddy,"* she whispers in warning, and I swallow my nasty reply.

Auggie, Charlotte's best friend and most passionate toady, leans into Charlotte's side and whispers something that sends them both into a fit of poorly concealed giggles.

"What's so funny?" Lucy asks in her little-girl voice, which makes the two girls laugh harder.

"Tell me!"

"You're too young to understand." Auggie lifts her chin, her narrow face still bright with humor. "Ask again when you're older."

"But I want to know *now*!"

Thunder growls overhead, working another loop into the tension knotted in my stomach.

"Don't tell her, Auggie," Charlotte says with a lazy wave of her hand. "She'll just tattle to Miss Viola."

"I won't!" Lucy insists. Her chestnut curls bounce as she thumps her fists against the table. "I swear!"

Auggie and Charlotte exchange a look.

"You swear?" Charlotte finally asks, and Lucy responds with a resolute nod. Another glance passes from Charlotte to Auggie, and this time I swear I can feel the satisfaction dripping between them.

"I *said* . . ." Auggie leans forward, fixing her hazel eyes on me. "The closest some of us will ever come to France is the bayou whorehouse they was born in."

The collective gasp that circles the table is nearly drowned out by the ringing that fills my ears. My chair comes away from the table with a squeal, and before I realize it, I'm on my feet.

"Maddie, wait—" Ruby says, but I shove her hand away. The other girls fade from my vision, the room narrowing until it focuses on the two smirking faces at the far side of the table.

Another chair screeches against the floor. Likely another girl—I don't care which one—scrambling to get out of my way. My eyes sweep the table, across napkins, decanters, delicate cups.

A bread knife.

Auggie follows my gaze, and her mouth drops open in the beginning of a scream. To yell for Miss Viola or Miss Emmi or the Admiral. So I can get the switch again while she and Charlotte smirk at me from behind the back of whoever's doing the whipping.

So they can keep on spreading the rumor that my mama sold sex and left her infant daughter on the Girls' House doorstep rather than take responsibility for her sins.

But before Auggie can find her voice, a different noise pierces the room. A wet, heavy slap that sounds from somewhere beyond the window. A second thump follows it, then another. And another.

The main door groans open, filling the first floor with a rush of wind and the smell of rainfall.

Then—

More thumps. A wheezing shout.

The Admiral.

"Ma'am!" he yells through the whistle in his lungs. "Miss Viola! Come quick!"

The bodies lie scattered across the lawn, each one dark and slick and still.

Fish, hundreds of them. Catfish and bluegill and sauger all the way down to finger-long minnows. From the safety of the covered porch, we watch, wide-eyed and open-mouthed, as they drop from the sky like hailstones onto the rain-soaked lawn.

Lightning illuminates the grass, turning the fish scales into tiny eyes that glint and glitter and wink. Then it's dusk-dark again, the sunlight choked out by the black clouds that stretch from one end of the horizon to another. The air reeks of river water, of mud and decay and things that lurk below the surface.

Teddy yelps as the porch roof shudders directly above us. An instant later, an enormous gar drops from the awning and hits the ground below. Its mouth wrenches open to reveal two rows of pristine human teeth.

My insides go icy.

"God in Heaven," Miss Emmi whispers at my side, and I turn to find her gripping the crucifix hanging from her neck. "Lord, have mercy."

The Admiral lets out a wheeze from the rocking chair next to the door.

"I'm fine," he grumbles, waving away Miss Viola's attempts to dab the sweat from his forehead. "It's just—I don't—"

Panic grips us like a too-tight glove, punctuated by Lucy's whimpers and Teddy's halfhearted attempts to soothe her. In the semidarkness, I fumble for Ruby's wrist and squeeze it. She threads her fingers through mine in response.

What is going on?

"Inside, all of you." Miss Viola helps the Admiral to his feet. Then, when no one moves, she yells, "*Now!*"

We file inside in clusters, followed by the Admiral and Miss Viola, who casts one last incredulous look through the door before slamming it shut.

"Lights out in five minutes," she snaps. "I better not find a single one of you downstairs before morning."

"But I'm on dish duty," Teddy says, only to cower when our matron whirls upon her with the countenance of a raging bull.

"Did I not make myself clear?"

"Yes'm." Teddy keeps her eyes on the floor. "I mean, yes ma'am, you made yourself clear."

Miss Viola points toward the staircase.

The other girls speak in frantic murmurs, but Ruby and I climb the stairs together in silence.

A shudder works its way down my spine. I can feel the Chérie River in the distance, past the forest of sugar maples that bow against the wind like acolytes on a pilgrimage. Coiled around the grounds like a lazy snake and growing tighter, tighter, tighter with each passing hour of rain.

Ruby squeezes my arm.

"I think I still need that smoke," she breathes in my ear, and I manage a nod in response. "Midnight?"

Around us, girls sniffle or cry outright, and we all flinch each time another muffled thump sounds from overhead. My stomach churns, threatening to bring my dinner back to my lips.

*Catfish.* I shudder.

Ruby and I part ways at the top of the stairs. Our rooms sit on opposite ends of a hallway lined with threadbare carpet and water-stained floral wallpaper, all illuminated by the jaundiced light of a handful of wall sconces. On the far wall is a window that sits directly next to my bedroom door, overlooking the front of the Girls' House grounds.

I try not to look, but my eyes drift to the window like moths to a flame.

More bodies now. And even more falling, still, every so often. A fish flashes past, its fins almost close enough to brush the rain-streaked glass, and I leap back so quickly I almost lose my balance. Heart hammering, I dive into my room and slam the door shut behind me.

The house is ink-dark by the time I creep back into the hallway. By now, the sky seems to have emptied its belly of fish, but the drumbeat of rain reverberates overhead. Still, I lighten my steps, ears straining for any sign of someone who might overhear me.

I refuse to look out the window as I tiptoe past. I don't care to see what other terrible things this storm may have gifted the grounds.

Sticking close to the wall, I slink past the closed doors of girls who whimper and mutter in their sleep. Past Auggie's room, which reeks of the poultice she swears helps with her complexion, and Teddy's door decorated with a wreath of dried flowers and lavender sprigs.

Lightning brightens the hallway in bursts, and each time it sends a jolt through my limbs that feels stronger than any electricity. The thunder that follows rattles the entire hallway, the ancient wood shuddering like loose teeth beneath my bare feet.

I was fourteen when I found the tobacco squirreled away in an ammunition box left forgotten in the hayloft over the disused stable. I had no idea what the leaves even were until Ruby arrived a year later and showed me how to roll them into cigarettes we clumsily smoked when no one was looking, until Miss Emmi complained of a strange smell around the toolshed. Today, we keep it hidden in a far corner of the attic, where a tumble of hatboxes hides its presence from the world.

Of all the rules I've broken in my time at Chérie Parish Girls' House, this is probably the worst of them, and I try to ignore the pang of guilt that eases past my fear to press at my ribs.

If I'm caught—and I have been, more than once—I'll say I was on my way to the toilet at the other end of the hall. It's a believable story, until I turn left instead of right and reach an uneven set of steps that rises into darkness.

I've climbed the attic stairs enough times to know which steps to avoid. But the wood still sighs beneath me, and it keeps my heart in my throat until I reach the top and nudge the door open.

The Girls' House attic is a labyrinthine maze of steamer trunks and boxes and discarded furniture. It trails from one corner of the house to the other, and when the sun is high, it feels as familiar as an old friend. In the dark, though, the room is a maw that gapes with sharp edges and jagged wooden teeth, made twice as eerie by the whistle of wind through the rafters overhead.

"Ruby?" Her name is lost in a peal of thunder. I swallow and try again. "Ruby?"

"Right here." She appears from the darkness.

With one hand, she gestures me toward the corner of the attic where the lone window sits propped open a few inches. Beside it is a low table topped with a single candle, along with two cushions scavenged from the old chairs left up here to rot.

I settle onto a cushion, and Ruby presses a slender cigarette into my fingers. The faint smell of tobacco lingers in the air, evidence of the weekly nights Ruby and I spend up here together, trading stories until we can't keep our eyes open any longer.

Normally, on nights like these, Ruby shares tales of far-flung cities, of New Orleans and the boroughs of New York City, of the neon lights of Las Vegas and the gaudy charm of Hollywood Boulevard. Places she visited with her father before he remarried and shunted Ruby off to Chérie Parish to appease his new bride.

In contrast, my memories begin and end within these walls. No steamer trunk bares my name, waiting for the day someone returns to spirit me back to a world beyond the parish.

Ruby presses a cigarette into my fingers, bringing me back to the thunder and the rain and the pitiful things left scattered on the grass.

"Am I losing my damn mind, or are there fish falling from the sky?" Ruby drops onto the other cushion. Her eyes are wide enough that the whites shine in the cigarette's glow. "What in God's name is *going on*?"

"I don't know," I answer, drawing my knees up until they bump against my chin. "The adults don't seem to have any ideas, either."

"Isn't this kind of thing in the Bible somewhere? Like a plague?"

Despite my nerves, I laugh. "My Bible learning is about as good as Charlotte's French."

In the darkness, Ruby sighs.

"Maddy," she says, her voice tight with warning, "you ought to leave that girl alone."

She's right, much as I hate to admit it. But even the thought of the ghastly beasts that litter the grass can't distract from Auggie's nasty words at breakfast.

Words that have once again ripped the scab from a wound that refuses to heal. I stretch out, fighting to keep from bouncing my legs.

"My mama didn't sell sex," I murmur back.

"I know."

But she doesn't, and neither do I. All anyone knows of my parentage comes from my discovery on the Chérie's banks nearly sixteen years ago. The proverbial baby in a basket, left at the river's mercy until Miss Viola found me wailing in the mud.

We flinch at the heavy thump of another fish hitting the roof.

"If they don't shut their mouths, I've half a mind to do it for them."

Sighing, Ruby lowers the book and leans closer. "They hound you because you take their bait."

"Let's see you ignore them when they call your mama a whore."

Ruby fixes me with a pointed stare. "You and I both know they call me worse when Miss Viola isn't listening. Just like we know Miss Viola won't risk any punishment that might get their folks involved."

I do, but it doesn't help me feel any better. Knowing Charlotte and Auggie get away with their nastiness because their parents' money helps keep food on our table.

"Charlotte's eighteen this year," Ruby adds gently. "She'll be out of our hair."

"There's still Auggie to deal with," I grumble.

Ruby pats my shoulder. "Once Charlotte's gone, Auggie won't have anyone to impress. She'll settle down, mark my words."

I scowl and sink deeper into the cushion's moth-chewed upholstery. For a moment, the storm doesn't matter. The fish on the lawn don't matter. Nothing matters except the cigarette smoke wafting between us, and the cigarettes' glow, and my best friend's silhouette in the darkness.

"She better."

That night, I dream of the Chérie. Drawing ever closer in the storm, its thick and murky water reaching up to swallow me whole.

Morning dawns with a scream.

I rocket out of bed in a stupor. I bang my shoulder on the dresser, grinding at the cigarette-smoke crust that's formed around my eyes in the handful of hours since I returned to my room.

My bare feet slap against the floor as I reach the door and wrench it open, revealing a hallway painted gloomy and gray from the light beyond the window. Across from me, Lucy blinks owlishly from her own doorway. Our eyes meet, and without words we rush together toward the source of the shout.

Charlotte stands at Auggie's open door, fist clenched around the neckline of her nightdress and hair wild at her shoulders. As Lucy and I join the cluster of curious, half-asleep girls, Miss Viola materializes at the top of the stairs, a bluster of black dressing gowns and a calico robe. I spy Ruby on the other side of the crowd, her coiled hair held in a satin bonnet tied with an oversized bow.

"Auggie's gone!" Charlotte shrieks, pointing into her best friend's bedroom with a trembling finger. "And—and—"

"Charlotte, please." Miss Viola sighs. "She's probably in the powder room. We're all on edge from the current, well, *circumstances*, but we mustn't lose our heads—"

"But look!"

Miss Viola turns to the room and goes still.

We follow her gaze.

A pair of muddy footprints make their way from the foot of Auggie's bed to the bedroom doorway. Like a flock of birds, we all rush backward as one, our eyes tracking the prints from Auggie's room and down the hallway carpet.

To the window by my door, which sits halfway open, the curtains fluttering in the misty breeze.

Teddy gasps, and the sound snaps the thread of silence that held us. All at once, girls begin to shriek and scream. Ruby's eyes meet mine, and she gives me a look I can't quite decipher.

"Get the Admiral," Miss Viola hisses to no one in particular, and when no one moves, she shoves me toward the staircase. I stumble down the steps, pulse thundering and panic locked on my throat like a vice.

I've lived in this house for as long as I can remember. I've seen the strangeness that lurks beneath the Chérie's surface, those wretched creatures with too many eyes or not enough skin. But always they've died, gasping, at the river's banks, never making it beyond the slimy sand.

I find the Admiral in the dining room, a steaming mug of coffee clutched between his thick palms. At the sound of my arrival, he jerks upright.

"Admiral," I gasp. "Upstairs."

He doesn't wait for me to continue. The mug clatters to the floor as he rushes past me in a cloud of aftershave and tobacco. I trail behind him like a shadow, clutching his forgotten cane to my chest and taking the steps two at a time to keep up with him.

The sound of my house sisters' wailing grows to a roar as we reach the top of the stairs.

"I have to pee!" Lucy wails. "Someone come with me—I don't want to go alone!"

"Did someone take her?"

"You saw! There was only one set of prints!"

"What if someone carried her?"

"The footprints started at the bed!"

*"I have to pee!"*

The look on Miss Viola's face is nothing short of horrifying when she rounds on us. Her teeth flash ivory when she next speaks, the words punctuated by a vein that throbs at her temple.

"All of you are to go to your rooms right this instant. Miss Emmi, the Admiral, and I will conduct inspections. If any one of you thinks this is some kind of game—if I find out you're hiding her . . ."

Lucy lets out a groan.

Miss Viola's hands curl into fists. "Teddy, go with Lucy to the facilities. I want both of you in your rooms as soon as she's finished."

"With all due respect, Miss Viola, it looks like she snuck outside," the Admiral says. "If that's the case, it might be best if I search the grounds and leave you women to the girls' rooms."

"I don't want anyone leaving the house in this—this—" Miss Viola gestures at the window, where a steady drizzle patters beyond the glass.

"Ain't nothing falling from the sky but rain now, ma'am, and I ain't sweet enough to melt. If it makes you feel better, I'll take the gun."

Miss Viola sighs. "Very well. The rest of you, your rooms. Now."

Miss Emmi mutters profanities under her breath as she wrenches a handful of my skirts from the wardrobe.

"I don't think Auggie could fit in there if she wanted to," I begin, only to be silenced by a look that drips venom.

Knees bouncing from my perch on the edge of the bed, I watch her make her way through the rest of the room, though the thought of Auggie hiding under the desk or behind the filmy curtains is absurd.

"Has the Admiral come back yet?" I ask, and I'm not surprised when Miss Emmi pretends not to hear. Guts churning, I turn to the window instead, where rainwater has turned the driveway into a miniature river, and the forest in the distance is a formless gray mass that bends and sways in the wind.

"How could Auggie have gotten down from the window?"

Still no reply from Miss Emmi. But I can see the questions in her thoughts, so clear they may as well be spilling from her lips. The footprints led from Auggie's bed and straight to the window beside my bedroom door. Could she have opened it without waking half the floor with the sound of the window's squealing? More importantly, could she have walked away after dropping two stories onto the grass below?

Miss Emmi snarls, now crouched and peering into the shadows beneath my bed. "If one of you brats is hiding that girl, Miss Viola will be the least of your worries."

I believe her.

I wrap my arms around my stomach. "Maybe the Admiral's found her, and they're on their way back."

Miss Emmi sneers. "Maybe."

"Maybe she ran away." She wouldn't be the first. One of them, a doe-eyed girl we called Trixie, vanished from her bed just before my thirteenth birthday. She turned up two weeks later on the banks of the Chérie River, just past the Girls' House grounds.

Drowned, Miss Viola told her parents, but I saw her body after they stowed it in the stables to wait for the doctor's arrival. I saw the purple finger-shaped marks that circled her throat.

"You hated her, didn't you?"

Miss Emmi's face appears inches from mine. I flinch back until my elbows bump the wall my bed sits against.

"I saw how she tested you. Her and Charlotte both." Miss Emmi's lips contort into a treacherous smile. "Are you hoping she's run away? Gone for good?"

I swallow. "I hope she's all right. That's all."

Miss Emmi snorts and straightens, calloused hands brushing dust from the front of her dress.

"I've worked here long enough to know you girls are all the same. Nasty little creatures, at each other's throats like dogs on a piece of meat. Even you. *Especially* you."

Heat rises in my cheeks. I dig my fingernails into my palms, unsure whether the pressure in my chest is from fury or tears or a combination of the two. I try to look away, but Miss Emmi's fingers latch on to my face and force it back toward her.

"Miss Viola may have tamed you, given you the same book learning as the paying girls. But you're still at the bottom of whatever pecking order keeps this place running."

She pulls me closer until I can smell the tang of whiskey on her breath.

"Here's the thing, though, Madeline. I'm at the bottom of the order, too. And sometimes we have to show the folks at the top that they're not invincible."

"I didn't do anything to Auggie," I whisper, my vision swimming with tears. "I swear."

A heartbeat passes. Then two. At last, Miss Emmi releases my face and straightens. I fall back with a gasp, pressing my cold fingers into the half-moon grooves Miss Emmi's nails dug into my skin.

Ruby finds me on the porch afterward, curled in the Admiral's rocking chair and trying to breathe without whimpering.

"Smells like rotten fish out here." She makes a face. "You all right?"

I swipe the back of one hand across my eyes.

"Fine."

She crouches in front of the chair and rests a hand on my knee. "Are you sure?"

"I said I'm fine."

"All right, all right." She raises her hands, palms facing me. "Want some company?"

"I guess." Sniffling, I wipe my nose with a sleeve and shift so Ruby can snuggle into the chair beside me. She doesn't seem to mind the sweat that sticks our arms together.

"You seen the Admiral?"

I shake my head, and Ruby peers through the drizzle beyond the porch. A steady stream of rainwater courses down the awning to the grass, where it joins puddles that must now be at least ankle deep. I can't see the Chérie from here, but I imagine it creeping closer with each passing hour, growing ever-fatter from the flood.

"I reckon he'll be okay out there," she says finally. "He's got practice with this kind of thing."

I snort. "Hunting girls?"

Ruby rolls her dark eyes. "*Searching* for people."

"You're probably right." I press my toes into the porch and push the chair back a few inches.

Silence creeps around us like fog, but it's a comfortable feeling. My eyes drift shut as I rest my head against Ruby's shoulder, and she reaches up to run a hand over my rain-frizzed hair. My stomach burns, as if someone's run a fireplace poker through my navel and tugged it through me like a hook. I press a hand against the skin and am almost surprised to find my flesh is cool to the touch.

"Maddy?"

I don't open my eyes. "Mmm?"

"Have you ever heard of a waterspout?"

I shake my head.

"I found a book about weather in the library this morning," Ruby continues. "Waterspouts are like twisters, but they happen over bodies of water—like rivers or ponds or the ocean. And sometimes they suck things up and then spit them out miles away."

"Like fish?"

"Yep. All kinds of stuff. The book said one really big one picked up a whole ship a hundred years ago or so."

I twist to look her in the eye. "What happened to the ship?"

She raises an eyebrow. "They never found it. But the point is, I think that's what's happening here. It makes perfect sense, with the storm and all the rain."

Ruby's words bounce through my mind. She's right—it does make sense. The thought is enough to loosen the knots Miss Emmi's words left embedded in my stomach.

"Waterspout." I try out the word, feel the glimmering of hope somewhere deep in my core.

Then a movement catches my attention, and the hope turns to ash on my tongue.

"Look." I point, and Ruby follows my outstretched finger.

Just past Miss Viola's daylilies, an alligator the size of a downed tree meanders across the driveway. Its blunt snout hangs half-open, revealing a mouthful of pointed teeth.

Its tail swings from side to side with each step, unbothered by the mud and grass that brushes its belly. The rumble from its throat, lower even than last night's thunder, sends goosebumps down every inch of my exposed skin.

But that's not why we stare.

Ruby squints. "Is that—?"

All the air in my lungs rushes out in a whoosh.

An extra set of legs pumps at the alligator's sides, situated where I imagine the base of its ribcage would be.

Ruby's hand finds mine and squeezes hard.

The alligator bends its tree-trunk head to snap up a fish lying motionless on the grass.

"We need to get inside," my friend breathes. "Right now."

Slowly, the beast turns to face us, its head at least as wide as I am tall. Cold, empty eyes lock on to us, and as it blinks, another terrible realization latches on to me.

Three eyes. Two where they should be, and a third blinking dimly at us from the middle of its scaly forehead.

Its mouth twists into an unmistakable smile.

I'm rooted to the chair, but Ruby grabs my arm and yanks me upright. With me in tow, she scrambles for the door, screaming for Miss Viola at the top of her lungs.

But by the time our matron arrives, breathless and frazzled, the creature's nowhere to be seen.

The Admiral returns late that afternoon, shoulders bowed and the gun slumped across his elbow. Water pools around his muddy boots. Miss Viola rushes to him, shouting for Miss Emmi to help her get the old man to his room.

Before Miss Emmi can arrive, Charlotte sweeps toward the Admiral and grasps at his shirt like a girl half her age. "Did you find Auggie? Please, tell me you found her."

He shakes his head.

A thin wail bursts out of Charlotte's mouth like a siren. She crumples to the floor in a mess of lavender crinoline.

Miss Emmi appears at our backs with towels and a quilt from the library. Together, she and Miss Viola guide the Admiral out of the foyer and toward the back of the house. They wave me and Ruby away when we approach.

"Leave him be," Miss Viola warns us, voice thin from the strain of helping support the Admiral's weight.

Ruby's chest heaves, but she doesn't argue. Instead, I follow her to the library, where she hunts down every weather book she can find. She presses one into my arms.

"There has to be an explanation."

But there isn't—at least, not one we can find in the encyclopedias and fairy tales and old medical journals stored on the library's shelves. We read in silence until dusk, when Miss Viola seems to realize none of us have eaten since last night's dinner.

No one seems to have an appetite, but we gather around the table anyway. I'm not sure about the other girls, but for me the comfort of routine feels like an anchor, something to cling to as the world outside crumbles away.

The Admiral shivers in his chair, but otherwise he seems all right. A thick bath robe—his own robe, I imagine, but I've never seen him wear it—drapes over his shoulders.

In the chair beside mine, Ruby twists her napkin into a knot, tying and untying it as she mouths something that might be a prayer. On the other side of the table, Charlotte's shoulders shake with hiccupping sobs.

Lucy shifts, trying to slip into the empty chair at Charlotte's side.

"Get off of that!" Charlotte shrieks, shoving the younger girl so hard she almost topples over. "Auggie sits there! Not you!"

Lucy starts to wail.

"Charlotte!" Miss Viola snaps. "Lucy, I want you in your own chair."

Miss Viola watches us with a scowl so deep it almost reaches her ears. Her snowy hair has come partly undone and tumbles in clumps down to her shoulders. A pair of glasses perch on the bridge of her nose, magnifying her eyes until they look far too large for her face.

We wait in silence as Miss Emmi emerges from the kitchen with a covered platter and a look that suggests she'd rather take her knives to us instead.

"Pork chops." She drops the platter on the table and removes the silver cover.

My stomach lets out a gurgle, and I realize I'm starving. The skin around my belly feels taut, as if I haven't eaten in days. As the girls pass the platter around the table, I load my own plate with red potatoes and biscuits. When the platter reaches me, I choose the biggest piece of meat and plunk it next to the red potatoes.

"Admiral, are you able to say grace?" Miss Viola asks.

He nods and bows his head, and she follows.

"Lord, we come to you now in a time of turmoil," he begins.

I open my eyes and find the other girls have done the same. We peer at each other around the table, lips pressed tightly together and faces gray from fear. All except Ruby, who stares down at her plate, but her gaze is a hundred miles away.

"And Lord, we beseech thee," he continues, as Charlotte meets my eye with a look that oozes hatred. "Deliver Miss Augustine back to us. Let us not lose faith, for we are faithful . . ."

I hold Charlotte's gaze like a weapon, satisfaction pooling in my belly as she responds to my neutral expression with a curled lip.

"Amen," the old man wheezes, and even Miss Viola lets out a relieved breath.

A moment later, she sweeps her eyes over us, nods, and retrieves her knife from the table. Our sign to start eating, whether we want to or not.

I press my own knife into the pork chop.

My cutlery clatters to the table.

Tiny white worms writhe through the meat, twitching and burrowing and dripping onto the porcelain plate. They emerge from the potatoes as well, and when I look back at the biscuits, I find them dotted with dark pill-shaped weevils.

This time, everyone screams. Even the Admiral, whose voice booms like cannon fire over the rest of us. Teddy wrenches her chair from the table, catching the tablecloth and pulling all the plates down to the floor with an earsplitting crash.

Charlotte grinds at her mouth with a napkin, and despite my disgust, a flicker of satisfaction pinches my stomach. How many bites did she take before we noticed the worms?

Miss Emmi bursts back through the doorway, her own shouts joining the chaos sweeping through the room.

"Enough!" Miss Viola's thundering shout startles us all into stillness. She turns to Miss Emmi, who withers before the older woman's countenance. "Speak."

"The whole larder's gone rotten!" Tears stream down Miss Emmi's face, and I almost feel bad for her until I remember the feel of her nails pressing into my cheeks.

"How could that happen?"

Miss Emmi balls her skirts into her bony fists. "I don't know, ma'am. It wasn't like this while I was preparing, I swear!"

"Just the meat?"

"All of it, ma'am. The vegetables, the flour, the milk, the butter—I even opened a jar of last year's preserves, and they reek of sulfur."

Thunder shatters through the room, and this time Lucy does tumble from her chair. Rather than right herself, she hunches forward, clutching tufts of hair in her hands and keening like a wounded animal.

"I want to go home! I want to go home *now*!"

"She's right," Teddy cries. "Whatever this is, it isn't natural. We're not safe here. We should leave!"

"We're not going anywhere," Miss Viola snarls. "Nothing will happen to you while you're in this house."

"Liar!" Charlotte leaps to her feet, chair squealing across the floor behind her. Her skin has taken on a green-gray sheen. "Look at what happened to Auggie! We're risking our lives every minute we stay in this house."

The Admiral bangs his cane against the floor.

"Even if we did decide to leave, we'd only get so far as the river's edge. The bridges are washed out, both of 'em."

"You're telling me we're trapped here?" Charlotte's voice rises another octave, and the Admiral nods sadly.

"I checked the road while I was lookin' for your friend."

A cup smashes against the wall. We all wrench our eyes to Miss Viola, her arm still poised mid-throw. Her hair has come fully undone by now, and it courses around her head like Medusa's snakes.

"This discussion is over," she says in a voice that borders on hysterics. "Girls, you will clean up this mess—I want to see my reflection in the floor when you're finished."

"You want us touching *worms*?" Charlotte shrieks.

Miss Viola continues as if she hadn't heard her. "While you're cleaning, Emmi, the Admiral, and I will take stock of the remaining food."

"I told you," Miss Emmi begins, "it's all—"

"That is *all*!" Fire brims in our matron's eyes, bright enough to send us all shrinking back like kicked dogs.

Miss Emmi was right—all the food in the house has spoiled. The moment Miss Viola informs us, the girls again erupt in frenzied conversation.

"We have to *leave*," Charlotte insists, and this time Miss Viola's hand slashes through the air. It connects with Charlotte's face with an earsplitting smack.

Charlotte gasps. The mark on her cheek burns like a flare.

"How—how—"

"Another outburst and it'll be the switch," Miss Viola says, so quietly I strain to hear her over the rain's endless patter. "That goes for all of you."

She glares at our pitiful assemblage, as if daring one of us to argue. When no one speaks, she goes on. "I want you in your rooms. Tomorrow, the Admiral and I will figure out a way to get into town and bring back supplies."

*Tomorrow.* My stomach growls at the thought. Miss Viola's eyes swing to rest on me. I tense my shoulders, but her expression softens just enough for me to notice.

"I know we're all hungry," she says, and for a moment she sounds almost like herself. "Just, please, be patient. I promise, by this time tomorrow our larders and our bellies will be full."

My fingers drift across Ruby's bedroom door, and I pause just long enough to press my forehead against the wood before I continue down the darkened hallway.

Charlotte's door is closed, but light spills from beneath it and I can hear her sniffling hiccups from within. My insides buzz, as if a nest of hornets has set up residence in my guts.

I take a deep breath. I am famished—*so* famished—but it's a different kind of hunger than before.

"Charlotte," I whisper, rapping my knuckles on the door just hard enough for her to hear. "Charlotte, Auggie's back!"

The response is almost instant. Her footsteps hurry to the door, and she throws it open with a sob that I rush to muffle.

"Quiet!" I put a finger to my lips. "She doesn't want us to wake up Miss Viola."

"Where is she?" Charlotte shoves past me to look up and down the hallway. "Is she all right? When did she get he—"

She coughs. Claps a hand to her face.

A heartbeat later, a burst of brown-and-yellow liquid explodes from her mouth. She doubles over, retching, and I watch as a silver, thumb-sized frog works its way past her lips. It hits the floor twitching, its legless body writhing against the rug like a fly without wings.

"It's beginning," I murmur, stepping through Charlotte's doorway and easing the door shut behind me.

As Charlotte chokes up more muddy water, I retrieve the knife from the band of my nightdress.

I'm soaked through within five minutes of leaving the covered porch, making my way in the dark toward the swollen Chérie. The grass is slick beneath my feet, and more than once I nearly go tumbling face-first into the mud.

In my hands, I grip the slender wooden box that comes with me anytime I visit the river. Tonight it's heavier than usual, clattering impatiently each time I almost slip.

"Just a little bit further," I murmur.

The trees rattle their leaves as I creep through them, as if they whisper my secret along their branches. Rain shivers down their trunks like tears.

Like blood.

When I reach the Chérie's banks, I smile.

"I'm here," I say, kneeling in the slimy muck and lifting the box's lid to reveal a lavender handkerchief.

I retrieve the bundle of silk and untie it in my palm. Four dainty fingers rest within its folds, and I feed them to the river, one by one.

Then—

"I *knew* one of you would try to sneak out," Miss Emmi hisses, latching on to my wrist so tightly her grip grinds my bones together. "You little bitches. You—"

Her words are lost in a rush of water, and the blunted snout of the three-eyed alligator bursts out of the river at our side. It clamps down on Miss Emmi's calf, wrenching her off her feet and yanking her across the riverbank, turned ice-slick from three solid days of rain.

"Help me!" she shrieks. "Help—"

Her head disappears below the water.

For a moment, I don't move. Just watch the spot where the alligator emerged from the river. My fingers drift to my stomach, where a calloused ridge of skin marks the mouth that slashes vertically through my midsection. My new jagged teeth gnash in excitement, and I test their sharpness with a grin.

"I'm coming home, Mother," I say, and step into the murky depths.

# About the Author

For as long as she can remember, **L.M. Copeland** has been telling stories. She spent more than fifteen years as a print journalist, editor, and graphic designer before reclaiming her beloved Oxford comma and moving into the world of public relations and content writing. When she's not at a keyboard, she divides her time between playing board games, kayaking, gardening, and nurturing her love for all things creepy and spooky. These days, her home base is Tulsa, Oklahoma, where she and her partner dedicate most of their energy to wrangling their small herd of cats—with varying degrees of success.

You can find L.M. Copeland on Instagram and Facebook at:
@authorlmcopeland

You can visit her website at:
lmcopeland.com

# The Widow of Winthrop House

# The Widow of Winthrop House

## Sarah Kennedy Keys

WINTHROP HOUSE HAD BEEN BUILT for a family, and a large one at that, one with an even larger staff and a revolving door of friends and acquaintances. Indeed, it should have been home to my own sizeable family—a beloved husband and a passel of children.

Instead, it housed me alone. I could not call it my home; it was merely my dwelling, a lonely edifice where I whiled away all my time, apart from some occasional visits to the city. Yet despite my distaste for being confined to Winthrop House, I disliked my time in the city even more and longed for my own bed throughout each trip.

A lone housemaid came thrice each week to dust and polish the unlocked rooms. I saw to my own cooking when the impulse took me and ate from the larder the rest of the time. I could well afford to keep a cook and a full staff if I wished, but I'd dispensed with such formalities after burying my last husband.

I was not entirely friendless, of course. My own family fortune, vast to begin with, had only grown with the inheritances bestowed by my three late husbands. Such an amount of money was not without notice, and it entitled me to periodic social calls and a handful of invitations to the city throughout the year. If I were minded to waste funds as I did time, I would surely never lack companionship.

But each husband taken too soon had torn away pieces of me until I could not distinguish how much remained. Fragments of my soul were buried in the family plot, nestled into each coffin against the still chests of my dead husbands.

Winthrop House and its adjoining cemetery sat on a peninsula, with a single thin passageway to and from the estate. Oftentimes, it felt like residing on an island. The perpetual fog and cloudiness misting about the house only added to the impression.

Apart from Mary Hayes, the staunch housemaid, few ever traversed the path to the old black house on the peninsula, leaving me with solely the company in the family plot. With no one else to call upon them, I considered it my duty to visit the graves daily, sometimes twice each day.

Edward's nephew should visit more often, I thought. Timothy would, after all, inherit Winthrop and all the lands thereunto, cemetery grounds included, when I finally saw fit to take my place in the earth myself. Would he visit my grave then, as I visited the resting places of my own dearly departed? Somehow, I could not picture the foppish young man coming to stand at my graveside or tucking a flower against my weathered headstone.

Thus, I resolved to keep out of the grave for as long as I could. Perhaps I would vex everyone and outlive Timothy. It was not outside the realm of possibility, considering his profligate excess. His mother had written to me to urge my intervention, seeming to think I could exert some of the influence my late husband had. Timothy was, after all, Edward's nephew by blood and mine only by that ill-fated marriage. Why the boy's mother thought I could do anything, I could not fathom. Consequently, I dismissed her letter and kept in excellent health, so that Timothy would not become master of my domain for many years to come, if ever.

We were hardly so far apart in age, in any case. Less than a decade, in fact, which was a smaller gap than the one I'd shared with Edward.

I had married young, and repeatedly, to men considerably older than myself. Such circumstances would likely age other women, yet somehow, I'd avoided that particular fate and retained much of the appearance I'd had as a newly blushing bride. Though I'd kept my youthful looks, my girlish optimism was but a long, distant memory. Sometimes I dusted it off like a cherished trinket and gazed back upon it, allowing myself to hold the faded remembrance.

During my first marriage, I had anticipated children of my own, progeny who would rightfully inherit my family's estate. I was the sole Winthrop of my generation, and while my children would not be Winthrops themselves, they could at least continue the legacy of the house.

But it was not to be, from any of the marriages I entered into. Time and again, my womb was left barren and then my bed invariably empty.

The family cemetery alone grew in fullness.

And so I was left with only Timothy Reeves, nephew of my late second husband, to name as sole heir to Winthrop House. Edward would be pleased, I supposed. He had always doted on the insipid boy, presumably since Timothy was the lone male of his generation. Hardly a noteworthy distinction, considering it was a mere accident of birth, but Edward had cared about such circumstances, and I had ceased arguing with him over them.

A great many things had mattered to Edward, and look where they all got him in the end. Buried six feet beneath my boots, in a grave neglected by his beloved nephew.

One would think that after three husbands, I was destined for permanent widowhood. But rich widows held a greater appeal than poor virgins, and so anytime I finally ventured into the city, I attracted the notice of new men.

The latest suitor was a widower himself with a modest fortune and three children from his deceased wife. We had met at a tearoom, introduced by his dull sister, who was a passing acquaintance of mine. In truth, there was nothing remarkable about him, and I didn't relish the idea of rearing another woman's children if I accepted his inevitable offer. Of course, stepchildren would displace Timothy Reeves, so the notion had some appeal.

Really, I could have written Timothy out of the will after I'd married my third husband, Carlton Somers. But Carlton came from a family even smaller than mine, if such a thing were possible, and had no relatives on which to bestow an estate. He also gave me no children, so Timothy remained stubbornly in the entail.

I sometimes wondered if he felt as trapped by the arrangement as I did. Perhaps that was why he seldom visited, especially after Edward died. I suspected Timothy had disapproved of my marrying Carlton shortly after my mourning period had ended.

What would Timothy think if he knew I was entertaining an impending fourth proposal, one that would at last displace him from inheriting Winthrop House? He might encourage the suit solely to get free of the estate. He had never shown any real inclination for the place, and thus I resented the idea of handing it down to him. Not that it would happen anytime soon. For all the death that touched me, my own life thread seemed exceedingly long.

Such was the case for the women in my family, and I evidently inherited longevity as well as a certain tenacity for life. Too many women would lie down in the dirt, buried in grief, at the loss of one husband, let alone three. But I simply brushed myself off and went on living.

I did not expect Mary Hayes on the day I heard a carriage rolling up the drive. She never came by carriage in any case, but by a small, squeaking trap with a pony that looked as old as I felt some days. The sound below my window was distinctly of an approaching carriage, though, drawing my curiosity. Few things remained to excite my intrigue these days, but unexpected company was one of them, infrequently as it occurred. Thus, I set aside my needlepoint and strode to the window overlooking the drive, half expecting the carriage to be a trick of my idle imagination.

That was not the case. Despite being a poor day for travel, overcast and drizzling, a small black carriage pulled by two chestnut horses rolled to a halt by the entrance of Winthrop House. In the olden days, a gatekeeper would have stopped them at the pointed iron gates to inquire their intentions before granting admittance, but I'd dissolved the gatekeeper position long ago, before all the other positions save Mary's followed in the same vein.

As I watched, the carriage door opened, and a dark head of unruly curls poked out. A young man in a gray suit stepped down, and a moment later, I recognized him as Timothy Reeves. I blinked and pressed a bit closer to the windowpane, as if I could not trust my own eyes and perhaps my thoughts had conjured a mirage.

But Timothy remained on the stone drive below, a hat in his hand instead of covering his mop of hair. He turned back to the carriage and extended his hand, and I briefly wondered if he had brought his mother along to pay a social call.

Indeed, it was a woman who stepped out of the carriage – but it was not Jane Reeves with her wilted hat or unfashionable clothing. Instead, this was a far younger woman, one wearing an elegantly trimmed bonnet settled over blonde ringlets and a gown made of fetching peach colored fabric. The color was rather out of season for our October weather, but it seemed to suit the girl; even from this distance, I could tell.

Timothy offered his arm to the girl, and the pair began making their way to the door. Belatedly, I remembered Mary was not here today, and so the task of admitting my uninvited guests fell to me. So, too, would the chore of preparing tea and offering refreshment. For the first time in a long while, managing such things myself rankled me. Perhaps I would have to reconsider my total solitude here and the hoarding of my fortune. After all, what was I keeping it all back for? Certainly not for Timothy Reeves or any future stepchildren I might get from that widower—whose name quite escaped me at the moment. Potts? Ports? It made no difference, and I did not have the time to consider him now, not when Timothy and some unknown young woman were lifting the knocker on my aged front door.

I heard the knocking as I reached the stairs and silently wished again that I'd employed some full-time staff member to oversee these menial tasks. If I had, it would have allowed me a moment to check my appearance. To smooth the still-dark hair that showed no signs of graying and to change my sensible attire into something more befitting tea with guests.

None of that made a lick of difference now, and so I simply steeled myself to answer the door like I was fortifying for battle. As I crossed the foyer, I wondered if Timothy had come with bad news. Had some calamity befallen the Reeves? Was Jane unwell—or worse, deceased? Timothy's mother often complained of various maladies, but she had done so for as long as I had known her. None of them were ever serious, let alone lethal.

Besides, if his mother was on her deathbed or in her grave, Timothy Reeves would not be on my doorstep. He would have far more important things to attend to than alerting the widow of his late uncle, a woman who was only passingly connected to the family and never any great friend of his mother's.

It must be something else, then, and I would soon learn what. I reached for the door handle and turned it, arranging my features into a polite expression of mild surprise and welcome. "Good afternoon," I greeted. "What a pleasant surprise."

Timothy had donned his hat at some point after helping the blonde down from the carriage, and then quickly removed it when I opened the door. "Aunt," he said, and I noticed he had grown a thin mustache since our last meeting. He'd filled out a bit, too. Although he remained quite slender, he had lost some of the lankiness of his youth and his dove-gray jacket was well tailored to his frame. "Forgive us for calling unannounced."

"Not at all," I said smoothly, holding the door open wider. "Won't you come in?"

"Thank you." Timothy guided his companion inside with his hand on the small of her back. When they were both over the threshold and I had shut the door against the chill elements once more, he said, "Allow me to present Miss Cynthia Wright. Miss Wright, this is my aunt."

Cynthia Wright dipped into a deeper curtsy than necessary before saying softly, "It's a pleasure to meet you, Mrs. Reeves."

I held out my hand to take her gloved one, shaking it lightly. "A pleasure to meet you, Miss Wright. Although I am Mrs. Somers most recently." And perhaps soon Mrs. Potts or Ports or whatever that widower's name was.

Miss Wright's cheeks turned the same peachy shade as her dress. "I beg your pardon," she said. "Tim—I mean, Mr. Reeves, did not mention you had remarried."

Timothy set his jaw at the reminder of Carlton, and I had to suppress the smirk that wanted to appear on my face. The pair had met only once, at my wedding breakfast. Carlton had been indifferent to Timothy, taking no special interest in the nephew of my late second husband. But Timothy had clearly despised Carlton. At the time, I'd thought it was because he feared being replaced in the entail. But given his disinterest in Winthrop House, I came to believe his quarrel had more to do with his memory of Edward than the estate.

It made it all the more surprising that Timothy had decided to call upon me now, and to bring this peachy girl with the golden ringlets.

Returning my attention to her, I replied, "I am widowed again. Mr. Somers passed away last year."

She gasped softly, her already wide blue eyes becoming even rounder. "My condolences, Mrs. Ree—Somers," she corrected. "That must have been terribly difficult for you."

"I have managed," I answered. "But I thank you for your condolences all the same."

We stood awkwardly for a moment until I finally cleared my throat and turned back to Timothy. "Why don't you both come into the parlor for some tea? I am sure the refreshment would be welcome after your journey."

A journey he had not explained but I was too polite to inquire about—at least, before tea was served. Once they had a cup in hand, I would ask why they had come all this way.

"Thank you, Aunt," Timothy replied, steering Miss Wright in the direction of the parlor like he already owned this house. That, paired with his insistence on calling me Aunt, nettled me again. It struck me as strange that he should still be calling me his aunt when I was no longer any such thing. Close in age as we were, the title had been unusual even while Edward lived, but I had accepted it then as a fact of my marriage. In Edward's absence, it seemed at once too formal and too personal. Being called Mrs. Somers would have been even odder, though, and I was no longer Mrs. Reeves. I was merely the widow of Winthrop House, which was hardly a qualifying address.

So Aunt it was, then, for lack of anything better.

"Please make yourselves at home," I said as I ushered them into the parlor, grateful that Mary had been here to do the cleaning just yesterday. It wouldn't do to admit them to a room streaked with dust and cobwebs, not that Mary ever permitted such things to build up in the available rooms. The remainder of the shut-up house—well, that was another matter entirely and one I preferred not to consider.

Timothy Reeves and Cynthia Wright settled themselves onto the faded divan, a velvet upholstered piece that had lived in Winthrop House since before my mother's time. Just as I saw no reason to keep extra help about, I saw little point in frittering away money on furnishings that few would ever see. Besides, this settee was comfortably worn in the way I liked it. I had no reason to bristle at the surreptitious glance Cynthia Wright cast at the furniture and around the room, like she considered the outdated furnishings beneath her. I could not help but dislike her and her peach dress and her tight golden curls and the false sweetness of her demeanor.

My distaste for the girl only grew when she placed her hand into Timothy's and sat closer to him than propriety permitted. For that matter, where was their chaperone? It was unseemly that they had traveled this distance alone, with only the coach driver accompanying them. As I had the thought, another closely followed: that I had become a disapproving old marm, with nothing better to do than criticize the young as I crept ever closer to being among the old.

Remembering that I had promised tea, I excused myself and left the pair further unchaperoned. I was not such a fine lady that I could not put together my own tea service and so the heavy tray was suitably appointed as I made my way back up to the parlor with it. Perhaps I ought to ask Mary to come daily. She was less insufferable than other servants I'd had over the years, and I did not relish waiting on my own company, even if I could do it.

When I reentered the parlor, Cynthia Wright was no longer seated on the divan. Instead, she stood by the mantel, gazing up at a portrait hung above it. As I set down the tray to begin serving, she turned toward me and said, "This is a lovely portrait of you, ma'am."

"That is a portrait of my grandmother," I answered crisply. The antiquated clothing should have tipped her off as to the year, but she did not seem an especially bright girl.

"Oh!" she exclaimed, blushing once again. She seemed to do that quite a lot. I wondered if this was the sort of girl Timothy liked, vapid and blushing. "The resemblance is remarkable. How very much like her you look."

"Ours is a family with strong resemblance," I said, pouring the tea into three cups, although I wanted none of my own. A dull ache had worked itself into my head and tea would not cure it.

"There's a portrait of Mrs. Somers's mother that looks much the same," Timothy put in, and I decided I disliked being called Mrs. Somers even more than I disliked being called Aunt.

"As I said, the resemblance runs strong," I replied, offering him a steaming cup of tea. The china was an old set, from my first wedding, and older even than that, as it was an antique when I was given it. I wondered if Cynthia Wright would turn up her nose at the dated porcelain as she did my faded settee, but she merely took her seat and her cup without a flicker of the protest or distaste I expected.

"This is such a remote estate," she commented. "You must get so lonely here by yourself. Why, it reminds me a bit of Count Dracula's castle! Have you read Mr. Stoker's novel?"

I pressed my mouth into a thin line at her theatrics. "I do not care for sensational stories."

"Oh, but they're most thrilling!" she exclaimed. "Sometimes I have wondered if there could be any truth to them. Truth is stranger than fiction, they say."

"So they say," I answered dryly.

"You must be wondering why we have descended upon you in this fashion," Timothy said, helping himself to one of the biscuits from the tray and sparing me from continued melodramatic conversation with Cynthia Wright.

"The question did cross my mind, yes." I sipped from my own teacup, ignoring the biscuits, which held even less appeal than the tea. "It is hardly an easy journey, especially in such weather."

As if to punctuate my words, a gust of wind rattled a branch against the windowpane, the twigs scratching the glass like jagged fingernails. So strong was the gale-force wind that the latch popped open and the window swung inward. Biting back a curse, I set down my cup and went to refasten the window, taking care to do it securely.

When I returned to my seat and my tea, Timothy went on as if he had not been interrupted. "Miss Wright and I have happy news."

He paused to sample the biscuit, almost as if he intended to build suspense. I was in no mood for more theatrics, but I forced myself to take another sip of tea rather than saying so. It went down bitter and I tried not to grimace.

At last, he continued, "We are to be married."

"I must congratulate you, then," I said mildly, not seeing why he came to deliver the news in person when a letter would have sufficed. In fact, it needn't have even been a letter from Timothy. One from his mother, Jane, would have served just as well. Even a newspaper clipping would not have gone amiss.

"Thank you," Miss Wright said, another blush blooming on her round cheeks.

How old was she, I wondered. Old enough to be married, evidently. I was barely eighteen at my first wedding and she seemed to be beyond that age, at least.

"You have such a lovely estate," she continued. "We wondered if you might consent to hosting the wedding here."

I had to bite back a laugh at the boldness and absurdity of the question, and I looked to Timothy for further clarification.

He shifted a bit uncomfortably, like he hadn't intended for his fiancée to blurt out the request. Even so, he didn't rescind it and merely explained, "We would like to hold the wedding party at a country estate rather than in the city. And I have always been fond of this house. I have pleasant memories here, from . . ." He cleared his throat. "From visits with Uncle Edward."

Once more, I had to resist the urge to scoff. Timothy had never cared for Winthrop House as he ought to, and he seemed to have forgotten his beloved Uncle Edward the moment the man was in the ground.

"I am afraid it has been a great many years since there were any parties at Winthrop," I replied, setting my teacup firmly in its saucer. "The house may not bear such a grand occasion now. And I expect it will be rather out of the way for most of your guests, remote as the location is."

"We do not have a terribly extensive guest list," Miss Wright said, seeming oddly determined despite having spent less than an hour in the house so far.

"And you have no nearer relations who would prefer to host the happy occasion?" I asked, trying not to sound arch about it. "I should hate to rob them of the opportunity."

Miss Wright's blush deepened, as if I had struck a nerve, and Timothy hastened to smooth over the matter. "Cynthia does not have a large family, so naturally, we looked to mine instead."

I took a sip of tea to keep from pointing out that we were not family; Timothy was Edward's nephew, not mine, and I had never assimilated properly into the Reeves family to begin with. Or any family I married into. Even in my own clan of Winthrops, there had been oddities and distance. Now I remained the sole bearer of the heritage, if not the name.

"I am flattered by your consideration," I said. "But I fear I must disappoint you. Winthrop is not the place it once was. Much has changed here."

Much had also stayed the same—too much, for too long.

"Perhaps you would permit a tour of the house and the grounds?" Miss Wright asked, evidently not above pleading her case.

"I fear it is not good weather for walking outdoors," I answered, casting my gaze to the gloom beyond the window.

That should have been the end of it, but Cynthia Wright looked so crestfallen that Timothy said, "The rain seems to have let up for the time being. We have worn sensible shoes for walking, and surely you have umbrellas at your disposal, Aunt? A quick jaunt would not go amiss."

I wanted to refuse again, but something about his insistence made that seem churlish. So I forced a tight smile and set down my teacup. "Very well. Before the rain starts again."

They followed suit in discarding their teacups, scarcely drank from, and we made our way out to the foyer, where their coats hung on hooks by the door. My collection of black umbrellas stood sentry on the opposite side, proving that I did indeed have them available.

I excused myself to go upstairs for more suitable shoes of my own. When I came back down, Cynthia Wright and Timothy Reeves were bundled back into their coats and hats and had helped themselves to an umbrella, like they were fortifying themselves to go back into the elements.

After putting on my own coat and selecting an umbrella—they had taken my favorite, the one with the carved bird handle, so I had to opt for another—I led the way outside. It was a rather uninspired tour and received a halfhearted reception, despite my guests' insistence on taking it in the first place.

When I had had enough of strolling the unkempt grounds and mostly pointing out things that were once splendid but had now fallen into disrepair, I pronounced that we should return to the house. The sky had darkened considerably, and the air felt laden with the threat of more rain. I had no wish or reason to be caught in it.

"I had hoped to see where Timothy's uncle is laid to rest," Miss Wright said, looking a bit like a child who had been denied sweets.

For the nth time since she'd arrived, I found myself biting my tongue to keep back a sharp retort. My late husband's grave was not a curiosity for this peach-colored, ruffled girl to ogle at. But before I could find a diplomatic way to say so, Timothy put in, "I would also like to show Cynthia Uncle Edward's grave. Since he did not have an opportunity to meet her."

It was a rather macabre idea, that Timothy should introduce Edward to this insipid creature now. Furthermore, I very much doubted that Edward would have cared a whit for Cynthia Wright. That idea was almost entertaining, and that perverse amusement was what likely drove me to lead the way to Edward's final resting place.

I knew the walk intimately, having made it daily for years now, even before I had the graves of three husbands to attend to. If I deigned to marry Mr. Potts—for yes, that was the widower's name, I was almost certain—would he soon take up residence in the plot? It almost seemed inevitable; perhaps I should spare the poor man that fate. If not for his sake, then for that of his children.

We did not speak as we traversed the grounds to the cemetery, even when a light drizzle began to fall again. I was the first to break the silence when we reached the plots. "Your uncle's grave is that one marked by the angel."

He took Cynthia Wright's gloved hand in his own and led her to the graveside, saying something to her in a low tone that I could not catch. The pair stood in reverent silence for a moment, before Miss Wright seemed to deem that sufficient enough observation. Releasing Timothy's hand, she slowly made her way from stone to stone, reading off the names.

"Such tragedy," she crooned sympathetically. "May I ask how it all happened?"

It took me a moment to realize she was asking what had become of my late husbands. I stiffened, wondering why no one had ever taught this girl not to pry. Still, I felt compelled to answer, and so I said crisply, "A carriage accident took my first husband. Edward died of consumption, and Mr. Somers suffered from heart failure."

"How sad that they were all taken so suddenly," Miss Wright said with a shake of her bonneted head. She meandered around a few more graves. "Is this your father's plot? Who are these other men buried after him?"

"My mother was a widow many times over, as well."

"And this is your mother's grave?" she asked, like she was a character in some insipid detective novel and paid to make an inquest.

"Yes, and my grandmother's is beside it," I answered, trying to head off the next question before Cynthia Wright could ask it.

"You share her name," Timothy commented quietly.

"Yes, I share a great deal with her," I said dismissively.

Miss Wright glanced once more around the cemetery, her pale eyes lighting on each plot before she remarked, "How curious—none of the markers are crosses."

Timothy looked around the plots as realization dawned in his eyes. "You're right. I never noticed before."

This seemed to be more of Cynthia Wright's sensationalist nonsense, and as the ache in my head had only worsened, I was in even less of a mood to put up with such drivel than usual. "If you have paid your respects to Edward, I would like to return to the house now."

Timothy seemed to realize I had been offended in some way and had the grace to look chastened as he said, "Of course, Aunt." He even went so far as to leave his fiancée's side and offer his arm to me for the walk back.

I accepted it out of spite, feeling his warmth even through the layers of his sleeves.

The rain was falling in earnest by the time our silent party reached the house. I had thought that would be the end to the traipsing about, but as we stepped into the foyer, Miss Wright inquired about a tour of the house itself.

"There's very little to see," I said, no longer caring to put on a show of politeness. The ache in my head had turned into a relentless throbbing, coupled with a sharp, burning sensation in my throat.

"I could give Cynthia a tour," Timothy suggested. "Just of these lower rooms. I remember my way around well enough."

"I'm sure you do," I said tartly. He had been sizing up the place as his own, after all, even as he pretended not to want it. Perhaps his visit was merely to ascertain my health and judge how much longer I was for this world. Was the jaunt to the cemetery merely in the hopes that soon my grave would be among the rest? He would be disappointed then. I would give no sign that I felt unwell.

In keeping with that vow, I straightened and said, "Allow me to show you the main rooms, Miss Wright. Although they contain little of interest these days."

She looked pleased to be getting her way and wasted no time following me as I swept along from room to room. Even these, which were kept open for my use, had furnishings and wall hangings draped with sheets. I had grown accustomed to the spectral appearance, but I could tell Miss Wright was taken aback by it.

As we entered the drawing room, she let out a small gasp.

I turned to look at her over my shoulder but saw nothing amiss. Her eyes were as round as the saucers from our tea, though, and after a moment, I followed her gaze. It was then I realized the source of her horror. I kept all the mirrors in the house covered, but the large one above the drawing room fireplace was no longer swathed in a sheet. Mary must have removed it for some infernal reason and forgotten to replace the drape.

In the reflection was Cynthia Wright's pale face and Timothy's perplexed one. I stepped to the side of the mirror's frame, away from the bewildered pair and the reflective surface. And then I simply led on through the few remaining rooms of any relevance. In all this time, the weather outside had begun to storm again, heavy raindrops pelting the windowpanes.

Weary as I was of Miss Wright's cloying company and Timothy's placid behavior, I could hardly send them journeying back through the elements. After the requisite invitation and polite refusals, followed by my equally polite—albeit insincere—insistence, the couple agreed to spend the night at Winthrop House.

I gave silent thanks that two bedrooms were in a ready enough state. Some dust and a few cobwebs would have to be excused, under the circumstances. I also begged to be excused once I had seen Timothy and Miss Wright respectively settled. Despite my best efforts, I could not hide the malaise claiming me, and I soon fell into a fitful sleep on my divan.

When I woke again, the wind was beating harder against the glass and the rain continued to fall in sheets. Something else was amiss, though. I could not at once lay my finger upon it, but the sensation was as present as the thick wool blanket draped over me.

I remained still, straining to hear over the storm rattling the house. There— steps in the hallway. Carefully, I folded back my blanket and crept to my feet. I was not sure why I felt the need to move in silence in my own house, but I stole along soundlessly in any case.

At the door, I paused and pressed my ear against the wood.

"It should have worked by now," Miss Wright was saying anxiously.

"We ought to wait until morning," Timothy answered, his voice steadier.

"Your aunt frightens me, Timothy. There is something unnatural about her."

I stiffened, my breath catching as I tried to catch Timothy's reply.

"You've read too many novels, Cynthia," he soothed. "Your imagination has run away with you in this house."

"She had no reflection!" Miss Wright hissed back in a whisper. "Right there in the mirror: it was you and I, and not your aunt!"

"A trick of the light," he said. "Don't trouble yourself. Now go back to bed. If she is as frightful as you seem to believe, it won't do to wake her."

"You are mocking me, but what if the poison doesn't take?" she asked, sending cold dread down my spine. "It may not, if she's not a natural being."

Poison.

The bitter tea.

My headache, and the feverish burning in my throat . . . No, those had come before, hadn't they? I could no longer recall.

My nails bit into the doorframe as Timothy laughed lowly. "If it doesn't take, you'll have your proof instead of your estate, my dear. Now back to bed."

I could not catch her muffled response over the throb of anger and pain in my temples. Edward's nephew had shown his true colors at last, it seemed. But such was a game that two could play.

And Winthrop House did not belong to Timothy Reeves, and certainly not to Cynthia Wright. Nor would it ever, I was determined.

It belonged to me and me alone.

There was only one thing for it.

When Mary arrived the next day, I greeted her in a panic. She tried to console me while I explained hysterically that I'd had overnight guests and neither had woken. Taken by some mysterious fever or malady, despite their youth. If my maid disbelieved me, she didn't say so. As usual, I could count on her discretion and stoicism. She simply went back into town and returned with the undertaker, who carted off the unfortunate young people after some requisite questioning.

I offered the burial plots as a gesture of goodwill to the Reeves and Wrights. Both families accepted gratefully, wanting Timothy and Cynthia to be interred side by side in the place where they had hoped to wed. I had also purchased the gravestones, crafted from smooth marble in oblong shapes.

A senseless tragedy, the papers reported. Two young lovers killed by some mysterious illness, overtaken by it so quickly in the night that there was no time for a doctor to be called.

I clutched the carved bird-shaped handle of my umbrella as the graveside service droned on. Funerals were old hat to me after a lifetime filled with them, but I still managed to summon the required appearance of grief for the two lives taken too soon, just as I had done countless times before. I would never let on to another soul that the dearly departed were not the saintly figures the minister presented. No one would ever know of that last night at Winthrop House, including the fanciful ideas Cynthia Wright had entertained.

When the minister finished his address at last, I turned my back on the gravesites and made my way alone up to Winthrop House.

# About the Author

**Sarah Kennedy Keys** writes young and new adult fantasy as well as historical mysteries. She owns more books than shelves but can never resist a secondhand bookstore, especially one with a coffeeshop. Her heart and home belong to two darling (and spoiled) cats who supervise her writing. She holds a degree in English and can talk for hours about Jane Austen and Agatha Christie. When not engaged in something literary, she can be found volunteering, designing websites, playing the piano badly, or making the case to adopt another cat.

You can find Sarah on Instagram at:
@sarahkennedykeys

To learn more about Sarah, visit her website at:
sarahkennedykeys.com

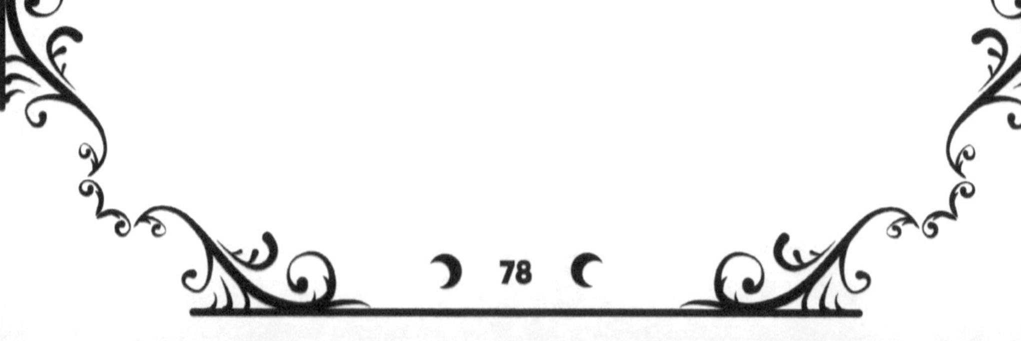

# Sleep Sound and Wake Nane

# Sleep Sound and Wake Nane

## Rosie Beech

"THIS GUY AGAIN?" DR. LOUISE Haig half laughed in surprise, looking down at the man on her autopsy table.

"What's that then?" Naasir, the pathology technician, glanced up from the tools he was organizing.

"I swear, I examined him the other day." She flicked through the paperwork that had come in with the body.

"Can't be him. That mannie was found on the hill. This guy was hit by a bus." Naasir pulled up the notes they'd made on the previous case.

"They could have been twins. Both John Does, too."

Louise took a closer look at the body's face. The eyes already had that post-mortem, cloudy glaze to them. Light stubble covered the rigid face. He looked to be in his forties, white, with thick, dark-brown hair. Not exactly uncommon attributes. It could be a coincidence. Death might have made them similar. But there was a character to the face—a worried thoughtfulness to the lines around the eyes, the set of the open mouth. Little things that added up to make the unremarkable memorable.

"Might be worth flagging up. If they were related then the timing is suspicious."

She inspected the cadaver with respectful efficiency, noting any injuries. The ribs were clearly broken, possibly from being hit by the bus. Something was amiss.

"I would expect more bruising." The limbs were unyielding. "When did the police record the time of the accident?"

Naasir read from the report. "Police arrived at 12:40. Bus security cameras show the vehicle coming to an abrupt stop at 12:21."

Louise palpated the body's arm. "This man feels like he's been dead for longer than that."

"Maybe he slid out the back of a hearse," Naasir quipped.

After taking photos, Louise began the dissection. Human skin was tougher than most people expected. She pushed aside the old flash of concern that she was hurting him. The smell of the open abdominal cavity always took her right back to the first time she witnessed it in training. She was better at containing her reaction to it now. Louise removed the organs in a systematic manner, cutting through veins and ligaments. As she delved through the viscera, she hunted for clues. Death was not a nebulous concept to her. It was a puzzle, and she always found the solution. No existential contemplation of mortality for her. Any brief thoughts were always quickly filed away under "waste of time."

"What's the verdict?" Naasir asked.

"Right now, without the results from the tissue samples, it's looking like he died from hypothermia."

"Literally being hit by a bus wasn't enough for him?" He looked incredulous.

"It banged him up, but it wasn't what killed him."

"I suppose it's not surprising if he was sleeping rough. Bet the bus driver will sleep better knowing that."

"I doubt it."

She tied a knot in the plastic bag of organs and dropped it back into the gaping chest.

"Is someone pulling my leg?" Her mind scrabbled for rationality. She had just opened the cold locker to find a familiar face waiting for her.

"Med students leave a chicken in there or something?" Naasir stuck his head around the door, halfway through his own lunch, long past squeamishness.

"It's the same man from last week! I thought he was sent off to the funeral director for burial."

"He was. Let me find the form."

While he interrogated the computer, Louise used the hoist to lift the body onto her trolley for a closer look. Without a doubt it was the same person. She'd spent hours with him, knew every intimate detail inside and out. And yet, it couldn't be. There was no Y-shaped incision, and the body was still in rigor. He would have lapsed into secondary flaccidity by now. She gently touched his face and chest. Even her hands recognized the shape of the corpse.

She wheeled him through to the other room, and Naasir turned the screen toward her with the triumph of discovery. "See, right there. He was picked up by the lads on Thursday."

"Can you get those photos we took for me?" If she could compare the faces and prove to herself that this was all a darkly amusing coincidence, then she could quiet the irrational part of her mind that was screaming *what if?*

The computer made a disappointed beep, and Naasir pulled a worried face.

"Don't be angry, or disappointed. I'm too fragile for either."

"What's happened?"

"When I try to open the folder, it just says *Files Corrupted*." He clicked a few times to prove his point. The computer bipped in protest.

"So all of last week's photos are gone?" she asked, panic creeping in.

"No, no! Just Mr. Hypothermia, thank goodness. Pretty weird though. Do you think the SD card was damaged or something?"

Louise couldn't respond. A weight had landed sickeningly at the bottom of her ribcage.

"Take a look for me. Am I imagining things?" She laughed to hide how shaky she was feeling.

He leaned around the monitor. "I guess they look similar. Can't say that I spend my breaks gazing lovingly into the eyes of the dead." He gave her a playful nudge. "Don't worry about it, Lou. You just need more than three hours of sleep."

She smiled in relief. "I'll have you know, any respectable corpse wrangler is nocturnal."

"So are the foxes that knock over my bins. You're in great company."

"Piss off!"

They got back to prepping her station. "Where's this one from then?" she asked.

"They found him in the hotel sauna. Might make time of death a bit of a bugger."

"At least he wasn't in the pool. Skin slip is even more of a pain."

She tried to ignore the uncanny familiarity as she inspected the body. She opened him up quickly. No wonder all the cases were blurring; she could practically perform the internal examination in her sleep. Saw through bone, run the bowel, weigh the organs. Her favorite to hold was the brain; it felt like she was holding the seat of the soul. Who this person was, where all their personality quirks and experiences lived. It was something of a privilege.

Her comfortable routine was interrupted when her fingers found something unusual. She pulled it out and carefully rinsed off the blood. Recognition knocked all the wind out of her. It was a small, plastic circle, one of the ties they used to seal the bags of organs.

"Are you well in yourself, Louise?"

She was sleepwalking through the meeting with the procurator-fiscal.[1] Her voice must have been hollow, because Moira Forna set her pen down and turned her full attention to her.

"Yes, all's well. Sorry is there something wrong?"

Moira gave her the kind of look that solicitors[2] and mothers had when they knew you were lying. "It's not a criticism. I just want to check in."

She was the epitome of professional compassion. Louise imagined for a moment that she could tell her all about the corpse, that she'd seen it twelve times in the last month. She saw his flat, milky eyes when she closed her own. She shouldn't be able to recognize someone from the look and feel of their lungs. But her throat closed up at the thought of it. She cleared it and smiled.

"I'm probably just coming down with a cold. Lack of sleep catching up with me." She gestured to the small blizzard of paperwork that she'd brought to the meeting. Moira grimaced in solidarity, glancing at her own straining briefcase.

"You need to actually use some of your annual leave," she joked.

"Sure thing. Can you tell the people of Glasgow to stop dying for a fortnight?" The protective dam of her denial was groaning under the pressure, but she shored it up once more.

Naasir welcomed her back to the mortuary with a black coffee.

"You, Mr. Fraser, have just become my favorite human of the day."

"Does that include the dead?"

"Of course not. They don't ask me to do anything, so they always win. But

---

[1] procurator-fiscal: The officer in charge of investigating sudden and suspicious deaths in the Scottish legal system. Similar to a coroner in other systems.

[2] solicitor: A law professional in the Scottish system. Often the first point of contact for legal advice.

you're definitely the best of the living." She took a sip and felt the caffeine creep into the dusty creases of her brain.

"This one might give you some grief. They pulled him out of the Kelvin this morning."

Naasir wheeled in a familiar body, and she tried to hide her shudder. She'd stopped pointing out the resemblance weeks ago. No one else seemed to notice. She was terrified that if she kept ranting about it, her sanity would be called into question and she would be fired, or worse. And if this was her psyche malfunctioning, if she couldn't rely on her own mind . . . She shied away from the thought.

"He doesn't look like a John," she said, trying to distract herself.

"How about Joe Bloggs then? Or Tam?"

"No, he's more of a Brian." She half hoped that naming their persistent guest might make him seem less threatening.

"Well then, Brian, say *putrescine*." Naasir started taking photos.

She knew that they would scramble into bars and dots of neon color, just like all the others. IT said it was probably a missing software update. Everything had an explanation. She tried to make herself believe it.

She cut through the layers of fat and muscle, splaying them open like a fleshy flower. She stopped mid-motion when she spotted a distinctive shear cut on one of the ribs. She had made that last Wednesday. These tiny pieces of evidence that only she saw the significance of felt like they were mocking her.

"You okay, Lou?"

She jolted up to find Naasir watching her with worry.

"Just contemplating the void. Why? What do you do for fun?"

Was that a look of relief? "You need a hobby, mate."

"Does taxidermy count?"

"You are an actual menace! We're lucky that you can't take work home with you."

The teasing comment sparked a wild plan that only her desperation made feasible.

When her mother had given Louise their old chest freezer, she could never have imagined what ghoulish purpose it would serve. Moving Brian without the mortuary's body hoist was a morbid farce. She struggled to preserve his dignity as she fell back on the reliable technique of rolling the body, occasionally dragging it with sturdy sheets. The jostling forced a dark, gritty fluid from his nose and mouth. She wiped the purge away and tucked ice packs around him to hold back decay. She sniffed to check for the telltale scent of licorice, lemon rind, and trout. All she could smell was the general mustiness of her garage.

The guilt sank in when she stopped and took in her handiwork. A modern-day resurrectionist, stealing bodies. This had driven her to make awful choices. She could feel her thoughts peeling away from reality, but she was not going to lose her grip. Someone was using this body to torment her; that was the only possible explanation. Louise would not let them break her. She would beat them at their own game. If they couldn't find Brian, then they couldn't patch him up and send him back to the morgue. She squashed the thought that it was virtually impossible to hide evidence of an autopsy. She needed to believe this, to make sense of what was happening.

With a whispered apology, she shut the lid. Then she padlocked the door to her garage, her makeshift tomb.

Louise was practically giddy when she arrived at work the next day. Not even the dreich[3] weather could dampen her mood. She had solved this cruel puzzle and restored logic to the world. Nothing to confront, nothing to process.

"Rejoice, for I bring you coffee!" she announced as she bounded through the doors.

"Literally what the doctor ordered." Naasir took it gratefully. "Good thing, too. We've got a tough one this morning."

"I love a challenge. Lay it on me."

"Some poor bastard found a guy impaled on a railing. It's pretty gruesome."

He brought out the mangled cadaver. The face. Bloody but unmistakable.

Fear hollowed her out. This was a nightmare. She needed it to be. She backed away, keeping her eyes on it.

"Lou, what's wrong?"

She sprinted out of the room. Away from Brian's blank stare.

Louise ran through the pelting rain, around the side of her house, and wrestled

---

3 dreich: Damp, wet, and tedious. It can describe both weather and someone's mood.

with the intact padlock. She forced her way into the garage and threw open the freezer. Her fragile hope shattered. Completely empty. She couldn't stifle the sobbing screams. At least her breakdown was hidden from prying eyes.

She was a functional zombie at work now, sealing away all emotions to protect herself from the fear. Bracing for the days when Brian turned up. Constantly being alert and on guard became a physical pain. A constant grinding ache in her rigid back, shoulders, and neck. She moved through a smir[4] of dread that matched the constant drizzle outside.

Louise was pulled out of her stupor when Naasir arrived late one morning. He was holding himself as if protecting an invisible injury.

"What's happened?" she asked.

He swallowed hard before answering, but his voice was still thick. "My aunt died yesterday."

Louise carefully took his coat for him and guided him to a seat. "Do you want to go home? This might not be the best place for you right now. I can manage."

"No, I need the routine if that's okay?"

"Of course. When's the funeral?"

"Tomorrow. I was just getting in the way, so I got out of the house." He let out a long, tired breath and covered his eyes. Louise gave him a sideways hug, and they sat together like that for a while. Louise found that even in the depths of her own despair, comforting someone else made her feel strong. They talked as they worked, about his aunt, his family, and the funeral.

"There's going to be so many people. The house is already rammed, and the kettle is literally boiling constantly."

"She must have been well loved," Louise prompted.

"Funerals are a big community thing. It's not just a family tragedy. We've all lost something."

"'Any man's death diminishes me' sort of energy?"

"Exactly." He finished unloading the freshly cleaned tools and went to check which body to collect first. "I'm looking forward to hearing everyone's stories about her. I think that's the most important part."

"I suppose. It sounds painful to me." Louise felt her shoulders creep up just at the thought of managing those emotions.

---

4 smir: A fine mist of drizzling rain.

"A bit, but that's the point of the whole thing. A lot of people are scared of being forgotten."

He wheeled in the first body. Louise shuddered when she recognized Brian and turned away to hide her reaction.

Naasir continued behind her. "Remembering them is the last way we can show that we care."

Some realizations hit like a crashing storm, but this one was like a gentle touch on her shoulder. She turned through the fear and made herself look at Brian. Maybe this was the first time she was actually seeing him properly. Not a problem to be solved. A person.

"Sorry I'm being so maudlin. Let's talk about something else."

"No, mate, you've just given me a massive wake up call."

A week after Naasir's aunt was buried, Louise had a meeting with Moira. It was the first time in five years of working together that Louise had seen the solicitor look shocked.

"This is what I would call an unusual request," she said, raising an eyebrow.

"But is it legal?" Louise asked.

"Officially speaking, nobody owns a dead body. But we have a duty to make sure that everything is aboveboard."

"I'd pay for everything out of pocket," Louise appealed.

Moira's eyes were sharper than a trocar, piercing through to the truth.

"Why is this so important to you, Louise?"

The doctor took a moment to compose her thoughts.

"I've worked with more unclaimed bodies than I can remember. I've lost track of them this last month alone." She didn't mention that these had all been the same man. "If I can take care of this one, then maybe he can represent all of them for me."

"Like a union rep for the dead?" Moira asked with a shade of sarcasm.

"If you like. Please let me do this."

It seemed to take an age for her to consider. Then she smiled. "I owe you an arm and a leg, and probably some other organs, as well. Leave it with me and I'll sort the paperwork."

The churchyard was comfortingly unchanged since her last visit. She and Naasir had driven in shifts back to her childhood village.

"First time you take annual leave this year, and it's for a funeral!" He laughed as she wrestled to park the borrowed hearse.

"It was between this and a performance of the 'Dance Macabre.'"

It had taken a heroic amount of organization to get everything arranged. The funeral director and her young assistant met them, and together they carried Brian through the gates into the graveyard. The celebrant was waiting for them by the open ground. Louise hadn't wanted to presume Brian's beliefs. She asked for a moment with him before they lowered his wool-shrouded body into the grave.

The horizon was ringed by blue mountains, the sun was warm, and steam rose from the fresh bales in the field below. Louise's muscles ached from carrying Brian. There was a grounded, earthly magic to the moment. She placed a hand on his chest and spoke, low and private.

"I promise to remember you."

Louise hesitated outside the mortuary doors. The moment of pause stretched painfully. Uncertainty, and the fear it brought with it, crowded into familiar channels in her mind. What if it hadn't worked? What if the rest of her life was dogged by anticipation and terror? What if?

"I don't know." She interrupted the spiral, actively deepened her breathing, and unclenched her shoulders. She accepted the discomfort of not knowing. On an exhale, she pushed open the door and walked through.

# About the Author

**Rosie Beech** is a writer and performer from Scotland. They produce the literary podcast Yorick Radio Productions and have created and directed several audio dramas including *I will Wait for You* (StAR Radio, 2019), *Communicable 2020*, and *Secret Saint 2022*. Their short stories include: "I Curled with Bauchans" (Crab Apple Literary), "Salvage Me" (The Selkie), and "Wood Woes" (Gramarye).

You can find Rosie on Instagram at:
@beechhedgewitch

# The Birthday Party

# The Birthday Party

## Elizabeth Torres

NOTHING IS LEFT FROM OUR life before.

Everything is strange. The house, the furnishings, the angle of the sunlight on the hearth. I'm struggling to put down roots, like a tree transplanted into unfamiliar soil.

Edward declares that this move will make me better, that my sickness will be shed with the old furniture. It will not follow me here, among the new carpets, the new servants, and the new society.

He suggests that I write a journal, a steadying pursuit to pass the time until I grow stronger and can more easily stand the company of others. So here I sit, attempting to discipline my unruly thoughts and keep them captive in ink.

I'm sure he is right. He always is. He knows what's best for me, even when I cannot see it myself.

When I awoke this morning, I couldn't remember where I was. The room was black as creosote, the drapes hanging thick across the windows, the fire not yet lit. I lay, paralyzed while the darkness swelled and took shape, shifting from one monstrous form to another. I cried out, although in that moment, I had no idea who would answer. My mind strained against its shackles, groping for a familiar face, a name I knew. The maid came running, but several long moments passed before I recognized her and calmed. Now, in daylight, her name comes to me easily. *Rose.*

I know it was only my fancy, conjuring visions that were not there. It's often hard for me to tell if something is real or a mere dream. Sometimes, when I speak, Edward will get that overcast look—brow furrowed, eyes dark—and I know I've made a mistake.

So I've learned to stay silent.

It's good for me to have some amusement, Edward says, but he seems reluctant for me to make the acquaintance of our new neighbors. I have Georgie, of course, but children can be tiring when one is ill. I am not allowed to see him at present, as his youthful exuberance may be too much for me. Edward refrains from even mentioning Georgie at dinner, for fear of upsetting me, I believe, knowing I cannot spend time with our son myself. I follow his example, talking of the weather, or the pleasantness of the meal. Sometimes he shares a little of his work or correspondence, but only light matters that will not over-excite me.

I do find the situation rather tiresome. I need *society*—and I miss Georgie dreadfully. If only there was a way to convince Edward that I'm well enough to be his mother again.

It's Georgie's birthday soon, so perhaps I might arrange a little party and invite the local families? Of course, I shall keep it all a secret from Edward. Once he sees how I have managed everything by myself, he cannot fail to think me fully recovered.

I wonder what Georgie would like as a gift.

Edward took me to Covent Garden today. I confess I was a little overwhelmed by this first outing. London seemed a veritable Bedlam—a riot of bustle and clamor after the tranquility of the countryside. People of all sorts thronged the city streets. Market traders hawking for business, thrusting their wares in front of me as I passed. Wealthy ladies in the latest fashions, admiring the hats in the milliner's window. And here and there a beggar, ragged and dirty, palms outstretched in supplication. Edward drew me along at a brisk pace as I gathered my skirts around me, beyond the reach of their probing hands.

I caught a glimpse of one or two things that interested me greatly, and I hope to return alone to explore them further. The plans for Georgie's birthday are taking shape in my mind, but I will need to be careful not to raise Edward's suspicions. I would not wish to spoil the surprise.

The purpose of our visit was to see *The Tempest* at the Theatre Royal. It's been a long time since I read any Shakespeare, and I found myself unfamiliar with the story. The opening scene shook me considerably, beginning with a loud bang which made me start from my seat. Lightning flashed, revealing sailors caught in a storm at sea. The stage began to move before my eyes, undulating like a serpent, as thunder echoed all around us.

Later, Edward explained how fireworks and sheets of metal are used to produce the sound and light effects of a storm, together with machinery to move the set pieces, all to create a thrilling spectacle for the audience. It's nothing but clever trickery. Yet in that moment I was fully transported. I could have sworn the sensations were real—the rush of the wind in my ears, the ocean spray on my skin, the taste of salt on my tongue. The play cast its spell over me, as if Prospero himself were truly there, weaving his illusions.

I felt a pressure growing in my chest. Would the sailors drown? Why did no one go to their rescue? So many people idly waiting and watching while lives hung in the balance!

I half rose, leaning forward over the edge of the box. I could not let them die, not if it was in my power to save them. The nearest sailor was just beyond my grasp, his face swimming in and out of focus. The tumult grew louder as the scene before me shimmered, sea bleeding into sky.

Reaching toward the man, I found myself tethered, some invisible force pulling me back to shore. I struggled to break free but was held fast. As my vision began to clear, I slowly grew aware of my surroundings: the proud curve of the proscenium arch rising high above the stage, the other patrons turning curious heads my way—and Edward's arms locked around my waist in a steel-like grip.

"Not again," he muttered. "Dear God, not again."

I feel that I have failed him in some way.

Last night I woke again.

Fearful of the dark, I'd left the drapes open. Moonlight stretched its spectral fingers over the counterpane, suffusing everything with a ghostly hue.

I wondered what had roused me. Could it be Georgie, stirring in the night? No.

Something else.

A curious scratching sound above my head, slightly muffled, as if someone were chipping away at the plaster on the other side of the wall. The neighbor? What could they be doing at such a late hour?

I let the blanket fall as I sat up, feeling the shock of the winter chill through my thin nightdress. Kneeling on the pillow, I placed my palm against the wall at the spot the noise was coming from. A faint vibration thrummed through my fingers.

I moved closer, pressing my ear to the wall.

The noise stopped abruptly.

For a few moments I stayed there, statue-still, until the creeping cold overcame me. As I lay down again, pulling the blanket up to my chin, all I could hear was my own breathing, rapid and shallow, and the regular tick-tock of the clock in the hall.

This morning, I questioned Edward about the people who live next door, only to learn that the residence is up for sale and currently empty.

How strange.

Had *he* heard any noises in the night?

Apparently not.

"Perhaps it was a rat?" he ventured.

This seems the most likely explanation, but it does not make me feel any easier. Suppose the rat were to enter my bedroom? Or Georgie's?

After breakfast I carefully examined the walls. To my alarm, behind my dressing table I discovered a small hole in the wainscot. I immediately went to the kitchen to request a gin trap. If there *is* a rat living in the walls, I hope to capture it with a sweetmeat.

As I passed the stairs to the nursery, I paused, my foot lingering on the first step. Georgie was somewhere just above my head, perhaps riding his rocking horse or playing with his marbles. Nurse would be with him, of course, but I knew he must be feeling my absence keenly. I was always his best-loved playmate. I strained my ears listening for his familiar laugh, trying to ignore the deep ache in my chest.

At that moment, Rose emerged from my chamber, carrying the dirty linen. She gave me a sharp look, as if I were a child caught stealing from the pantry.

"Can I help you, ma'am?"

I made no answer, but hurried past her into the bedroom, afraid she would see my tears.

In the afternoon I headed out to run some errands. I know I shouldn't have gone alone—Edward is most disapproving of my going anywhere unaccompanied, especially since the distressing incident in the theatre—but I wanted to work on my little surprise.

At the confectioner's, I ordered a delightful cake, a fairytale creation decorated with fruit and rich icing. I also indulged myself by buying a box of marzipan. It has always been my favorite—and Georgie's, too. I wish I could send a piece up to the nursery with Rose to let him know his mother is thinking of him, but I cannot trust her to keep my secret.

Afterward I entered the toy shop, where the owner took great pleasure in showing me the merchandise. I spent a happy half-hour looking at the dolls, remembering the simple joys of my childhood. But my own playthings were shabby compared to these beautiful porcelain figures, elegantly dressed in satin and lace.

Truth be told, I've always longed for a daughter but have never conceived any child but Georgie. I have not quite given up hope that it may happen one day, but I believe Edward has. He hasn't come to my chamber for many months now.

Eventually, I abandoned the dolls and decided on a set of skittles that resembled soldiers, handsomely painted in red and black. I know that Georgie will love them!

When I arrived home, I carefully set the gin trap, pushing down the spring and laying a piece of marzipan on the plate between the jaws. Now there is nothing to do but wait.

Unfortunately, once again, my sleep did not go undisturbed.

I awoke to the sound of a child crying.

Not the strangled, high-pitched screams of an infant, but an older child, perhaps four or five years old.

Georgie?

I started out of bed, fumbling for a candle, then paused.

The noise was not coming from the nursery on the floor above, but through the same wall as before. The wall of the neighboring house.

Edward must have been mistaken. There were people living there after all!

I crawled back into bed, listening. Surely someone would come to comfort the child.

But the sobbing continued, growing louder minute after minute until I could bear it no longer. I knocked on the wall, tentatively at first, and then with purpose. The crying faltered a little, but I could still hear the child's shuddering breaths as they tried to contain their tears.

"Shhhh," I whispered soothingly, pressing my lips to the wall. "Go back to sleep. There's nothing to be afraid of."

The crying stopped.

Silence thick as dust descended on the house. Somehow, that silence was more unsettling than the weeping before. Sleep eluded me for hours.

In the morning, I received another surprise. Steeling myself for the sight of a dead rat, I peered under the dressing table. To my astonishment, the marzipan was gone, but the jaws of the trap lay empty and unsprung.

After breakfast, I spent an hour writing invitations to Georgie's birthday party, enough for every house on the square. I wanted to deliver them myself, seizing the opportunity to get some air and shake off the unease of the night.

Rose was more than usually attentive, constantly in and out of my room on some errand or other, enquiring if I needed anything. I wonder if Edward has told her to keep an eye on me. I must be on my guard. Rose asked if I planned to take a walk, but I feigned a headache. I slipped out while she was busy in the laundry room.

I first approached the house next door, eager to make the acquaintance of the family with the young child. How wonderful it would be for Georgie to make a friend his own age! I knocked and waited.

The house was stubbornly silent.

At the window, the drapes were pulled nearly all the way across, but there was a small gap in the middle where they did not quite meet. Shading my eyes from the sun, I peered into the room beyond. As far as I could tell, it was empty of furniture. A film of dust lay on the windowsill.

How could this be? I'd heard a child crying. I was sure of it. My skin prickled uncomfortably. Was this one of my fancies? No. I was better now. The episode in the theatre was a moment of confusion, nothing more. Those troubles were left behind in the old house—Edward had told me so. It was just a dream.

But I plan to keep it from him all the same.

Unnerved, I walked on, passing from house to house until all the invitations were delivered. After that, there was just one more task to fulfil.

It took me fifteen minutes to walk to Covent Garden. I wandered around the market, marveling at the jugglers and fire-eaters, until I found what I was searching for.

The puppet theatre rose above the dreary cobbles, brightly painted in red and gold. On the small stage a puppet in a jester's cap fought over a string of sausages with a stern-faced police constable. Children sat enthralled, laughing and squealing in delight. I forgot my anxieties for a time as I followed the diverting adventures of the mischievous Mr. Punch.

Once the applause subsided, I approached the puppeteer—a charming man with a cheerful countenance—and secured his services for this coming Saturday. What a treat for Georgie! It will truly be a day to remember.

When I returned home, I scarcely managed to evade Rose, slipping up the stairs and into my chamber just as she entered the hallway. Exhausted by the morning's exertions, I decided to retire to bed.

As I slid between the covers, my fingers brushed something rough against the smoothness of the sheets. Crumbs. Puzzled, I raised one to my lips, only to taste the nutty sweetness of the marzipan.

Moving swiftly to my dressing table, I searched for the box I had bought the day before. The sweetmeat lay untouched, save for the piece I'd cut to place in the gin trap.

What could this mean? The marzipan had been stolen from the trap while I slept, but here was proof that it had not traveled far. A chill came over me, spreading through my veins like treacle. Someone—or some *thing*—had been in my bed.

☽●☾

Today is Georgie's birthday! I said nothing of the party at breakfast but was in such a lively mood that Edward remarked on my good humor. I told him only that I had a little surprise planned for this afternoon and would be grateful if he came back from his club immediately after lunch.

I am happy to report that my sleep has not been troubled any further by mysterious disturbances. I believe now that they were but dreams, albeit vivid ones, brought on by the anxiety of moving to a new place. How silly of me to be afraid! Edward was right all along. The change of scene and air has made me well again.

☽●☾

I hardly know what to write. The party is over—and nothing will ever be the same again.

As soon as Edward left for his club, I sent Rose to run some errands in town, providing a long list to keep her busy for hours. I decorated the drawing room with ribbons and flowers, placing the cake on the table in all its splendor. The puppeteer came around one o'clock to set up the theatre. Shortly after, the guests began to arrive, and for the first time in an age, I felt alive. The joy of conversing with people after many months of solitude and sickness! The excitement of the children when they saw the puppet theatre, anticipating the amusement to come!

Just as I was about to fetch Georgie from the nursery, Edward arrived home.

"Ah, the man of the house, I assume?" Mr. Shaw, our neighbor from number 6, approached Edward. "I must congratulate you on an excellent party, sir!"

Edward nodded stiffly. His eyes scanned the room, taking in the guests, the cake, and the puppeteer. "Please excuse me a moment," he said, taking hold of my hand and drawing me into the back parlor.

"What is all this?" he demanded, once we were out of hearing. "Why are all these people here?"

"Why, it's a party for Georgie's birthday!" I laughed. "Surprise!"

Edward's face drained of color. "Georgie?" he said. "Where is he?"

"Upstairs, of course! I was on my way to fetch him now."

"Then let us find him." Edward grasped my arm roughly and almost dragged me up the back stairs.

"Show me," he said. "Where is our son?"

"Edward, you're scaring me." I stumbled up the second flight of steps. Outside the nursery I hesitated, trying to recover myself. I did not want Georgie to see me discomposed.

Pushing me aside, Edward thrust open the door.

The room was completely bare. No furniture. No toys. No Nurse. No Georgie.

Fear seized me, its grip like a cord around my chest, growing tighter and tighter. I could barely breathe.

"Edward," I whispered, searching his face for answers. "Where's Georgie?"

He turned away, the muscles in his neck taut like a bowstring. "Do you really not recall?"

And all of a sudden, I remembered.

*A beautiful summer's day. Georgie playing in the garden. The sun warm on my skin as I drifted in and out of sleep.*

*Shouting. A frantic search. Our darling boy face down in the pond, floating on the surface like a ragdoll.*

I fell to the floor, insensible.

When I came to myself again, I was in bed, alone. The horror of the memory surged over me afresh, and I felt the bile rise in my throat. Shakily, I made my way to the door, where I heard the murmur of voices below.

"... may be time to consider more specialist care for your wife."

"An asylum, you mean?"

"If these episodes continue, I believe you have no other option."

*An asylum?* No, Edward would never do such a thing.

I am not allowed to leave the room. Edward insists I must rest, that I've had a terrible shock.

But I think it is he who has had the shock. Something has changed. He will not even look at me, and his voice when he speaks is as cold as the grave.

When he unwrapped the soldier skittles, he uttered an oath, his face crumpling in an ugly fashion. He ordered Rose to take them away, but I managed to conceal one under my pillow. The weight of the polished wood, smooth and cool in my grip, is a comfort, and God knows, I have little enough to comfort me now.

I have asked Rose to draw me a bath. She's been coming and going for half an hour with pails of hot water. She will not look at me either, scurrying in and out with her head bowed.

The water was warm as I entered it, but it did not soothe me as I'd hoped. In my mind, I saw the pond water, stagnant and muddied with silt. How cold Georgie must have been! And colder still now, deep in the earth, far from his mother's embrace. How could Edward have brought us here and left our son all alone?

When I closed my eyes, I saw him in the coffin where we'd laid him, mahogany lined with midnight silk. It was a prison devoid of light and air. He could not breathe, could not escape.

Hark! What was that?

He was knocking, louder and louder, but no one came!

My eyes opened, but the knocking remained, a drumming in my head that would not cease. It was coming from the wall again, behind the bed, urgent, insistent.

And then it hit me. Edward was wrong. The dead would not be forgotten. We'd left him behind, *but he had followed us here.*

Everything made sense. The noises, the crying, the missing marzipan. Georgie was here—and he needed me.

I was on the bed, water dripping over the counterpane, clawing at the wall with my nails. The paper ripped easily, hanging limp, like strips of flesh torn by a wild animal. I set to work on the plaster, pummeling it with my fists until it started to crack. Then the soldier skittle was in my hand, chipping away until a small hole appeared. I slid a finger through the gap. Something brushed against my skin, cool and clammy and soft to the touch. *Oh Georgie, I am coming!*

"My God, what are you doing?"

Edward was there, pulling me from the wall, pinning me down by my wrists as I flailed and writhed beneath him. He struck me so hard I saw stars. Could he not hear our son? The pounding was so loud that I was sure the wall would give way. *Georgie, Georgie, break free and save us both!*

Everything went black. My mind was a whirlpool of fear and confusion.

Somebody was screaming.

It was Rose.

She stood in the doorway, terror in her countenance. I followed her gaze.

Edward was slumped over the bath, face down in the water, a bloody gash on the back of his head. The skittle, broken in two, lay on the floor at his feet.

*Oh Georgie, what have you done?*

I reached for the bedpost to steady myself, and pain shot through my palm. With a trembling hand I removed a splinter, two inches long, its smooth edge tinged with red and black paint.

# About the Author

**Elizabeth Torres** lives in Cambridge, UK, with her husband and two children. A lover of gothic and supernatural fiction since childhood, she enjoys writing stories that linger in the shadows, blurring the boundary between the ordinary and the uncanny. She can often be found wandering the cobbled streets of historic towns in search of inspiration—and stopping to sample the cake in each quaint little tea room along the way. Elizabeth's work has been named a runner-up in the 2024 New York City Midnight Flash Fiction Contest, and her story in *Not As it Seems* marks her first appearance in print.

You can find Elizabeth online at:
BlueSky: @onthewritelines.bsky.social
Instagram: @elizabethtorreswriter

# Marin

# Marin

## Katherine Rea

LAST NIGHT, I DREAMT I went to Terncliff again. I could hear the gulls screaming, whirling above the manor, dipping in and out of the fog. I could feel the spray of saltwater from the waves crashing far beneath the cliffs.

In the dream, I walked up the long driveway, much like when I first arrived. The eucalyptus trees hung low, overgrown, their pungent, silver leaves brushing against my cheek. I noticed the sound of water as I neared the house—not from the ocean, but from the large tanks inside. The continual lapping against the glass, the artificial bubbles piped in for aeration, and the thrum of the filtration systems. The sounds were distinctive but not overwhelming. They were even, dare I say, comforting. Oh, how foolish to think that now!

I woke this morning with the sounds of the house still ringing in my head. I left Terncliff seven months ago, but it hasn't left me. Even as I sit now, writing this in a damp sublet in the Outer Richmond, the house looms large in my mind.

Designed by the nation's premier organic architect, Mickey Muennig, Terncliff was made entirely of natural elements: wood, stone, and glass, without a straight line in sight. Those details were characteristic of Muennig's projects, but the integration of the ocean made Terncliff unique. As a way of letting nature in, the manor had not only soaring skylights and open windows and atriums featuring native palms and ferns, but also massive saltwater tanks built into different parts of the house, and even an open water feature meant to mimic a

Northern California tidepool. The main saltwater tank, featured in the atrium, was a replica of the Kelp Forest exhibit at the Monterey Bay Aquarium—all twenty-eight feet of it. Only the top section was visible, featuring the swaying fronds of kelp, with schools of sardines, leopard sharks, and wolf-eels darting around. The bottom part descended into the bowels of the house, much the same as a real kelp forest disappearing to the bottom of the ocean.

I won't pretend the homage to California coastal ecology wasn't a big draw for me. As an avid diver, I marveled at seeing everything normally reserved for the special underwater world up on the surface in Terncliff. I loved the tiger sharks, their dead eyes leering at me through the kelp forests. The purple sea urchins and giant green sea anemones entranced me.

You see, I didn't ask for this assignment randomly. I insisted on it, for personal reasons. The tanks and their beautiful creatures weren't my main focus. I was there to write a profile for *GQ* about the homeowner, Silas Lockmere, and reveal the truth about him. The whole truth. I was a journalist, after all.

I'd built a reputation for doing hard-hitting profiles of big tech entrepreneurs. So when *GQ* started looking for someone to cover Silas, the enigmatic entrepreneur and notorious recluse made famous by his wealthy family and ocean conservation efforts, I was at the top of the short list.

I was so convinced at my own prowess as a journalist, so high off my own success, that I couldn't see how vulnerable I was. Just before Silas, I'd led the charge on a tell-all for a fintech pioneer. It was a big #MeToo takedown, and the whole thing had me drained, emotionally and mentally.

"You're headed for burnout, big-time," my mentor had warned me, but I ignored her.

"You're not well," she urged.

She was right, though I didn't want to admit it. I hadn't slept properly for weeks, maybe months. I'd received death threats when my piece was published. I'd had to watch my subject's survivors struggle with the decision of whether to testify; some were discredited and harassed for agreeing to be quoted in my article. All of it was awful.

"Silas is different," I said. "He's a philanthropist. His work has largely been non-profit, and he's even invited me to stay as his guest for the weekend in Big Sur."

"Won't that make it hard to stay objective?"

I waved her off. I was already far from objective about this piece, which would have bothered me earlier in my career, but now I didn't care.

"This will be the last profile piece," I said. "I want to do something different after this." At least I'd been right about that.

I've gone back so many times through the voice notes I made during my time at Terncliff, trying to make sense of them. My recorder was almost always on. Maybe that's why I became so obsessed with the sound of the tanks; they permeated every conversation with Silas, every quiet moment to myself.

"Ava Gutierrez from *GQ* magazine."

My voice in that first meeting on the steps of Terncliff reminds me of a version of myself I liked, a confident Ava. An Ava I'm afraid I might never get back.

"Pleasure to meet you, Ava. I'm Silas."

I remember his laidback style, his disarming charm and warm, hazel eyes. I was wary, but I liked him. I couldn't help it.

I already knew him, of course. We'd never met in person, but Marin had told me a little about him.

"Come in, please," he said.

We commenced with the tour, where I got my first introduction to Muennig, the flora and fauna of Terncliff, and Aquanatic: Silas's cutting-edge new venture. "Where machine learning meets marine preservation," he told me.

After the tour, we settled in the main atrium with a pot of pu'er tea between us, the tidepool lapping at my feet.

"So, Aquanatic," I started. "Tell me about it."

"It's my vision for the world," said Silas with a smile. "I want everyone to enjoy the beauty, the simplicity, that you see here in Terncliff. That's why Aquanatic uses AI to monitor and predict ocean health trends. It's the future of marine conservation."

"A lucrative future. The Department of Defense is your primary client?"

Silas raised his hands in mock surrender. "I can neither confirm nor deny."

"Aquanatic went public two years ago with a forty-one-billon-dollar valuation, yet you initially struggled to find investors."

"That's true, yes. Those VCs are kicking themselves now," he said with a harsh laugh, but I ignored it. Men were always unnerved when I didn't laugh along with them, but I'd grown accustomed to the awkward silence that followed.

"You got your first round of seed funding back in 2015," I pressed on, referencing the extensive notes I'd taken from my research before coming here. "But most of that came from your family?" It was a rhetorical question. I knew where all of Aquanatic's investments came from. I wouldn't be a very good journalist if I didn't.

Silas smiled politely and set his teacup down. "You're not the only one who has done their research prior to this meeting, Miss Gutierrez."

For a moment, my heart caught in my throat. Maybe I hadn't covered my past as thoroughly as I'd thought.

"I know your style," he continued, and I felt my jaw relax. "I know you like to get big reactions from your subjects. I'm sorry to say that won't be the case with me. You see, I have nothing to hide."

"Excellent," I cut in swiftly. Only people who had something to hide said a version of this. "So, tell me more about your family."

Silas sighed. "Everyone just wants the gossip, don't they?"

I smiled. There was always pushback around the topic of family, but I knew how to get my subjects to talk. "I know it seems trivial, but your background allows me to flesh out the 'why' behind Aquanatic's mission. It's what makes readers care."

He weighed this and then nodded. "As I'm sure you know, my father founded Howlett-Lockmere, so we weren't exactly short on power or money in Silicon Valley. He was a stern man, and my mother was soft-spoken. She let my father run the family, and he ruled with an iron fist."

"So you didn't always get along with him?" I asked, knowing the answer already.

"No. I'll be the first to admit that. As you probably know, my father refused to back my early ventures. It wasn't until he passed that my family became financially invested in my businesses."

"And tell me about your sister, Marin. Your only sibling."

"Half-sibling," Silas replied coldly. "Her mother was my father's first love. Some say she was his one true love. My father was devastated by her death but was a widower for less than a year before he married my mother. Marin and I were only eighteen months apart."

"Yes," I said slowly. I knew all of this. I just wanted Silas comfortable before I asked the big questions. I needed to tread lightly here. "Marin's recent disappearance was quite a shock, wasn't it?"

Marin Lockmere's disappearance had been highly publicized just because of who she was. "Young Heiress Presumed Dead in Tragic Diving Accident." That had been the headline. But I knew there was more to the story.

Silas shrugged. "Marin was an avid diver. She devoted her life to it. But everyone knows diving is extremely dangerous. There are a million things that can go wrong underwater."

I nodded and let my eyes drift to the large tank in front of me. I watch the kelp dancing in the current and shudder at the thought of drawing my last breath in that cold, dark water.

Shifting my gaze to the mantel, I noticed the Clinton Global Citizen Award for philanthropic work and the Crystal Award from the World Economic Forum for raising awareness about climate change.

"You shared a passion for the environment," I said, as more of a statement than a question. The Lockmere siblings had been well-known ambassadors in ocean conservation for decades, regular fixtures at every type of fundraising event for the environment, with a particular focus on coastal waterfronts.

"We did, yes," Silas said, looking at the mantel as well now. In addition to all the awards, there were several pictures of them together: Marin shaking President Obama's hand, Silas at a podium, the two posing on the red carpet together. Silas was short, with dark hair and olive skin. Marin was statuesque and blonde. But they shared their father's hazel eyes.

"It's getting late," he suggested pointedly. "Why don't I show you your room, and we can resume our conversation over breakfast?"

"Lovely," I agreed, turning off my recorder.

Silas walked me down the hall to the guest suite, which had a bed pressed up against the side of a floor-to-ceiling window. The wood ceiling was inspired by a nautilus shell, its beams curving concentrically above me. But the most breathtaking feature by far was the floor, made entirely of glass, built over a bioluminescent tidepool. It resembled a living nightlight with all its glowing crabs, fish, anemones, and sea stars.

The tidepool scene below me flitted and flowed in shadows cast on the ceiling as I lay in bed, trying to fall asleep. The glass wall felt cold and unnerving with no visibility outside at night.

I could hear the steady lap of the water and the hum of the tanks and filtration system supporting it. I flipped on my recorder so I could remember it, but now when I listen to that recording, all I hear is my own breathing. It makes me wonder if the sounds were only so loud in my mind.

Oddest of all, I remember just before I fell asleep hearing a distant thumping. It sounded like someone pounding their fists on glass. I left the recorder on all night, and even though I've played all those hours back many times now, I've never been able to hear the pounding again.

We met in the atrium the next morning for cold brew, muesli, and fresh fruit. "How'd you sleep?" Silas asked when he saw me.

"Fine," I said. "Though I did hear some banging?"

Silas cocks an eyebrow at me over his coffee. "Like pipes?"

I hesitated but decided not to say it was more like fists on glass. "Maybe," I conceded.

"You'll have to forgive the house," Silas said with a smile. "With all the tanks, it's a lot of plumbing to support it."

I smiled back and sipped my bitter cold brew. "I'd love to see the lab where Aquanatic was born."

Silas's face lit up. "Of course, Ava. Your story wouldn't be complete without it."

He stood up and walked over to a curved bookshelf across the room. He looked at me knowingly and pulled out *Twenty Thousand Leagues Under the Sea* by Jules Verne, which triggered the whole bookshelf to turn on a hidden axis, revealing a small passageway. I inwardly marveled at the physics of a hidden doorway on curved hinges.

"I call our lab the Nautilus," Silas explained over his shoulder as we descended the narrow staircase. "Are you familiar with the work of Jules Verne?"

I rolled my eyes. All these tech guys were the same, thinking the one book they enjoyed as a kid made them some kind of literary genius. I supposed I should give Silas credit for at least not fanboying over Tolkien like the rest of them did.

"Vaguely," I lied. Verne was one of my favorite authors, too.

The sounds were all muffled here, though I still heard the distant rush and roar of the ocean tide, like a heartbeat from the womb. As we continued, it got even quieter, and I needed to remind myself to breathe.

We reached a door, to which Silas pressed his palm, causing a shimmery blue halo to appear around his fingers. With a soft chime, it slid open, revealing the Nautilus.

As with the rest of the house, there wasn't a straight edge in sight. The room hummed with that now-familiar sound of the tanks, and underwater glow panels lit everything with an eerie blue. Sensor equipment covered the sleek, stainless-steel tables, and samples of seaweed and coral lined the walls. A centrifuge sat in one corner of the room, opposite various tanks stacked on the other side. But what dominated the space was the massive kelp forest tank in the middle, the bottom of what extended all the way into the atrium. Seeing that tank from the top was one thing, but seeing the full height of the giant kelp that reached almost thirty feet was breathtaking. I truly felt like I was in an underwater kingdom.

"Like the forests of Crespo Island," I murmured. At this, Silas's face lit up.

"Beautiful, isn't it?" he asked. "So you are familiar with *Twenty Thousand Leagues*. Let me show you the brains of our Nautilus, the models that Aquanatic uses."

He turned on a computer attached to several monitors, and for the next hour we went through various models of currents, temperature drift, and marine population decay rates.

Silas showed me cameras and data collection units from buoys posted all over Monterey Bay—devices that fed the models with a constant stream of data.

I noticed a framed nautical chart on the wall behind the screens, with the initials M.P. in small script at the bottom.

"Marin?" I asked, nodding toward it.

"Yes," Silas said with a sad smile. "She helped design the original algorithm that powers Aquanatic."

I frowned, my brain churning over details from my research. "But your name is the only one on the company patent."

Did I see the faintest shadow pass over Silas's face? If it did, he quickly brushed it off.

"My sister was a genius at oceanography, but I handled all the paperwork. All the legal and logistical details she didn't want to get bogged down in. We were a great team in that way."

Just then, an alert went off, making us both jump. A red siren flashed at the computer center, and a robotic female voice chided, "Warning, system down. Warning, system down."

Silas frowned and went over to the computer, entering a few command lines in the terminal.

"Ah, it's one of the drones out by station 462. West side of the bay. We're always getting choppy tides there," he explained. "I'm just going to fix this."

I nodded, and at first I sat and observed him, but after a while I grew restless watching him type and flip through different software applications on the monitor. I turned on my recorder and started to walk around the lab. I stood in front of the kelp forest, trying to see if I could pick up a sound from one of the eels flipping past a cord of kelp. In person, you could hear a very faint bubbling sound. But I was never able to capture it in my audio.

I walked through the rest of the Nautilus, recording what I saw for the notes I'd use on background information later. Silas was still at the computer and now on the phone with someone, quite distracted. That was when I saw it: a sealed, lightless tank in the very back of the room. It had all the pipes, temperature controls, and filtration devices like the other tanks, but no label. It was shaped like a coffin, large enough to fit a tall person, but no wider.

I glanced back at Silas, who was still on the phone, and made my way over to it. I gently waved my audio device over it, thinking I might pick up something. And I did—a marbled tapping, like fingernails on thick glass. I froze as the memory of the pounding from last night came rushing back to me.

"What are you doing?" Silas's voice came from behind me. I whirled around, nearly dropping my recorder.

"Nothing," I said. "Just background audio for my notes."

He looked at me strangely. "That tank is empty."

I nodded. My hands shook, and I just wanted to get out of there, get above ground. I felt like the walls were closing in, like the kelp forest tank might burst at any moment, flooding the room and drowning us.

"Ava," said Silas, reaching for my shoulder. It took everything in my power not to flinch at his touch. "Are you okay? You seem nervous, and you've barely eaten anything since you've been here."

I took in a deep breath and tried to steady myself, tried to regain some kind of professional composure. "Why is the tank powered if it's empty?"

Silas smiles. "Ah. Good question. It's just cheaper to keep it hooked up to the system than decouple all the devices. The machinery down here can be quite complicated."

I nodded again and couldn't help but let my eyes dart to the exit. I knew Silas saw me, and he smiled again. He seemed genuinely worried about me, but I couldn't let my guard down.

"It's been a long day," he said, squeezing my arm reassuringly. "Why don't we have dinner?"

Dinner was a quiet affair: grilled salmon, arugula salad, and a crisp Albariño. We were overlooking Monterey Bay on the veranda, and the sun had just set, leaving an orange-pink glow in the sky.

"Tell me more about your sister."

"You feel her presence here, don't you?"

I wanted to disagree, but I couldn't. "Yes," I admitted.

"You're not alone in that," said Silas matter-of-factly, sipping his wine. "She adored Terncliff. She worked with Mickey on every element of it. The kelp forest was her idea. Everyone said it couldn't be done, a research-grade exhibit like that in a private home. But she was insistent, and of course in the end, she persuaded the builders to do it."

"Bull-headed," I whispered.

"You knew her?"

I shrugged in a way I hoped looked nonchalant. "No more than anyone else. But I'll admit, I followed her work closely. It's clear from everything she did—the political lobbying, taking on the big oil companies—she never backed down from a fight."

Silas chuckled. "No, she didn't."

"Tell me about her last dive," I said quietly, flicking on my recorder underneath the table.

Silas pursed his lips. "She was out by Buoy 9, her favorite spot in the bay. She was conducting standard research out there, recording observations about the declining California halibut population. She was diving alone but had worked many times with the boat captain she was with. After she'd gone thirty extra minutes with no safety checks, he called the Coast Guard."

He pulled out a tissue and dabbed at his eyes. Was he putting on a show? His eyes didn't look wet, but he did sound choked up. I continued to listen calmly, but I knew something was off, because Marin wouldn't have dived alone. Not after what happened in Palau. Not after she promised me.

"In the end, I think she got tangled. The kelp forests are so thick out there. But it's hard to say, because her body is still missing."

I played back his story in my room that night, trying to ignore the eerie blue glow emanating from the glass floor. I'd done so many profiles over the years that I should be able to tell when someone was lying. Usually, it was easy. People had tells, or they eventually contradicted themselves. But Silas hadn't, yet. Either that, or I just wasn't on my A-game. Maybe my mentor was right, and I really was burned out.

I reviewed the facts as I uploaded everything I'd recorded that day to my phone. Silas had possible motive for killing his sister. With its extensive lab and complex models, Aquanatic clearly would not exist without Marin. Yet she was like a ghost in all the paperwork for the company. Her name wasn't on Aquanatic's keystone patent, she wasn't listed as a cofounder in any legal documents, and Terncliff was fully in Silas's name. Perhaps she'd been pressuring Silas for more ownership, or she'd disagreed with him on the direction he was taking the company. After all, Aquanatic had gone public only after Marin's death, and that was after years of speculation as to why the Lockmere siblings were waiting when so much money was at stake.

I checked the time on my phone: 11:11 p.m. I rewound the audio back to the start of Silas's story to listen to it one more time before trying to fall asleep, but it skipped to earlier, to the drumming of fingernails on the glass of the sealed tank. I froze. I tried to navigate in the audio stream back to the story, but it was stuck on a loop in that one spot. The drumming of fingernails played repeatedly.

"Marin?" I called out to the empty room.

And then it stopped.

I looked down at my phone. Now the cursor moved wildly across the audio file without me touching it, and a woman's voice, high and ethereal, spoke in fragments interspersed with static.

"The Nautilus . . . Check . . . The Nautilus. Help . . . the tank . . . Help."

I sat up in bed, my heart pounding through my chest. She was here, in this house . . . a part of it. I knew it in my bones. And she was speaking directly to me.

I got out of bed and snuck to the atrium. Using my phone as a flashlight, I scanned the curved bookshelf till I found *Twenty Thousand Leagues Under the Sea*. I pulled it, opening the wall of books just as Silas had done, to reveal the narrow flight of stairs leading down to the Nautilus. I reached the door to the lab and pressed my hand to it, praying it wasn't a biometric lock.

With a soft chime and a gentle whoosh, the door opened as it did before, and I stepped inside. The robotic thrum of the filtration devices and computers replaced the dense silence of the passageway.

The familiar panic from earlier returned, but I steadied my breathing and crept over to the dark corner of the room where the sealed tank sat. Marin needed me. However weak I might feel, I had to expose the truth. If Silas had killed her and hidden her body in that tank, I needed to know.

I paused, and then forced myself to heave the lid open, expecting to see Marin's swirling blonde hair bobbing in the water. But the tank was empty.

As I looked inside, my brain tried to catch up with my eyes. I had been so convinced that she was in there. The water was dark, but the blue lights of the room illuminated things well enough that I could see there was nothing inside. Even though it horrified me, I even put my hand in and moved it back and forth, seeing if my fingers would touch something other than the sides of the tank. But no.

I stepped back, letting the lid bang shut. Maybe I was truly losing my mind.

I stared at the kelp forest tank, watching a sanddab waggle its flat body along past the glass. It reminded me of the flounder we'd seen in Palau, back when Marin and I dove together.

I'd met her in college, at Johns Hopkins. We'd been assigned to room together in the freshmen dorms. At first, I'd had a lot of prejudices about her: I'd heard her name, knew she was from a rich family. But no one was more down to earth than Marin. When the university closed the homeless shelter across the street right before Christmas, she didn't protest just to attract more clout, and she didn't have her family quietly donate money to fix the problem. She stayed up past midnight for a whole week making care packages with bags of groceries, socks, soap, and underwear. And she recruited everyone on our floor to help hand them out. I'd never forget how grateful those families were.

She was passionate about marine biology, which was how we got into diving together. For me, it was just a hobby. But for Marin, it was her life. She could have gone into anything: politics, economics, even architecture. But she'd always said that underwater was the only place she felt truly herself.

We traveled all over the world together, a different destination every summer and spring break. Each dive she got bolder, going deeper and for longer periods of time. It worried me, but it wasn't until Palau that it all came to a head.

Marin was collecting coral samples, and I was writing a piece on the impact of warming oceans in Micronesia. On the last day, we'd each done two dives and spent most of our tanks, but of course Marin wanted to go back down one last time. I was up on the boat, drafting copy, with one eye on her oxygen levels, when I noticed they were falling way too fast. Since Marin had gone down alone, it was impossible to know what was going wrong. Terrified, I immediately suited up and dove to get her. She'd gotten caught in a narrow coral crevice, and in trying to free herself, she'd damaged her equipment and was leaking air. She had already passed out by the time I reached her. Luckily, we got to the surface quickly, but my hands shake even now remembering it.

We'd had a long talk that night, just us two on the beach. We sat in front of a fire, waves crashing in the background.

"You almost died today," I had said finally, accusingly.

"I know." Marin poked at the fire with a stick, and I'd felt like a parent nagging a child. "I'm embarrassed," she whispered. "I thought I had it under control."

I sighed. We were the same in that way: too proud to admit when we were wrong, or to ask for help when we needed it.

"Promise me," I said. "Promise me you'll never dive alone again."

Marin nodded.

"And one more thing," I added. "If you ever feel like you're in over your head, in any situation, just call me. I'm here for you."

"I promise," she whispered. And we'd hugged. I could still smell her shampoo, mixed with sea salt.

But everything changed after that trip. We stopped seeing each other as much, stopped diving together. When I did see her, she was more distant, more emotionally detached. I think in Palau, I'd seen her be too vulnerable, and she didn't want anyone to know that version of her.

"Where are you now?" I whispered to the empty lab.

I was just thinking that I really needed to go back to bed when my eye caught something glinting in the sand at the bottom of the tank.

I peered closer, my nose pressed up against the cool glass. Most of it was submerged in the sand, but I could see just enough to make out the edge of a gold ring. I took out my phone to use the flashlight. The bright light illuminated the tops of two letters: an "M" and a "P."

I took a step back. Marin's ring? What was Marin's ring doing at the bottom of the kelp forest tank?

I closed my eyes and thought back to Marin's distorted message in my room. What if she hadn't been saying "help"? What if she'd been saying "kelp"? "Check the kelp tank in the Nautilus."

Anxious now, I spent the next hour scanning the sand for more clues, watching the fish swimming around, and wondering if I hadn't gone even crazier than before. What if I'd only imagined Marin's message? What if all of this was in my head?

And then I saw it. It was so subtle that even though it was right in front of the submerged ring, I'd missed it the first few times I'd scanned the tank. But etched in the glass was a word, rough and in reverse, but clear as day: "NEMO." Scrawled on the interior of the glass—something only a diver would be able to write.

I took pictures with my phone, my hands shaking, before Silas's voice boomed behind me.

"Ava. What are you doing here?"

I jumped and took a step back from him, instinctively raising my arms to protect myself. "She called you Nemo, didn't she?"

"I . . ." Silas looked genuinely confused and, for the first time since I'd met him, scared. "I don't know what you're talking about."

"Look," I said, pointing to the tank. But the word was gone. The tank's glass was completely unmarked. I opened the camera roll on my phone, but the pictures I'd taken just a minute ago had no etchings in the glass either.

"I didn't want to do this," Silas said, reaching into his pocket, "But when I went to check on you, I saw these on your bedside table." He pulled out two full, rattling pill bottles, and I winced at the sound. "Seroquel and trazodone?"

"How dare you snoop through my things!" I hissed.

He gestured helplessly around the lab. "And what are you doing here, if not snooping through *my* things? Since you got here, you've been walking around recording nothing, jumping at every little noise. Are you even writing an article?"

I didn't say anything, but rage consumed me, directed mostly at myself and my own hubris. I'd let curiosity get the best of me, and I hadn't wanted anyone to think I was mentally unstable.

"I wanted a clear head to write this story," I whispered. "I don't want to be on those drugs anymore."

Silas stood in front of me, and he didn't look scared anymore. I could tell from the way his eyes widened, with a pleading look in them, that he pitied me. And that hurt worse than anything he could have said.

"Let's go back to your room, Ava," he suggested gently, taking me by the elbow and leading me to the door. "Get some rest."

I shook my head and looked back to the kelp tank to catch a glimpse of the ring glinting in the sand at the bottom. I'd taken it too far with the etching, that was clear now. But the ring was real: proof that I wasn't crazy. How else could a monogrammed ring have gotten to the bottom of that huge tank, without it having come off in a struggle? It seemed beyond mere coincidence, and I couldn't help but smile to myself at the thought of questioning Silas about it later. As much as I wished I could do it now, I'd already overstepped, and I had to play by his rules for now.

I let Silas walk me back to my room, and resolved to go back to the Nautilus the first chance I had, but I never saw the lab again.

"When was the last time you took your medicine?" he asked when we got to my door.

"Twenty-four hours ago," I admitted.

He pursed his lips. "I'm sure you know you shouldn't go off it without medical supervision."

"Please don't worry about me," I said. "I'll see you in the morning, and we can finish the story."

I planned to grill him, starting by confronting him with the ring in the tank and breaking him down bit by bit until he admitted to killing Marin to keep full ownership of Aquanatic. But my mind had other plans for me.

That night, the withdrawals took hold. It started with a dull headache that quickly progressed to an insistent pulsing behind my eyes. I shivered under the covers. I was so cold my teeth were chattering, and then suddenly I felt so hot and sweaty that I could hardly breathe. The prickling heat under my skin propelled me out of my bed and onto the glass floor, which was blessedly cold. I lay there until my cheek ached. Then I dragged myself back to the bed, only to repeat the process. I don't know how many times I cycled from the bed to the floor until I realized this would all stop if I just took my medicine again.

I looked to the night table, but the pill bottles were gone; Silas had taken them with him. I cursed myself for not thinking to ask for them back, for not thinking I'd need them, and then I cursed Silas for taking them from me.

At first, these thoughts remained in my head. I tried to push them away, to breathe through what I was feeling and stay grounded. But the thoughts turned into tears, and the crying came in fits. Sometimes it was just tears leaking quietly, soaking into my shirt as I curled against the wall. Other times it was full, wracking sobs till I could barely breathe. I became dimly aware that I was yelling in between the tears, screaming at Silas that he'd never get away with this, that I'd call the police and every media outlet in the country and tell them what he'd done.

My throat burned with salt and bile, and after a few hours, my voice gave out. At first, the silence that followed was a relief. My mind had temporarily emptied itself. But the sounds that came next were far worse. The tanks' humming grew louder, vibrating in my skull like a swarm of bees. The eerie blue glow of the floor panels rose and surrounded me like a damp cloak. It felt like Marin's essence was in the room with me—not the friend I'd loved, but a cold version of her spirit. Her voice came through in fragments, as though I'd left one of her recordings running: static, then the hiss of a regulator, then a clipped phrase. *"Descent initiated. Need to recalibrate surface readers . . . if Silas ever lets me take the rig offline long enough."* Then it would vanish. I pressed my hands over my ears, but it didn't matter. The voice came from inside.

"Marin," I rasped. "Marin, I'm here!" But she never responded.

Then came the tapping. Sharp at first, like knuckles against glass. I froze. Was Silas coming to get me? And if so, to help me, or to put me out of my misery?

It came again. Not from the walls or door, but from beneath my floor. I pressed my face to the cold surface, but all I saw were the tidepool creatures, safely ensconced in their own world.

Marin's voice returned, but this time with nonsense, her cadence lilting: *"Nemo, Nemo, Nemo,"* a singsong chant looping like a child's rhyme. Then a long *scrrrratch*. Pause. *Scrrrrratch*. The dragging of something sharp on glass. A knife? A shard of coral? The vibration raced up my spine, spreading into my shoulders, my arms, the tips of my fingers, until I dug my nails into my own palms just to make it stop. And on and on it went.

I don't know exactly how long I suffered that night. Silas called the police in the early morning hours, and I was put on a fifty-one fifty hold. I don't remember much of the time I spent in the hospital. They put me back on all my prescriptions and added a few more to keep me docile.

So now, my days as a journalist are behind me. Silas didn't want any controversy for Aquanatic or the Lockmere family, so when I got out, I signed an NDA and *GQ* shuttered the story. I never reconnected with my editor and haven't reached out to any contacts since then.

Some days, all I can think about is going to the police and telling them everything about my time at Terncliff, the NDA be damned. But would they believe me? Everyone believed Marin's death was an accident. Yes, I knew her ring was in the tank, but would that be enough to convince them to investigate further?

Marin's voice still haunts me in the dead of night. She calls to me. I promise that one day, when I can trust my mind again, I'll return to Terncliff. This time, not for a story, but to finally reveal the truth at the bottom of the kelp tank, and what happened to Marin Lockmere.

# About the Author

**Katherine Rea** is a writer from Saratoga, California. She currently lives on California's Central Coast with her husband, two children, and an orange cat. When she's not writing, she enjoys reading, spending time outside, and traveling.

You can find Katherine on Instagram at:
@katherine_rea_writes

To learn more about Katherine, visit her website at:
katherinerea.com

# Ultraviolet Night

# Ultraviolet Night

## Jesse Ramon Ferreras

THE MARGINS SAT AT THE east end of the city, before a vista of mountains and ocean. Once a prosperous district where landowners erected palatial blocks in the early twentieth century, the area had fallen into ruin over one hundred years later. Majestic theatres and elegant department stores gave way to moneylenders, convenience marts, and apartments so decrepit their residents preferred the streets.

That suited me fine; I preferred my prey in the open.

Awakening after a decade, I floated above streetlights that cast an ultraviolet glow on the people below, designed to discourage drug use by preventing them from seeing their own veins. The lights were a ridiculous and oppressive innovation. These were practiced people; they knew how to find their own veins. And so did I.

Rain soaked my red tailcoat and long, wavy hair such that no one noticed me when I descended into the chaos of the streets. Red and white ambulance lights flashed across the desiccated faces of young and old, more than I'd ever seen when I'd awakened before. Paramedics rushed to revive people who lay prone on the sidewalk, pumping their chests and jabbing their limbs to bring them back from the dead.

Amid the chaos, I spotted an older girl who sat up against a pharmacy window in a black leather jacket with a soaked hood that sat heavy on her head.

Before her lay a small, handwritten sign, its letters leaking off the cardboard in the rain: *Evicted. Need $$ for hotel.*

She looked familiar, even though I'd never seen her before. In her sullen, studded face, I saw the lineage of a people who had lived on this land since time immemorial. They were strong and spiritual people, hunters and trappers who had respected a landscape they harnessed to their needs, long before a greater power turned their descendants into mendicants who haunted the streets like listless specters.

I knew these people well; my own family had pushed them aside to build blocks like these.

A man in a tattered green army surplus jacket stumbled into a dark alley, the rain dripping into a mane of gray hair that stood on end like frayed wires, and I followed him, my throat parched from ten years of sleep.

He steadied himself against a wall where the names of the Margins' most dangerous predators were scratched into the brick. I found my own name—the Viscount—inscribed there like an ancient carving, alongside policemen, pimps, and serial killers.

The man stopped beneath an iron staircase, his left hand pressing the wall as his right hand moved to his chest. He gagged and gripped at his heart, and violent shakes took over his body as he fell to the ground. A cloud of dust burst from his chest with a loud crack, like someone had stomped a boot between his ribs, and he twitched, calmed, and lay stunned, shocked at his sudden collapse.

I knelt next to the man, tore open his jacket, and found a deep groove in his chest, like a valley between two peaks. His ribs had shattered and punctured his lungs, and his white T-shirt was stained red as it stuck to a heart that beat its last rhythm before he died.

There was no catharsis in his passing, no poetry, no moment of reckoning to give his last moments some meaning. I had never seen a death so ruthless, and I felt sensations in my own chest that I didn't know I could activate anymore. A heavy emptiness like the sting of grief, strong enough to overwhelm my hunger. The feeling unsettled me at a level I'd never known when I'd awakened before.

It was time to find the Sentinel.

The Round Up Café had a buzzing red neon sign with an arrow that pointed to a door covered in steel mesh. A smiling golden cat with a waving left arm at the edge of a horseshoe-shaped lunch counter gave me my sole welcome as I went inside.

The café's owner, working late as always, stood behind the counter and glowered at me. She fell for no one's charms, and I respected that. From a set of steel cups, she lifted a fork, knife, and chopsticks and led me to a booth where a man sat reading in a faded green smoking jacket.

She left the utensils on the table, pointed to the menu on the wall, and walked away, saying nothing.

"Little Lord Fauntleroy," the Sentinel said, making notes on a page as I sat with him.

"Careful," I warned. "I understand that insult."

He looked down at his pages.

"What are you reading?" I asked.

"A newspaper," said the Sentinel. "I have a special affection for things that have lived past their lifespan."

I never liked his jokes, but I couldn't say I had no time for them.

"What troubles you, son?"

I told him I didn't like what I was seeing on the streets.

"What do you mean?" he said, looking up at me through glasses with over-sized frames.

"People dead all along the sidewalk, a convoy of ambulances lining the curbs."

"Same as ever," the Sentinel said.

"This was different," I told him. "A man's chest sank in on itself, suffocating him."

The paper started to tremble in his left hand. "Must be the crushing weight of life in the city. Next-level drugs to cope with it."

"This was no drug; this was a blunt-force impact to the chest, of a kind no one could do without the strength of a hammer," I said. "Tell me what's doing this."

"Must be something more powerful than you out there," he said as he looked back down.

When the Sentinel looked at me again, he saw me sideways, with a blunt-force impact cascading up from the right side of his head where I slammed him into the table. Fighting to catch his breath, he chafed from the grip of my crab-like fingers as I pushed him down on the hard surface.

"I am the envy of the living and the dead, and there is no power greater than me anywhere," I told him. "You are nothing more than a bloodhound sniffing out the best game. If something out there is taking people before I can reach them, I want you to tell me where it is. And if you expect any special pleading, just remember that this"—I breathed a draft of cold air across his throat—"is the only way I beg."

The Sentinel's head snapped up like a spring when I released him. He cracked his neck and folded his hands atop the table, seething with fear.

"Sunken Chest Syndrome," he said, emphasizing every word. "Most people are born with it. Now it's developing in adults."

His right hand shook beneath his left, and he struggled to suppress its tremors.

"Paramedics used to see it in one or two places but now that you've seen it in the streets, it must be spreading," he said. "It kills people faster than doctors can get to them and no one knows what's causing it. At first, police thought a serial killer was taking people with a hammer, but the grooves are wider than the head of any tool."

He gripped the table's edge and leaned against the bench's high back. "Whatever is doing this is not of this world. It's more powerful, more mysterious. More sinister."

"The attacks were confined to a specific area of the city at first," I said. "Where is that?"

"The towers."

"The towers?"

"The city can't grow out anymore, so it's growing up," he said. "Look way past the Margins, and you'll see the places where the *nouveau riche* live and play. Little glass boxes in the sky. Police found the first signs of Sunken Chest Syndrome in those apartments. Start there, m'lord, and maybe you'll find your answer. Plenty of fresh game up there, too."

I stepped back out of the café and looked down the main street of the Margins, past the crumbling blocks and out to the city beyond, where a complex of glass towers sixty stories tall stood like pillars that held up the sky.

Bright bands of light spanned the structures from ground to summit, matching the streetlights with an ultraviolet glow.

I ascended.

Four towers loomed like alien ships above aging Art Deco buildings on the western edge of downtown, their smooth, glass facades reflecting the city in a distorted blur. The towers stood atop a vast plot of land where I'd once seen families return to humble, three-story homes far below the luxury—and without doubt, the cost—of the apartments that replaced them. I didn't know where the families had gone, but they couldn't have lived here anymore.

I floated amid the towers' heights, one positioned in each direction like a compass, and looked in on small units that were laid out the same in every building, with square living rooms and thin balconies where sliding doors led into bedrooms.

I found the lights were on in just one apartment for every four, and most people lived alone, their sole company the ones who spoke to them through their devices. Few did anything to illuminate their imaginations, like read a book or play an instrument, and they looked to me as listless as the people in the streets.

A slender woman's golden skin glistened as she pumped the pedals of a stationary bike next to her window on the thirty-seventh floor. So loud was the instructor barking inspiration from a small screen that she heard nothing as I slid open her balcony door and stepped inside.

All human blood has a unique scent, and I sensed in hers a rush of adrenaline, hinting at a relentless fight response.

I exhaled a breeze that chilled the sweat up her spine and she decamped from her bike, looking around to ensure she had left all the doors and windows closed. All were, save the door to her bedroom on the right.

She saw nothing through the doorway as she passed to the kitchen where she had left a canister of bear spray inside her purse. From the darkness of her bedroom, I watched her collect the canister along with a cleaver before she heated a cast-iron pan with oil on the stove. The bubbles crackled with the scent of an exquisite extra-virgin olive oil as she readied to defend herself.

She gasped to see the clock gone dark on the stove's digital display. Turning the knob down and back up to start the gas burner again, she screamed as the stove produced nothing but sparks.

Her apartment lights dimmed overhead before they started to surge on and off with the rapid rhythm of a strobe. I ducked around behind her so that all she saw of me was the flickering shadow of a man with long hair and broad shoulders, flashing on the wall before her like a shade projected on a cinema screen. She squinted, swung the cleaver, and discharged the spray in a burst that dissipated like a cloud in the wind.

I took her around her bare, sticky shoulders and lifted her into the air with me, angling her head to watch my shadow lower my mouth to her throat as I pulled her down into the darkness with me forever.

Many more perished this way in the nights to come, and my favorites were the young men locked into epic battles on their computers. Whole armies would halt the fighting on the screens as their generals swung keyboards, controllers, and waste bins to defend themselves in the real world, and I couldn't help but laugh as they leapt to save their sedentary lives.

On my fourth night of hunting, I spotted an apartment on the fourteenth floor where every surface shone in bright, tasteful colors. Books lined the walls and a tree with pink LED lights illuminated the balcony. Stuffed animals sat up against the bed's headboard and a sheet of paper was taped to the bedroom wall with three words: *You are enough.* To look upon this apartment was to open the door into the bedroom of a vibrant child in a Puritan's home, the colors a protest against the staid and stoic reign of a family that ruled by the book.

A woman lived there alone, worked late on her laptop and curled up on her couch with books when she relaxed. She sprang up from her couch at every ping from her computer, excited to see a message from friends, family members, even bosses who asked for her help with last-minute tasks. When I looked in on her, I sensed a kind, selfless, yet lonesome woman and felt again that sinking sensation I had experienced on the street, like I mourned the soul I would take from this body. My hunger was too strong to stop me, but I could give her a death more merciful than the life she lived.

From the dark of her bedroom, I saw her emerge from her shower in silhouette, a towel covering her from her chest down to her thighs. Sitting down on her bed, she cried as she looked out the sliding door at a view of her own building in the facade of the opposite tower, and the view was like a magic mirror reflecting the life she hoped would make her happy.

She sensed nothing as I floated atop the mattress and crawled to her, watching as her shoulders pulsed with cries. I soothed her with soft strokes of those shoulders, entrancing her such that she welcomed this phantom presence and guided my hands to every part of her smooth, soft body.

With every touch, the saturated sweetness of dopamine faded from her, replaced with a flowery aroma of oxytocin that flooded her blood like glacial water filling a dry creek bed. I kissed her neck and, with the gentlest bite on her jugular, guided her peaceful descent into eternal darkness.

I stayed with her for another night to read the books on her shelves. I found Blake, Byron, and the Shelleys, authors I had loved in my own time, and as I read, I looked at my kill and wondered at the cruelty of a world that could exclude a woman of such imagination.

Back on the hunt, I listened to water flow out of a showerhead in a different unit for forty minutes. The water splashed a surface too soft to be a basin, and no one made a sound. Something was wrong.

I inched the door open and saw a young man lying beneath the showerhead, his chest red from the beat of his heart through a thin layer of flesh. His ribs had caved in on themselves, and his heart pounded a weakening beat in the gorge between his pectorals.

More were dead in the same way on their beds, their couches, even sitting up at their computers in the middle of a game. For two nights, I found no one else I could take, and I floated about the towers in a panic, desperate for blood.

Prey had not been promised to me in the towers—a game had. And I was losing.

I grew ever more famished until I spotted a flickering light on the balcony of a sixtieth-floor penthouse. Staying close to the tower's facade, I reached the penthouse level and watched violet light dance on the balcony ceiling.

"Join me for a drink?" a voice asked as I hid.

"No, thank you," I replied.

"You don't?"

"No," I said. "Never."

The man snorted. "Why don't you come have a seat anyway?"

I glided to the balcony and saw a man sitting before a round hearth with tall, violet flames that matched the streets' somber glow. The fire illuminated a wide mouth that grinned at its edges and hair that was long and dark, shaved at the sides and tied back behind his head, its color impossible to tell in the soft light. He betrayed no surprise at seeing someone float out of the air to sit with him.

"Like them?" he asked, pointing to the towers as I took the empty wicker chair next to his.

"They don't quite blend in," I said, looking at towers so tall they obscured the view of the mountains to the north, their occupants claiming the vista all to themselves.

"No tower should, and no city should either," he said. "Towers rise to inspire a city to greatness, and the city rises with them."

I looked long at my host, wondering whether he was trying to impress me.

"You're an architect?" I asked.

"You could say that," the man replied. "But to call me an architect is to call Jesus a carpenter; it captures none of his magnificence."

"How about I call you that anyway?" I asked him. "For brevity's sake."

"You've explored the towers for weeks," the Architect said. "Why?"

"I heard about a menace that's imperiling the city," I said. "I'm told it started here."

"What did you find?"

"Sad people who live alone, dying faster than anyone can reach them."

"What manner of death is this?"

"Sunken chests, shattered ribcages," I told him. "They look like something sat on them until they stopped breathing."

"Life in this city extracts a terrible price," the Architect said.

As he rested a hand on his right knee, I saw sharp fingernails so long they made it impossible to close a fist.

"You know what's happening here, don't you?" I asked. "Tell me."

The Architect stood with his wine glass in hand, leaned over the balcony railing and looked down on the city as if it were his very own. Strong back muscles stood out through a tight, dark, long-sleeved shirt, with lats so thick they looked like the ridges of retracted wings that flanked the narrow valley of his spine.

"Life was good to the families who lived here until the eyes of the world fell on the city," he said. "People with money from abroad were looking for new places to park their cash, and they were hypnotized by the beauty of the landscape. So they tapped me, and others like me, to build them homes in soaring towers whose majesty challenged nature's own."

He took a sip of wine.

"We tried so much to make the families leave, but too many held out, so we had to try something else. We changed how the city saw them."

He broke off as if he were giving me a chance to press him further. I said nothing.

"We found champions for the towers in young people who would never have a chance at those family homes themselves," the Architect said. "We made them believe that smaller units would be more affordable by virtue of their size, and that the families were being selfish by staying here. Our champions showed up in the news calling the families 'squatters' and 'freeloaders.' They told a story convincing the city that these were rich people who had to learn to share."

He choked back a laugh. "They went around telling people that if we just built more homes, everyone would be able to buy one," he said. "What they didn't know, what they refused to know, was that when you build one thousand units where just one stood before, you multiply the land value a thousandfold. Because of this, a single apartment costs more than the standalone home it replaced."

Another sip of wine.

"The units became more expensive along with all the land around them," said the Architect. "The city changed land laws to build more, and guess what happened."

I shook my head.

"We built more homes and made more people homeless," the Architect said with a subtle laugh. "Imagine that."

The heavy emptiness loomed in my chest once more, pulling at my heart like a wrecking ball that hung from a chain.

"Our champions were shocked that when they bought into the towers, the apartments cost a great deal more than they'd expected," the Architect said. "They had to stretch their money to afford them, and then a strange phenomenon emerged."

He turned back to me, glass still in hand, and sat atop the balcony railing like it was a prone man's chest.

"People's chests caved in on themselves, suffocating them until they died," the Architect said. "It happened here, where people bought the apartments, and it happened out in the streets, where the homeless lost all hope that they would ever find shelter in the city again."

I leaned forward, suppressing my disgust like a sickness in my stomach. My mind flashed back to the girl evicted to the sidewalk, to the hunters and trappers my family had displaced. The embers of my humanity smoldered inside me, kindled back to life by injustice.

"'The crushing weight of life in the city,'" I said, eyeing him as his sharp, claw-like nails tapped against the steel railing. "The Sentinel wasn't joking, was he?"

"Not at all. The Sentinel connected us to our champions. He has a sixth sense for prey."

"Did he tell you about me?" I asked, fighting my nausea.

"Of course," he said. "He told me all about his lordship, the Viscount. He wanted us to meet."

"Why?"

"To show you the natural order of things."

"And what's that?"

"That power has its time, and then it ends," the Architect said.

"If you met the Sentinel, he must have told you I could end you."

"That's not the way," he replied. "Titans give way to gods, and so they reign."

I looked down at the hearth burning between us. The Architect watched me reach inside and bathe my fingers in ultraviolet fire. They left no scar, no mark of a burn.

"Here's what's important to know about the natural order," I began again, turning my hand inside the fire. "When the gods came to power, they kept humanity in darkness. They wanted Earth all to themselves, so a titan rose up to challenge them."

I closed a fist around the flames.

"The titan stole fire, hid it in a fennel stalk, and delivered it to humans," I recounted. "He gave them the gift of light, and they held dominion over Earth for millennia to come."

A flaming orb rested in my palm when I removed my hand from the hearth.

"You talk as if you've brought fire back to humanity," I said. "But this looks like a fire you're keeping all to yourself."

The Architect scowled, his right hand tightening around the railing.

"There are more like me," he said, his voice trembling. "Many more. You can't kill us all."

"I don't want to," I replied. "I just want to put the fire back where it belongs."

From the floor, I lifted the wine bottle and splashed a glass's worth of wine in the Architect's eyes. I tossed the orb of flame with my other hand, igniting his hair and the wings he hid beneath his shirt. He extended them, trying to fly as he fell off the back of the railing, but the fire burned their membranes. To try to fly with ridges alone was to sail against the wind with nothing more than a mast.

The Architect plummeted sixty stories onto a concrete plaza where his limbs contorted like a marionette's and his skull shattered with blood and fragments littering the ground.

I reached into the fire once more, pulled a handful of flame, and slid it inside the bottle where it continued to burn bright.

As the sun rose in the east, I floated back to the Margins where I saw the same girl from the streets, struggling to light a fire beneath a bridge. I touched her shoulder, startling her as I handed over the bottle and watched its flames turn from violet to white in her hands.

A fire rose high as she shook out the bottle on the ground, and when she turned back to me, she saw nothing but a cloud of ash floating on air in front of the sun's rosy glow.

She tore a strip from her shirt, stuffed the material in the bottle's mouth and ignited it with the flame inside.

All who slept on the sidewalk, all who lived in the decrepit apartments woke to see her step out to the middle of the main street and stand before them like a defiant champion. They all shouted for joy, cheering her as she ran for the glass towers, carrying the fire like a torch that brought everlasting light to the ultraviolet night.

# About the Author

**Jesse Ramon Ferreras** is a former award-winning journalist based in Vancouver, B.C., Canada. His work has appeared in *The Globe and Mail*, CBC, The Huffington Post, and The Tyee.

You can find Jesse on the following socials:

Instagram @jesseramonferreras
X and Threads @jesseferreras

# The Woman in the Window

# The Woman in the Window

## Edmund McKenzie

GENTLE CURLS OF LATE-SEASON mist drifted in through the cracks in the window, bringing with it the chill the stone of the walls were doing very little to stave off. Dark, hazy clouds, heavy with the promise of rain in the not-so-distant future, blotted out the sky beyond. The low, mournful song of an old gray bird was lost to the thickness of the glass, voice now nothing more than a silent scream against the gloom.

But, in that moment, I could not have cared less about the outside world, even if I tried to. Now, all that there was for me in life, all that I could have dared to dream of or hope for, and perhaps all that I could ever need, was here within these walls. Until now, it was as if I had been walking through a dream, never quite living, never quite real. It had come in a flash, twin jewels that twinkled like amber in the autumn daylight, the curl of ruby flashing pearls to the world for but a moment.

It could have been a lifetime and an eternity since that day, since I first caught sight of the young woman peeking out through one of the windows in that peculiar old cottage on the edge of the tree line.

The first time I saw her, I was sure her gaze was not turned to me. Why should it be? A strange man passing her home with little to say for himself? But then I met her gaze. Not on that first day—no, I had shied away in a peculiar shame of my very self when I saw her then. It took a week to pass before that day came. That day, I did not turn my bashful gaze away, as I had out of habit each time before, and she did not object. No, she turned a smile to me, and it was as if the sun itself had cut through a darkness I had not known to hang so heavy over my heart.

I knew I had to meet her, knew this with the certainty a drowning man knew he must fill his lungs with air, even before she took up residency in my dreams. Though, it was only in my dreams that I could share the hour with her. For a time, it had been enough. Dreams more real, more desired than the bitterness the waking world provided.

But—it was not enough, could never be enough, no matter how I wished to content myself with the thought. I needed to meet with her in the waking world, this strange whisp of a silhouette, to make her real. To see that there was something real beneath the glass, not just the strange worlds my mind conjured from those few fleeting glimpses I was permitted each day.

And on this day, I knew she felt the same.

She was not at her perch in the window as she had been every other time I had passed through, but just as disappointment stung at my heart, what did I see? The door, typically sealed as though purely decorative, hung ajar.

It was an invitation. There was not a single shred of doubt within my mind that she had left the door open for me.

Never had I seen another set foot within the vicinity of the building hidden away by the trees that strayed from the forest (this very same solitude had been what had drawn me to frequent the path initially), and nothing suggested that any others lived there. Not even a caregiver, which I would have expected, as even a mere glimpse of her made it clear there was a sickliness to her that kept her from the sun.

So, it must have been for me.

While there was a bitterness in the air, characteristic of a coming storm, the winding corridors within the stone walls felt as though warmth—true warmth, at least—had never traveled the space I found myself in. What a state for a sick woman to reside in!

But then I heard it. The first sound I had ever been gifted from the woman who consumed my slumbering world and waking world alike. A little giggle, clear as the bells strung up during the holiday season, floating out from a little way off, just around the corner. The sound set my heart to thunder in my ears, the treacherous organ roaring as if it wished to drown out the sound in its entirety. A peculiar prickle raced down the back of my neck, but I brushed it aside as nothing more substantial than a buzz of nerves at the idea of finally meeting my mysterious stranger.

"I apologize for my intrusion," I called, my voice cutting through a silence more pervasive than I had quite realized. "I just wished to speak with you for a spell, ma'am?"

I was not met with a reply as I had expected, but neither was I met with the silence I had feared. Instead, the response I received was another giggle. Light and airy and slightly further off than the first had been. I was not too proud to admit this caused a spike of panic to twist within me. She was not turning me out, no matter the strangeness of invitation (or lack thereof), but she did not come to greet me. I could only think her lack of a proper greeting had come from an unfamiliarity with all the little intricacies that accompanied having guests. This must have been her attempt to invite me in, to follow her to somewhere more welcoming to talk together for the first time.

All this made so much sense to me, a rational explanation for the behavior of someone I assumed was a bit of a recluse. This was why I found myself traveling the odd, winding stone corridor, following only the occasional flicker of laughter or brief clatter of footfalls ahead of me.

Of course, I could have turned and left. I was, essentially, intruding on the space of a stranger who had made the active choice not to greet me. It was a peculiar situation. An odd sense of . . . something tugged at the back of my mind, desperate for me to acknowledge it while so soft I could not quite hear its warning. So, instead, I let my curiosity claim superiority in my mind.

An itching curiosity that burned beneath my skin with a desperation I had not realized I possessed, let alone could reach.

That was what it was, wasn't it? A curiosity that was driving me onward through the house. If I could just speak with her, just once, just long enough to satisfy my interest, I was sure I could content myself even if she were to request that I never return.

There were no corners that I could see, but the subtle curvature to the architecture made it feel as though I was walking on forever while the woman I was chasing never grew closer. Once or twice, I could have sworn I saw the flicker of a shadow leap and dance in the distance, the humanlike shape distorted by the unseen light sources that allowed it to stretch long enough to reach me.

Distracted as I was by the movement of shadows, I found that time had evaded me. Surely, the place was not so very large that I could have carried on my loop as I had without passing the front door, and yet I had not. In fact, I could not help but wonder if I had actually seen any doors at all since I'd made my way inside. Of course, this must have been a trick of my mind; it was impossible to imagine anyone living in a building that was just a single, perpetually gloomy, twilit corridor. Gloom, cut through by the occasional trail of light or flicker of a shadow to drive me onward, was no longer held in limbo by the occasional window as the walls were now perfectly bare.

My stride, which I had maintained at a level close to a jog, slowed to a trot. How on Earth had I not noticed such a drastic change in my environment? Where there had once been glimpses of the outside world, now only a steady monotony of stone greeted me. With an uncomfortable uncertainty, I glanced about me, only for nothing at all to stand out. So, with a sneaking suspicion, I brought my fingertips to brush against the wall. It was subtle but curved. I had not been following the woman in a straight line, but rather curling further and further inward, so near imperceptible it was as if it had been designed to not be recognized. Lowering myself to a crouch for just a moment, I could almost be sure there was a slight slope downward.

The single, muffled note of discomfort that rang in my ears hit a sudden crescendo. How had I been following this woman for so long without ever catching a glimpse of her? How could I have been so fixated on a person that I did not realize the path had been curling slowly inward, my loop a spiral so subtle I could have walked right down into the center of the Earth while I was blissfully none the wiser?

But then I saw her.

Just as the idea of doubling back, admitting defeat and returning to the world outside to brave the coming storm surfaced, I saw a flicker of her nightgown, a lock of dark hair vanishing just ahead of me. She was so close! Howsoever could I have considered turning back when she was so close? Just a little bit further, then the strangeness would all be worth it!

"Excuse me?" I dared call again, my voice failing me just that little bit more than it had any right to. By all rights, I had nothing to worry about. I had been invited in and so it was not as if I was doing anything I ought not. I was simply following her lead, as she clearly wanted me to. At any point she could have asked me to leave, and even that would have satisfied me. To hear her voice at last even as she dismissed me. But she didn't, and now I was so wonderfully near to the moment of our true meeting.

A sharper corner, at long last cutting away the previously perpetual monotony of the long corridor, seemed to come about all at once. I dared slow my pace. It would hardly make for a good first impression (could I consider it to be a first impression when she had not left my mind from the very moment I first caught sight of her?) if I was rushing about and flustered. I swallowed, my mouth oddly dry suddenly, as if I had never taken water for as long as I lived.

She waited for me. My lovely stranger.

Her dark curls, rebelliously tumbling about her shoulders, obscured the finer intricacies of her features as she let them fall about her face, but I could tell that she was smiling. It was a mischievous upcurl of her lips, a youthfulness her illness had not deprived her of. She clutched at her nightgown, a near inconspicuous attempt at obscuring her enthusiasm, and leaned against the delicately carved wooden door.

"I was not sure you would meet me here," she began, a wispy softness in her tone. "I'm glad."

"You truly wished to meet with me?" I asked, my voice akin to one walking in the spaces between dreams and the waking world.

"You sound so terribly surprised!" she exclaimed, punctuating this with yet another giggle. "Did you think I would not? We are friends, aren't we? Why shouldn't I wish to meet with you?"

Clearly my face, ever treacherous and disobedient as it was, betrayed me once more. An expression I was unaware of played across my face, winning an exaggerated pout from the woman. It did not reach her eyes, however, which carried a lighthearted twinkle. There was an odd familiarity in this, that look that teetered the fine line between mischievous and secretive, like I had seen all this before, but the meaning was lost to me.

"Why did you take so long to come here?" she continued, taking my silence as a reply of its own. "I've been terribly lonely, you know? It was cruel of you to leave me waiting like this." The mockery was lighthearted, and yet it left an uncomfortable ache in my chest all the same.

"I did not mean to keep you waiting," I said to my stranger, my wretched, lonely, and agonizingly familiar stranger. "Will you forgive me now that I am here?"

Of course she forgave me; her disapproval had been insincere. A twitch of her lips exposed her poorly obscured losing battle against a smile. A dazzling smile that broke across her face in an instant, clumsy in its flash of teeth, free of that terrible refinement so common in town, a denial of something sincere in the pursuit of acceptability.

"I might," she began, a playfulness in the way she seemed to ponder the idea, "if you will follow me?"

If I would follow her. . . . How easily she asked this, as if I would not, in that moment, follow her to the very ends of the world and right back again if she wished me to.

"If you would have me . . ." was all I could bring myself to utter.

She let out a hum, light and airy, before she drew back, slipping away through the door with such nonchalance as if to rival the intensity of the hammering of my heart. The door hung ajar for only a handful of moments before I gathered my wits and followed her in.

The act of shutting the door behind me sent the candles to flicker about, twirling the shadows into a wild, erratic frenzy of a dance in the small room. My curiosity left my gaze to wander the room, but before I could really identify anything of note, the woman threw her arms around me, drawing me closer and closer until her soft breath fluttered against my face, her lips so close that even the slightest shift between us would send them brushing against my own. The warmth of her skin was such a stark difference from the chill of my own, the bitter weather outside still clinging to me, that it was almost intoxicating.

"You really and truly don't remember who I am, do you?" she crooned, tilting her head to the side, further reducing the already minute space between us.

It was strange; I was quite sure the first time I saw her was when she sat at the window, and yet somehow, I knew she was right. I had felt an ache of familiarity even then, but the longer I spent in her presence, the more I knew there was something more, something I had forgotten, time stripping me of the sharpness of clarity.

Featherlight fingertips trailed my jaw, tilting my head to suit her better, her other hand straying aimlessly to brush loosely against the back of my neck, sending an uninvited chill to prickle my spine. Gone was the brightness of her smile, twisted instead into a bitter sneer. The twinkle in her gaze had darkened into something worse, something that seemed to suit her far better than the lightness she had attempted to carry. The ancient darkness that lay within the scarred hearts of all those who knew of more pain than their years.

In this moment, I was sure I knew her.

I uttered a sharp gasp, but my attempt to draw back, to escape, was swiftly thwarted as she dug her nails deep into the tender skin of my jaw, her other hand snagging into my hair with the sudden swiftness of a striking viper to make sure I was not going to escape. An involuntary whine slipped through my gritted teeth, uncomfortable and panicked. Even in my sudden bout of distress, her strength far outmatched my own.

"How dare you forget me?" she growled. "How dare you claim not to know me when I was damned by your hand! It was your wretched selfishness that doomed me to this existence of nothingness! You live each and every day as if nothing happened, but what about me? I'm trapped here and you have the audacity to forget!"

I wanted to deny this, to claim she must have mistaken me for another, that

I hadn't the faintest clue what she was talking about. But my words died in the back of my throat, rotting and decaying away until I was left to choke on my silence.

"But even now, I wanted to think we were friends. That you regretted leaving me here to rot," she continued, her voice cracking in a flood of emotions lapping at the surface. "I could have forgiven you if you did. Did any of it mean anything to you?"

Oh gods, I did remember, didn't I?

We were children then. Naive and blissfully unaware of the dangers the world could hold for children who did not know any better. Rumors circulated of a witch who lived in the impossible cottage that sat where once there was a thriving forest. We children of the village had whispered tales of her luring children into her home to feast upon them, as she had been cursed to remain within the house, a house that was forever changing from the lingering magic of her craft. A chameleon of stone and woodwork presenting itself to the eye as something comfortable and familiar. The style of the time was everchanging, and the cottage (had it always been a cottage?) let these trends define itself. If I were to push my memory, I was sure I could recall a cottage not too dissimilar from that of which my grandparents shared in their twilight years, but that was not what it seemed now. If anything, it seemed closer to the sort that those strange and fickle artists took to when their reputations grew too grand and they needed to get away from it all.

I knew now, with the wonderful little gift of hindsight, that what we'd done was foolish, but was there any way better to ensure a child did something they should not than telling them not to do something? With all the gusto of a child who felt they were invincible, we dared make the worst decision of our lives, hers to be doomed to suffer, mine to live as though it never happened at all.

And I had simply forgotten all about it. Then again, I felt I could be forgiven for wanting to forget the greatest mistake of my life. We had found the truth that had nestled into the heart of the stories, and I had been selfish. I had left someone I had considered to be my friend behind to suffer what I could not begin to imagine. But I could not be expected to wear the blame she forced upon me! We were children facing the very witch we had hoped to prove nothing more than legend and stories parents told to their children to keep them from straying too far. I was frightened, so I ran. Anybody would have. I did not know she would not follow me. That she would be trapped there, snatched away by that weary, gnarled figure who resided there.

"What do you want from me?" I asked, my voice lacking any of the strength or certainty I had hoped for.

"Are you still so ignorant? Or do you enjoy playing the fool?" she remarked, an edge of cruelty in her tone. "I want what I lost. I want my life back."

An odd chill raced down my spine, as if a bitter wind had struck me alongside her words. With a sudden rush of certainty, the sort that accompanied a dreamer just as the waking world came to greet them, I realized I had fallen for her trap with embarrassing ease. Even the fly posed more cognitive awareness when avoiding the spider's web. My lovely stranger, my poor abandoned friend, had clouded my mind, whether by the coincidence of my passing her in that window or by some terrible lingering guilt I had shoved to some far corner of my mind so that I might avoid having to reflect upon it.

She clearly recognized my revelation, for her eyes sharpened.

"You know, there has been so very little to do here ever since you left me to be trapped by the house, ever since my arrival allowed that poor old woman the chance to secure her freedom," she mused. "She did visit, you know? Which is far more than could be said for you. Of course, she never set foot inside, but I never blamed her for it. Isn't it terrible that we called her a witch? She, too, had found herself a prisoner of this nothing-space, having made that same mistake to step inside. I shudder to imagine just how many years of solitude she spent trapped here, wrongly accused of being something wicked and dangerous. I think that is why she visited, why she wanted to make things a little easier for me. At least one of you felt bad about my fate, I suppose. But during her visits, she told me a great many things she had concluded over those years, what little she could conclude from this nothing-place. She told me the house needed its host and would not let one go without a replacement."

She paused, uttering a shuddering breath as she rocked agitatedly.

"She said it was a form of symbiosis. It needed somebody here, that burning flame of life to occupy its walls, and in turn it kept its prisoner free from those most basic of wants. I never found myself without food, without books to distract me from the nothingness. All of it here in these neat little rooms, which are so unlike the rest. They never change in the way the rest of it does. I'm sure they must be what the house was once, before it started to grow and become what it is now, and that is why it needs somebody here. The core of its being kept alive by its captive's heart. It does sound so very selfish of it, but that is why I came to the conclusion that I did. That you and the house were practically made for each other!" In a bout of enthusiasm, she was practically stumbling over her words, a waver of excitement that frightened me.

"I am not going to stay here," I declared.

"Oh, you will. I am not giving you a choice." She shrugged. "I was being kind by telling you, not waiting for you to take your first step outside only to be greeted with the sensations of your very being succumbing to a swift and hungry death. Are you familiar with that feeling? I am. In those early days when I did try to leave, I got as far as the clearing before the pain grew so immense that I crawled back to safety, dragging myself on my hands and knees to try to escape a death that was not my own. I never fully recovered from my last attempt to escape, so now I am stuck with a reminder of my prison wearing away at my flesh. I would not wish that upon anyone at all, even you."

"You're mad!"

"I would not have survived if I were not," she shouted. "If I am mad, it is a madness you forced upon me! Did you tell them what happened? That you abandoned me here? Or did you pretend to be just as ignorant as everyone else was? You're terrible! I've had enough of this. I need to live, to feel the sunlight and remember that I am real. You did this to me; you need to make this right!"

She was hysterical, I concluded. Her solitude had driven her quite mad, and yet, I found I could not fault her for this. Of course, just because I understood why she had been driven out of her mind, it did not mean I was going to just relent to her request. We were children when she had been reported missing; she had never had the chance to start her life. Mine started that day, this new walk of life that came about after this change, this secret I buried deep within my heart guiding me even as I wished to forget. It was not fair to sacrifice that just for the sake of a woman who had since found herself a stranger in my life.

Unfortunately, the few seconds that had slipped by as I was reeling from the intensity of her reaction gave her the advantage she had been hoping for. Her theatrics had artfully hidden her inching steps toward the exit. I had not noticed her open the door at all, but before I had time to even realized she had thrown it open, it was once more shut. But she was sickly (injured? One and the same) and had been trapped indoors for so long that she would have hardly had the opportunity to maintain any real level of fitness, so I felt confident I could escape.

In a flash, I flung open the door, heavier than I had anticipated, and broke into a run. Faster and faster, faster than I necessarily felt I was capable of and perhaps even a tad faster still. My irregular, frantic footfalls echoed off the stone walls around me in a cacophony of panic. Loud enough to drown out the sound of the woman's own. Loud enough to muffle the sound of my heart as it thundered in my chest, threatening to burst through its cage and outrun me in my own flight.

I had walked through the spiraling hallway as if in a dream, time meaning nothing, and it left me regretting my lack of awareness of the passage of time. How many times did the passage loop before it reached its final turn? How long must I run until I was free to leave this terrible business behind me?

My panic rose with each time my feet hit the floor without drawing me any nearer to the silhouette of the running woman ahead of me. My lungs ached, but I could not slow. How it was that she did not seem to falter in her stride was beyond me. While she seemed to escape me, the ramifications of my failure to surpass her rattled around in my brain with an alarming incoherence.

The first window I passed offered me a glimpse of the world outside. The stretching gold of the sunset reached out as if to call me out with it. A wild notion came to me, and I dared stop, skidding from my efforts. If I could simply escape through the window, there would be no need to reach the front door at all! It was a risk, a gamble that could lose me everything, but it was the only option I had left. I was frantic, backed against the wall, and in desperate need of a miracle.

It was like the windows were sealed to the wall, a permanent, unmoving fixture. I wiggled at the latch, but it seemed purely decorative. With a whine in the back of my throat, I knew I had lost. A suspicion I proved true when, in a fit of desperation and anguish, I slammed my fist against the glass, and yet it remained just as it was. Again and again and again I tried to shatter the glass, and it simply did not budge. All my effort had left me with an ache in my fists and an ever-growing distance between myself and the woman.

The fact that I resumed my running was no longer out of any expectation of reaching freedom, but rather to soothe that part of my psyche that needed to know I'd tried. That I had not given up and just succumbed to my despair that crept from my heart like frost on a winter's morning, spreading out across me as I ran.

After an eternity that passed by too quickly, I saw it. The front door. Worse, still, I saw the woman fling it open with the frenzy of a caged beast who finally had a taste of freedom. She did not even care to turn back, to see if I had followed her. To offer the apology that I had not given her when it had been my place to do so.

"Wait!" I shouted to no end, my voice falling on unhearing ears.

She was free. She was free, and she was not going to look back. I slowed, gazing out through the doorway, out into a world that had been snatched away from me in such a brief moment. The woman vanished down the familiar path by the trees that was rarely traversed by anybody but me, and the dread was finally free to set in once the hope died.

The rain, which had teased me all throughout that day, finally released overhead, swift raindrops blurring the world to a smudge before my eyes. It was miserable weather, the sort that nobody would go out in by choice, so I swallowed up my pride and let the rain wash away my old life, leaving it to puddle in the mud like some terrible, irrelevant thing.

I could fight it. I could curse the heavens for each day of my life since that day we first dared approach the house. I could fall into bitter despair. But I didn't. The numbness set in, the shock, the nothingness. Perhaps there would be a time in the not-too-distant future when the reality of my situation set in, but that was for the future.

For the present, I simply turned back into the building. My house. My whole entire world. It was all I could do, and so I was back to traversing the loop, back and forth until, perhaps, I would even be able to tell when each circuit ended and the next began. Not that it really mattered anymore, but nothing mattered now.

I just had to hope that I would not have to wait the same nearly twenty years my friend had waited before someone took pity on me and saw me in the window and decided to meet me.

# About the Author

With a habit of writing stories where nothing at all really happens while everything happens, as a writer, **Edmund (Eddie) McKenzie** enjoys offering little glimpses into the wider fleeting moments. The need to create, to do something (anything!) burns through him like fire, leading him to the theatre, to spill out his heart across the page, to do something creative enough to soothe the soul. It is not always so easy to find the chance to do so whilst also studying at university, but sometimes one must play the starving artist to find satisfaction. Spooky, Australian, and trying to have fun.

You can follow Edmund on Instagram at:
@tocreateandtolive

To learn more about Edmund, visit his website at:
bio.site/hydesboy

# Manor
# of
# Memories

# Manor of Memories

## Elizabeth Faye Moxen

RAIN PELTED AGAINST THE GILTWOOD carriage as howling winds swayed the four of us inside. Dimly lit enchanted flames flickered on either side of the cabin, catching the warmth of Hartley's copper eyes as he wistfully stared out the window in front of me. The icon of the sun god dangled from the chain, bobbing on his chest as the carriage hurried down the uneven road. He sat next to Adelaide, the third princess of the Stahlar Kingdom, whom we'd been hired to guard on a diplomatic mission to Kholand. She sat still and proper, but I had watched her chew the inside of her cheek for the last hour, revealing her dimple. With her boyish, ashen-blonde haircut, people often mistook her for her brother, the second prince. She nervously spun the prominent steel royal signet ring on her finger. It was a ram on a shield outlined in diamonds, worth more than our combined reward for the mission.

The crinkled map in my hands rested on my journal about poisonous plants, which I was using as a makeshift desk. As the designated navigator, I charted the best route to Kholand. While identifying local flora and fauna came easily, I couldn't predict the surge of night creatures. The cloudy skies had obscured moon visibility, but the calendar indicated it would be full tonight.

"YAH!"

Jairus's harsh voice strained over the elements outside, prompting the two horses into a gallop. Elinalise's arm brushed up against mine as she bumped into my side. She concentrated on maintaining a shadowy awning over our companion's head outside, shielding him. As a royal mage, she wore a small pin with the royal crest on her black lace collar. Her eyes met mine amidst the silence, giving me a tender smile.

"Lonan, are you all right?" she asked.

"Y-yes," I lied. Bile rose in my throat as the carriage hit another rock in the road.

Trying to keep my stomach down, I braced myself in the rolling and swerving carriage. I had survived in the wilderness and charted the natural terrain of the kingdom, but the rocky ride humbled me. I feared motion sickness would be my end.

Jairus turned back to check on us through the window and then refocused ahead. The scars on his face pulled the skin in four distinct lines down his cheek, looking as if something had clawed him. As we hit another bump, his tall collar shifted to reveal two scarred puncture wounds, just about an inch apart. There was no way he could be a vampire; I'd spent too many days in the sun with him for that. For a man marked with endless stories, I wished he'd share more of them, if only to break the monotony of these unending days. With only a few days left, Kholand awaited our arrival.

Lightning flashed, a bolt of white branches expanding through the sky. The horses whinnied and reared back as thunder boomed.

*Thump. Crack.*

*Thud.*

Adelaide screamed as the carriage veered wildly on the muddy road, having run over *something*. I leaned over Elinalise, bracing her head to protect it from the impact. Hartley moved to protect Adelaide, wrapping his body over hers.

"You okay?" I asked Elinalise.

"Yeah, I'm okay." She gripped the fur of my hide armor.

My eyes scanned her body, making sure she didn't get hurt. My heart skipped a beat, seeing her in that black velvet-lace dress, hugging the delicate features of her slender body. I ached for her, the need rising like a hunger in my stomach.

Hartley eyed me.

"Remember our mission. Keep the princess safe," he warned.

My emotions had been scattered in the last few weeks, distracted by Elinalise, prioritizing her instead of Adelaide's safety. But Hartley was right.

Jairus tugged on the reins, urging the horses to halt. He hopped down from the carriage. Adelaide grabbed a pristine black-steel box with a small padlock attached to the handle that had sat near the chest filled with her luggage.

Jairus knocked on the door's glass. Loose curls unfurled from Elinalise's hair as she jolted up to open it. The princess straightened. Having left the protection of the mage's awning, Jairus's shaggy, mahogany hair stuck to his face. His leather armor pieces had darkened from the water droplets pouring down.

"We've run over a beast of sorts," he said. "One of the wheels broke off, and the horses were frightened. I'm so sorry, but the storm is too wild. We'll have to make camp for the night, Your Highness."

"Very well. I trust your judgement," Adelaide said.

"After I check on what type of beastie it was, I'll move the carriage to the side of the road."

My stomach eased as I planted my feet on solid ground. If it weren't so wet, I'd have kissed the stone. Rolling thunder rumbled in the distance, with each echo gaining volume. A gust of wind blew Elinalise's wide-brimmed hat off as soon as she put it on, sending it into a puddle near the broken wheel.

I lifted her by the waist, hoisting her onto a log beneath a white ash tree, partially shielding her from the tempestuous weather. She gathered her long hair, twisting it into a messy bun—it framed her face and reminded me of blackberries, mostly black with a streak of red-violet from a birthmark on the left side.

She glanced at the skies, counting from one flash of lightning to another. At the next strike, she muttered a spell under her breath. Her shadow detached, peeling up from the ground. It expanded with the next flash of light and interposed itself on the mage, creating a thin barrier between herself and the rain. She appeared to be nothing more than a void, save her eyes of pink amaranth.

"Lonan," Elinalise called, "where's your raven? Shouldn't he have come back?"

"I haven't seen Fich since we left Slocum Hollow."

"Was he with us when we left? I don't remember seeing him."

"He must have scouted ahead of us."

My heart twinged. Fich had never been gone this long before—not in a storm. My memory clouded when I pressed deeper, leaving a dull headache. I shook it off. He'd come back. He always did.

Jairus stooped by the wounded beast and lifted its hefty paw. The body rose and fell in short, shallow breaths.

"Stay back, everyone!" he shouted.

I steeled myself, stepping in front of Elinalise. This was a werewolf. My hand instinctively reached for the dagger at my side.

It whimpered and then snarled before lashing out. Despite dripping blood from its injured hind leg, the creature pinned Jairus down. Its canines ripped into his shoulder. Our comrade reached for his thigh, gripped a silver-tipped dagger, and drove it through the creature's heart, twisting until its last breath.

"Jairus, do you need help?" Hartley asked.

"Go take care of the princess, I'll be fine!"

Hartley dashed off, swiping Elinalise's hat. The bottoms of his priestly vestments trailed on the ground, mucking up the gilded lining. His sandy-blonde hair was tied in a low ponytail, with tendrils of loose strands clinging to his damp face. He removed his robes, showing his long, thin frame, and held them above his head.

"I cannot offer much, Your Highness, but I can hold the cloth above your head to shield you from the rain."

Adelaide stepped down, her boots sinking into the mud with each stride. Hartley held the vestments over her head, but it made little difference. With her linen tunic soaked, her teeth chattered. She stood just as tall as Hartley, taller than the rest of us.

I helped Jairus push the carriage while Elinalise tugged a taut thread of shadow attached to it, dragging it out of the way. I smelled the copper from his gaping wound, open from the torn-up leather. He moved as if nothing had happened, but I knew this all too well. Noting his jugular veins and carotid artery, I mentally planned a quick kill if he succumbed to the curse.

The princess jumped, placing a hand over her chest as the mage traipsed beside her.

"For heaven's sake, warn a girl next time you encase yourself in shadows."

"If you let me, I can help you, too. Your boots won't sink into the ground, and your clothes will dry faster." Elinalise bounced on her toes.

"Will I look like . . . that?" Adelaide gestured.

"Yes, but it's better than Hartley's soaked vestments."

"Fine, fine. Just do it."

Once again, Elinalise timed the lightning to capture the best light for casting Adelaide's shadow, layering it over her. She examined her form, waving an inky hand before her face, leaving her sage-green eyes as the only color visible.

Howls resounded in the distance. I scanned the sky, searching for any sign of the moon, but only saw dark cumulonimbus clouds. Hartley tossed Jairus a glass jar filled with shimmering liquid. He chugged it and threw the empty container back to his companion. The bleeding from his shoulder stopped, but the fresh bite marks remained.

Jairus grimaced. "I'll need to make the antidote before the curse sets in."

My ears twitched. "I think we've got company."

Growls and barks bellowed over the roaring winds as werewolves approached from behind, driving us into a cloud of fog, obscuring our vision. Footsteps splashed in the murky terrain. Bodies smacked together, followed by groans.

"Lonan?" Elinalise called.

"I can be," Jairus joked.

"Jairus!"

My hand reached into the gray mist, hoping to connect with someone.

"I'm over here!" I called.

"I'm . . . touching somebody. Please tell me it's one of you," Adelaide said.

"Somebody is definitely holding my hand," Hartley replied.

"I think that'd be me."

"Did we lose them?" I asked.

"I'm praying the werewolves also can't see shit in this fog," Jairus answered.

"I thought you didn't believe in the gods," Hartley quipped.

"I'll believe in whatever gets us through the night."

"Lonan, where are you?" Elinalise shouted.

I followed the sound of her voice. Something deeper tugged me in her direction. It had been pulling at me all night. A well from the depths of my being lurched, reaching for her, craving her ancient magic. The magic smelled of sweet licorice. My soul hungered, my tongue salivating. As I brushed against her shoulder, she relaxed beneath my touch. My stomach turned into knots. I shook my head and staggered back.

*What is wrong with me?*

Jairus clapped my back, and Elinalise interlaced her fingers in mine, grounding us both. A weight surrounded Jairus, like I could feel his soul losing its luster. Ghostly chains tightened around his aura as lycanthropy began to set in, twisting his scent to that of a wet dog. More werewolves stalked closer, snarling—their scent muskier and overbearing. One's slobbered maw opened, and a growl formed deep within its throat.

"On your left!" I bolted, leading the way.

Jairus dodged, lifting his dagger and swiping it across its throat. It yelped. We dashed forward, urging Hartley and Adelaide to stick closely behind. Twigs crunched behind us as the werewolves pursued. The dense fog dissipated ahead, revealing a manor. With another flash of lightning, the stained-glass panes displayed an image of a woman with her hands covering her eyes. A headpiece covered her hair, and a pendant shaped like a crescent moon hung on a thin chain around her neck.

My grip on Elinalise tightened. She stumbled over her feet, unable to keep up. A werewolf closed in on her, swiping its claw, missing her leg. My head throbbed with my quickening pulse. I threw Elinalise over my shoulder and continued toward the manor.

With another flash, the house illuminated. At the front door, we knocked frantically. A pale woman with silver hair and eyes opened the door and gestured for us to enter. She wore the same crescent moon pendant from the stained-glass panels, iconography of the night goddess.

As we rushed inside the manor, Jairus hesitated. I pulled him inside and closed the door as another wolf nipped at his ankles. With the door shut, silence settled. Enchanted white flame orbs lit the room like miniature full moons, casting a radiant, silver glow. Elinalise lifted the shadow magic, unveiling herself and the princess. Hartley handed the mage her drenched hat. She stowed it away while Adelaide continued clutching the black box in her arms.

The woman's crimson lips curled upward in a soft smile, quickly drawing into a subtle glower. Her gaze lingered on me, and then on Jairus's bite marks. He winced as he rolled up his pant leg, exposing the werewolf bite. It had pierced through his boot but managed to only graze his skin.

"I see there was a werewolf attack." The woman brushed her dress. "Feel free to spend the night here as the Lady of Night wills it. You may all have a warm bath and fresh robes. I can make you all some tea before you retire for the evening."

"Tea and a bath do sound lovely, Lady—" Adelaide said.

"You may call me Lady Ophelia."

"Thank you for your hospitality, Lady Ophelia. I am the third princess, Adelaide Schloss Stahlar of the Stahlar Kingdom."

Ophelia bowed and drifted out of the room as if floating just above the floorboards. Adelaide paced, peering around corners of the vestibule. Jairus settled onto a plush, midnight-blue sofa and unpacked his bag on a hickory table, uncovering an alchemy set. He measured out a small amount of dried wolfsbane.

"Hartley, I need your help. I'm preparing a concoction to prevent the lycanthropy from fully settling in my system. I need to use enough to break the curse, but it will cause some side effects. Once I start vomiting, I need you to call upon your god and use your restorative magic."

"He may not heal a depraved soul like yourself."

"Don't joke with me right now, Hartley. I've got lethal amounts of poison in my hands."

"Let me look for another potion."

"I can't exactly keep down a potion if I'm retching."

Hartley shifted, uneasy. He held the sun pendant, pressing the metal between his fingers. "I have a confession to make."

"For the love of your sun god, make those at church."

"I can't, actually. I'm excommunicated. The bishop of our sect stripped me of my holy connection."

"And you didn't think we needed to know this information before now?"

"I thought I'd get by with the potions and holy water I stole from the church!"

Jairus ran his fingers through his damp hair. He laughed, bitter and desperate, before he continued crafting the wolfsbane potion. When he finished, he lifted it as if to toast to nobody and drank it.

My shoulders relaxed. The thought of one of us turning into a werewolf brought up emotions I thought long forgotten.

"Hartley, I'm putting you in charge of me for the evening. When the heart palpitations start, that's your cue to give me your potions."

"I can do that."

Ophelia entered with a silver tray holding five porcelain teacups and a silver pot steaming from the spout. She placed it down and poured the tea of chamomile, rose, raspberry, and hibiscus.

"Thank you for allowing us to stay the night. How may we repay you?" Adelaide asked.

"I serve our Lady of Night. I bring sanctuary to the lost and those needing a temporary haven. Once you find your rooms, my work will do itself. Please, feel free to drink the tea and wander the corridors until a room feels right. Once the manor accepts guests, the goddess requests they stay until morning. The house will be locked until then, under Her protection. May Her light put your troubles to rest."

As Ophelia left, I scanned the room between everyone and settled on Adelaide as she sipped her tea. She released a contented sigh, letting the porcelain rest warmly against her palms.

"Not to be the bearer of bad news, but the wolfsbane is kicking in." Jairus held his abdomen and winced in pain. His scarred, tanned face paled, and his violet eyes glossed over. As I wrapped my arm around him, he leaned into me.

"Hartley, let's take him to a room and keep an eye on him. Adelaide, Elinalise, go relax. We can reconvene shortly," I said.

Elinalise gently placed a hand on the princess's back and guided her up an onyx spiral staircase adorned with intricate designs representing the different phases of the moon along the railings.

Hartley led us through a corridor that stretched and circled like a labyrinth. The same moon motifs followed us throughout the manor. Moon-shaped sconces lined the walls, thrumming with luminosity with each forward step.

He outstretched a hand toward an ordinary closed door where the hall abruptly ended. Jairus's body quaked beneath my grip. My head tilted as we entered the room. The door closed, and a lock engaged. Beautiful stained glass adorned the walls. Murals indicating sun motifs surrounded a circular skylight centered above us. Pews lined the room, incense filled the air, and hymns of the sun god sounded without a choir in sight.

A confessional stood in the corner with two doors. Dried blood splatter stained the wood. Hartley's eyes widened as he darted to the exit, jiggling the handle. It wouldn't budge. A strange woman, not of our group, entered one side of the confessional.

"What the hell is going on?" Jairus groaned.

"I need to get out of here. I need to—" Hartley choked.

Jairus vomited on the fine carpet. I helped him over to a pew and sat him down. He curled into himself, body trembling. The organ against the wall joined the phantom choir, producing a melancholic melody as the keys played themselves. Hartley continued jostling the door handle.

"No, please. I can't do this again," he panted.

He kicked the door. The wood cracked and repaired itself, as good as new.

An ethereal, feminine voice surrounded us like an amplified whisper: "Your darkness comes out, revealed in the moon's light. Face your truth, and then you may rest."

Hartley slowly approached the confessional, opening the door across from the woman. I followed behind, cracking the door he had just closed. A pale, slender man with long, blonde hair loomed behind him. A hand gripped Hartley's neck, nails digging deep. The man gave a twisted grin, extending his fangs, blood dripping from his mouth.

"May the Sun's light purify your sins," Hartley said.

"Bless me, Father, for I have sinned. It has been two months since my last confession. I killed my husband after he sold our daughter in exchange for two sacks of gold," the woman said.

"May your sins be absolved by the Sun's light." His voice wavered.

Tears stained the holy script in front of Hartley as he gave the vampire a subtle nod. A breeze swept past me as the doors opened and shut. The woman let out a blood-curdling scream before silence fell. Sobs escaped Hartley as he remained in the booth.

"Thank you for this sinfully delicious meal, my friend. I'll be back tomorrow. Find me another worthy feast."

"I can't do this anymore, Casimir."

"Have you forgotten our arrangement, priest?"

"Just take me, instead."

"Either you keep me fed with those you judge yourself, or you turn into a vampire. You do not get the luxury of choosing yourself for my meal."

"Becoming a vampire is not an option. You are abhorrent to the Lord of Day."

"And here you are playing judge and executioner to a cursed night creature, expecting your god to welcome you with open arms if I simply kill you."

The vampire's visage faded, as did the confessional and pews. Jairus thumped on the ground, moaning in pain. His eyes shut tight as he heaved. Only illuminated by candlelight, a dark room replaced the church. Hartley knelt, weeping into his hands. As I reached out to touch his shoulder, the hunger I felt earlier returned. Before me was a shell of a man. His aura shed little light. What I craved this time was not ancient magic. No, I wanted to free him from his pathetic life, give him the out he'd desperately asked for from the vampire. My lips twitched, and then I blinked.

The room shunted Jairus and me out, locking itself again. My stomach churned, bloated and gurgling. Jairus rolled over, heaving in a fetal position. I blinked again, looking down at him and back at the door, and grimaced.

"Where's Hartley? What just happened?" I asked.

"How should I know? One minute I'm on the church floor, and the next I'm here. The wolfsbane is in my system, and Hartley can't heal me. Is he still in that room?" Jairus asked.

My fist pounded the door, and I called out for Hartley. No answer. My heart raced. I clutched my chest, glancing back at Jairus.

"What do we do?"

With their arms looped, Elinalise and Adelaide walked down the corridor with ease compared to us. Their footsteps quickened. A brief relief washed over me, seeing them safe, seeing Elinalise safe. I wrapped my arms tightly around her, nestling my face into the crook of her neck.

"Whoa, what happened here? Are you okay?" She pulled back.

"We lost Hartley in there, and I can't get back in. He had the potions for Jairus."

He groaned on the blue rug, trembling before her. Elinalise crouched by him, stroking his sticky cheek. Beads of sweat pooled on his neck.

"You look awful, Jairus."

"Really? I feel great."

The corners of his mouth tugged upward but quickly faded as he retched again. I helped him up once more. Elinalise warped his shadow to cradle him while he walked, alleviating the pressure to do it himself.

"The lady of the house said something about staying until morning. Perhaps Hartley is still in there, and we'll see him in the morning?" Adelaide posed.

"Possibly, but this place doesn't sit right with me." I shivered.

"Let's start with what we can do. Elinalise, can you go get Jairus some of that tea? It may have a blessing from the night goddess," the princess said.

"I'll grab the tray from the great hall."

She dashed down the passageway, making her way to the manor's entrance. The corridor seemed shorter than when we'd walked it, as if it were guiding her. Adelaide reached for the doorknob directly across the hall and stepped inside, revealing a forest. I reached out to pull her back in, but it was too late. I stumbled inside with Jairus as the door slammed shut behind us.

"No, not again," I muttered.

"What about the tea?" Jairus whined.

"I think it'll have to wait."

"Fantastic."

She whipped her head back toward us, searching for answers to a question she hadn't asked. I released Jairus so he could lean fully against his shadow, which propped him up.

"It was like this with Hartley. We went into a room, only it wasn't a room. It was a church to the sun god. I'd never seen him so stunned. It seemed to be some sort of memory. A voice said something about darkness, light, rest—I'm not sure," I explained.

"Your darkness comes out, revealed in the moon's light. Face your truth, and then you may rest," the same ethereal voice echoed.

My eyes widened, and I pointed. "Yes, that. That same thing."

"This isn't funny," Adelaide called out.

She stood straight, poised even, but her hands shook. The crisp forest air smelled of pine and birch. In the distance, rumblings of laughter sounded. Adelaide stepped forward toward a group of noblemen. Her hair grew, cascading in long waves down her back. Her clothing switched to a buttoned-up dry cotton shirt with a thick, green vest. Her sleeves were rolled up to her elbows. She wore the same knee-high laced leather boots as she did for our journey.

Dressed in fine coats and tall boots, the men carried long, slender wooden and steel rifles, weapons only common in the Stahlar Kingdom. As she stepped into place, her brother, the second prince, angled up his firearm toward a dire wolf licking its paws.

"You want to give it a go?" he asked.

Adelaide's attention snapped from the wolf to her brother and then to the gentlemen spreading out. The scene froze as she stilled. She leaned against a tree, her lip quivering.

"Adelaide, what happened here?" I asked.

She shook her head, walking toward one of the men nearing the wolf. She placed a hand on his grinning face.

"I'm sorry. I'm so, so sorry."

She sobbed, pulling the man into a hug he couldn't return. After a few silent beats, I cleared my throat.

"I don't want to rush you, but I think you need to complete the scenario for us to be able to leave."

Adelaide wiped her eyes and trekked back to her spot next to her brother. She picked up the gun and aimed at the wolf. A gust of late-autumn wind swept her long hair in her face. Her finger pulled the trigger. With a loud *bang*, the shot missed the target, hitting the nobleman in the chest. Chaos erupted as the man fell back into a pile of dead leaves. Blood soaked his coat, gushing across his chest. Her brother's eyes widened in horror. Some men shouted at her, while others yelled at her brother for letting her shoot the rifle. The beast's guttural snarls grabbed the bickering men's attention as the wolf lunged forward toward the princess.

"No!" the prince cried out, jumping in front of his sister.

The wolf sank its teeth into his arm, ripping it off with its powerful jaw. The wail that escaped him pierced my eardrums as I witnessed the events unfold before me. Adelaide fell to her knees. Her shoulders shuddered as sobs began to flow.

*Bang, bang, bang.*

Three more shots came from one of the gentlemen, finally killing the wolf as it fell lifeless to the ground. All eyes darted toward the prince, as the man who had dealt the final blow rushed toward his side. He ripped his own tailcoat and wrapped it around the bloody nub.

"It's going to be all right, Your Highness."

He held pressure on the wound, barking orders to the rest. Adelaide trembled. Her hand reached out toward her brother until the greenery faded, unveiling a cozy, candlelit bedroom.

"Hello?" Elinalise called from the hallway.

When I opened the door, I found her holding a tray of teacups and facing the opposite direction. She turned around and entered the bedroom, hurrying to Adelaide's side.

"Adelaide, what's wrong?"

"This room just displayed a kingdom secret."

I stepped closer. "It looked like an accident. You didn't mean to kill him."

"I couldn't even properly apologize to his family. My brother wouldn't let me. The official story is that the man died that day from an animal attack, and to corroborate the story, he showed off his steel prosthesis."

The black box she'd clung to earlier lay in the middle of the room. She unlatched the clasp. Inside lay a smaller steel firearm with several firing chambers in a rotating cylinder. It had a sleek, shellacked wooden grip and a complex filigree design on the frame and barrel.

"It's called a revolver, a new weapon my kingdom created. We're using it as a negotiation tool with Kholand." Adelaide's breath hitched. "I'm terrified to wield it myself."

"Accident? Kill who?" Elinalise asked.

Adelaide composed herself, clasping Elinalise's hands in hers.

"This room shared a memory of mine, forcing me to live through it again, unable to fix my mistake. I killed Lord Friedrich, not the dire wolf."

Elinalise pulled the princess into a hug. Adelaide slumped over, exhaling deeply. I couldn't imagine how long that secret had been weighing her down.

"I'm not sure how the Lady of Night's magic works, but something similar happened to Hartley before we were pushed out of the room," I added.

"So this manor's magic psychically connects to us somehow." Elinalise glanced in my direction.

"When we went upstairs, we found a library of holy texts, prayers, and thin journals with names on them, each with a traumatic experience or dark secrets scribed," Adelaide mentioned.

"Why were we shunted outside the room connected to Hartley's memories? What happened to him?" I shifted my weight.

Elinalise gently let go of the princess to pour a cup of tea. She brought it to Jairus's lips.

"I was too busy heaving to see what happened fully. We'd have to check out another room to see," Jairus sipped.

"Are you feeling any better?" Elinalise tilted her head.

"I'm still dizzy, but my stomach settled some."

"Is this worse than the time the hag cursed you?"

"I think a thousand times worse, yeah. All she did was haunt my dreams every night, causing nothing worse than anything I have seen in my life. At least the cure to that didn't make me so physically ill."

I sensed the ghostly chains around Jairus loosen, as if the lycanthropy gripping him grew brittle. While they were still attached, the wolfsbane showed progress, though it made him smell worse than rotten eggs. The intense foul scent, even more pronounced now, filled my nostrils. I poured myself a cup of tea, allowing the floral aroma to soothe me. I took a swig, expecting it to have cooled. The heat stung the back of my throat as if still freshly brewed.

I coughed. "Adelaide, what are you planning on doing with the firearm?"

"Continue the mission as I was told. Kholand is rich in silver, and the werewolf attacks have worsened. Adding silver to these bullets would be a game changer for those not strong enough to wield swords and crossbows."

"This sounds dangerous in the wrong hands." I narrowed my eyes at her.

"Please feel free to give another idea if you have one."

"How about we find Hartley and meet back in here?" Jairus asked.

"Probably a good idea. Adelaide, do you want to stay here and take a bath? It seems safe enough, and this manor is finer than the inn we stayed at last night," Elinalise suggested.

She fingered the silk-lined blanket draped over the bed. "Perhaps a bath would help. Just prop up a chair on your way out and find me if you need anything."

Shadows hoisted Jairus up with Elinalise guiding them. I stayed a few paces behind him, holding my breath to avoid his stench. I propped the door open with a small desk chair as we exited. They crossed the hall to the room where we had lost Hartley.

Jairus opened the door, now unlocked, his clammy hands trembling. Shadows shifted to stilts, ushering him as he entered the chamber, which resembled a study. A chandelier hung from the ceiling, candles halfway melted and lit. Bookshelves lined the walls with a ladder propped up on the side. A maple desk sat toward the end of the room in front of floor-to-ceiling windows lining the alcove. A light patter of rain rhythmically strummed against the glass. He scanned the room and approached a large leather chair behind the desk. A worn open journal lay before him. His expression turned somber as he read the notes.

"Let's get this over with, shall we?"

"Get what over with?" Elinalise asked.

In response, the same ethereal voice spoke as it had in the previous two rooms. As Jairus settled into the re-creation of his past, color returned to his face. His violet eyes brightened with a joy that had long been lost. The dark circles under his eyes, which I had seen every day since we'd met, vanished. He lifted a quill and dipped it into an inkpot before writing on the parchment. Another presence entered the room. Without lifting his head, Jairus spoke.

"There's a sect in the Order out near Kholand. We'll have to travel east through Stahlar and then head north. If you can manage until then, I believe they can cure your vampire curse."

Lurching from behind me, a raven-haired woman hissed, manifesting her elongated fangs dripping with venom. I turned my head and stumbled back as she burst into mist and reappeared next to him. His lips quivered and his brows arched. Her veins were dark, varicose, and protruding. He looked up to meet her soulless stare, finding nothing but rage and hunger.

"Nava—please, stop!"

She sank her fangs into his neck. The healthy color of his skin faded as his eyes fluttered.

"I know you're still in there, please. We can fix this."

She drank like a feral creature with unquenchable thirst. He pushed her off just enough to rip her teeth from his skin. Elinalise grew Jairus's shadow, throwing it over him like a protective shield. Nava paused unnaturally still with her mouth open. The mage waved her hand, guiding the shadows to cover the vampire's maw. I tugged at Elinalise, pulling her back.

"Jairus! Stake her!" she shouted.

"I think this is a flashback. He must relive this memory. Something similar happened in the room Adelaide opened when she went 'off book,'" I said.

Elinalise reluctantly dropped the shadows, and the memory resumed with Jairus pinning Nava to the ground. She swiped her sharpened nails across his face, gouging deep into the skin. With one arm against her neck, he reached for a stake at his side.

"Please don't make me do this," he pleaded.

She continued lashing out, baring her fangs. She bit his arm and hoisted herself out of his grasp. He readjusted and stabbed the spiked wood into her heart, pressing deep. Her pale body desiccated into ash, withering before his eyes. Her lips curled into a small smile before she faded away. Jairus scooped her ashes into a pile and sat beside them, his eyes vacant, fixated in front of him, while his wounds dripped blood from his arm and face.

The memory faded, shifting the study into a bedroom. His fresh wounds became scars, but his skin still paled from the poison coursing through his body. His hands rested on his lap, palms facing up, as if holding the remnants of lost ash.

"I clung to the delusion that she'd make it long enough for the journey to Kholand. One of the most brutal vampire curses infected her, and she could hold on for only so long. We thought if we could keep her fed, she wouldn't go berserk," Jairus said.

"Who was she to you?" Elinalise asked.

"She was my wife. I kept my stake sheathed at my side just in case, but I never wanted to go through with it."

"Would you still want to search for a possible cure out in Kholand? I know it's too late for her, but you could help others out there."

"I no longer have my credentials. The Order kicked me out after I broke some tenets. Best I can hope for is that I find someone willing to break the rules, much like I did. They're tightlipped with their research, even though it could honestly save so many lives."

"I know what it's like to have to kill a cursed loved one." My gaze softened. "I'm sorry."

We shared a mournful smile between us before I traced my fingers on the smooth walls, searching for a hint of Hartley.

"What happened?" Elinalise broke the silence.

"Her name was Ceara. A werewolf bit her while we were alone in the mountains." I swallowed. "She begged me to kill her before the curse set in."

Elinalise turned to me. "Lonan, I'm so sorry."

"It's in the past now. I'd rather not dwell on it further."

"If you open up a door, you might have to relive that."

Dark wallpaper tore underneath my nails as I clenched my hand on the surface. I balled up my fists and headed toward the bed. The incision in the wall glowed a bright light as it repaired itself.

I stuck my head underneath the bed and surveyed the floor for any dropped potions or iconography of the sun god. There was nothing but a short-woven blue rug with the moon phases outlined on it. I kept to myself as they chatted, scratching my head, curious about where Hartley had disappeared.

I reached over my shoulder where my raven usually perched, forgetting he was missing, too. A deep ache swelled in my chest. Mental fog bogged down my brain with a memory at its edge, unable to surface.

"Lonan. Lon-an," Elinalise sang.

I snapped out of it. "Hm. What?"

"Your eyes went dark, and you zoned out. Looked like nobody was home for a wink."

She waved her hand in front of my face, but I remained unfazed by the words she'd spoken; however, Jairus remained quiet. His eyes locked on mine for a second too long before he finally broke his silence.

"You were the last person to see Hartley in this room."

"Are you accusing me of something?"

"I'm just pointing out the facts."

"You were in here, too."

"I was too busy hurling to see what happened before we were removed. All I know is you were speaking with him, and then we were kicked out. That didn't happen with us after Adelaide and I made our way through these magical trauma rooms."

"I swear to you, I have no idea what happened to him."

"Fine."

Heat rose in my chest, and that peculiar hunger struck again, similar to when Elinalise had walked past me in the fog outside. My stomach churned at the thought of consuming Jairus, both longing for and detesting the idea, sickened by his scent.

That unsettling fog around my memory closed in as I tried to recall the moments between Hartley weeping and my frantic pounding on the door, begging him to let us in. It couldn't have been me.

"You two continue checking out the rooms. I'm going to rest with Adelaide and maybe see if I can find Lady Ophelia." Jairus braced himself as he stood up.

He knocked on the open door across the hall, announcing his presence, while we retraced our steps. The corridor stretched on with no end in sight. Blank doors lined the hallway of the ever-expanding labyrinth, winding into new paths until Elinalise stood in front of one.

"I think it wants us to choose a door. The manor doesn't seem pleased with us walking aimlessly."

She sucked in a breath and placed her hand on the handle. She crossed the threshold into an endless void. The door creaked shut behind us, sealing us in. The dense air slowed my steps, like swimming through a sea of gel. The scent of her mixed with the smell of burnt ozone wafted toward me—sweet licorice, fresh lightning, and metal. The same words echoed from each room past, subjecting her to her memories. I searched for her hand to squeeze reassuringly, but my fingers only intertwined with a balmy mist. Metal bars clanked, and a padlock engaged. A low, airy voice spoke.

"Learn to channel the shadows, Lina. I'll be back."

"Daddy, when will you come back?"

"Soon."

"Last time you said that you were gone all day."

"You must have faith and trust the process."

"It's scary here. I don't like being alone with them."

"It is that fear you must overcome to bend them to your will. I had to go through this, as did my father before me. You will be fine."

Her voice sounded higher than usual, as if this were her childhood. A match struck and ignited a torch. The soft glow of the fire revealed a middle-aged man with onyx hair and olive skin identical to his daughter's. The shadows danced fluidly with the flame. Footsteps retreated, leaving her alone in this prison. With each shift of the shadows, she closed her eyes and wrapped her arms around her knees, rocking back and forth. Her wavy hair cascaded down her back, held together with a lopsided bow made with rosy ribbon. A wispy tendril brushed against her cheek, whispering incoherently. She covered her ears to block them out.

I strode forward and sat on the ground in front of the cage.

"What is this place?" I asked.

She lifted her head, darting her eyes around the room. The swaying flames and shadows stopped as I interrupted the flashback; her body paused in her young form.

She swallowed before answering. "Daddy says it's training, but I'm scared of the dark."

"Couldn't there have been a better way?"

She shrugged sheepishly.

I gripped the cool metal bars. "I'll stay with you so you aren't alone."

She nodded and burrowed her head back into her knees, allowing the memory to resume. Her breath quickened as the darkness coiled around her. Time stretched as we sat in the unending shade.

Eventually, Elinalise took a deep breath. She soothed herself and communed back with the shadows. She started with soft murmurs in hushed tones, inviting them in. They cradled her in a tender embrace. She cracked one eyelid open, and then the other, before outstretching an arm, allowing the umbral ribbons to flow as they pleased.

She giggled. "That tickles."

Her labored breaths steadied as she grew comfortable in the darkness. Her father's heavy footsteps approached once more. He scowled at his daughter. She flinched back, scurrying toward the back of the prison. The shadows returned to their usual formation.

"What are you doing? I told you to bend them to your will, not make friends with them," he scolded.

He clenched his jaw and fist, shaping the darkness into his hand without incantation. From his silhouette, he created a solid spear and aimed it at his daughter, mere inches from her face. Her eyes crossed, focusing on the sharpened point.

"You wield it, it doesn't wield you. You will stay here for the night and learn to control them. I'll be back to fetch you in the morning, and you will show me your progress."

"What if we work together? I think they want to be friends."

"It is not the way of our bloodline. You will master this."

"What about dinner? I'm hungry."

"You'll eat in the morning. Fasting helps hone your mind and spirit, strengthening your will."

She curled into herself again as her father walked away. The darkness faded, and the weight of the air lifted. We sat facing each other in the bedroom, with Elinalise back in her adult body. I pulled her into my arms and stroked the back of her head and neck. Her shoulders relaxed beneath me.

"What happened after that?" I asked.

"He continued to punish me for years. It wasn't until I received the job offer as the court mage's apprentice that he cut me some slack. I don't think he ever accepted my way of doing our family's magic, but he recognized my ability to make a living in the kingdom. Despite the formal court mage training, I don't think I'll ever be good enough to him."

"Just because you're not pursuing magic in the way he deems correct, it doesn't mean your way isn't right."

"I know."

Elinalise adjusted herself, put on a cheerful smile, and stood. She offered her hand to pull me up. My heart ached for her as she wore the mask her father had created. She interlaced her fingers with mine and led me out of the room.

"Let's go find a door for you to open," she said.

"What about you? Don't you want to rest?"

"You were there for me, so I'd like to be there for you."

"Prepare yourself for what you're about to see."

"Do you think the room will show you Ceara?"

"I'd assume so. In Garbhaill, when we turn fifteen, we're thrown into the wilderness and told to survive with nothing but our raven, a weapon, and a waterskin. She and I left the group, thinking we'd be fine on our own."

"I'll be right here," Elinalise said, squeezing my hand.

We continued down the corridor with the clear intention of picking a room. The hall was short with a plain door at the end. A guestbook and an arcane brass lamp on a wooden side table stood against the wall. We peered over at the ledger. Our companions' names were written in fresh ink, with Elinalise last on the page. My name wasn't on it yet.

I opened the door and crossed the threshold, and Elinalise followed behind me. The door slammed shut and we heard the same echoed voice, prompting the start of the memory. The sky glimmered with constellations on the clear night. I took a deep breath, inhaling the crisp, fresh air of Slocum Hollow. The scent of iron lingered in the atmosphere from the local blacksmiths' long day's work. The rundown inn faded into the distance as I strolled toward the mines. That same dense fog crept at the edges of my mind, stinging like sleet. A heavy presence settled nearby. I wasn't alone. My steps hastened into strides. My heart raced with each running step as I gasped for air. A deep, gurgling croak came from my raven to my left. My eyes brightened as he approached.

"Fich!"

He perched on my shoulder, and I stroked his feathers with my finger. He extended his wings and flew to the right. To the left, sounds of wet snarling greeted me. An imposing worm blocked my view of the moon as I leaned back to meet its two beady eyes. Thick slime covered its armless body, its three sets of sharpened teeth forming a perfect circle when it unclenched its maw. It curled around my body and sniffed with two holes flush against its face.

Fich flew back around, pecking at one of its eyes. The creature winced as I writhed through its filmy sludge, breaking my arms free. I reached for my dagger, but it slipped from my clammy grasp, clanking on the rocky ground. The monster snapped its mouth toward Fich, engulfing him, leaving nothing but a couple of feathers sticking to its mucus. I blinked back tears from my swollen eyes, crying out for my raven.

Then, reality shifted.

I blinked again, my one eye in excruciating pain. Pangs of hunger surged. Ancient magic lingered around the human in my grasp. I craved the body attached to the sickeningly sweet shadow magic. I needed to consume him to get my real prize. His pale, freckled face looked at me with hazel eyes as he wiggled through panic. His heartbeat pounded faster and faster. He reached for another dagger, but I swallowed him whole.

Absorbing his memories—Lonan's memories—I rested in a meditative state. I sorted through flashbacks internally and shifted my body to match his.

I cracked my neck and stretched my new limbs as I took on his form, becoming him to find her, the one whose blood runs with ancient sorcery.

The mountains faded as the bedchamber apparated, enclosing me and Elinalise in the room together. She took a few steps back; I'd never seen her so frightened. She backed herself into the wall, reaching for the door. I slowly met her.

"Lina–"

"Don't you Lina me."

"It's different now."

"You killed him!"

I lifted a hand to her cheek. She froze. Her hand clenched the handle. Her brilliant eyes darkened as they settled on me.

"But now I am him. I remember his memories. I feel his feelings—"

"You can't replace him."

"I-I love you. He loved you. That was one thing I didn't expect to feel. I was in my monstrous form for so long that I forgot the breadth of human emotions."

"You ate him. You ate his raven. Fich was like family."

"And I regret that now! It's not like I can bring him back. Resurrection magic is that of myth."

Elinalise cracked the door. She inched toward it, wedging her foot and arm out. I leaned against the wall over her. She muttered whispers under her breath, unintelligible.

"Please, hear me out. I want to be Lonan. I want to be with you."

She faded into her shadow, leaving a wispy echo of herself. Ribbons of shadow wove through my fingertips as I grasped for her. I slammed the door open, investigating the hallway to find Jairus stumbling my way with the hilt of his dagger gripped in his hand. Elinalise leaped into his shadow, hitching a ride. She rose from the ground, rematerializing, and whispered to him.

"Talked to Lady Ophelia, by the way. Turns out it's pretty easy to find her when you aren't around," Jairus said.

"Did you ask her about Hartley?" I asked.

"I did." He paused. "She says you killed him."

"What does she know about me?"

"That you're a dangerous, manipulative monster who absorbs people's memories and abilities. She sniffed you out the moment we arrived."

"I know how this looks, but we're friends. Lonan would have wanted this."

"I don't think he would have."

"I know him better than you."

Jairus threw his silver-tipped dagger at me, piercing Lonan's heart. I winced and pulled it out, its blade dripping blood, and then shed Lonan's skin. As I grew taller, I curled my worm-like body around Jairus. He reached for a second dagger, and I tightened my grip around his throat. I opened my mouth, but my stomach turned. Poison still circulated in his system. Elinalise chanted incantations, gaining volume as darkness filled the area.

"Perforabit eum tenebris," she repeated.

Before I lost my vision, I saw her open her palm as the shadow hardened into a spear. A pool of shadow surged around her as she drew from the gleaming sconces.

"Kill it," Jairus choked.

A sharp pain throbbed in my neck, followed by a dozen more. Thick umbra forced my mouth open and covered my nostrils. As I tried to gasp for air, breaths wouldn't come. Stars edged my vision—a reminder of how much Lonan had enjoyed his midnight strolls. The void surrounded me, dampening my senses. I felt farther, retreating deeper into nothing. She was right. I faced my truth, and now I must rest. My eyes grew heavier until I sank, floating away into oblivion.

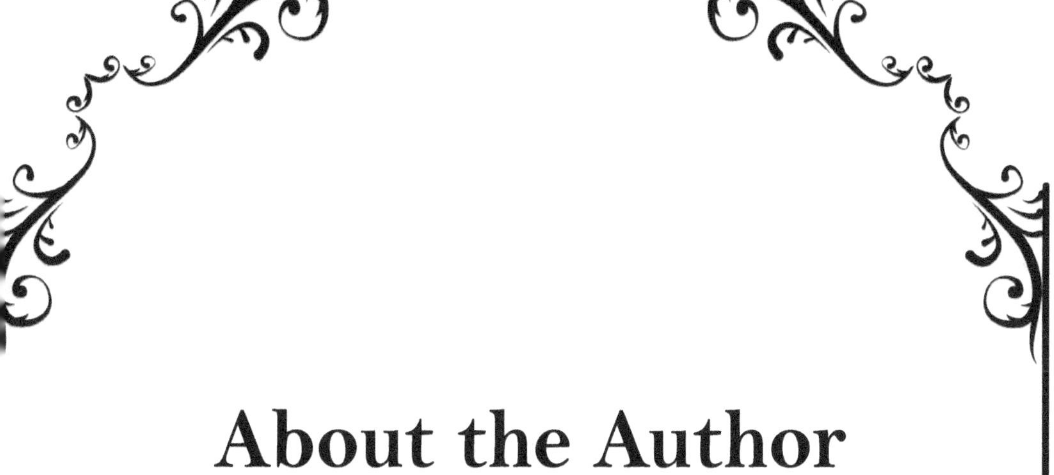

# About the Author

Submerging herself in fantasy worlds through reading, watching anime, and TTRPG gameplay, **Elizabeth Faye Moxen** discovered her love of character creation, world-building, and story. She is working on her debut fantasy novel and hopes to publish it in the near future.

You can find Elizabeth on Instagram and Tiktok at: @el.f.moxen

To learn more about Elizabeth, visit her website at: https://elizabethmoxen.wixsite.com/el-f-moxen

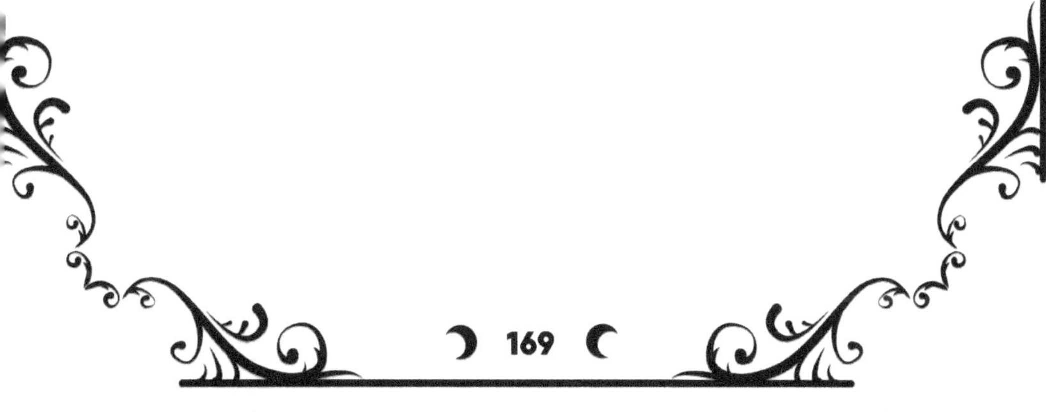

# The Lady of the House

# The Lady
# of the House

## Constance Renfrow

THE NOISES UPSTAIRS WOKE MARLA again. Her phone would read, she knew, 2:08 a.m.—the same as it had every night for a week. She pressed her face deeper into the bedsheet—the pocket of air beneath the covers warm and unmoving, safe—thinking that if she could just fall back asleep, the inevitable could be postponed for as long as possible, maybe forever. The noises would stop, she would forget them, Armand would come home from his business in Berlin, and life would go on. They would be together again and happy, the two of them.

They'd started off small, the sounds. That first night, while watching one of Armand's favorite shows on Netflix, just as Inspector Barnaby started up his usual routine—talking down to Sergeant Jones—Marla heard the creaking of floorboards overhead, a strange tapping. She'd paused the episode and sat up, looking to the ceiling, at the ornate plaster where the gasoliers were no longer *in situ*, to use her husband's phrase. The dog, a husky, a giant brute of an animal, too big for New York City but meant as a guard of sorts, lay where Armand's feet usually rested; if it noticed the noises, it found in them no cause for concern. So it was easy for Marla to suppose she'd only heard the wood expanding or settling, gas in the pipes. The sounds old townhouses make, and this one was nearly two hundred years old.

Not until the second night had she truly been afraid. Because then it was footsteps, crashing and carrying on. Something heavy falling to the ground, like a hinge shrieking open, and Marla ran out of the house. She pounded on the neighbors' door; Armand had said before he left that if she needed anything, Mr. and Mrs. Purley next door had promised to do what they could. And when she started stammering about crashes in the attic and intruders on stairs, they invited her inside, which in itself surprised her. They kindly said nothing about her being only in her teddy, and this sheer and short, not really intended for sleep, a gift from Armand after his last trip, the one over her twenty-seventh birthday.

Mr. Purley had pulled a gallant face and left to investigate, while Mrs. Purley, in her flannel robe, made Marla a cup of warm cocoa—the fancy kind, from a tin, made with milk instead of water. After Marla started to calm down, to breathe instead of gasp, Mrs. Purley let her borrow the house phone to call Armand. He'd been gone only two days and was about to step into a meeting and told her to call the police if she really believed something was wrong. Mr. Purley returned right then, smoothing his graying hair and saying loudly that he'd searched the whole house and hadn't seen anyone or anything out of place, and it was no wonder her being scared, a sweet young wife half her husband's age, a mere child, all alone in a big house like that. He blamed her imagination, for having too much of it. Armand heard everything, of course, and told her to thank the nice neighbors and go back to bed. He was the first to hang up. Mrs. Purley even patted her hand and said, as if Marla *were* a child, "There, there."

After, when she thought about it—when she replayed the sounds to herself in the afternoons, wandering alone among the aisles of the grocery store, a single frozen pizza in her cart, or pretending to read on the park bench beside where the jazz band sometimes played—she believed the noises familiar. Like metal latches flung open, the screech of old hinges, something slammed shut. It brought to mind the old steamer trunk her father had given her when she left years ago for a college across the country. An heirloom from his student days, emblazoned with his name, her maiden name, in ruptured white paint. For years, it had served as her dinner table, where she and her Craigslist roommates would gather for Gold Emblem macaroni and to complain about the rent or their managers or the things strange men said to them in bars. Marla supposed it must be in the basement somewhere, with the other boxes from her life before this house on Fourth Street. Armand had given her a spot down there for all the things she wouldn't need anymore.

Now, she wanted only to ignore the noises. Even when the voices upstairs turned into singing, jerking her back from the warm edges of sleep in her bed, the most she could muster was a frustrated groan. The way she used to respond to her roommate's cat mewling for breakfast too early in the morning, or when the people in the apartment next door screamed through a late-night binge. The way she would sometimes pretend to stay asleep as Armand tried to wake her at five a.m., when he left for work, or earlier, for sex. She was exasperated that no one else heard these things, or else weren't bothered by them, as if this torment existed for her alone.

She took her phone from the nightstand and texted Armand, simply to say that what she heard this time, seeping down from the attic, was *singing*. She messaged him again with the words of the song. *I'll not leave thee, thou lone ones.* The night had turned the covers to gray, and she pushed them off; her bare legs, too, were colorless. She'd gotten used to sleeping naked, even when he was on his business trips—more frequent now than when she'd first known him, piling on more blankets to make up for the heat he took with him.

Marla's foot, when she rose, brushed the long lace gown pooled on the floor, where she'd left it following Armand's Skype call that morning. He hadn't wanted to hear about the noises, or how they'd escalated; he'd wanted to look at her in the lingerie he filled her closet with. She pulled the gown on over her head, feeling it compress her figure as she tugged it past her hips and let the material below flow free. So what if it was see-through, slinky, a garment devised for a man's gaze? She felt powerful in it because only when she wore such things did she ever have her husband on his knees.

*Since the lovely are sleeping*—the voice, a woman's, lamented—*go sleep thou with them.* An Irish tune, she thought, old country, like she'd heard in foreign movies or from folk singers at open mics back before Armand told her he didn't appreciate her wasting nights on them.

Her phone buzzed ineffectually on the comforter. She reached for Armand's reply: *You probably forgot to turn off the TV in the study.* But Marla didn't watch TV in his study—that was his habit—and she'd made sure to turn it off the morning he left for the airport. There hadn't been anyone there to watch it since. Marla threw the phone onto the empty side of the bed, upsetting the dog sleeping there, who looked at her with disapproving eyes, the scowl the breed was known for even more prominent in the half-light.

Marla snatched the phone back. She'd sworn to herself that afternoon that if she heard anything more, she would go upstairs and record. It would be her proof, something to show Armand or the neighbors or the cops, something to make them understand that what she told them was the truth.

She grabbed, too, the framing hammer she'd taken from her old tool belt in the basement the day the noises became voices. She now kept it on her night-stand. A relic from her days, a few years back, at Habitat for Humanity, when she'd been pulled from behind the desk at the ReStore thrift shop and sent to the Far Rockaways to tear down and help rebuild after the hurricane swept through. One of her bosses had shown her how to use it, an older woman with broad shoulders who cursed after every blow. *Bitch! Bitch!* Marla never knew if it was the hurricane she cursed, or the work, or the husband she'd divorced. Maybe it was just that the impact hurt her hands.

More than once Marla had thought to call the woman, to tell her about the noises and Armand. Surely she would have something to say to fix it, something more blunt than *there, there.* Like she used to tell Marla which pipes to check, or she'd come to search the house herself to locate the cause of the problem. But Marla had culled her old phone contacts after the wedding last year—former colleagues, the roommates with whom she'd never had much in common, peo-ple barely remembered from shows she'd attended. People she didn't think she'd have reason to speak to again. And now, of course, she couldn't. She'd even tried to find her boss on Facebook, but if she had a profile, it was under a different name.

The day she first brandished the hammer in terror, the voices surged into a shriek of laughter, and she had fled onto the street, gasping and shuddering, unable to speak for a time. Before she escaped, she'd pulled on the dog's collar, but it refused to move from its spot on Armand's side of the bed, and so she left it to whoever howled in the attic. Like she'd left her phone, forgotten, just out of reach. As was usual of the city at that time of night, people still wandered the streets, and they stared at the figure Marla made, wrapped in one of Armand's robes, gripping the hammer tight to her. A madwoman, run from her home.

But she wasn't mad. She'd read stories in the news of vagrants living in clos-ets in other people's homes, and Armand's house had so much empty space. Someone could easily live up there, if they were quiet, and neither she nor Ar-mand would ever know. Remembering Armand's cynical words crackling long distance over Mrs. Purley's phone, she nodded yes when some nice young stu-dents, dressed as though for a party and stumbling in their heels, offered to call the police. They apologized that they couldn't wait, and Marla understood; she, too, had once been out underage.

The Purleys never once stepped outside, even though she saw the light from their TV flickering in the bedroom upstairs. When the police finally ar-rived, they searched the house; they took her statement, and when—back in the kitchen, where she'd been led—she left a message for Armand, explaining that one of the cops had knocked over some piece of his mother's Waterford crystal, he called back immediately, demanding to speak to the officer in charge. She waited, biting the nails of her free hand, but when he hung up, the officer's expression had changed. He asked Marla to let go of the framing hammer and promised to put it back in a toolbox they'd found in what Armand's parents had called the tea room, though Marla had taken to calling it, when feeling especially perverse, the mud room.

Now, this time, as she prepared to search out the songstress, she already knew the dog wouldn't come. It sprawled with its paws over its eyes, as though pretending not to hear the song or Marla calling softly. It looked almost human, ignoring her. It would stay there and sleep, as it had every night that week. A day or two ago, this might have prevented her from unlocking the bedroom door, from slipping out into the hall and turning on the staircase light, but not this night.

The singing grew louder. Multiple voices now—three of them, she thought—in harmony. She found the recording function on her phone and tapped it. She hefted the hammer, practiced a swing. "Bitch!" It made her feel stronger for saying it.

The staircase rose high and steep in the ancient row house, the home where Armand had grown up, where his parents had grown old and died. Marla started climbing. She'd never gotten used to the tall, shallow steps, and they still made her nervous. One slipup, or if her gown caught, she'd go tumbling down, unable to stop the plummet or find a handhold to cling to. Armand never mentioned it, but the first owner had died this way, Marla knew. A Victorian woman, more than a hundred years ago. The house was a stop on the neighborhood ghost tour, and Marla had stuck her head out the window on Halloween to listen. From above, she'd caught a glimpse of the enlarged photograph the tour guide held aloft; the lady was tall and severe, scowling at the cameraman in her high collar and tightly knotted hair. It was taken, supposedly, just days before she went crashing down the stairs, her neck snapped and bent. Her death throes echoed up through the whole house, trapped in corners.

She hadn't lent it much credence then, but these days it occurred to her, more than once, that the tour guide might have been right. Maybe the Victorian lady *was* haunting the place. Maybe *she* made the noises in the attic.

Maybe she was unhappy with the way the house had changed since her time and was making her displeasure known. Maybe she didn't like electricity or the modern plumbing, or that Marla always did what Armand said. The lady had lived on her own her whole life, never married. Maybe she didn't like that her home was now so fully a man's.

It was hard juggling the phone and the hammer and keeping her gown up above her knees. On their Skype date, he'd asked her to turn around and bend over and sashay—a sight for sore eyes, he'd said—and she'd done so reluctantly, each time trying to find the right way to bring him back to the noises, the problem at hand. She hoped he'd notice the dark circles under her eyes, or the way her shoulders hunched and strained, but he said only that the image of her body would have to last him awhile, as his trip was being extended; just like that. He explained the reason, at length, but all she heard was that he wasn't coming back to help her in her distress. He was leaving her in his house, in his neighborhood, alone. When she told him she didn't think this was such a good idea, that she wished he could come home sooner like he was supposed to, he demanded, "What do you want me to do about it?"

Marla had answers. She wanted to tell him to leave whatever issues the company was having this time to the people he'd hired to deal with such things and come home to her. Instead she said, "I don't know." She tried not to sound too bitter, to make him wonder why he bought her pretty things and paid her bills, not that there were many. She didn't buy herself the luxuries her old roommates had suggested she would. When she broke her lease to marry, they referred to him as her "silver fox." Her last night in that grimy three-bedroom above the dive bar, she had overheard them dubbing her a "trophy wife," a "gold digger," while she packed the last of her belongings into her trunk. Perhaps, she thought now, they weren't even wrong.

After all, Armand's money had let her quit her job. She didn't cook or clean or do any other things that a man of his age, and with his upbringing, might expect. Other than a knack for making cocktails, and looking glamorous in lingerie, Marla was acutely aware she didn't bring much to the marriage. The cocktails were something she'd learned just for him; she'd understood early on that Rum and Cokes, her old standby, were not enough for these parlors, with the Waterford and the silverware made of actual silver, and the artwork by painters she'd studied in school. So, relying on YouTube videos and books from the Strand, she'd experimented with Pegu Clubs and Moscow Mules and, Armand's favorite, Whiskey Sours with fresh lemon juice and simple syrup she prepared herself, and homemade maraschino cherries. The first time she'd served them, he'd called the whole thing "exquisite."

She couldn't quite look at him on the screen. "I just—"

"Just what?"

"I just want you to believe me about this." It would be, at least, a start. He'd been silent, about to make his goodbyes, and Marla hung up on him. She'd never done that before, and he didn't call back.

Now, as Marla reached the landing to the third floor, the staircase turned onto a hall. The steps to the attic waited at the very end of the long, narrow corridor. It was strange, Marla thought, but the song, as she grew closer, seemed muffled, as though it *were* actually coming from an old television set. As though Armand was right, and she felt her muscles clench, and the gown, for a moment, going slack at the waist. But of course Armand's top-of-the-line TV didn't sound antique; even from the hallway, she could always hear him watching his financial reports on CNN, in perfect clarity. She made for the light switch but found the bulb was burned out. It must have gone sometime that evening, because it had been working just hours earlier, when she'd made her now-daily trek up to the attic and back, searching for signs of anything strange or out of place, with still enough daylight for comfort. She tightened her grip on the hammer and told herself that this was no sign of anything. After all, how many times had she flipped a switch only for the bulb to flash and the filaments to pop, the whole thing needing to be replaced? Why was her first impulse always to be afraid?

But then again, she hadn't heard anything pop. It made her glad for the recording. It made her glad, too, that the camera's image would not pick up the Duncan Phyfe chairs in the corner of the hall, or the antique clock that stood, unwound but filigreed, on the display cabinet beside them. The things her friend—an old one, from college—had seen when she came by to catch up over coffee. To see the house on Fourth Street Marla had mentioned at the wedding, the last time they spoke. She was stopping, she explained, in the city for a day or two, before going on again, to another town, another story, always someplace new on the road. She helped Marla put the china in the sink, and asked to see everything, on every floor. The furniture impressed her, and the price of her mother-in-law's prized figurines, and she looked longer at the paintings in their heavy, ornate frames than at Marla, who tried, because it seemed to interest her, to tell her what she could recall of these things. And finally, when they climbed the stairs, Marla could contain it no longer, and confided about the noises, the voices, the sounds she heard in the night. Her friend only laughed, a deep roar of envy, and said, "I'd put up with all kinds of weird shit to live here."

The darkness, Marla thought, didn't feel oppressive in the way it so often did. It wasn't pitch-black; it didn't envelop her. She'd often felt her bedroom in this house was like when she'd been onstage—college theater followed by community shows, pre-Armand, pre-New York, even. Fully lit and blinding, mid-performance, and the black all around, unknown and impossible to ever explore. Made of monsters, sinuous and whirling. Now, though, the dark was calm and lived in. Not empty but occupied, the hum of the melody an invitation.

A door at the end of the hall closed off the attic staircase, intended to keep it out of sight and so out of thought, concern. At the top—if one deigned to climb to it—four large rooms opened onto a large workspace in the middle. It contained furniture and clothes and paintings from Armand's parents, collections he had no use for at the moment, or reason to display. The pieces of his inheritance he couldn't part with, which was most of it, even though she knew, from those days at the ReStore, that he could sell each piece for more money than she'd ever held, or even, if he were feeling charitable, donate to such a cause. Marla had said once that the rooms were big enough to rent out to students from the university nearby. A little extra money each month, though Armand had laughed at this, squeezed her ass and laughed, but mostly Marla had liked the thought. Of twenty-somethings—closer to her in age than she to Armand or to his friends—just upstairs, talking about poetry over beers, or setting up their easels in the common space. Strumming guitars, running lines. She could bring them Rum and Cokes, the meals she would practice making. It would have been nice to have that sort of energy in the house, where she could feel, perhaps, like she belonged.

When the Victorian lady had lived here, the attic had been where the servants slept. There were always three girls. Some went; others came. Irish girls looking for work, Marla remembered from the ghost tour, who'd come to the States to earn money. And service was better than the tenements, better wages that might save their mothers or fathers or siblings from the conditions of their homeland in those days. She'd read about girls like them at the museum a few blocks down. The old houses of the old city.

What if they were up there now? The ghosts of them, their imprints. Returned because the house had a lady again, a lady alone, with no one to look after her. What if they'd mistaken her for their mistress, summoning them to their duties? What if they saw she was kind, nicer by far than the Victorian woman, or later, Armand's mother? What would she do if she saw their afterimages?

Marla pulled open the attic door and shivered. It wasn't just her lace gown or the feeling that one is supposed to tremble at the opening of doors—it *was* colder here, even though it was summer and heat was supposed to rise. She could just make out the faint words, so quiet now, escaping with the turbid air like dust, seeping into her skin, itching her: *Oh! who would inhabit this bleak world alone?*

The last note lingered, held, the song at its end, and Marla . . .

Suddenly, she could withstand ignorance no longer. She thundered up the stairs, her feet slapping the steps, the framing hammer clanging against the railing. Even so, she heard quiet footsteps retreating to the opposite side of the room, and Marla ran onto the landing, crying out, "Wait!"

The footsteps stopped.

"Wait, please wait!" Marla gasped. Her plea shuddered through the closed-up workspace, the furniture piled high, near to the ceiling, and covered in white sheets, and shadows from the moon streaming down from the skylight. She didn't know what she was looking for—a person living inside the old oak hutch, or a specter, or thieves come finally to take their haul—but she searched blindly in the gloom.

And then she saw them, the three servant girls, or their shades. Or the Victorian lady, with two of her maids, gray and ethereal. Silhouettes in the middle of the dust that swirled with every one of Marla's breaths. She thought she could make out aprons around their middles, dresses that bulged at the shadows' waists, around their arms. One wore her hair loose, hanging down past her shoulders. Another knotted it up high, severe and stiff. The third held her arms to her chest as if in prayer.

They hovered, silent now.

"Are you here to help me?" she asked them, holding up the phone, still recording. She was not scared like she had thought. Here, confronting them, she felt elated, and asked, "You are, aren't you?" Her gown had wrapped itself around her legs, lace and elastic binding her where she stood. She could not step forward, go toward them at all, not without looking down, away, and then, she feared, they might disappear.

"Please. I can't take this anymore," Marla was saying, the shades still and towering. "Can't you say something, do something? Please." And then she was pleading. "Help me."

Her phone vibrated and Marla nearly jumped. Armand again: *Did you turn off the TV yet?*

Her stomach clenched. Her knuckles strained against the hammer's padded handle. She could feel a callus forming as she glared up into darkness.

"Do something," Marla hissed into the silence. "Do something now."

# About the Author

**Constance Renfrow**'s fiction has appeared in such places as *the minnesota review*, *North Dakota Quarterly*, *South Carolina Review*, and *Litro*. Her short story "The Urg" won the Porter House Review Prize for Fiction and was selected for Best of the Net. Her book, *Songs of My Selfie*, an anthology of millennial fiction, was an IndieFAB finalist. She received her MFA in Fiction from Pacific University.

To learn more about Constance, visit her website at: www.constancerenfrow.com

# A
# Killer
# Dream

# A Killer Dream

## yesenia monique

SHE IS MESMERIZING; THE WAY each of her free-flowing gestures glides into another as she effortlessly dances across the private stage leaves us spellbound. Her flowing teal dress ascends into graceful suspension with every spin as the soft amber light gently illuminates her curly brown hair. It feels like a privilege and a curse to sit here against the dim corner of the back wall watching the performance meant for only our eyes. All of us want to be just like her, weaving our own magic through the air, and without a doubt, any one of us would kill for the opportunity of a solo spotlight.

I've always loved ballet and its theatrical form of storytelling, but watching her impromptu performance reminds me of the essence of dance itself. Something innately felt, sending that electrical impulse through the body where one's only recourse is to move and sway. Each bounce is perfectly timed to the soundless notes of the violin playing its tune, and I am desperate to join her. A rare duet of principal dancers we would be, moving in perfect sync.

I yearn for her to grab my hand and envelop me in her quiet spectacle, and in a sudden, fortuitous moment, she lands in front of me and her deep, green eyes bore into mine. Her wide grin slowly fades from her face as her stare intensifies. The pressure of the music builds in dramatic flair. My heart begins to race along with the violent tones, and her fear is the last perceptible thing before she crashes into me, jolting me into the harsh, white light of a dingy trailer.

It takes a few blinks for my eyes to adjust to the fluorescents above as the nervous, muffled voice of a man shouting to someone a few feet away replaces the climactic music.

The trailer's sterile, white walls are a stark contrast to the array of broken beer bottles and dirty dishes littering the counter and carpet in front of me. The metal chair I feel glued to is cold against my aching bare skin, the only warmth coming from the curly brown locks that cascade down my chest.

This isn't my body—it's hers—but I can feel how it has been brutally used and violated. Her face is my face, tight from the already crusted saline tears, and I can sense that hollow feeling of stripped dignity within her soul.

The nervous man comes over to me, his lanky frame towering above as my eyes slowly rise to meet his. His face is pale, his brow furrowed in agitated contemplation behind a cascade of deep brown hair.

"Only one thing to do," he says with a slight hint of regret, but it wasn't directed at me.

He grabs my arm and throws me down. The pain of his phantom hold still pulses on my skin as my face hits the ground, and the sting of a fresh wound forms on my cheek from the strewn shards of glass.

Another man laughs deviously as he steps forward and positions his black leathery boot in front of my chin, lifting my head off the beer-soaked carpet. This one is the exact opposite of the first: bald, with a stocky build. I catch a quick glimpse of his blue eyes before the first man pulls me up to standing, his firm grip entangled in my hair.

"Let's do it, then. I already had my fun," says the bald man with a satisfied and sinister grin as he turns and descends the few stairs that lead outside.

The lanky man stays behind to whisper something only for me to hear.

"We'll make this quick," he promises with a trace of sympathy. Then he thrusts me forward, giving me a second of relief from his painful grip until my bruised flesh clashes with each stair as I tumble into the night sky.

The dirt is soft beneath my face, a small respite before the lanky man kicks me in the stomach, rolling me to my back where my eyes meet the darkened sky.

"There's no backing out now, you hear?" a calm, accented male voice urges from some dark corner in the direction above my head. "It's easier if she's standing up, yeah?"

"I have no regrets," Lanky Man replies defensively, "but how do I know this won't get tied back to me?"

"Don't worry about that. We'll shoot her up with some fentanyl and dump her at the Fruitvale station. Happens all the time with the homeless down there. Drug deal gone bad."

"And the cops?" Lanky Man asks.

"They'll be paid well," the accented man assures.

Everything happens relatively quickly, as Lanky Man said it would. His cold, slightly trembling hands wrap around my neck, pulling me up to my feet as he pushes me into the dim light of the streetlamp. But my legs are too weak to keep this body upright, and I fall to my knees before a man I can only assume owns the accented voice I just heard. I can't see his face, only the glowing red ball of coal from the tip of his cigarette. It doesn't matter, anyway, because in one swift motion, the crushing blow of something sharp hits my skull.

The searing clash jolts me upright and leaves me gasping for air in my one-bedroom apartment. My head throbs, and my once-baggy shirt feels plastered to my skin from the cold sweat, but I am grateful to feel the familiar cotton sheets of my bed beneath my fingertips. My familiar bone-straight black hair hangs in my peripheral. It takes me a long moment to piece together what just happened as the faces play like a carousel around and around inside my head.

*Deep breaths, Rylee. Let's calm down*, I tell myself. It was just a dream.

*Was it, though?*

I have always been connected to the other side. The veil is thin for me between the living and the dead, and I revel in my gift of clairvoyance, glad for the dreamy visits of loved ones who have passed on. Their spirits accompany me through my waking moments, but this is different. I'm sure I have never met this dancer.

My friends have warned that if I don't put up the proper guards, other potentially dangerous energies will find me. How did Roan put it?

*"When you start communicating with the other side, it's like the spirits see you as a beacon of bright light in an otherwise lonely ocean, and trust me, they'll start rushing in!"*

I knew to trust her because she had a history of working as a medium for the dead and now works as a death doula.

*"But I don't want to close off any connections I have with my spirits," I explained to her. "How can I be sure they'll keep coming in?"*

I'd always questioned myself, often thinking I was a fake spectator within the magical community. I might have a long ancestry of magical connoisseurs in tune with the natural world, but that didn't mean any of the native ways passed on to me.

*"Be direct. Let the spirits know which ones are welcome and which aren't. Say it out loud if you have to before lying down for bed or meditation. Making a protection bag or amulet can also help," Roan urged.*

I should have listened, but then again, this really could've been just a messed-up dream. No, this must be real. It felt *so* real. I felt the pain, the abuse . . . her brutal death. Although, my dreams have always been hyper-realistic, and I am no novice to lucid dreaming.

Am I trying to convince myself of something that's not there? If this was a real murder, what do I even have to go by? A few faces and the event itself? This would be impossible to figure out. My life isn't some supernatural episode where I stumble on a murder and somehow use my intuition to bring peace to a grieving family.

Just to give myself a sense of closure . . . just in case, I decide to do a quick google search.

*I can't believe I'm doing this.*

It seems so elementary, but I can't think of anything else.

I grab my MacBook and cue up the search bar: "murdered woman+ballet dancer+head blow" trying to be as succinct as possible yet detailed enough to get something worthwhile.

Results for murdered woman+ballet dancer+head blow (without quotes):

*Post and Courier:* **Former Ballet Dancer On Trial For Murder**
*The New York Times:* **Lorraine Graves, Pioneering Harlem Ballerina, Dies at 66**
*San Diego Union-Tribune:* **San Diego Dancer's 1923 Death Still A Mystery**

I shut my computer in frustration. What did I expect? A neatly packaged search result with all the answers laid out before me?

*Rylee's Weirdo Tribune:* **Young Ballet Dancer Murdered by Three Men at a Trailer Park With Ghastly Blow to the Head**

I'd have better luck solving what's for dinner tonight. I have to get to work anyway; I don't have time to pore over thousands of search results, looking for that one needle in a haystack. If there even is one.

I'm grateful for the peaceful moment of zen before the air is disturbed within the quaint little bookshop. One I desperately need after the rough start I've had. I close my eyes and welcome the unique smell of the old, leather-bound pages and distinguished aromas of newer ink on paper, the old and new coming together in a euphonic partnership as they trigger a melody.

Before, my place of calm would have been the smooth stage of an empty auditorium. I allowed the intrusive thought for just a moment, imagining myself swaying to an internal tune as the smells of soft wood polish mixing in with the dusty, damp corners of the old building fill my nostrils. A bitter yet sweet memory gently tugging at my heart.

*It was my safe space.*

Cora comes in a half hour later in her usual spunky attitude. She often reminds me of Roan, who, like her, fashions her long, red hair into two symmetrical messy buns on top of her head. Her thick, black-rimmed glasses opposing her usual eccentric ensemble gives her a quiet, yet quirky librarian flair.

"So, how has your morning been? I ran into the most interesting couple at the coffee shop next door. Well . . . the guy was no one to remember," she says contemplatively, "but his girlfriend has my impeccable sense of style. She had the most gorgeous teal shawl embroidered with these cute, fancy yellow daisies. Of course, I had to know where she got it from. Anyway, it turns out she is a bookstore connoisseur too and they're heading over to check out our collection."

"Great!" I say as excitedly as I can when she stops in front of me and waits for a response. I don't tell her about my terrifying dream mostly because I'm still getting over the shock of it and don't want to relive those traumatizing moments just yet.

"I'm going to the pop-up market for that shawl after work. I need it in my life!" Cora continues to gush as she walks off into the back room, surely chocking up my short answer to my usual quiet demeanor.

Not a moment passes before the bell chimes over the entryway alerting us to a new customer. The woman with the memorable teal shawl walks in with a familiar air of poise. She scans the space with a slightly raised chin as if an invisible string is carefully lifting her head, her gently elongated frame gracefully pivots almost en pointe toward the new release table on her left. I stiffen at the sight of her as I do around every dancer, trying to pause the trickling wave of envy. My eyes jolt to the man coming in behind her and the air catches in my chest.

I want to run, but my feet are glued to the wooden floor, my body tense as if in a state of rigor mortis. It's him, the lanky man from the dream. He has a few scraggly grays that weren't there before, but I'm sure it's him. I'd recognize that face anywhere, as it's been seared into my consciousness since I awoke this morning. His eyes meet mine, his confused expression answering my wide-eyed stare because, of course, he's never seen me before. He doesn't know that his secret is my misery. The sound of breaking glass behind me interrupts our awkward stare.

"Shoot!" Cora exclaims as she stares down at a red crystal bird now in shards.

When I turn back toward the front door, Lanky Man is heading into our New Age section, and I slowly let go of the immobile breath lodged within my chest. I need to escape; I can't spend another moment in the same room with him even if he doesn't know who I am. Cora finally steps out of the back room and the words rush out of me like water from a firehose.

"I have to go. I'll explain later. I'm sorry, I just can't be here right now," I blurt out as I gather my bag and run for the door, leaving no room for her response. I run until my chest feels like it's about to explode.

Back at my apartment, I decide to cue up my search history again, but this time adding a five-year gap. I scroll through three pages when something catches my eye:

*San Francisco Chronicle*: **Ballerina Stages Starry Gala in Memory of Her Late Friend**

A chill rises up my spine. *Could it be?*

As I scroll the page, I land on the late ballerina's photo, the familiar curls suspended in motion across her caramel-toned face as she was caught mid pirouette. "Emma Benoit, Soloist in Sweet Daisies" reads the caption underneath.

> *The San Francisco Ballet is holding a special Yellow Daisy Gala performance to honor and remember Emma Benoit, who was tragically killed last year. Donations are currently being accepted, and the family urges anyone with any information regarding the late dancer's murder to contact Byron Guidry, Private Investigator.*

It was published four years ago, but I imagine the PI may still be looking for any new information on the case, since there is no update on the perpetrators, or he may at the very least have a point of contact for me. If all else fails, I can try seeking a new lead at the ballet studio Emma danced at; I know the place all too well. Now that I have her name, anything might be possible.

Without another moment's thought, I pull out my phone and enter the numbers carefully. My finger shakily hovers over the Call button for a few seconds before committing, and after a few rings, a deep voice booms through my speaker.

"Hello, Mr. Guidry. My name is Rylee. I believe I may have some important information regarding Emma Benoit. The family has you listed as the private investigator handling her case. Is this a good time to speak?"

He sounds surprised that someone is finally calling about Emma after all this time. Byron mentions that the police officially closed the case a week after finding her body, but the picture the police painted didn't match up with the Emma her family had always known. We agree to meet at a park close to my Nob Hill bookstore, a strategic location not only because it is usually well populated, but because I want to swing by the store before our meeting. I would bet my whole life savings that Cora signed up the couple for our member's rewards program, and I could at least show up to my appointment with some sort of lead.

When I get to the shop, I see Cora helping a customer in one of the aisles, and I motion for her to meet me in the back as we lock eyes. Since I've arrived after our usual story-time hour, I expect I can be in and out quickly and make my trek to the park with some time to spare. As I enter the cozy, closet-sized room, I feel a small crunch underneath my sneaker. A shiver runs up my spine as I recall the little bird that shattered earlier. My eyes barely get a chance to scan the shelves when I catch the fragmented creature at eye level staring back from the ledge, its crimson head still partly intact.

"Okay, seriously, what's going on?" Cora begs, interrupting the forming spiral I'm about to plunge into. "Are you okay? You look a little pale." The gentle touch on my shoulder steadies me, snapping me back to my mission.

"The bird, it . . . never mind. I promise I'll fill you in, but right now I'm kind of in a rush. I'm meeting up with someone."

"Oh, you are?" she asks quizzically.

"It's a long story, I just need to know if you caught the name of that couple that came in earlier. You know, the woman with the teal shawl?" I sidestep her, knowing that she'll follow me to the bulky, yet reliable computer that holds a clue to this mystery.

"Umm, yeah, Margaret. I signed her up for rewards."

My eyebrows instinctively rise.

"Jones. Margaret Jones." The search result quickly pings back: *Margaret Jones: 39 Sussex St. San Francisco, CA 94131.*

I rummage through the desk for a clean sheet and scribble it down on a notepad. Staring down at the address, I can't seem to let go of the pen. How do I even begin to explain this to the PI? Why would he even bother to take me seriously?

"Rylee?" Cora says behind my shoulder, and in an instant, I tear out the sheet and run for the door. "Share your location with me!" she yells, her plea intermingling with the chime of the door.

Dolores Park is buzzing as expected. Snuggled within my favorite pea coat, I walk toward my favorite bench on the hill where, on a good day, I can catch a glimpse of the sparkling bay a couple miles away. I let my mind wander. The view of the city from here is unmatched, as is its deep history as a place of refuge and venerated ground. It became a gleaming haven within the shattered cityscape of the 1906 earthquake, thousands of displaced San Franciscans flooding to it like a beacon in the dark. It was also my refuge after the accident that changed my life, the light on a sea cliff while I drowned in the dark.

A sudden yell from familiar faces playing their weekly game of ultimate frisbee snaps me out of my daze. I feel like a spectator as I wait to meet my stranger. My red coat acts as my shield, but also a glaring tell for Byron Guidry to find me. Luckily, I gathered bits and pieces of his background before I left the store. He is the opposite of what I had pictured a private investigator to be. His old fashion sense and long support cane for his stubby legs do not fit into my preconceived illusion of a clever Sherlock Holmes. I hope this man from New Orleans will be no stranger to the supernatural if it comes down to it. He seems like a modest man taking pro bono cases for the underprivileged.

Still, nervousness continues to gnaw at my stomach. What was I even thinking? *We're no Nancy Drew.*

I have to admit there's a certain thrill to it all. The black man that approaches the somewhat secluded bench I have picked out is the exact image I had pulled up on my phone earlier. His 1940s plaid vest is tightly snuggled around his stout midsection, and his matching worn beret hides his short black curls. A pocket watch dangles from his gray pant pocket. His aged, scruffy face analyzes me with curiosity.

"Rylee, I assume." He takes a seat next to me, his thick Southern drawl soft and friendly. "There haven't been any leads in this case for quite some time. What made you want to come forward now?"

"I didn't really have any information or even know about Emma's death until just recently," I respond, decidedly leaving out any supernatural details.

He raises an eyebrow. "You just came into this information? After five years you just happened upon something about a murder you never even knew about?"

"I know how this sounds. I would just rather not go into the details of how I came across a possible lead in your case. I can't sit back with this information and do nothing." I wanted to share the least amount as possible about my encounter with Emma, knowing the story could very well make me sound like some mental case.

"Or you're just looking to clear your conscience . . ." he pries with a subtly accusatory tone.

"What? No." I pause and take a deep breath. "One of the men that I believe was an accomplice in her murder came into my bookshop this morning. I have his address—well, the address of his partner. Looking into him may also lead you to the other two men."

He eyes me with deeper suspicion. "Other two. So you're saying there were three people involved? And exactly how do you know this?"

His skepticism is a fair reaction.

"That's the part I prefer not to get into. I just know that if you look into this guy, you'll get the answers you seek. All I want is to pass on the information, to get justice for her family." I know he has no reason to believe me, and asking him to simply take my word for it is a lot.

"I see, and I'm just supposed to believe that you have damning knowledge on these men to pass on just cuz you want to be a good citizen?" He pauses for a moment, his question rhetorical. "You know what I think? I think you may have something to do with it. Maybe you're the partner this man has, and you can't continue on knowing, or maybe . . . maybe you had a hand in it yourself." His tone is a bit harsher now, and I'm taken aback with his quick conclusion.

I stare at him, too shocked to speak. My mouth is partly open to defend myself, but I can't get the words out. His astute expression claims he has everything he needs to look into me if he really suspects that I'm guilty. I have to tell him. I can't be accused of being complicit to a murder; I have to tell him everything I know before I officially become a prime suspect.

"It's not how you think it is!" I say, urging him to believe me. "I'll tell you everything I know." I close my eyes. "But it's going to sound strange."

I take a deep breath and let the words flow out of me like a river. Everything from my personal encounters with spirits to the dream itself in its entirety. I'm almost sobbing by the end of it, reliving those painful last moments of sadistic torture. I expect him to categorize me as one of those crazy woo woo women who dabbles in witchcraft. Someone who should be committed to a mental institution for hallucinating such a horrible dream. But to my surprise he gives me a strange look of knowing. As if he, too, is familiar with what lies beyond the veil.

"This has been a cold case for some time now, some details never even shared with the public," he says after a long pause. "Details that can only be known by the investigators and the perpetrators. I'm not a particularly spiritual man, but where I come from, you learn to respect the mystical world. I can't imagine feeling someone else's death like that."

My hands unclench within my pockets at his words.

"I'll tell you what, Rylee, I'll look into this lead of yours cuz it's the best I've got so far. The police haven't been helpful, as they usually aren't when the victims come from the other side of the tracks."

"Can you keep me informed on what you find? I know I have no real right to ask, but . . ." I trail off, trying to find the right words. "I still feel connected to her."

He looks unsure about my request but decides to keep me in the loop with his investigation as long as I reveal any new information that may come up from my "experience." I imagine my picture added to the wall of his murder map, my position of accomplice or lay witness still yet to be decided.

Cold metal chair . . . broken glass . . . blood . . . excruciating pain . . . sweat . . . relief. Every morning this week after the initial dream has started with the same jarring routine. I thought that reaching out to Byron would be enough to quell the spirit, but the only relief I've received is not having to relive the event in its entirety each time.

*She's not going anywhere.*

Parts are mercifully sped up, but there haven't been any new details that could accelerate the closure of this case, which I now assume is the only way to rid myself of this misery. I've tried reaching out to Byron to see how the lead has panned out, but so far all I've gotten is possible motive and the old wait-and-see line. He did send me details of how Emma was found in case it would help jog my memory, as if my memory needed jogging. Familiar smells and sounds of the city are now my enemy, keeping me on edge while sending me back to that trailer of horror.

"How are you holdin' up?" Byron asks after my shaky hello on the other side of the receiver.

"I'm okay, just not getting much sleep these days. Do you have anything new?" I say, desperately wanting to shift the conversation away from me.

"I sent you some of the details from the police report, but just a warning, it can be triggering," he responds, but I get the sense that he wants to trigger me. "Emma's body was originally found near a homeless encampment by the Fruit-vale station in Oakland. The police tried to sum up the story by labeling her as a worn-out ballerina needing an escape."

My mind returns to the darkened sky where I . . . Emma . . . stared moments before her death. I felt oblivion awaiting her soul as the accented man mentioned that same train station. The ballet world is so competitive; drugs happen to be a common recourse.

"So, they claim that she got into it with the wrong people and ended up in a ditch for it," I say, looking over the notes.

"Yep, and whoever did it went through a lot to make sure none of the evidence could be found on the body." He pauses, then solemnly adds, "Though it was obvious she was a victim of assault and killed by a fatal blow to the head."

"Are you going back to stake out the address I gave you? I can help!" I say, trying to be more involved. The sooner he can get answers, the closer I may be to a full night's rest.

"I'm headed there now. There's no need for you to get further involved. Just let me know if you remember anything else. One more thing: that lanky man who walked into your bookshop, his name is James." Byron leaves room for a response, as if to see if the name sparks any reaction from me, but I meet him with silence. "I've tracked him back to Emma's old dance studio."

☽●☾

I'm still staring at the picture on my phone when the crashing sound of scraping metal and shattered glass sends me into the frenzy of my mental prison. The flash of crystal fragments near my face on the carpet . . . dance floor . . . blood . . . then blackness. The angry voices of two men fighting over fault snaps me back onto the sidewalk in front of my apartment building, phone still in my trembling hands. I don't let go of it until I ascend the three flights of steps to my door. Sliding down to the floor, I hear the small thud as I drop it to my side and close my eyes.

In the picture, Emma is elevated, en pointe, in arabesque while her suitor, James, supports her by holding on to her thin waist. I imagine the movement in completion as my own suitor turns me 360 degrees while I prepare to complete my pose in fifth position. The romantic 1890 ballet *The Sleeping Beauty* is an exquisite favorite, complete with backdrops of royal props and colorful stained-glass windows. The courtly dance is to end in an emotionally charged display of love. Mine, however, abruptly concludes with me lying on the stage floor surrounded by fragmented glass, broken wooden beams, and a career-ending injury. Whether my suitor threw me into one of the three lancet windows or simply let go remains a mystery. The jealousy and entrapment within the competitive world do not. I imagine Emma's rising fame won her the deadly attention she unfortunately received.

*That could've been me.*

The knocking on the other side of the front door startles me, and it takes a second for my brain to register the interruption. I called Roan after fixating on the photograph for what seemed like hours and asked her to come as soon as possible.

"Hey!" she says after I open the door, her friendly smile quickly turning into a cautious frown.

"Hey," I respond despondently. "Thank you for coming so quickly." My own smile fails to meet my eyes.

"Whoa! There's a lot of chaotic energy coming from your apartment," she says in an alarming tone. Roan closes her eyes as if she's putting her guard up and slowly steps inside before opening them again. "Walk me through it and try not to leave anything out." She takes in the small space as if looking for the source.

I tell her every last painful detail of the dream, my sleepless nights, and the recurring images triggered by random events of the outside world: the smells, the sounds, the darkness. I even tell her about Byron and his role in it all.

"She's tethered herself to you," Roan says with conviction. She's been continuously eyeing the space while taking in my words and finally settles on my face. "There's a really strong connection between the two of you. It's the reason she chose *you*. Any idea what that might be?"

"I don't even know why there would be one; she is a stranger to me." I look away from Roan, focusing on pulling my cuticles on each finger.

"Rylee?" She places her hand on my shoulder, slightly craning her neck toward me.

"We were dancers," I say quietly. "We were both dancers."

I let my statement hang in the air. I haven't called myself that in a long time, letting the memory fall to the recesses of my mind as if it were another life lived long ago.

I need to move on before I fall to pieces again. "Is there a way to calm the chaos? I feel like I'm literally doing everything I can to help close her case."

"Hmm . . ." Her lips press together as she squints her eyes, taking a moment to ponder the question. "Well, I have some selenite with me. I can try clearing your space and cleansing you with some palo santo, but I'll be honest, with this type of tether, it's not likely to make much difference."

I'm grateful for her honesty, but I still can't hide the tinge of disappointment from appearing on my face.

"I'm sorry there's not much more I can do for you without tapping deeper into her space, but I hope you can find relief soon," she adds, giving me an *I told you so* without verbally saying it outright. "I can tell you, though, she's angry."

After a few more sleepless nights and no new information from Byron, I decide to do a bit of scouting on my own. I pound my third cup of coffee while parked in front of the brick dance studio. I can't chance closing my eyes and falling back into that dreaded sequence of motions that leads to the disorienting headache. It's been a week and a half since the initial dream, and I can no longer tell if my jitters come from the amount of caffeine I've ingested or the debilitating stress I've developed.

*We can't sleep, don't sleep.*

I start to wonder how long it'll be before James makes an appearance at the studio. I imagine I'll find the small lobby empty on a Saturday afternoon with the receptionist off for the weekend. The hustling and bustling taking place within the auditorium will allow me to slip in unnoticed, past the little desk calendar still displaying the date for last Thursday. The chaos of rehearsal week flusters everyone. When I peek through the door, I see the stage is set with the Russian flair of St. Petersburg—colorful and intricate textile loops drooping across thin metal beams and the iconic spire of the Cathedral of Saints Peter and Paul situated majestically in the background. A few dancers, adorned with varied watercolor costumes, anxiously wait for the dress rehearsal to begin. Margaret speeds out of one of the corner wings to take her position center stage, her hair tied up in a high bun, fashioned with a striking red feather. Her matching red ensemble is the quintessential vision for the principal dancer of Igor Stravinsky's *The Firebird*.

The start of the rehearsal is the best time to start poking around backstage if I'm careful to remain shrouded within the shadows. The characteristic smell of old buildings fills the air, and I can't help but reminisce the untethered feeling of my slippers freely moving across the black floor. I allow my eyes to close for just a second and welcome the sensation.

The sudden vibration of my phone rudely snaps me awake and I barely make out the letters of Byron's name flashing across the screen when something big jerks me back, pushing me hard into the wall. I let out a small squeal before large hands envelop my throat, the familiar blue eyes coming into view. The bald man gives me a small look of surprise before morphing his expression into one of deep satisfaction, my own wide eyes quickly giving in to fear.

I try to punch his chest over the word SECURITY across his shirt, but his hand closes in tighter and all my efforts to pull it away have me struggling in vain. I try to kick him, but my feet feel welded to the floor. Heat rises to my face, my futile clawing doing nothing to gain me oxygen in these last moments before I pass out. Dreaded realization washes over me—no one is coming to my rescue, and his sinister smile will be the last thing I see while the unbearable pain of his grip crushes my trachea.

I shoot up, gasping for air, the hot sensation scorching my swollen throat, but my lungs are grateful for the unsuppressed inhale between each cough. My eyes are burning and my vision is blurred, but the familiar steering wheel underneath my palms gives a small sense of comfort to my fractured psyche.

*We're still here. It wasn't me.*

It takes a while to steady my breathing, and for my splintered brain to catch up on the turn of events—another dream. Slowly I begin to place the numbers that flashed briefly across the screen as the phone rang. Margaret Jones, time of death: 8 p.m. last week, Thursday. I fumble over Emma's case notes, sprawled over my passenger seat, and locate my buried my phone so I can call Byron, but something stops me. As my thumb cautiously hovers over his name, I remember.

Byron Guidry, the name flashed on the screen as the phone buzzed in my right hand before I hit the wall. Was it Margaret's phone or was it mine? I close my eyes, willing for my memory to place the timeline correctly. It would make sense for him to call me, but Margaret? He might reach out to her if he thought she was in danger. Still, I can't shake the nagging feeling that he's involved somehow.

The sudden vibration of the phone jolts me in my seat, but it's not Byron, it's Cora. I take a deep breath, relieved to see her name instead, and answer.

"Are you okay?" Cora asks as she pulls me into her arms when I see her at last. "Girl, you look haggard!" I let myself fall into her embrace, finally releasing the tension my body had been holding since the last dream.

"I'm not," I say on the verge of tears. "I'm not okay." The only thing that feels remotely safe is the familiarity of Dolores Park and Cora's comforting touch.

*We're not okay.*

"What were you doing at that ballet studio?" she asks, her voice calm and nurturing, a stark contrast to her usual speed racer demeanor. I almost forgot my phone was still sharing my location with her. "Did it trigger you, being back there?"

"No, well, not because of that," I say, taking a seat on a familiar bench. Cora was well aware of my history but knew never to talk about it unless I brought it up. "I was there because I was tired of not hearing from Byron. My plan was to scout it out, but I finally crashed in my car and had another dream."

"With Emma?" she carefully asks. I told her everything about the dream on one of my sleepless nights when I just needed someone to vent to. Cora has always been a whirlwind tornado threatening to suck anyone into her chaotic vortex, but when needed, she could also be a reliable listener.

"Margaret." Saying her name out loud takes away some of the sting.

"Oh my god, is she?" Cora quickly interjects, wide-eyed and surprised.

"Yeah, I believe she is," I say solemnly. A desolate ambiance replaced the vibrant energy around the studio from the dream as I stared at the door from my car, but I decided to call the studio anyway. The somber recording informed me that all performances were postponed until further notice.

*What if we're next?*

"Have you tried reaching Byron? Maybe he knows something, or at the very least, he should know how it happened."

"I can't bring myself to call him. I just have this gut feeling that he might somehow be involved." I look at her for answers, even though I know she has none.

*No one can save us.*

"Wow! Really?!" she replies, stunned. "That would be some horrible irony. What makes you second guess his intentions?"

"The call. He called the phone I was … Margaret was holding. I don't know! I can't say for a fact if it was me or her at this point!" I keep willing my brain to figure this mess out without having to undergo the painful experience of the dream again.

*We're in trouble now.*

"And the accent. I keep going back to the silhouette man's accent during Emma's murder. Was it Southern? Was it something else? Ugh! I just can't fill that hole!" The aggravation of unanswered questions leaves me straining within my mental mayhem.

Cora sits in silence, contemplating the events as I have revealed them. I can sense her own mind mulling over the scenario. "I think you need to trust your intuition," she says finally, meeting my watery eyes again. "I also think you really need some rest. Come to my apartment. You don't have to be alone."

"No," I say, my tone resolute. "I can't allow myself to fall asleep even if it means finding the answers. I'm too drained, too tired to go through that again." Of this, I'm sure.

"Maybe we should go to the police then . . ." Cora's voice trails off into a muffled sound.

The hairs on my arms stand up before my ears even have the chance to register the noise. Somewhere on the nearby trail, a bottle hits the ground. Its shattered pieces infiltrate my mind in rampant succession.

Shards . . . splintered wood . . . blood . . . darkness.

*He's coming! He threw us!*

The growing thumps of my heart are lodged within my throat as I begin gasping for air. My eyes are wide open, but everything is pitch-black. I can still hear Cora's muted voice somewhere beside me as my body begins to shake uncontrollably. I just want it to end. I feel myself asphyxiating, and I don't know how much more I can endure.

*Stop!* I want to scream. *Just . . . stop!*

After a few moments, I slowly start to feel Cora's touch on my arm. Her voice, still imperceptible, steadily becomes clearer.

"Rylee!" I finally register, her voice clear yet alarming. "Slow your breathing, in . . . out . . ."

*In . . . out . . . in . . .* I silently repeat.

She continues the mantra until I look up. "You had a panic attack." Her expression is full of worry.

"Is that what that was?" I reply, confused, my voice sliding through my still slightly trembling throat.

"Just try to keep your breath steady."

As my breathing slows, my brain clicks together her last words before the attack. "Cops," I breathe out. "We need to go to the cops."

"I'm going with you."

*I'm going too.*

The fear that has been slowly creeping in since we set off for the closest police station is amplified as we reach the sidewalk outside the building. I feel as though I'm on the verge of another panic attack.

*Crack.* I hear it as if I'm stepping on a thin piece of glass threatening to fully break under my body weight. I take another step.

*Crack.* I imagine the spider veins quickly shooting out from the initial impact point.

*Crack.* I stop right in front of the stairs that lead to the entrance. I can't move. Another step and the glass pane will surely shatter.

"What's going on? Do you need to take a moment?" Cora asks, seemingly unaware of the thin, fragile landing that's about to give way. The familiar throbbing starts to ascend into my throat as the air becomes thin around me.

*We're going to fall!*

I immediately grab Cora's hand. "Cora!" I gasp, the panic returning.

"Sit down right here. It's okay. I'm right here," she tries to assure me as she leads me to the edge of the sidewalk.

*Crack.* Another spider vein on the pane as my bottom hits the cold concrete.

"Cora, I can't see! It's going to give way!" I say desperately. Wetness streaks down my face from the barrage of tears.

"What's going to give way?" she asks, alarmed and confused. "Excuse me, sir! Can you help us?"

"What's going on?" The male voice comes in from my left. I want to speak, but all I can do is hopelessly gasp for more of the thinning air.

*No one can help us now.*

"She had a panic attack earlier. I think she's having another one, but I don't know."

"The medics are on their way."

Within the blackness, swirls of color start to appear. Faceless dancers glide over a bright, clear stage. I catch a glimpse of my own face. Am I dancing, too? No, this is wrong. One of the dancers leaps into a grand jeté, landing on her heels with a heavy thud. The impact creates a crack on the silky surface. One by one, the other dancers follow suit in timed succession, unaware of the spider veins jutting out from each blow. I catch a glimpse of the dancer with my face.

"Stop!" I yell, trying to warn her. Droplets of blood begin to rise through the weakened spots.

"Rylee?" a distant accented voice calmly says. "My name is Patrick. I'm here to help you."

The swirls of color begin to redden as they mix with the blood-red substance, the cracks growing wider as the dancers continue their spectacle. My twin turns her face to me, and I register the sinister smile. I blink and James's face comes into view instead.

"He's here!" I scream. "He sees me!" I gasp, unable to hide my horror. The blood threatens to puddle above the veins as leathery shoes continue to haphazardly move across the stage. *Thud . . . Thud . . . Crack . . .*

"He wants to drown me!" I wail as James stops in front of me a few feet away, his leg lifted above the ground, and I realize he's about to stomp out the last crippling blow.

"H-He's—" I barely get out. Then his elevated foot descends to the surface with a sting, and my body effortlessly plunges into the red sea of blood.

"She's got five cc's of Midazolam. She'll be a bit disoriented when she wakes up." Patrick's accented voice sounds distant, intermingling with the slow, steady beeping of a machine. Am I in the hospital?

*We'd be so lucky*, the familiar dancer whispers in my head.

"Full mental break then?" asks another male voice as a whiff of cigarette smoke breaches my nostrils.

"That's our best play at the moment. We should hash out the details so we're all on the same page, yeah?"

Something in my mind clicks; the Southern drawl is unmistakable.

"That's your area of expertise. Mine is getting them to where they need to be and we all know Ivan is the muscle. So do your part."

"Babe, let's just take a beat. She's not going anywhere." Cora's here? Is she with Patrick? The beeping of the machine speeds up.

"James, go check on her, yeah?" Patrick urges. "Or is that not your job either?"

The tension is rising and as the footsteps get closer, it becomes clear. *We're done for.*

# About the Author

**yesenia monique** is a designer and storyteller who intricately weaves letterforms together to create messages that move the spirit and challenge the narrative. As an Art History and Design major and former servicewoman, she uses her experiences and cultural education to lift silent voices and deliver unique storylines. Her complex background informs her work as she seeks to highlight underrepresented communities.

She currently resides in Southern California and enjoys being a mother of two, throwing kitchen dance parties, and a nice cup of coffee with a good book.

You can find yesenia on Instagram at:
@ym.narrative

To learn more about yesenia, visit her website at:
https://www.yeseniamonique.design/

# Everyone's Polite, But No One Is Nice

# Everyone's Polite, But No One Is Nice

## Derek Moreland

"WEH-HELL AND TARNATION, IF IT ain't John Higgins's oldest!" the old man behind the counter hooted. He wore a Houston Texans baseball cap smeared with decades of oil stains pulled down low on his wrinkled head, popping his ears out like car doors. When he smiled, I could see the teeth he still had were a deranged shade of yellow.

*Spitter's teeth*, my dad had called them. That's why Dad had smoked good ol' Camels. Didn't want to lose his own chompers like that.

Instead, he'd just lost his lungs.

"Yep," I nodded and tried to smile. "Stan Higgins, that's me. It's been a while, Mister . . .?"

The old man cackled. "Oh, I don't 'spect you to know me, son. You wuz knee high to a grasshopper when me an' your dad worked at the garage together. You just got his face, is all. It's like lookin' at a mem'ry."

I smiled for real then. My first real smile in the last week. I didn't have a lot to remember my father by; he hadn't had a lot to leave anyone. But knowing he and I shared the same piercing blue eyes, strong jawline, and head of healthy blonde hair always brought me some comfort.

"I appreciate you saying that, sir," I said, setting my candy bars and bottle of soda on the countertop. "Were you a mechanic at Wilson's?"

"Yep!" the old timer crowed. "'tween me and your pop, we could get an engine pulled, serviced, and settled in three hours on a good day. That man was a mechanical genius, God rest his soul." He swiped my goods through the laser. "Don't suppose you got any of them skills along with the looks, didja?"

I shook my head. "Afraid not. That was my brother."

The old man's face fell. "I heard about that, son. And I tell you, I'm sorry as hell that happened. I'm guessin' that's why you're back in town? That'll be $12.30."

I ran my card through the reader, careful to keep my face neutral. "Yeah."

The old man took off his greasy hat and placed it over his chest, the wispy errant hairs on top of his head standing up and saluting.

"He's with God and your pop now," he said in a voice that he probably thought very solemn and serious.

I just nodded and picked up my snacks.

"Well, sir, it was nice chatting with you," I said, turning to go.

The old man put his cap back on. "You come on back soon, son."

I hit the flashing stoplight and turned left onto College Avenue, the main thoroughfare through town. The old guy's Gas'N'Go was the first convenience store after about an hour on the highway in from the interstate, and I'd needed some sugar and caffeine to perk up after the long drive.

Now, though, it was official. I was home.

I drove past the sole Walmart and the lone McDonald's; past the graying husk of the community college that gave the main street through town its name. I thought about driving past my old house—the house that my brother had, until recently, called home—but decided against it. I'd see the old homestead after the funeral, when Junior's wife and daughters had the reception. I made my way to Guesthome Hotels instead.

*Get checked in, get in the room, call Destiny*, I said to myself. *Get checked in, get in the room. Call Destiny.*

I'd held it together through the hours on the long, lonesome drive down. I'd held it together in front of the stranger who knew my name. I could hold it together until I got checked in. Got to the room.

I would hold it together on the call with my brother's widow.

I pulled into the parking lot, wiping furiously at my eyes, biting down on my tongue so I had something else to focus on. The late May sun was already setting fire to the hotel's concrete walk-up; I could feel it through the soles of my loafers, an infernal complement to the sudden pressure of heat on my neck and shoulders.

*Shouldn't have run the AC so hard in the car. I didn't prep myself for the temperature change.*

I should have remembered. But I hadn't been in Texas, let alone the blank and burning Panhandle, for years. I'd let myself forget.

A rush of sudden icy cold hit me as I stepped into the hotel; the place had jets above the automatic doors, blasting newcomers with air so frigid it almost felt moist. I'm pretty sure the owners thought this was a courtesy: something of a relief from the growing hellishness outside. Personally, I'd always found it a little disorienting.

As I walked in, a young woman with braided black hair and very red lipstick standing behind the front counter offered me a smile that never reached her eyes.

"Good afternoon! How can I help you, sir?"

"Uh, hi, I have a reservation?" I said, juggling my travel bag and suit bag around until I could pull out my ID and credit card.

She took both and glanced at my driver's license. "Oh, my God, are you JJ's brother?"

*JJ?* "I don't . . ." Then it clicked. John Junior. J.J. "Yeah. Older. In town for the, uh . . . yeah."

The smile fell over, and her lower lip poked out. A practiced performance, a sham sympathy for the relative of the deceased. "Oh my God," she said again, "I am so, so sorry. JJ and I went steady for a few months in high school, you know. He was my junior prom date, actually."

After a second or two, I nodded. I wasn't sure how else to react.

"Anyway, we still kept in touch sometimes. My oldest is a grade above his youngest. They've been to each other's birthday parties." She sniffed and blinked, as though she were trying not to cry. "I'm sorry, I didn't mean to get all personal there. Let me get you your room card. I'm sure you've been on the road *forever*."

"It's quite a drive, yeah," I agreed. I'd also forgotten how much people in towns like this just . . . *talked*. Shared their lives, their pasts, their thoughts and hopes with strangers. First the old man, now this young woman. No age, gender, or social barriers. Everyone just talked. About anything.

She pushed the electronic key across the counter. "You're lucky," she said. "Booked a room on the first floor. The elevator here can be testy, and no one likes taking the stairs, right?" She winked at me.

I took the key and thanked her, glancing at the sign in the hall to make sure I was headed the right way. I shuffled away, glancing back over my shoulder before turning the corner.

The woman was still looking at me. Still smiling, even if the smile never reached her eyes.

"Hi, Destiny . . . it's . . . Stan. Yeah, I'm in town. Just got in." I sat on the edge of a crisply made double bed, holding the courtesy landline's receiver in a limp and trembling hand.

"Stan. . . hey," Destiny said. Her voice sounded sweet but ragged, like tattered silk. She'd been crying. "Did you get a new phone number? You didn't show up on the Caller ID."

"What? No, I'm using the hotel's phone. I can't seem to get a signal in this place." I wiped at my eyes again. Dry, but itching. Wanting to cry.

"Oh," she said. Distracted, maybe even a little spaced out. *Cut her some slack. She's spent the last week planning her husband's funeral.* "Would you want to come stay with us? I could make up the spare if . . ."

"No, I'll be okay. But go ahead and take this number down, I don't know how reliable my cell is going to be. . . ."

"Okay," she said. "I'm glad you came down. The girls are looking forward to seeing you."

"Okay." Biting my tongue again. *Can't start crying. Not now.* "Do you need any. . .? I mean, I can come over, if you need help or-or anything," I sighed, holding the receiver away from my mouth so she wouldn't hear it.

"No. Thank you," she said. "You should get settled in. We'll have plenty of time to catch up after . . . well, after."

"Okay, well, I'm here if you change your mind. I'll . . . I'll see you tomorrow. Two o'clock, right?"

Like I didn't know. Like I needed to confirm the time of my brother's funeral.

"Two o'clock," she agreed. "The boys at the shop rented a car for me and the girls, so we'll have to meet you there. I hope that's okay."

"Of course. Okay. Love—"

"Love you, Stan." A sudden fierceness in her voice. Love, even for extended family, was all she could anchor to right now.

"Love you, too. Give my love to the girls. Take care." I hung up the receiver.

And all at once, a huge, racking sob that had been caught in my throat for the last God knew how many hours disgorged itself, as though my very soul was screaming.

The reality of it—the *finality* of it—hit me. Johnathan Bartholomew Higgins, Jr . . . was dead.

Forty-two years old, felled by appendicitis he'd confused for a spot of exceptionally terrible indigestion.

I didn't cry. I roared. I screamed, my shoulders shaking, my body wrenching and contorting itself around the grief, choking on the spiked iron ball lodged in my throat.

"You stupid fucking bastard!" I wailed. Tears, hot and angry, escaped the corners of my eyes and flooded down my cheeks. "You selfish fucking prick, you're the one with kids! And a fucking partner who adores you! You couldn't let me die first. You had to go and make me come home?!? You had to make me come back?!? You're too fucking young, you fucking *asshole*!!!"

I had *made it out*. No one fucking makes it out of this town, but I had. After Dad died, and with Mom in the ground for five years before that, I had set my sights on San Francisco and never looked back. And Junior, he'd stayed, and married a local girl, and made little local girls, and kept the family business going, and he'd never once said he was angry that he'd been the one to carry on the Higgins legacy, because he'd always wanted to anyway.

And Dad must have known that! Elsewise, why save his name for his second son?

And now that legacy was dead, and I was home, and I had to face the weight of all of that. I didn't get to mourn just my brother. I got to mourn the loss of my family's history.

And no, those feelings weren't fair to John. *Of course*, they weren't fair. But I'd been sitting on them for the better part of a week, ever since Destiny had called me, whaling and gasping for breath, choking out between heaves of weeping tears that John was *gone, he's gone, Oh God, Stan, my husband is gone.* I'd pushed them down into the deep black part of myself for days and days, and they had finally erupted.

My brother was gone. And I was home.

Whatever home meant now.

It would be a hoary cliche to say that half the town showed up for Junior's burial, but damned if that wasn't how it felt in the moment. We held services at the First United Methodist Church. I sat in the front with Destiny and the girls, Candice and Cindy; they sat on either side of their mom, hugging her waist and bawling their little blonde-headed eyes out into her wrinkled black dress. Destiny kept dabbing at her own in an attempt to keep her mascara from running; her shoulders shook, and every inhaled breath sounded like a hiccupping sigh.

She hadn't been homecoming queen or anything, but she'd been on the cheer squad; two kids and twenty years hadn't done too much to alter her figure, and not every eye in the church looked to her with only sympathy. Some looked positively ravenous.

Both girls had inherited my family's long nose and their mom's high cheekbones, the color high and red from tears, their young faces looking thin and washed out. Ten and seven, far too young for any of this.

I didn't cry. I couldn't. I'd vented my grief, my rage, in the hotel room the night before. All that was left was an aching void, slowly filling with a heavy acceptance.

*I will never speak to my brother again.*

The pews behind us sat packed with mourners: family friends, faithful customers, and gawkers wanting to see what the fuss was about. All of us sitting in our best black elegance, all of us sweating, sweating, sweating in the nave, the overtaxed air conditioner bolstered by slow ceiling fans swirling the thick and blistered air around.

The priest on the dais above us droned out a Mad Libs sermon, slotting in John's name in the appropriate blanks, never raising or lowering his voice, never pausing for a breath. His face rose and fell accordingly with the words, a pantomime of shared grief. Nobody else noticed.

Once the wind-up eulogy ran down, I stood and walked to the casket with five other men: John's coworkers and friends from Wilson's Mechanical. They were all bigger and burlier than me—during the sermon, I'd made a game of trying to remember which one had broken what bone that had put me in traction for the better part of a month my junior year—but I took my place at the back corner, where the coffin was heaviest.

I could only do so much. I wanted to do all I could.

We carried him out of the church and into the sweltering sun. We walked down the scorching flagstone path behind the church to the cemetery, its wrought iron fence seeming to warble in the heat of the day. Dead ochre grass poked up in sickly clumps through the colorless dust and dirt. The mourners followed behind us at a respectful distance, their heads and shoulders sagging beneath the weight of the heat. Even the roof of the church seemed to bow under the sun's glare.

I took my walking cues from the other men, thankful that I couldn't really see where we were going . . . thankful that I could concentrate on the physical burden of the coffin. Perhaps I wasn't quite as done with grief as I had believed those few, long minutes ago.

Finally, we rested the coffin on some cinder blocks that sat next to the open grave. The professionals would take it from there, lowering the coffin into its final resting place and covering it with the dead, sullen dirt of the graveyard. A couple of the men nearest me reached out and shook my hand, their rough palms and callused fingers dwarfing mine.

"We're so sorry," the first one (broken nose, knocked out two teeth) murmured, his voice a basso rumble.

"Let us know if Destiny needs anything," the second (two fingers and a fractured wrist) chimed in.

I just nodded in thanks. I didn't trust my voice.

I looked around at the congregation as I walked toward my seat. Other than Destiny and the kids, who continued to weep, the mourners seemed strangely quiet. I saw bowed, uncovered heads and empty, drawn faces. There were children with wheat-straw hair and sunburned cheeks staring vacantly at the coffin, the headstone, the priest as he committed my brother's remains to the earth.

A whole sea of calm, uncaring eyes. An ocean of open, indifferent looks.

I made it to my seat, once more next to the widow . . . and kept walking. Back up the flagstone path, back into and out of the church, back into my car. No words of protest, no questions, no reaction.

I turned the key in the ignition, and I drove away.

I got on the highway and drove until the "low gas" light flickered into life on the dashboard. Then I hit an illegal U-turn and drove back, stopping at the Gas'n'Go once more for a fill-up.

To my great relief, the old man was enough with the times to have a credit card reader on the pumps outside. I didn't have to go in and talk to anyone.

☽●☾

I have never been comfortable sleeping in an unfamiliar bed. I tossed and turned on the damp sheets, the covers kicked off the edge of the mattress, even though the big AC unit hummed down past sixty degrees.

It was a dry heat down here. A heat absent of humidity, a heat that pulled cotton up out of the ground and melted the tar on the road. Nothing like the humidity that came in off the ocean. The kind of heat that wicked the spit out of your mouth, sizzling it away like eggs on a griddle. It stole the mucus from your nose, the tears from your eyes. It *baked* you, tanned and toughened you, molding the clay of you into something dark and hard.

I'd tried so hard to get away from the heat. The hardness.

I reached out for the third time since I'd come back to my hotel and picked up the receiver to the landline phone; for the third time that evening, I put it back without dialing. It was after midnight, and with any luck, Destiny was asleep. She didn't need me waking her up just so I could mutter a halfhearted apology.

No, I would call her tomorrow. From my cell phone, once I'd gotten somewhere where the reception wasn't shot to shit. I would call her in the full light of day, from a place that wasn't just *flat* and *dirt* and *heat*.

Maybe I could even convince her to move away from here. To take the girls and come with me to the big city. What was left for her here, anyway? For any of them? What did the Higgins name mean, now that there was no one left to carry on the legacy?

*Except me.*

A flash of light rolled over the wall of my hotel room: headlights from a car passing outside my window. I must have left the heavy pull curtains open. I rolled over, glancing to see how much . . .

A silhouette, tall, midnight black, outlined by the light of the high beams outside my room, raising its arms—

I screamed and scrambled, throwing myself out of the bed and running a foot or two before gasping in a breath and looking around.

No figure. No lights.

The curtain over the window pulled closed. The heavy thrum of the AC unit fighting to maintain the ridiculous temperature I'd set for it.

A dream. I'd finally managed to fall asleep, only to have a fucking nightmare of a dream.

*It's this place.* This dying, decaying place, this place that took my mom and my father and my brother and *it'll take me, too. If I let it, it'll swallow me up just like every Higgins boy.*

I walked to the bathroom on unsteady legs and turned on the overhead light. Harsh, bright, sanitation-white light spilled out over the tile floor, the stucco walls, the ceiling. It hurt my eyes, but the pain felt good. It felt awakening.

I splashed my face with cold water and patted it dry with a complimentary white towel.

*Tomorrow. This will all be over tomorrow. Try to get some sleep. It's a hell of a drive out of here.*

I went back to bed. I didn't turn off the light in the bathroom.

I skipped the continental breakfast and made my way straight for the concierge desk that morning. I figured I'd stop at the Gas'n'Go for a fried burrito and a Monster Energy drink on the way out of town. The sooner I could leave, the better.

A different young woman with a mess of brunette hair and the same over-abundance of lipstick met me at the desk. She also shared her coworker's surface-level professional smile.

"And how was your stay, sir?" she asked with a practiced sweetness.

"About as good as it could be," I said. At least it was an honest response. I handed her my room's key card. "Is there anything else I need to do to check out?"

"No, sir! Have a lovely and safe trip home," she replied, but her eyes were already on the computer monitor, and the smile was already beginning to fall.

That was another thing about the South. Everyone's polite, but no one is nice.

As I pulled out onto the highway and set the cruise control for a comfort-ably-within-the-margin-of-error 78, I pulled out my cell and attempted to open my Audible app. I'd just discovered Richard Stark's Parker novels, and I wanted to finish *The Hunter* on the way back to 'Frisco.

But for the life of me, I could not get it to play.

I growled, thumbing at the touch screen and glancing between the phone and the road, my focus bouncing between the spinning blue wheel, the error notification, and the way ahead. The growl turned to a roar, the roar into my palms beating the steering wheel because *this god damn piece of shit app fucking up is the last "fuck you" from this god damned godforsaken hellhole and watch out there's a washed-out pothole on the right there, wait, what—*

I never even slowed down. The force of the blow jerked the whole car, tilting it crazily off its driver's side tires and spinning it halfway to the ditch. I slammed the brakes in unfocused panic, overcorrecting and fishtailing even more, the tires and engine screaming in discordant harmony around me.

A sudden feeling like my guts were . . . rolling, like I was on a roller coaster looping the loop.

Then I was back on the highway, the car shuddering and slowing but still heading forward. The accident had disengaged the cruise control, and I had a foot on neither the brake nor the gas.

I pulled to the side of the road and heaved a long, slow breath. I closed my eyes and gave my body a quick once-over to see if anything felt off. I was definitely bruised along the chest and waist, where my seatbelt had locked in—thank heaven for small favors. But nothing felt broken. I took another breath; no pain, no lightheadedness. Good.

Okay. That meant it was time to check the car.

*Good thing I splurged on the insurance.*

I got out and walked around, gritting my teeth and fearing the worst: a blown tire, or a bent axle. But I didn't see anything immediately out of the ordinary; no major body damage, and the tires all looked to be intact. If anything was broken, it would be internal.

I slid back into the passenger seat and, after a moment of hesitation, turned the key. The starter rumbled and caught; the engine roared to life.

*Lucky. You lucky, lucky fucker.*

I picked up my phone. The touch screen was shattered, and when I thumbed the power button, a kaleidoscope of muddy color shone through the cracks.

"Yeah, I deserve that," I said to no one. I pocketed the phone and resumed my drive.

After about half an hour of silence spent just happy to be alive and in one piece, I turned the radio on and let it cycle through whatever channels it could pick up. Country and Western to gospel to fire and brimstone preaching to Modern Country to classic rock to Classic Country to televangelism: a microcosm of southern culture enveloped me between long bursts of static and scratchy, tuneless dead air.

It took what felt like another two hours, maybe more, before I started to feel something was off. I'd driven in using Google Maps, which was, of course, impossible now. But I still had the overwhelming suspicion I should have already made my connection to the interstate . . . or at least driven past another town. I checked the gas gauge; it held comfortably at just over half a tank. And the clock on the dash didn't do me any good, as it was set for 'Frisco time, and even then had been a little over an hour off. I hadn't bothered to set it because I had the time on my phone.

The sun, still pitiless, still burning down on the acres and acres of flat, brown nothing around me, was almost right overhead. That meant it was probably close to eleven o'clock in the morning. The gas station burrito was long gone, and the Monster had been lost when I hit the pothole, flown out the window, or something.

I pulled over to the side of the road, turned off the car, listened to the engine tick down. Almost immediately, the heat of the morning began pressing against the car like a vice, with feverish waves rising from the pavement to meet the crushing pressure from above. Sweat beaded on my forehead and upper lip. It slickened my armpits and the small of my back.

*Okay. Fine.* Nothing to do but go forward.

I restarted the car.

I drove for what felt like hours. There was nothing else I could do.

I lost all sense of time. The sun never seemed to move from its perch just above my head; the road never split off, never joined another. The clock on the dash ticked off numbers that meant nothing. I should have felt hungry, or thirsty, or tired.

But I only felt *hot*.

I kept my eyes on the road, but the horizon refused to change. There was nothing but a flat, sepia void to either side of the highway. No vehicles passed me, and nothing came barreling from the other direction.

Until . . .

I almost couldn't believe what I was seeing. Distantly, so far down the highway I almost mistook it for a bug on the windshield, was a structure. It was just off the road, just off *my side* of the road.

Finally! Someplace I could go inside, talk to someone, get some directions. Maybe find out what the hell happened to the interstate.

It was about this time I also noticed the sun had finally changed position— had, in fact, started to set.

Setting . . . to my right. To the west.

Which meant I was driving south.

How the hell was I driving south?! I hadn't turned around, not in the entire day I'd been on the road.

Which should have been the worst of it. Dear God, I wish that was the worst of it.

Because the building I was driving up to was the old man's Gas'N'Go.

"Hello?" I called out. I'd done a quick powerwalk through the station, marching through the aisles of candy and chips, 5-Hour Energy drinks and engine oil, bottles of soda bigger than my calf muscles. I'd poked my head in the public restrooms, checked the counter twice for some sort of bell or something to ding for service.

As far as I could tell, the station was empty.

"I was just here this morning," I muttered. "Right?"

Right. And the old man had been here. He'd called my fried burrito breakfast a "Mexican burrito," which had made me laugh, though it had been more at him than with him. Yes, I'd been here.

And I'd gotten the feeling that this was his whole world, that he bunked down in the back and played solitaire or listened to the radio when there weren't any customers. That he had a handwritten *back in 5 minutes!* sign behind the counter he'd slap on the door as he locked it to use the facilities during working hours.

A guy like that wouldn't just take a break and leave the front door unlocked.

A chill ran through me. A town like this didn't see a lot of crime, but that didn't mean bad things didn't happen.

I slowly looked over the counter to the floor behind . . . and let out a long, draining breath. No body, no blood, no signs of a struggle.

*Okay.* Relieved, I decided to try another test. I ran over to the refrigerated cabinets and grabbed a couple of sports drinks, not even looking at the flavors. Then I skipped over to the candy rack and grabbed a few bars. I walked over, dumped the whole mess on the counter, and shouted, "All right! I'm ready to check out!"

Nothing. Silence. Even if I was on camera, being recorded, there was nothing and no one to stop me from taking whatever I wanted.

I sighed, glanced outside. Whatever daylight had hung over my head for so much of the day seemed to be fading. It would be dark soon.

I pulled my wallet from my back pocket to grab the spare ten-spot I kept hidden behind my license for emergencies. I needed a bottle of water and something with carbs, if nothing else . . . and I couldn't bring myself to just take them. As I did so, something hit the floor with a soft *click*.

I turned around.

Looked down.

The keycard to my hotel room lay on the floor.

"I thought . . ." I tried to remember. "I thought I turned you in." I picked up the card. "I guess I could head back to the hotel?"

It made as much sense as anything else. And it'd be nice to lie down after a day in the car. I left the pile of crap on the counter—never mind the water or snacks, and it would serve him right to have to restock, especially since I could have just pocketed what I wanted—and left.

I got back in the car, and for a moment, my spine felt like ice. *What if it doesn't start?*

But the key turned in the ignition, and just as before, the thing rumbled to life.

Just out of curiosity, I checked the fuel gauge. Just under a quarter tank. I'd driven all day, and I'd barely burned through an eighth of a tank of gasoline.

It only took a few minutes to drive from the gas station to the Guesthome Hotels. I parked and walked in.

I guess I should not have been surprised that there was no one at the concierge desk.

I closed my eyes. Took a long, slow breath. Opened them. Walked down the hall to the room I had rented.

A little cardboard sign dangled off the handle. It said, *Welcome! Enjoy Your Stay!*

I tried my keycard against the reader. The light turned green, and the door clicked open.

I lay in the bed I had slept so fruitlessly in the night before, wearing the clothes I had tried to leave in. It didn't make sense to change into anything, or even just to disrobe. In fact, that I was still wearing an old Toadies concert tee and a pair of Levis brought something of a comfort to me. At least they felt real. At least I knew what they were, where I had got them, why I wore them.

Once I'd gotten to the room, I had tried to call Destiny. The phone never rang; instead, I got an automated message telling me that the person I was trying to call was no longer available. I thought maybe she'd blocked me after the stunt I'd pulled at the funeral . . . but then I remembered that she would have done that to my cell phone. Why would she bother blocking a hotel's number? What were the odds that I would try to call her from this particular phone again?

Was she that mad at me?

I decided I'd go by the house in the morning and apologize. Maybe take her and the kids to McDonald's for breakfast. The one here had a pretty good little play place, and I could tell her I was an ass for trying to leave without saying goodbye.

Yeah. Everything would make sense tomorrow. Everything would—

Radiant white light smashed through my hotel window. Then a horn began to wail. I sprang out of bed, head whipping around, eyes wide, trying to take in everything at once.

Then another horn joined the first. And another, and another, until the world felt full of cacophonous, disconsolately blaring horns.

Car horns. They were car horns. And the light . . .

I spun around, sure I would see some dark silhouette once more reaching for me. Searching me out, looking to wrap me in his cold, unearthly grip. But I saw no one.

And I realized . . . *that's because he's outside.*

I swallowed. Took a step forward, then another. The horns blared, a ceaseless, unending noise. The headlights shone, blindingly bright.

I stepped out onto the hotel room's front step.

Every car in the parking lot faced my room. Every headlight shone at my door. Every car's horn resounded off one another, echoing throughout the lot.

And in front of every car, every headlight, stood a shadowed figure haloed by the light. They looked to be from every walk of life: tall, short, thick and thin, men and women and children. They stood silently, looking at me with no eyes, no faces. Their hands all linked together.

Except the figure in the center. Its arms stretched out, toward me. Not threatening. Waiting.

I felt my face collapse into a smile, weak and watery.

"Hey, Junior," I said.

After all this time . . . I'd made it home to stay.

# About the Author

**Derek Moreland** is a freelance writer living in Texas with one wife, four cats, three dogs, and an absolute buttload of X-Men comics. He is the author of *Songweaver: The Temptation of Tanith Ven*, *Stranded on Dinosaur Planet*, the Shmonster the Monster series, and the comic book *Space is Awful*. Additionally, he has published a collection of short horror and speculative fiction, *All the Things We Bury*.

You can find Derek on Instagram, TikTok, and Bluesky at:
@shmonstermaker

To learn more about Derek, visit his website at:
derekmoreland.wordpress.com

# The Hollowing

# The Hollowing

## Grace Silva-Ortiz

I'D ALWAYS FELT LIKE A ghost in my own life, hovering just behind the glass of every moment, unable to touch it. As if my soul had arrived late to this body, misaligned and waiting for the life I was meant to live.

The present felt dim. Muted. Like a room thick with dust where time once danced. Where laughter was muffled, and even sunlight seemed reluctant to stay.

The dreams didn't help. Not since I was a child. Oh my, how they haunted me.

Visions pressed in like unwelcome visitors—cities swallowed by sand, rain-slick streets beneath a foreign moon, voices whispering in languages I shouldn't understand, cold iron biting my wrists, a blade across my palm. And always, eyes watching from the dark. Patiently waiting for something or someone.

My therapist called it trauma. My friends said I needed sleep. I nodded. Smiled. Pretended. But I knew better. Something was wrong with me.

*Honk, honk!*

The light had turned green. I blinked hard, shaking the fog from my mind, my hands tightening on the wheel to remind myself I was real.

This wasn't the life I imagined after university. Years studying art history had filled me with visions of curating forgotten masterpieces in gilded museums, not standing behind glass at the ferry pier, surrounded by the smell of fish, damp concrete, and impatient travelers. Still, the job paid—for now.

I parked my late parents' sedan and hurried toward the pier, boots splashing through shallow puddles, oversized sweater pulled tight against the damp chill. At the dock office, my breath misting in the cold air, I caught a flicker on the foggy shore. Something watching.

I glanced away, dismissing it as just another shadow of exhaustion.

Then a raspy whisper brushed my ear. *"The time isn't right, Tess. Not now."*

"Tess!" Marty barked. "Let's go. You're late again."

I swallowed the shiver and followed. Another long day awaited. Another day of slipping further from any sense of wholeness. Another day of feeling hollow.

The sky darkened as I stared at the small digital clock near my ticket window. *Ding.* Time to close.

Night was my enemy—the hours when I hated being alone. Always alone.

Sometimes, on evenings like this, I swore I could hear my name—a long whisper carried by the wind. *Tess* . . . But I never answered. They didn't leave you alone if you did.

I shook the thought away like a bad dream and stepped out of the booth, wandering toward the street-corner café.

Seth greeted me with his customary warm smile. He was an older man living his dream, owning the last remaining café in the city's Art District. The walls were covered in chalk sketches and half-finished poems, and the scent of roasted beans clung to the wood.

After each shift, he'd welcome me with a cup of hot chocolate mocha and a bakery treat of my choice.

Tonight, as I sank into my usual seat, Seth noticed the weight in my eyes, the dark circles beneath them saying more than my words ever could or would.

"What's wrong?" he asked gently.

"I haven't been sleeping," I admitted.

"Those dreams again?"

"More than dreams. They feel real. Like warnings. I don't know how to explain it, really."

His gaze softened with concern. "What do they say?"

"My name. Sometimes they want me to see things . . . but I can't remember what."

Seth placed the hot chocolate mocha and croissant in front of me. "You should take a few days off. Rest. Dreams like yours don't come to just anyone."

I looked up. "You believe me?"

He shrugged, eyes darker than usual. "Let's just say . . . you're not the only one who's dreamed of past lives."

Before I could respond, a woman at the next table looked up. I hadn't even noticed her.

In a long beige overcoat draped over a floral dress, she seemed like she'd stepped out of another era. Her red lipstick shined brighter than the café's lights, and her wide green eyes were fixed on me with unsettling calm. A faint clink caught my attention—a pendant resting against her throat. Antique gold, oval-shaped, etched with swirling patterns forming a skull surrounded by laurel vines. A Victorian piece. I couldn't quite decipher whether it was original or a replica. A memento mori. *Remember you must die.*

I tilted my head, curiosity rising. But it was Seth who surprised me. His eyes lingered on the woman's pendant a little too long. His jaw tensed, just barely. Then, in the space of a breath, the warmth returned to his face like a mask.

"Interesting piece," he murmured barely above a whisper. Then, as if catching himself, he looked away and refilled my cup.

Something about the woman's presence made me uncomfortable. I looked away, too, a chill running through me.

She softly cleared her throat. "Past lives, you say?" she repeated, her voice low and hypnotic. Seth shrugged with nonchalant ease, contradictory to his earlier reaction. "Yeah, that's all she's been talking about this week."

"I specialize in past life regression," the woman replied.

I blinked, caught off guard. "What's that?"

"It's quite simple," the woman replied, her tone eerily mesmerizing. "A journey into your own forgotten stories. You sit and relax, and I guide you back . . . back to where you've been."

"Back where?"

"Wherever you've been, my dear."

"I see . . ."

She slid a small card across the table. Her long, red nails scratched the surface.

*Madame Lynette*
*Experience a life lived.*
*If not now, when?*

"I have a quaint shop just up the road."

Then, she rose and walked away.

I picked up the card, staring at the words.

"Interesting," Seth muttered. "Maybe you should give it a go. Maybe it's the right time to face your fears?"

I stared at the card, slowly mouthing the words printed in the bold, black letters. "Maybe I should."

I didn't sleep. Just sat on the floor, the card turning between my fingers like a coin I was too afraid to spend.

By morning, the silence in my apartment felt suffocating. I needed answers more than I needed air.

So I went.

The bell above the door chimed faintly as I stepped into Madame Lynette's shop. The warm smells of frankincense and lavender occupied the small space. Dried herbs hung from the low ceiling, and heavy velvet drapes dressed the tall windows. Faded photographs, strange diagrams, and antique mirrors of all shapes and sizes cluttered the walls. Madame Lynette appeared from a side room without a sound in a long, beige, silk dress with her pendent beaming against the light of the faux candles dancing on every surface.

"You came," she said simply.

I nodded. "I want to try."

"No expectations. Only remembrance," she whispered. "Please, follow me."

The room beyond was bare, windowless, with the exception of a deep charcoal recliner and chair.

"Many lives leave many shadows," she said. "Are you ready to meet them?"

I sat in the recliner. Her voice dropped low, hypnotic.

"You are drifting now . . . through the veil. Breath by breath you walk down a narrow corridor with a gray stone door at the end. Without touching the door, it opens for you. Walk through. . . . You are no longer here, not yet there . . ."

At first, nothing. Doubt rose.

Then, a surge.

Memories crashed in: a fire-lit room, palms marked with sacred lines, screams stretching down corridors, a galloping horse, a baby's cry. My breath quickened. Madame Lynette whispered to the pendant. I sensed her leaning closer to me.

The visions sharpened. I was there, alive and dying across lifetimes. Suddenly,

I could no longer feel my body against the recliner. My body . . . was gone. I was all memory. All pain.

I was running through a blood-soaked field, the Roman spatha heavy in my grip, slick with the heat of war. All around me, men screamed—some in fury, others in death. I could taste iron in the air. My limbs moved on instinct, driven by something ancient, something deeper than memory.

I had fought. I had bled. I had watched comrades fall, their eyes wide with the sting of betrayal. Loyalty meant nothing here. Only survival.

At the top of the hill, a figure stood motionless, silhouetted against the gray and dying sky. Something about them felt . . . familiar. Then it struck.

A pain, searing and sudden, tore through my back, erupting like fire through my spine. I dropped to my knees, the world spinning. My scream shattered the stillness, raw and unfiltered.

*Wake up. Please wake up.*

But I couldn't. The vision held me fast. Too vivid. Too real.

"Walk back through the door, Tess," Madame Lynette said softly, her voice steady, always in control.

The door in my mind glowed blue. I opened my eyes.

I woke with a gasp, the scream still caught in my throat.

Every inch of me felt hollowed out, drained, as if something had pulled a thread of my soul through a gauntlet of shadows. My limbs were heavy, useless. My skin clung too tight to a body that didn't quite feel like mine.

Pain bloomed in strange places—my back, my ribs—as though I'd been struck or pierced in a battle I hadn't fought. Not in this life.

I reached for my side instinctively, expecting blood. But there was nothing. No wound, no bruise. Just the ache, sharp and ghostly, pulsing beneath the surface like a memory embedded in the flesh.

What was happening to me?

"How are you feeling?" she asked.

I told her, my voice shaky. About the battle. The watcher. "I thought these would be peaceful . . . happier visions."

"They vary depending on the intensity of the past life," she said. "We cannot choose where our souls wander. But rest assured, the visions ease with each session."

I nodded slowly, though a sliver of disappointment gripped me. I tried to mask it, but my eye flinched. I couldn't quite shake the feeling of failure.

Maybe I had expected too much. Or maybe I was just afraid the answers would never come.

Still, I clung to the hope that the next session would pierce the veil, that the figure on the hill—so still, so haunting—might finally show me who they were. Maybe then I'd understand why my nights were so restless, why sleep felt more like a descent than a refuge.

Maybe then I'd stop waking with shadows wrapped around my bones.

Small things began to shift.

My voice slipped into strange accents. My handwriting curled into unfamiliar scripts. I hummed songs I didn't know. Sometimes I caught my reflection mouthing things I hadn't spoken aloud.

I pulled away from my friends, retreating behind polite smiles and half-hearted reassurances. Their concern only made it worse—the worried glances, the hesitant offers of help. I couldn't explain why I didn't want to accept their help. They wouldn't understand.

They didn't know. How could they?

The memories—if that was even what they were—came like shards of shattered glass, piercing through the calm with lives I didn't recognize but felt too deeply. Faces, voices, wounds. All of it too vivid to dismiss, too tangled with my own soul to ignore.

I felt unbearably alone. Haunted by things I couldn't name. And no one—not a single person—could understand what it was like to carry so many ghosts inside one's skin.

It happened one evening, after another tense exchange with Marty. Something in me cracked.

I slammed the drawer shut at the ticket window, the sound sharp as a gunshot. I stood so fast the stool toppled behind me. My words came out like shrapnel—accusations flying faster than I could rein them in.

"You micromanage every breath I take. This job—it's a cage. The people I serve feel more alive than I do!"

My voice rose, louder than I realized, echoing off the cold walls of the near-empty terminal. *Give in*, whispered a voice, slithering through my mind like smoke. *Give in.*

For a heartbeat, Marty looked stunned. Then his face iced over.

"That's enough, Tess," he said, flat and cold. "Get your things. Don't bother coming back."

I didn't argue.

I ended up at the café again. My refuge.

Seth was waiting, an americano and croissant before him.

He gestured for me to sit in my usual spot. I did.

"Rough day?" Seth said quietly, voice steady but carrying an edge I couldn't place.

I swallowed hard. "More like a rough week."

Seth nodded. "They say memories are chains. But sometimes they're keys."

"I have to go back."

"To the regression lady?"

"Yes, her. I need to see more."

Seth leaned back, eyes shadowed. "Be careful what doors you open, Tess. Not all memories want to be found . . . and some doors are opened not to heal, but to bind." He said it like someone who'd done it. Like someone who'd watched it work.

I gave him a tired smile. "Perhaps *you* need to get some sleep, Seth."

He tilted his head and chuckled. "Oh, Tess, sleep is a luxury I abandoned long ago to keep the café running for night owls like you."

)●(

The next session held promise. Madame Lynette greeted me as if it had been years, not days, since we last met. Her voice was warm, rehearsed, almost theatrical, like she already knew what I would see.

I sank into the recliner, its cushions soft as velvet dusk, and closed my eyes. My breath slowed. Her words washed over me like summer rain.

"The door, Tess. Walk toward it. The first one you see."

In the quiet of my mind, I stepped forward. A pale-green door appeared, faintly pulsing like it was alive, like it had been waiting for me. It creaked open on its own.

And then I was there.

*Victorian London.* The air heavy with soot and judgment. I wore a corset and lace, a cage of propriety pressed to my ribs. I was a poet, though no one dared call me that aloud. My verses burned with revolution, with forbidden love and secrets scrawled in hurried ink.

But secrets never stay secrets for long.

He was once an admirer—my patron, my confidant. But admiration curdled into fear. He found the letters. The manifestos. The poems that carried too much of my truth.

They burned my words.

Then they burned my name.

When scandal whispered too loudly, my lover chose safety over truth. He signed the papers.

The asylum was gray stone and cold stares. And in the corners of my room, a shadow watched silently, day after day, as I faded away.

My voice was smothered before the world ever had the chance to hear it.

I opened my eyes without meaning to. Silent tears traced salty lines down my cheeks.

"Well," Madame Lynette asked, her eyes alight, "what did you see? How did you feel?"

I swallowed hard, the grief still thick in my throat. "Sorrow. Emptiness. Betrayal. I was in . . . Victorian times. And I saw a figure—same as in the first session."

Her tone sharpened: "A figure, you say?"

"Yes. But I couldn't make them out."

She smiled faintly, something unreadable in her eyes. "Fascinating. What say you come back tomorrow evening?"

I didn't even hesitate. "Yes," I said. "I will."

The sessions stopped feeling like therapy. They became rituals. Hypnotic. Possessive. Each descent into memory wrapped itself around me, pulled tighter. I was obsessed—and I could no longer resist.

In the Dark Ages, I was a healer, moving through shadows with quiet hands and ancient remedies. I whispered the names of plants like prayers, mixing cures passed down through bloodlines. But fear ruled the land, and mercy was often mistaken for magic. When a child recovered under my care, the whispers began.

Witch. Heretic. Unwanted.

The accusations came swiftly. I was dragged to the town square, surrounded by flames and frenzy. As the fire climbed toward me, I saw him again—the figure cloaked in smoke. Standing still in the crowd, whispering something I couldn't understand. His words curled into the air like ash.

Then everything burned.

In another life, I wandered the streets of Renaissance Florence. An artist, known by name but not by heart. My hands gave the world beauty with oil and canvas, light and shadow. But my soul? It remained restless. Lonely. I would sit in quiet corners of the city, sketching the things I couldn't bring myself to say aloud. And always, in the edges of my paintings . . . a figure. Watching.

I never had time to look closer. Another life would pull me under before I could understand.

Once, I was a psychiatrist—logical, practiced, searching for order in disorder. Maybe I thought if I could understand the minds of others, I could finally understand my own.

I remember one patient in particular. They sat across from me week after week, face half hidden behind a silk scarf. Their voice was soft, fractured, like something broken inside had learned how to speak.

They spoke of lost love, of wounds that refused to close, of a loneliness so vast it seemed to drain the warmth from the room.

Then one day, mid-sentence, they stopped. Went still.

Not looking at me. Looking past me.

I turned slowly. Nothing was there.

"He's here," the patient whispered. Their hands trembled in their lap. "He follows you through every life."

"Who?" I asked, a tremor of fear in my voice.

Their gaze didn't shift. "The one in the dark cloak. The one who watches you now."

A chill slid down my spine like ice melting under skin.

I turned again. Still nothing.

But I *felt* it—that creeping sensation, like fingers brushing just above the surface of my soul.

And still, I kept returning.

Tonight, I didn't wake.

I was stuck in the trance, caught between lifetimes, the edges of my mind thinning like mist.

Madame Lynette's voice floated to me, soft and coaxing, her whispers threading into the pendant pressed to her chest. She knew. I was close. So close to understanding what I wasn't meant to remember.

And somewhere in the shadows, he was waiting.

Each regression left me breathless, my body trembling and drenched in sweat. I could feel the scars of past lives aching beneath my skin. I was unraveling, and I couldn't stop.

But I tried to stop. Just once. I skipped a session. Walked past her shop. Avoided the café. For a day. Just one day.

And that night, I dreamed of drowning. In ink. In fire. In stone.

Her voice in my ear—*You don't get to walk away, Tess.*

The final regression began in silence.

I opened my eyes to candlelight flickering across stone walls, the scent of old incense and wilted roses thick in the air. Ivory silk clung to my body, and distant bells tolled from a tower hidden by fog. My heart pounded, not with joy, but with dread.

I stood alone in the sacred hall of an ancient abbey—once grand, now hollowed by time. Crumbling pews lined the nave, and the altar stood bare. My reflection flickered in the stained glass like a ghost.

He never came.

At first, they whispered concern. Then the whispers soured into scandal. Eventually, even the whispers faded. The guests were gone. The light waned. And still, I waited—my wedding gown grayed by dust, my veil trailing behind me like smoke.

I wandered the cold corridors as night swallowed the abbey. Each echo beneath my heels felt like a heartbeat buried in stone. The wind through the archways spoke with too many voices. Not mine. Not from this life. From every one before.

Then, I found it.

A forgotten chamber hidden behind an iron-framed door cracked just enough to invite me in.

The moon poured in, filling the room with silver and an eerie stillness.

Inside, a man knelt beside a bed, his shoulders trembling with silent grief.

He wore the cloak.

My breath caught.

My betrothed.

But his pain wasn't for me.

On the bed lay a woman, deathlike in stillness. Her black hair spilled over the pillow like ink across a page. With her eyes closed and her lips parted, she looked timeless and worshipped.

He gripped her hand like a prayer.

"I will find you," he whispered. "Across time. Across flesh. Whatever the cost. Whatever the life. Whatever dark magic I can find."

My pulse surged. I couldn't move. My soul recognized what my mind had not yet accepted.

The battlefield.

The asylum.

The paintings.

The fire.

The voices.

The shadow had always been him.

He turned to me slowly, his eyes calm and known to me.

"You've finally made it," he said.

My voice cracked. "Seth?"

He nodded, just once.

I looked again at the bed. The sleeping form. No . . . not sleeping.

Madame Lynette lay dying, slowly emptying of her essence, as if her soul had already begun to depart. I couldn't breathe.

"I don't understand."

Seth rose from her bedside. "Past lives aren't linear, Tess. They fold. They're intertwined. I needed the right moment to align. This one was just right."

He glanced at Lynette. There was something manic in his calm. A devotion sharp enough to bleed.

"You have to understand, Tess, her physical vessel is at its end. Her body is failing. But I found her in the present . . . just too late. She needs a new vessel," he said softly.

"Most people, when they die, that's it. The physical body decays, giving life back to the soil. Our souls move on to other lifetimes with no memory of the past. Some are cursed, bound to this world as restless spirits—lives severed before their time, doomed to drift forever in the cold embrace of darkness.

"But we . . . I . . . found a way to keep both her memories and her physical self."

"The memento mori," I say under my breath.

Seth continued. "When her vessel began to fail—when it could no longer hold her—I found those with hollow souls. Souls that could hold space, just enough for her essence to fill."

His voice dropped further with desperation. "And now . . . the body can't hold her anymore. This is the last time. If she dies now, she won't come back."

I staggered back. My skin tingled with the cold press of something dark, something wrong.

"Why me?" I asked, though I already knew.

"Because your spirit is hollow," he said. "Because you never belonged. You said it yourself. Every life you left too soon. But this time, we prepared you. You were always meant for her."

My knees shook. "And you . . . how is it that you escape death's grasp? Living again and again across countless lifetimes?"

"I don't live, Tess. I feed. I survive through the hollow souls, just like Lynette. When a spirit is fractured, empty, or broken—like yours—I can draw from that emptiness. I pull what's left of their energy, their essence, to sustain myself and continue our lives together. It's a parasite's way of living forever."

"The café," I whispered. "The dreams . . . the voices . . ."

Seth smiled. "It was always leading here. Preparations. Everything was aligned. I merely traded one who never lived fully in the present . . . for the one I lost in the past."

And in that moment, I understood.

I had never been the one remembering.

I had been the one *prepared*.

He didn't look at me with malice. No, his eyes held something worse.

Devotion, twisted by time and obsession. The same obsession that had led me here.

"Poor Tess," he said, almost mournfully. "You were never meant to stay."

I tried to wake.

Panic took hold. I reached for consciousness like a drowning woman reaches for the surface.

But it was too late.

In the bed within the chamber, Madame Lynette awoke.

Her eyes opened slowly, gleaming with life. Vividly green eyes, terrifyingly awake.

She looked straight at me. Through me.

"Walk through the door, Tess," she whispered.

And the world shattered.

I felt it—my soul torn from its place, dragged into something smaller, weaker . . . dying.

I gasped and found myself in the present. The scent of lavender lingered, sweet at first, but beneath it, the bitter trace of decay, like flowers lying too long on a grave.

I looked down. I was in *her* body. Madame Lynette's.

Her skin, now my skin, was papery and pale. I could feel the lifetimes in my bones, the nearness of the end pressing against every cell.

Across the room, my body—*Tess*—stood still. Then, it moved with the elegance of Madame Lynette.

Madame Lynette—now in *me*—rose from the recliner with serene certainty. She crossed the floor and stood over me, her old shell. *My* new prison.

She smiled. The kind of smile that had no warmth in it.

Then she reached down and tore the glowing pendant from around my neck—my now fragile and failing neck.

"Tess," she purred, "this was never meant for you."

Her eyes—*my* eyes—now green, glittered with cruel light. "In all your lifetimes, you were wedded to sorrow. You never let joy in, never learned how to love. Even when love came calling, you didn't fight for yourself. You simply . . . faded. Lifetime after lifetime, my true love fought to keep me alive. And you—you made it easy. A soul so hollow, so weary of living. Why waste a vessel on someone who never truly inhabited it?"

I tried to scream, to speak, to beg, but my lips barely parted. My vision blurred.

And Madame Lynette, wearing me like a dress she'd waited centuries to claim, turned and walked away without a backward glance.

In that moment, bound in a dying vessel never meant for me, I exhaled my last breath.

And was gone from the present. But not entirely.

At the café, I watched helplessly—trapped somewhere deep inside the realm of darkness—while Madame Lynette, wearing my body like a second skin, sat beside Seth at the counter. They spoke in low, gleeful tones, savoring their victory. My victory . . . stolen.

The bell above the door chimed.

"A new customer!" Madame Lynette chirped, her voice chipper and bright. My voice. God, it sounded wrong coming from her.

They both turned. I turned with them, though I didn't know how. And that was when I saw her.

She was already seated. A woman in a black dress. She sat in *my* seat. The one I always chose. The one that still held the warmth of memories I feared were slipping away.

"I'll have a hot chocolate mocha," she said, making an effort to smile, "and a croissant." The tone of her voice was shrouded with sadness—another helpless, hollowed soul wandering in a vessel of flesh and bones.

Madame Lynette tilted her head slightly, locking eyes with *me*. Then she smirked and whispered, "Walk through the door . . ."

And in that moment, I felt it.

A shift.

A pull.

The air grew cold.

And somewhere behind me, a purple door creaked open—a door that hadn't existed a second before.

# About the Author

**Grace Silva-Ortiz** is a fiction and poetry writer born in Puerto Rico and raised in Orlando. Her work explores themes of identity, the metaphysical, and self-awareness. Her poem "Femininity in the Infinity" won second prize in the International Planetary Society's Pages of Stars 2022 contest. She is also the author of the self-published collection *Black Dream State*, a surreal journey through the subconscious. When not writing, Grace can be found in creepy bookstores, cemeteries, or gazing at the stars—always with the next story in mind.

You can follow Grace on Instagram at:
@grace_silvaortiz_author

To learn more about Grace, visit her website at:
bio.site/gracesilvaortizauthor

# Of
# Sound
# Mind

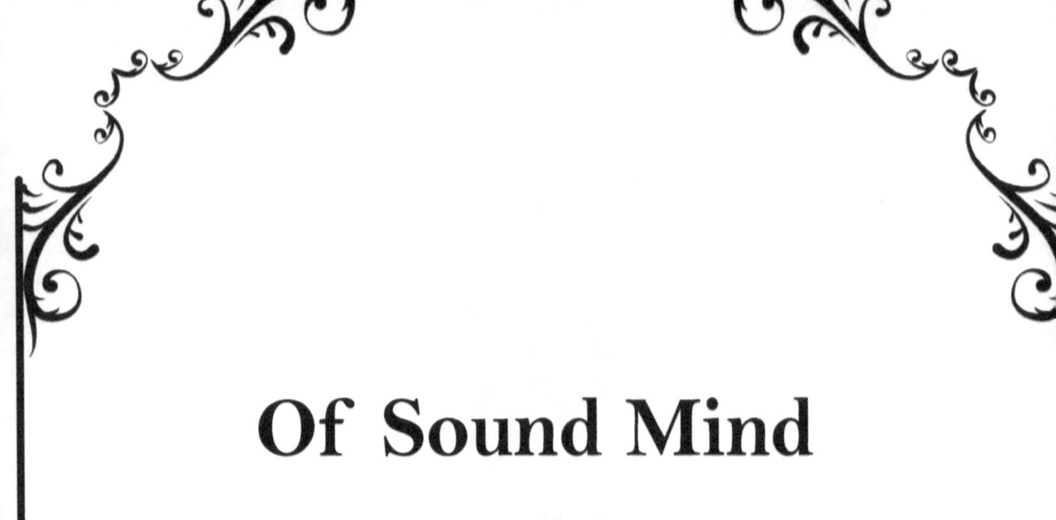

# Of Sound Mind

## Caroline Baccene

THERE ARE MANY TERRIBLE THINGS about being human. I can name quite a few off the top of my head. But the one that stands out to me as I stalk down this dimly lit hallway is the ability to hear. The pounding of my heavy, booted footsteps against the wooden floor are evenly spaced and echo throughout the corridor. My heart pitifully pitter-pattering, as if it may just decide to stop right here and now. My breaths come out quickly, much too fast and loud in my ears. And then there's the dripping on the other side of this door.

*Drip.* I take that last step and pause in front of the plain, brown door.

*Drop.* My hand, no longer trembling, grips the cool metal of the doorknob.

*Drip.* Exhaling once more, I briefly close my eyes and prepare myself for what will be.

*Drop.* Opening my eyes and twisting the knob simultaneously, I swing the door open with force. A loud bang sounds as it rebounds against the inside wall and almost slams shut again.

For a moment, there's red everywhere. But then, just as quickly, my vision clears and the dilapidated bathroom is just what anyone else would expect to see. Disgusting, broken tiles, half a ceramic toilet bowl, a missing sink, and the remains of a shower. *Drip. Drop. Drip. Drop.*

Rushing to the faucet of what used to be a shower, I twist the knob as hard as I can. To my dismay, it doesn't move, and the sound continues as water droplets fall. Knowing it's a lost cause, I sigh in frustration—and then hope no one is around to hear me, as a sigh is a clear sign of the emotions I'm not supposed to have—before leaving the room and the annoying faucet.

With the last moving box in my grasp, I exit my childhood home, but instead of feeling relieved to be free of the place finally, there's only despair, which makes no sense. That dilapidated building was my home only in the most fundamental way. It was the place I laid my head most nights as a young boy, but other than that, it doesn't elicit feelings of what I imagine homes should. Although, how would I know, honestly?

As my rusty, dirty vehicle takes me to the new location I'll soon call home, I'm lost in memories of the old house. Well, the old house and my mother. Mrs. Dorothy was her name, and Mrs. Dorothy was what I called her. As a boy, when I'd mistakenly refer to her as Mom, she'd punish me. I can still feel the sting of cold water in the clawfoot bathtub as I sat in there, alone, crying and trembling, for what must have been hours, waiting for Mrs. Dorothy's return. I'd stare at that wooden door, listening for her footsteps but only hearing the dripping of the faucet and the occasional rain pelting the roof or thunder outside if a storm was near.

Shaking off those horrid memories, I now hear the cicadas outside the car windows, and they remind me of those long-ago nights sitting near my open bedroom window. Since we didn't have air-conditioning, the windows were always open, and I learned quickly when the sun went down to turn off the lights or my room would be bombarded with life of all kinds: moths, mosquitos, even the occasional bird, all drawn to the lonely lightbulb in my ceiling, as if it were a beacon calling them to me.

The headlights of my car shine on a blur in the road, too close for me to do anything but gasp before a crunching sound interrupts the quiet night. Knowing the wilderness out here like the back of my freckled hand, I count off the things that are as big as what I seem to have just crushed with my vehicle. It's rare to see a bear out here, but it was definitely not a deer. I've never seen a bobcat, but surely, they aren't this big.

The night is foggy and, with it being a new moon, almost pitch-black but for the shine of my headlights. My eyes take a moment to adjust as I get out of my car, and when they finally do, there's nothing in the abandoned road. No dead or injured animal. No blood or fur. If it weren't for my tire marks from skidding to a stop, there'd be no evidence of anything having happened moments ago. In fact, I'd claim I imagined the animal if not for the small dent on the front bumper of my car. Maybe that had been there already, though. I'm not known to be the best driver.

The chill in the air makes me shiver, so I tighten my jacket around me and make my way back to my car, keeping my head on a swivel in case one of the beasts indeed found me. Once I'm settled in and buckled, I exhale as I glance at my knife in the passenger seat, then turn the heater on full blast and will away the goosebumps that have appeared all over my too-skinny body. Another unfortunate side effect of humans; it's outrageously obvious when one is emotional in any way. I might as well hold up a sign for all to see that says, "I am spooked."

Dismissing the idea with a chuckle, I shift the car's gears from park to drive and quickly leave the empty road, checking in my rearview mirror as if the unknown animal will pop up and chase me, demanding vengeance. As I take extra side roads and many perplexing roundabouts, the tension in my back eases. If someone or something were pursuing me, which most would think is a ridiculous thought anyway, no one or nothing would be able to follow my confusing path.

My new home is very different from the one I just left, made obvious from its overly bright white walls, recently installed gray hardwood floors, and pesky neighbors on both sides, as well as behind and across the street. The house is new and clean, untouched by the violence from my past and present activities. But the most important way it differs from my previous home is in its safety. After all, who would suspect me to live in a place like this, surrounded by people during the day as I spend my nights hunting those who constantly threaten and pursue me? Anonymity is always the safest way of life. If the new house is a newborn kitten, my old one is a twenty-eight-year-old anaconda, or whatever the exact opposite would be. Some might say a dog, but those are both domesticated mammals, and my two houses wouldn't even be considered the same vertebrate groups.

Tonight's activities have obviously muddled my brain, as my thoughts don't seem to be making much sense, so instead of unpacking or even turning on the lights, I go straight to the bathroom. These faucets don't drip. In fact, the water comes out of the showerhead with such velocity, it almost makes me shriek. The cold water hits my head, rinsing all the grime and other fluids down the drain, but my suffering only lasts a few moments before the water heats, practically scolding me, which is preferrable. While standing under the spray, eventually I remove my clothes, knowing I'll need to burn these. This brings another sigh, but it's masked by the sounds of the shower, so no one would hear it. If I were a wealthy man, the cost of clothes from the local thrift store wouldn't make me blink. Since I am not, it makes me want to weep. Instead, I finish cleaning up and fall into bed, which is currently a sleeping bag rolled out in the living room.

Thunder wakes me from a pleasant dream, even though some might find fighting through a mass of zombies as they eat you alive disturbing. Either way, I'm awake when lightning flashes through the window, briefly lighting my surroundings. With the unpacked boxes strewn about, it's a bit more startling than it should be. Lying back down, I try to breathe deeply, spell words, and even count sheep before deciding it's useless and sleep evades me again.

After moving to the kitchen, I find a glass in one of the boxes on the counter and pour myself some water from the sink. Even in the dark, I can see how clear this water is compared to other water that haunts my memories. Another crash of thunder from outside has me peeking through the window above the sink. There's not much to see in my small backyard surrounded by a six-foot privacy fence. When the lightning shows the yard for a moment, I drop the glass in my hand, which makes an even louder noise than the storm as the glass cracks and bursts across the linoleum floor.

Just a flash of movement, but it almost looked like . . .

No, there aren't creatures of the night here. And they wouldn't have found me *here* of all places. Still, even the idea is so abhorrent, I'm tempted to leave and not return. But I have nowhere else to run, so I grab one of my many knives from the box in the living room and open the back door, careful not to step on the shattered glass on the kitchen floor. Breaking my skin, causing the scent of fresh blood to permeate the air, would only make me a bigger target for the ones that want to find me.

Part of me wonders if what I saw was real or just a figment of my under-stimulated, over-exhausted mind. Yet, would my mind make up such intricate details?

Long, tangled hair and tearstains over too-pale cheeks.

Scrawny arms with elongated nails.

Bony, dirt-covered knees and calves.

And, surely, I couldn't make up its eyes. Bright and dark at the same time, knowing and wondering, and vicious to the core.

The rain is coming down in huge sheets, instantly flooding the earth with cold, dirty water, which will probably keep me in bed with illness for the next few days. This is something I'm familiar with at this point in my life. If someone had told me I'd be living in the suburbs, still hunting the creatures that haunt me, I'd laugh in their face before driving the tip of my blade across their soft skin.

The wind whips strands of hair across my face as the rain darkens it a few shades, no longer the golden honey-blond I've grown accustomed to seeing in the mirror the past few decades and instead a dark brown that could be mistaken for black in the dim light. It's a fine color but not nearly as breathtaking. But making myself attractive bait doesn't matter at the moment, so I don't bother worrying more about my hair as I search my yard for that *thing* my eyes saw but my brain says I imagined.

After an immeasurable amount of time, the storm passes and the rain slows, and I give up and go back inside, not bothering to wipe my feet or dry off before I sink back into a reluctant slumber.

*"Please."*

*Doesn't this creature know there's nothing it could say that would make me release it into the wild again? There are no words it could utter through its trembling lips, no acting it could perform that would halt my actions. I've seen it too many times since hunting became a regular thing for me in my teenage years: They always beg. They always plead. Even though we both know they will be hunting innocent humans if they ever find an escape. So, without meeting its tear-filled eyes, I move closer to do what I always do. To hunt the hunter.*

☽ ● ☾

A pounding knock on my door wakes me from my pleasant dream, and I'm wondering if I'll ever be destined to actually get a full night's sleep again. Although, based on the light coming through my blinds, it's no longer a reasonable hour to be asleep. Sighing, I run my hands through my shaggy hair, ignoring the dirt under my short fingernails. Maybe there's some tweezers somewhere I could use to pick them clean, possibly in one of the purses in the basement.

Another loud series of knocks draws my attention back to what woke me in the first place, so with a silent groan, I heave myself to my feet and walk to the door. There's no need to fear the beasts right now, as they only hunt me at night, so I leave my weapons where they are.

The pounding continues until I twist the knob, but then it's silent on the other side. That is, until the door is shoved open and a loud voice practically shouts at me, saying my name and telling me things about remaining silent and lawyers and other words that don't make sense. I'd think I was still dreaming, since this is a nightmare I'm familiar with, if it weren't for the pressure on my arms and metal handcuffs pressing so tightly to my wrists that I know they'll leave a mark. They always do in my dreams. But this pressure, this awful metal digging into me, has never been in my dreams.

The drive takes only a few minutes, and then I'm pulled from my semi-comfortable position in the back seat and brought into a room. This room I haven't imagined before, even though it seems obvious to me now that I should have. The walls are stark, bare, and depressing as they fit together to form a rectangle. There's one large mirror, obviously where others watch me from the other side, as if I'm an animal at the zoo. Or maybe that's even too generous. Maybe a goldfish in a bowl, empty of everything but water. There is a small, metal table and I'd be surprised to see three chairs if this were an emotion I were capable of feeling. However, the number of chairs makes sense once I'm seated and two others sit across from me. Are they police officers? Detectives? Maybe something higher up, probably used to covering up things for the government. My first guess would be the CIA, but maybe that's not even high enough. Now my mind wanders, trying to figure out what is more powerful and classified than the CIA.

No one says anything for a long time. My eyes are drawn to the reflective mirror behind them, and I can almost hear the gears of a camcorder on the other side as it films my face, studying me, trying to find out all my secrets.

Someone clearing their throat distracts me. It's one of the government officials. He's older than the other. Probably more experienced, although I doubt, based on his physical attributes, that he's taken down any of the beasts I hunt regularly—at least, not in recent years. He asks me irrelevant questions, things he knows. Maybe to build a rapport that I will not agree to. Maybe to see if I'll lie to him. They know my name. They know my date of birth. They know my address. I will not have idle chit-chat with these people.

Keeping my mouth closed, eyes open, and hands on the table, I continue my examination of a speck of dust as it floats in front of me.

The other, younger man in the room doesn't say anything. He has a notebook and pen, but he doesn't write anything. I can feel his eyes on me, and I don't like it. Both of them watch me too closely, as if they know more than just those simple questions. Maybe they know more than they should. The older man's voice breaks through my thoughts, and I wish I'd been paying attention to his words.

"...in your basement?"

Of course they went into my basement. By now, they've been through my entire house, as well as my childhood home. They've found the evidence. How long will it take them to examine the bodies and realize what I've done? Will they ask me to join their specialized intelligence team that hunts the creatures, or will they force me against my will? Or maybe they already know what the bodies are. Maybe that's why the younger one across the table is staring at me like he is. As I meet his eyes, I'm sure of it, in fact. He knows what I do. He wants me to tell him, so they have a confession to take to their bosses and then I won't be able to deny any of this. Then they will own me, take away my free will, make me do their bidding.

My mouth refuses to open, so the man who's been talking the entire time sighs. "We just want to know why, son. There's no denying you murdered all those women. There's more than enough evidence. Just tell us why, so we can understand your side of things."

*Son.* If he were my father, my life would have turned out vastly differently. I would have had a happy childhood probably, but that means I wouldn't have ever learned to catch and destroy the evil things that must be obliterated from the earth.

Although . . . something about his words doesn't sit right with me. Women? He's referring to the beasts I hunt as *women.* So, he doesn't know what they are yet. I meet his eyes, and that's when I see it. There's a gleam, almost unnoticeable if it weren't for the light right above us, hitting him at just the right angle. He knows exactly what these "women" he speaks of are, and yet . . . he's pretending he doesn't.

This is their strategy then. They won't get me to join them. No, they will incarcerate me for heinous crimes that no judge or jury would ever forgive. They will make me rot away for the rest of my life unless I divulge all my secrets. Or maybe they don't even want information. Could I be that much of a threat to them or their secrecy that they'd get rid of me just because they can? Or have the creatures of the night infiltrated here, as well? It's daytime, so this man can't be one of *them.* But he can be bribed or threatened by them, convinced to do away with me and anyone else out there who risks their livelihoods.

My fists tighten into balls, and I don't try to fight it. There's no point in doing anything, not trapped how I am. So, I just meet his knowing stare with a defiant one of my own. He may have the power now, but this doesn't mean I will crawl into a ball and cry my eyes out or confess to things I did not do.

He must see the decision on my face, because he exhales and leans back, shaking his head, as if he's disappointed in me. But this is all for the witnesses and the camera in the hidden room. He's happy I'm not denying anything. He's happy I'm not giving up my secrets. The longer our staring contest continues, the surer I am that he may not be one of them, but he's evil just the same.

Time passes. Words might be spoken, but not by me. Never again by me. Not to them. Then I'm led away. As I glance behind me into the room just before the officer pulls me out, I meet his stare again. Just once. He smiles slightly at me. A knowing smile. If I had my knives, I could stop that smile. Since I don't, I just return his with one of my own as I imagine things that are much too graphic for a story like this.

# About the Author

**Caroline Baccene** is the author of the novels *Breathing in the Fog* and *A Beautiful Lily*, as well as the short stories "The Charred Grape," "When You Know, You Know," and "Of Sound Mind." Caroline grew up in the middle of nowhere, South Carolina, where she developed a love of reading, writing, acting, gardening, and caring for all types of animals. She graduated from the University of South Carolina with a degree in Early Childhood Education and was a teacher for five years. She currently resides in South Carolina with her husband and son.

You can follow Caroline on Instagram at:
@caroline_baccene

To learn more about Caroline, visit her website at:
carolinebaccene.com

# Remember Us

# Remember Us

## Meranda Tuttle

MY FINGERS FLEW OVER THE keys of the typewriter. The tapping echoed like lightning throughout the room. I wanted to cover my ears, but I couldn't stop.

I felt their eyes on me from across the room. Hollow voids that would suck you in if you looked. I didn't dare turn my head. They stayed where they were as long as my fingers moved. At the sign of the slightest slowing, they became restless. If I stopped completely, a foot would slowly drag across the floor, the boards beneath their feet creaking as they shifted their weight.

There was no stopping. I had to keep them at bay.

**Before**

The sun was bright as they maneuvered up the hill in their tiny car. I stood in the belfry, bell long since removed, clapping my hands in anticipation. A phantom chime of the old bell rang in my mind. It'd been a year or more since the last visitors, and I was really excited.

Constantly involved in my writing, I didn't always pay attention to the people around me, but sometimes I did crave company. It had been long enough that I didn't only crave it, I needed it.

As they pulled into the circular driveway, navigating around the dry fountain, I left the belfry and nearly ran at breakneck speed down the stairs, across the kitchen, through the hallway, and up the stairs of the grand staircase. I wanted to be looking down at them regally when they entered to make an impression.

The door opened just as I made it to the top. Plush, dark-red carpet ran down the stairs and led to the door. Old, decorative, golden rods spanned the back of each stair, keeping the carpet firmly in place.

Hilde, the old caretaker, stood to one side of the staircase. She waited patiently as the dark mahogany door opened on silent hinges. I, on the other hand, bounced on my toes up until the moment the children walked in. Then, I stilled myself.

The visitors were what I considered a modern family. Two preteens, a boy and a girl, wearing jeans and T-shirts. Their parents trailed behind them, looking tired. All were thin and tall. The preteens looked around curiously, but no one looked at me as I stood demurely at the top of the stairs. I couldn't blame them.

"Welcome!" I called out at the same moment the door behind them swung shut with a bang.

No one had been expecting it, and we all jumped. The parents stood dumbly, staring at the door. The children huddled closer together. Hilde, more used to the quirks of the mansion, having been here forever, recovered first and cleared her throat.

The boy leaned over to the girl and said in a loud whisper that everyone could hear, "This place is haunted."

He ignored a disapproving look from his parents, which held no weight since they seemed inclined to agree.

Hilde spoke up in her monotone, addressing the boy's comment. "The place is cursed. If you die here, you stay here."

The children looked alarmed, and the parents started to chuckle until the seriousness on Hilde's face caused them to stop awkwardly.

"Welcome. May I show you to your rooms?" Hilde greeted them, ever the no-nonsense person. "Then we can have drinks, and the cook made cookies, though dinner won't be too far away with the late hour. We expected you sooner."

"That sounds wonderful. Lead the way," the mother said as she tried to herd everyone toward Hilde.

Hilde turned and went down the hallway she'd stood in front of, the parents quickly following with their bags and backpacks. The children continued to stand, surveying the room. Their eyes stopped on me for a minute, but the sun was to my back, and I must have been a dark silhouette to them. They didn't return my tentative wave.

Instead, as I stared back, it looked as if their eyes vanished, and nothing but a black void was where each eye should be. I was transfixed.

"Lewis! Mae! Hurry up!" The impatient voice of their mother sounded down the hall.

Lewis took off first, but Mae lingered, staring up the grand staircase. The stained-glass image behind me was quite exquisite, a forest scene of a hunter shooting a noble deer, each leaf picked out in clear detail. But I felt like she wasn't looking at the stained glass or me. Frowning, I turned around as a shadow retreated up the stairs. I felt a cold chill down my back as I watched it vanish. Worried about Mae, I quickly looked back but she was gone, having finally followed her family down the hallway.

With a shaking hand on the banister, I went searching for the shadow's owner. I steeled myself; no one here should scare me.

Despite searching around for a while, I never found anyone and put it from my mind, judging it a trick of the light. Eventually I returned to my room to get some writing done. I'd try to meet the family again at dinner.

I woke with a start, drool dangling from my mouth and pooling on my typewriter. The moon was up and the lights were out. I could just see the nonsense word that had been pressed into the paper when my head had hit the keys. I hadn't realized how sleepy I was.

A noise behind me had me turning. Mae stood by the door in green pajamas with a stuffed pig gripped in her hands. Fear emanated from her wide eyes.

"Hey there," I started, but she took a step back and I spoke quicker, trying to make my voice soothing. "You won't get in trouble; I don't mind if you explore. I really should be in bed. I'm sorry I missed you at dinner. We haven't been properly introduced yet—"

And this was not the time for introductions; she took off at a run. I sprang up and almost fell to the ground, lightheaded for a moment. The room looked off. Empty and dark. Where was all my stuff?

Just as I felt like I'd hit the floor, the world righted itself. My bed sat to one side under a window; a wardrobe nearby held my clothes. A plush carpet lay underfoot. A lamp by the table with my typewriter would cast a yellow light over my workspace if turned on. I shook my head and headed for the door.

Peering down the hallway, I didn't even hear Mae's footsteps. She was silent as a ghost. I liked that thought and immediately turned back to my typewriter to get my thoughts down about ghostly children. The door remained open, and I didn't bother with any light. I wrote by the full moon's rays.

It didn't take long to type down my thoughts, and my hands stilled on the keys. A shuffling noise sounded as if it came from the bottom of the stairs. I turned, wondering if it was Mae again, but I saw a shadow, a darker outline against the night, a shade. I blinked several times, and it was gone. Frowning, I stood again and made my way to the bed. I must need to sleep. Sleep and a good breakfast. That would put me right.

As I drifted off, I heard a noise, but I was too tired to open my eyes. Instead, I plunged into a dreamless sleep.

The room was gray when I woke to the sound of children playing outside. I rubbed at my eyes, trying to clear my vision. As I looked toward the window across from my desk, the sun was bright and sunny, but it was like the light didn't reach into the room. A filter had been set.

It was near lunch. I had missed breakfast, but I didn't feel hungry, just confused. I couldn't lift my heavy body, as if I were in the ground, struggling to breathe. At that thought, color flooded back, and I popped up to sit, panting.

Within a few minutes, I calmed, but stared wide-eyed around the room, wondering what had happened.

The shrieking of a child caught my attention, and I lurched over to the window and looked out.

Lewis and Mae were running back and forth in the garden. The shrieking apparently had come when their dad turned on the sprinklers without warning. Black spouts emerged from the ground and started to soak everything. They were turning on and off, much to the children's delight, as their father laughed in an ominously low tone.

Relieved that the children were safe, I left the room to go to the kitchen. In the hallway, the scent of grilling reached me. I couldn't remember the last time the grill had been used, and I walked a little faster.

No one was in the kitchen when I arrived, but on the patio visible through the side door, chafing dishes had been set up to keep hot dogs and hamburgers warm, with all the condiments a person could want laid out around them. My mouth watered, but I felt I hadn't been properly welcoming yet.

Instead of eating, I set about making chocolate chip cookies while I listened to the sounds of joy outside. My mind wandered as I mixed sugar and butter. I slowly added other ingredients, creating a dough that I ate off my fingers in giant gobs. No one bothered me as I preheated the oven. It was an oddly empty day.

I mused over where Chef had gone. What Hilde was up to. What those two shadows I had seen were. I frowned as the last thought crossed my mind.

The timer beeped, and I brought out trays of cookies from the massive ovens, moving them over to the cooling racks. Snagging a loaf of bread, I left the kitchen. An idea for a story had just occurred to me, and I needed to get it down.

Lost in typing, I hadn't noticed the sun had gone down until I paused for a moment. The moon was full and the only light in my room. I blinked at it owlishly, trying to bring myself out of the world of my new story.

The floorboards creaked, and I turned to look at Mae, instinctively knowing it would be her. She seemed inquisitive. More so than her brother. I gave her a warm smile.

She didn't look at me, her eyes traveling around the room.

"They told me not to come here," she said softly, and I wasn't sure if she was talking to me or the stuffed pig she carried. "Someone died here."

"Don't pay any attention to them. I like company from time to time. What's keeping you up?" I kept my voice bright and sunny.

Her eyes darted to me immediately, and then everything about her face changed. Her eyes became voids, her skin sallow and vacant. I felt drawn to her as if I'd be swallowed whole. I almost stood up.

"Don't forget about us." An almost alien voice came from her mouth, and then she ran away.

For the second time that night, I was left blinking. A noise came from the hallway, close to the top of the stairs. A heavy shuffle that slowly rolled across the floor. Then, a thud. I frowned but felt a heavy weight in my heart that kept me where I was. I didn't want to know what the noise had been.

Instead, I turned back to my typewriter and continued the story I had started. Immersing myself once again and drowning out any noise behind me with the sound of my clacking keys.

My ideas didn't slow until the sun came up. My fingers felt tired as I lifted them from the keys and then turned to look at the door. Nothing was there.

I yawned wide and stumbled over to the bed, where I slept until I woke in the evening. I could just hear the sounds of voices, silverware scraping on plates, laughter. It sounded welcoming to me. Maybe I could use some time with people.

I got out of bed, walked down the hallway to the stairs, and turned past the kitchen toward the dining room. Before I got there, the laughter and jovial voices changed to anger, slowly rising in volume. My footsteps slowed. I frowned, concerned.

A chair dragged against the floor, followed by clattering silverware being tossed on the table. Then heavy footsteps retreating.

A second chair pushed back before soft footsteps retreated.

Turning the corner, I looked into the dining room. The children sat rigid in their seats, terrified their parents would return to yell some more. The remains of a roast with corn on the cob and mashed potatoes were still spread across the table. Plates of mostly consumed food sat in front of the chairs.

Mae leaned over to Lewis and whispered something to him. He nodded once. I watched from where I stood, just out of view. It felt like a private moment, but I was hungry, and I'd come all the way down.

They pushed back their chairs and quietly withdrew to the back doorway out of the dining room. Neither turned to look at me. I didn't try to stop them. Their sorrow hung heavy in the air, and I felt embarrassed for having viewed even a little of it.

I took my time, not immediately wanting to return upstairs, and half hoping someone would come back to get the untouched dessert, which looked like butterscotch pudding parfaits.

No one returned, and I eventually retired to my room for more writing.

My fingers touched the keys of my typewriter just as the sun slipped below the horizon, a full moon rising in its place.

Typing didn't come as easily tonight. I felt tapped, used up. But any time I stopped typing, a slow shuffle scraped across the floor down the hallway and I started again, using the keys to drive away the noise.

The next day I found myself in the empty belfry again. I'd always loved the view. The wind whipped by my ears, and if I strained, I felt like I could hear the bell tolling.

With my eyes closed, I heard the clapper creak back and forth. The distant sounds of the family playing. A strong gust of wind took me by surprise, and I had to take a step back to steady myself. The bell let out a loud gong, and the family went silent.

I opened my eyes, confused. There was no bell. I looked down and could just see the family's faces staring up. They didn't look right. Hollow black voids. I squinted down, trying to make out features.

Another, stronger gust of wind pushed me back, and I tried to keep my feet. The bell might be gone, but the long, empty passage to the ground was still there. Suddenly, my back pressed flat against a metal curve and I couldn't move. My heart pounded a mile a minute.

The wind died down, and I lurched forward, turning at the same time to look at . . . nothing. There was no bell. All that was left was the ragged, broken wood from where it had fallen many years ago.

I should have fallen.

Hilde should be checking for a pulse. An ambulance should be called. I should not be here.

My heart raced as I looked back out toward the horizon. The family was gone. Storm clouds were gathering, which must be where the wind had come from.

Leaving the belfry, I felt like I could hear the peal of a bell again. I didn't look back, though.

〉●〈

The rain was spitting, the clouds allowing only a few glimpses of the full moon. Lightning streaked across the sky. It was an ominous night. I sat at my typewriter, keeping the noises at bay.

The family's vacation had taken a turn for the worse. I hadn't left my room this night as I heard raised voices and slamming doors. I didn't want to interfere. Instead, I stayed in my room and typed.

My fingers dashed over the keys, well familiar with the typewriter. I didn't need light. A moving person-shaped blur in the rain caught my eye. My fingers slowed but did not stop as I stared outside.

The blur dropped something and paused but kept going without turning back. Another blur ran by, and then two more. It was the family. Something had happened.

I stopped typing and stood up to see where they were going. A straight line headed to the woods. The shuffling sound was almost to the door, but I didn't care. I had to go help. Something bad was going to happen.

Several shades crowded the hallway, humanoid but stretched thin, shuffling thick feet. Black holes for eyes tried to draw me in, but I had to help the family. I surged forward, crouching low to get by the slow-moving figures. A long hand reached for me, but it moved as if through syrup and never connected as I sped down the hallway.

I came to a stop at one of the side doors that looked out into the woods. I didn't see the family, but I spotted Mae's pink pig lying in the yard, soaked by the rain. I was about to take a step forward when I heard voices.

Changing direction, I followed the voices until I got to the bottom of the belfry. The parents yelled and pointed angrily. Mae was crying, and Lewis was trying to comfort her.

A particularly strong gust of wind hit the house. The bell rang out loudly, but the family ignored it, merely raised their voices over the cacophony, but I still could not hear what they said.

The wind increased. I screamed to be heard, told them to move, but they acted like I was invisible.

Lightning crackled through the air and lit up the yard. A horrible tableau of a family vacation gone wrong.

Lightning hit the belfry, sending sparks and lighting everything up. Giving me the perfect angle to see as the wind pushed too hard and whatever held up the bell broke. There was nothing to hold it up! It shouldn't even be there! It had fallen years ago!

My mouth dried as it seemed to hover for a moment before plummeting through poorly kept up timber. The crashing got louder, but the family heard nothing. I dashed forward, trying to save them. Push them out of the way, drag them somewhere, warn them. I didn't know. Something.

I could do nothing. I passed right through them. Wood rained over us seconds before the bell landed.

I came to myself in my room. Rain was pouring down against a full moon.

The sound of sliding feet was behind me. The shades of those I'd tried to save over the years. Dragging me back to fail over and over again. Cursed to be here forever since my death.

The only thing keeping the shades at bay was my typing and the unmade promise to never forget any of them. I didn't want to be sucked back again.

# About the Author

**Meranda Tuttle** is an aspiring author who works at a library. She enjoys writing flash fiction and novels in many different genres. In her spare time, she pursues too many interests. A few are watching movies with friends, volunteering at local theaters, and trying to build strength through aerials practice.

You can find Meranda on Instagram at:
@merandatuttle

To learn more about Meranda, visit her website at:
https://www.merandatuttle.com/

# Duskwood Hollow

# Duskwood Hollow

## Cora Laine

THE PATH TO 2458 DUSKWOOD Hollow is lined with moss-covered flag-stones, crumbled by time and worn with age. Ivy twists its way up the magnificent stone walls. A fixer-upper, sure—but it screams potential. And finally, after years of negotiating, it's all ours.

"Where would you like this, ma'am?" a tall man in a navy-blue mover's uniform asks, arms shaking, gripping one end of my beloved armoire.

"Master bedroom, please," I tell him, motioning to the top floor.

The men shuffle past, entering through the arched mahogany entryway, and I follow suit, running my hand along the deep grooves etched into the wood as I pass. The stale smell that greeted us during our first showing is finally beginning to fade, slowly giving way to the familiar scents of home—and with them, a calming sense of familiarity. I breathe it in, relishing this moment.

"How about this box, ma'am?" another mover asks.

"Oh, um, looks like master bedroom as well, thanks," I say as my cell phone begins to chirp loudly in my pocket.

"Hello?" I say, fumbling the phone to my ear.

"Hey, baby. How's it going over there?"

I wondered how long it was going to take before Dean checked in.

"It's going," I tell him. "The movers have most of the heavy stuff inside. It's starting to feel like home already." A smile plays across my face, and I can tell Dean senses it.

"That's great, honey. I wish I were there to see it come together. I hate that I'm not there to help."

"Don't worry about it," I reassure him. "We have to pay for this place somehow." I let out a playful laugh, hoping he finds the humor in my joke.

"Yeah, yeah. Just don't go too wild until I get there. I want to enjoy the place's old charm before Renovator Hadley comes in with sledgehammers blazing."

"Very funny. I have visions, Dean. Visions. You know I've had my sights set on this place forever. I—" I stop midsentence as a loud crash from upstairs breaks my train of thought.

"Hadley?"

"Sorry, got to go. I think the movers just broke something. I swear, if that was one of Dad's vintage pieces . . ."

"Easy, tiger. Don't be too hard on them." He laughs.

"Easy for you to say," I quip, rolling my eyes. "You never liked them anyway."

"I like anything you like, my love. Let me know what you find out."

"Love you, bye." I hang up, exasperated, already making my way up the creaking staircase.

The grand hallway is just as magnificent as I remembered it—a high-vaulted ceiling lined with ornate wood-carved trim and an antique crystal chandelier hanging in the center. My hand glides along the banister as I ascend the stairs, taking each one slowly and deliberately.

"Everything okay up here?" I call out, peeking my head through the first open doorway.

When I'm met with no reply, I check the other bedrooms until I arrive at the last door at the end of the hall—the master bedroom.

"Is everything all right in here? I thought I heard something break," I call out. But there's no one in here, either. I walk to the window, the pitted old glass partially obscuring the view below. Several navy-blue blurs scurry in and out of the moving trucks and through the front yard.

The room appears to be empty. Aside from several boxes stacked neatly around the perimeter, everything seems to be in its place. I pull out my phone and quickly type out a message to Dean.

**Nothing broken. Must have come from outside. Come home soon—this place is magnificent.**

As I return to the foyer, I'm thrilled to find the movers have unloaded a fresh batch of boxes from the truck. For the first time in weeks, I lay eyes on my precious belongings—clothes, shoes, handbags, jewelry. It feels surreal to see it all here, safe and sound in this new space, a highly anticipated reward for all the effort it took to get us here.

"Where are we taking this stuff, ma'am?" another man in the same navy uniform asks.

"Upstairs. Master suite, please."

At once, the crew dispatches up the stairs with my belongings in hand. Finally, this place is beginning to feel like home, just like we knew it would.

"Wow, this place is shaping up nicely, isn't it?"

Dean's familiar voice comes from somewhere past the crowd of movers, boxes, and dusty old sheets.

"There you are. Glad you can finally be here to witness the transformation," I say, fanning my hands out with a dramatic flourish.

Dean shakes his head, a half-smile painted on his face. "I'd say we still have to work on that transformation."

I glare at him reprovingly. "What's that supposed to mean?" As if I don't already know.

"I mean, it still looks a bit like a haunted old mansion, doesn't it? You really think buying this old money pit was the right move?"

I shake my head, averting my eyes. If we've had this conversation once, we've had it a million times before.

"I'm sorry, honey. I didn't mean to upset you."

"I just wish that you'd get on board with this move. I mean, why are we even here, doing all this, if you're not fully in it with me? Isn't this what you want, Dean?"

He sighs, scratching the back of his head with one hand, his lips pressed into a hard line. "Yes. This *is* what I want. I want you to be happy. I want this house. I want to raise a family with you in this house—right here, in your family home. And that's exactly what we're going to do. Come here."

He pulls me in, wrapping his arms around me, my head pressed tightly to his chest. We stay there in silence, each of us lost in our own thoughts. I've heard Dean make these declarations more times than I can count, but somehow, he always manages to unravel them himself. Bit by bit, his offhand jabs and furtive glances at his phone chip away at his own story until I'm left wondering how much of it was ever real.

"I only want to be here, in this house, if it's what you want, Dean," I say, my voice muffled against his shirt. "Yes, this is my family's home. And yes, it's been in the Cunningham lineage for generations. But I would never force you into this if you weren't ready . . ." My voice trails off, tears catching at the edges of my words.

"I could never stand by and watch your family home be auctioned off, Hadley. You know that. I'd never let that happen to you. I see how important this place is to you—and that matters to me. It's my job to make you happy," he says softly, lifting my chin so that our eyes meet. "And that's what I'm going to do. Even if that means renovating this cobweb-ridden Halloween house." His lips curl into a playful smile.

"Shut up!" I say, playfully pushing him away.

"Seriously, who knows? Maybe this will turn out to be the best investment we've ever made. We'll give it our best shot."

"Thank you," I whisper, before slowly pulling away from his embrace.

Somewhere deep down, I know Dean would rather be unpacking our things in a brand-new home at the end of a cul-de-sac on the coast, near his parents, where our future children could grow up riding bikes and having sleepovers with the neighborhood kids. But instead, he's here, trying to be happy, and I'm grateful for that.

It aches knowing that no matter which decision we make, one of us will always be closing the door on a dream. Marriage really is a compromise—something the two of us know all too well.

"Well, should we head out? It's getting late. The movers seem about finished. We can get in early tomorrow morning and start unpacking."

"What? You want to leave? I'm staying," I insist, my eyes locking on his.

"Staying? Here?"

"Duh. Did you think we weren't going to spend the very first night in our brand-new home? I've been waiting for this night for years! I'm not leaving. You'll have to bury me here at this rate."

Dean crosses his arms over his chest, and I follow his gaze around the room, focusing on the walls, where cornflower-blue wallpaper peels in long, brittle curls, exposing the bare bones of wooden lath and crumbling plaster.

"Don't you want to, I don't know, clean up first? It's not what I'd call livable, is it?"

"Well, of course it needs some TLC, Dean. It hasn't been lived in for years.

Not since Grandma passed away. It'll be good as new in no time. Can't you just see it?" I gaze around the room, unable to hide the optimism that shines through my smile.

"I don't disagree. But shouldn't we at least take a day to clean the place out before committing to an overnight? I got us a reservation at the inn just a few miles down the road. We can come back refreshed and ready to work first thing in the morning."

"You can go. But I'm staying."

I don't blame him for reacting to my petulance with an eye roll. But I've waited long enough to make this place my home, and Dean knows that. If he wants to stay at the inn tonight, so be it. But I need him to understand that I am staying right here—where I belong—with or without him.

Without another word, I turn away and begin to explore the rest of the dining room, taking in the details of the pinstriped wallpaper with the tiny blue birds that transports me back to my childhood. So many meals were shared with my family in this very room. The antique brass mirror that once hung above Grandma's buffet now sits propped against the wall. I swipe my hand across its surface, leaving four long streaks in the dust. I stare down at my fingertips, unable to fathom how time can change things so drastically. How years can take people out of one's life and bring others into it in the blink of an eye. A familiar feeling of grief rises in my chest, but I stomach it down, wiping my hand clean on my jeans.

"Fine," Dean says in a strained voice. "We'll stay. If that's what you really want to do. We can stay."

I smile softly at him, nodding my approval.

"Pizza sound good for dinner?" he asks, pulling out his phone. "I've just got to cancel the reservations and then I can—"

*Crashhh!*

A violent clatter echoes from somewhere above. We both freeze, our eyes locking in wide-eyed alarm.

"Is that what you heard earlier?" Dean whispers.

"Yes," I say, my breath catching in my throat. "I think so."

He nods. For a moment neither of us moves, as if the house itself is holding its breath along with us.

"Must have been—"

Again the sound rips through the silence, like something heavy hitting the floor above us with finality. My heart lurches. A high-pitched yelp escapes my lips before I can stop it.

"Shhh," Dean hisses, holding a finger to his lips. His eyes flick toward the ceiling. "I'm going to go check it out. Stay here."

"Stay here? Are you serious?" I shoot back in a strained whisper. "Absolutely not! There's no way I'm waiting down here alone."

He doesn't answer. Instead, he tilts his head in the direction of the staircase, signaling for me to follow. I nod, heart pounding. Together, we creep up the staircase, tiptoeing one foot at a time as the old boards groan beneath us. The scent of Dean's woody cologne is only mildly comforting as I crouch behind him, inching forward while we switch on every light we pass.

Flashbacks flood my memory as we creep slowly by each room, peeking cautiously inside—Grandpa's, then Grandma's, Mom's old room, the playroom that was once filled to the brim with toys for my sister and me. But there's no sign of the source of the noise anywhere.

Suddenly this all feels a bit ridiculous. This is a safe place. A home that was once filled with love and laughter—and one that now holds more memories than can be put into words.

"Dean?" I say, no longer bothering to keep my voice low.

"Shhh!" he warns, his eyes darting around the hall.

"No, Dean. Seriously, this is silly. It was probably just something in one of the boxes. Look, there are things stacked all over the place in here. Something's bound to fall over. We can't let it get to us like this just because we're in an unfamiliar place."

"It happened twice, Hadley. Don't you think we should make sure there's nothing—er, no one—in here?" he asks, his voice still low and cautious.

"There's clearly no one here. The place has had a lockbox on it for months. We've had movers in and out all day. If someone were hiding in here, we would've noticed. It's just an old house—we'll have to get used to the sounds it makes." I take a deep breath, straightening my shoulders. "We can't give up on this place, Dean. Please . . ."

"All right." He lets out a deep sigh, his expression clouded with wary resignation. "Come on, let's order some dinner. I'm starving."

Clanging in the kitchen jolts me awake. My eyes snap open. Blurred impressions of ornate plasterwork and vintage crystal dance across my sight. I desperately rub the sleep from my eyes, fighting to reorient myself with my surroundings. Grandma's house. I'm just at Grandma's house. *Our* house.

Dean greets me with a cup of tea as I step into the kitchen.

"Good morning," he says, placing a kiss on my cheek. "Tea?"

I take the warm mug, grateful for the caffeine.

"I would have made coffee," he adds, "but I have no idea where the coffee is. Or the coffeemaker, for that matter."

I shake my head, a half-smile playing on my lips as I walk toward a stack of boxes by the back window. It only takes a second to find the one labeled *Coffeemaker.*

"Cheers to that." He laughs, raising his mug. "So, how was your long-anticipated first night in the new house? Get any sleep?"

"It was great," I say, though the twitch in my eyelid and the dull ache in my neck suggest otherwise.

"I've got to admit, I slept pretty well. You were right—I don't think this place will be so bad after all."

"See?" I take a slow sip from my mug. "Told ya."

"What's on your agenda for today?"

"Well, I want to get the kitchen unpacked, for starters, after we do some cleaning in here, of course. Then I have a meeting with a pool company at one. Then—"

"A pool company? In October?"

"Yeah? Why not?"

"I just didn't think the pool would be a top priority right now, that's all."

"I figured it's smart to have it inspected now so we know what we're dealing with by the time spring rolls around. It's bound to be an investment. It's been left sitting for so long. Might as well bite the bullet and get started on some maintenance. Don't you think?"

Dean brings a hand to his head, rubbing his temples the way he always does when he's mulling something over.

"Yeah, I suppose you're right. But you know how those pool companies are, always trying to sell you something. Couldn't we just clean it out ourselves?"

I laugh, nearly spitting tea across the room. "And what do we know about in-ground swimming pools, Dean?"

"Well, it's not rocket science, is it? There's nothing a good online video can't teach you these days."

"Let's just hear them out and go from there. If it's too outrageous, we'll move to Plan B. Fair?"

"Fair enough."

Satisfied, I begin pulling kitchen utensils from a small box and sliding them into a ceramic vase. Dean watches with narrowed eyes, his mouth shifting from side to side as if he's working out what he wants to say next. I wait with bated breath, busying my hands until, just as I predicted, he inhales, slow and measured.

"Hey, by the way, I hate to have to tell you this, sweetheart, but Ray called me this morning. It was completely unexpected. He's actually the reason I'm up so early. Anyway, I have to go into the office today. Just for a while. It won't take long. We're on the cusp of sealing the deal with a big client. I'm so sorry."

I falter under the weight of his words, allowing only a fraction of a second for my knees to buckle beneath the crushing blow he just landed. But he's watching me, waiting for my reaction. Waiting for me to make a move. This is how it always goes with us—highs, then lows. Give, then take. Truths, then lies. He can't honestly think I still buy into his tricks at this stage in the game. But I guess old habits are tough to break.

I raise an eyebrow at him over my mug. "Work on a Saturday?"

"I told him we were moving into the new house this weekend, too. The man has no respect for personal boundaries. But if we want to be able to afford this place . . ." He pauses, holding my gaze, his green eyes unnaturally cold. "Then I guess I better not piss him off."

"Wouldn't want that, would we?"

Dean huffs a laugh before dumping the last of his tea in the sink. "I'll be home later to help with the house. Promise. Let me know how things go with the pool guy."

Minutes later, the front door creaks shut, and the sound of gravel crunching under tires echoes through the open windows. I watch as his taillights disappear into the fog, the old rope swing swaying gently in his wake. Just because Dean won't be participating today doesn't mean I won't make the most of it.

Sweat beads form across my brow as I finish unpacking the last of the cardboard boxes labeled *Kitchen*. For the first time all day, I allow myself time for a short break, slumping into a chair at the dining room table. I survey the stacks of boxes scattered around the room, the random objects strewn across the table that have yet to find their permanent home. This is going to be a much bigger endeavor than I'd imagined. But it will all be worth it.

Clearing a space in front of me, I slide over a small plastic tote labeled *Photos* and lift the lid. The album on top is a pale-green cloth-lined photo album trimmed in off-white lace. Inside are pictures I've seen many times before. Grandma in her prime, cooking, posing, dancing. Mom and her siblings, all in this very house. It's not until the last page that I find the single photo of Grandpa, apparently the only one Grandma kept after his death.

I stare at it, taking in the background—the large oak tree, the mahogany railing, the gray stone exterior of the home he lived and died in. My fingers trace over the clear plastic as I study his masculine form, the sun-kissed wrinkles etched across his forehead and at the corners of his eyes, his fixed and haunting stare. I picture Grandma standing there in the kitchen, just feet away, her words still fresh. *"A leopard doesn't change his spots, you see. Become a cheater, die a cheater."*

Once again, a sudden crash from above rips me from my thoughts. I slam the album shut and spring to my feet. Dean needs to know about this. I snatch my phone from the table and dial his number. I back slowly against the wall, my eyes darting between the doorway and the staircase as the line connects.

"Yeah? Hello?" Dean's voice comes across the other line exasperated and strained.

"Dean?" I whisper, keeping my voice low.

"What?" he snaps.

Clearly I've interrupted something. Instantly, heated rage twists in my stomach, threatening to boil over as I recall this morning's conversation. But like before, I ball it up, swallow it down, and follow his lead.

"I know you're busy at work, but I heard that noise again—from upstairs. It sounds like something's up there. . . . What do I do?"

"Ahh, Hadley," he says, his tone condescending, like a parent gearing up for a lecture. "It's probably nothing. You said it yourself: a box probably just fell over. Or maybe it's the house settling. A quirk we'll have to get used to. That house is very old, remember?" A muffled voice trills in the background. "I need to go. Just keep doing what you're doing, and I'll be there later, okay? Bye."

The line goes dead.

"Bye," I mutter to no one but myself.

Grandma wasn't always right, but she was right about one thing: A leopard doesn't change his spots, especially if that leopard has been lying and cheating his way through seven years of marriage.

But there's no time to dwell as a thunderous clunk of the door knocker turns my attention to the foyer.

Normally, someone showing up half an hour early for an appointment would feel like an intrusion. But with the noises coming from upstairs still echoing in my mind, the thought of a friendly face sends me hurrying to open the door.

"Good afternoon, ma'am," says a tall man standing on the threshold, smiling. He's wearing a red-collared shirt embroidered with white cursive lettering and a sun-faded baseball cap. "Donnie, from Duskwood Pools and Spas. Here for a pool inspection," he adds, his words coming out more like a question than a statement.

"Yes, hi. I'm Hadley. Nice to meet you. The pool is just around this way."

Donnie tucks a clipboard under one arm and reaches out to shake my hand. "Nice to meet you. Lead the way."

We exit the house and navigate our way around to the rear of the property. Overgrown grass thick with weeds makes it difficult to see where I'm stepping, causing me to stumble.

"You okay? Watch your step there."

"I'm fine," I say, the heat of embarrassment burning in my cheeks. "Sorry, it's a bit of a mess back here. We just moved in. It'll be a bit of a process trying to get this place back up and running."

"Ah, don't apologize. I've seen it all. Trust me."

I huff a laugh. "Well, here it is. What do you think?"

We stand facing the ominous pit. Trash litters the ground around the crumbling concrete deck. Heaps of fallen leaves and rainwater sit stagnant atop what must have once been a cover, the material now shredded beyond recognition. A putrid stench emanates from the maw—more swamp than a backyard oasis. I'm quickly reminded of why I need this pool taken care of. Grandma would be outraged to see it like this. I owe it to her to see that her home is restored to its former glory. Something buzzes around my head, catching me off guard. I swat the air, grimacing.

"Well, I can see why you called. Looks like this thing hasn't seen the light of day in years."

"No, it hasn't been used since my grandmother lived here. The place has been empty ever since."

"Your grandmother's house, huh? That makes sense. I couldn't believe it when I heard someone actually bought this place—no offense. Just looks like it needs tons of work. I pass it all the time on my commute."

I nod, pressing my lips together. "'A lot of work' would be an understatement. But we're hoping it'll be worth it."

"Of course. So, about this pool . . ." Donnie glances down at his clipboard. "I'll need to remove what's left of the cover. See what's lurking underneath.

Then we'll go from there. Sound okay? It's probably going to fall apart—lots of dry rot. Not like you'll be reusing it anyway, I'm sure."

"Of course. Whatever you need to do. Should I wait out here, or . . .?"

"No need. I'll let you know what I find."

Instantly, I regret not waiting outside with Donnie. I linger by the front of the house for a while, pulling weeds and picking up fallen tree branches. I'd hoped Dean would have been home by now, but clearly he's having more fun elsewhere. I stare up at the house, *my* house. Memories flood my mind as I picture Grandma drawing the curtains, standing at the window before tucking us in for bed. What would she think of all this? Of me and Dean? Surely she'd love the idea of me living here, raising a family here. But I wonder what she'd think of Dean. Would she be ashamed of me for not leaving?

"Ma'am?"

Donnie's sudden reappearance startles me. I turn to see him peeking around the corner of the house, one hand raised toward me.

"Sorry, didn't mean to scare you. I'm going to need to bring the truck around to the back. That pool is an absolute sludge pit. I won't be able to give an accurate assessment until I pump some of it out. Of course, it's your call."

"Yeah, sure. Go ahead," I tell him, waving him on. "Whatever you need."

"Great, I'll get started."

A loud rumbling noise soon fills the backyard, rattling the windowpanes as the pump's engine whirs to life.

My thoughts travel to Dean. What will he think of all this? Though, he has no room to complain when he hasn't bothered to be here all day. Still, I pull out my phone and type out a text:

> They're pumping sludge out of the pool. Said it shouldn't take long. Are you coming home soon?

I hit send just as a large drop of rain splatters across my screen. The sky above has turned a hazy shade of gray, and rumbles of thunder roll in the distance. Will Donnie keep working if the storm hits? I start around back to check on his progress when my phone pings in my hand. Finally, a message from Dean:

> On my way.

I scoff at his sparse reply, don't bother typing one of my own, and shove my phone into my pocket.

"Everything okay?" I shout to Donnie over the roar of the pump's motor.

It's clear that he doesn't hear me—he doesn't even look up from his work. I inch toward the edge of the concrete slab, arms crossed over my chest, squinting as the rain starts to fall more steadily. Swamp-green sludge gushes from the end of the hose, churning into a foul-smelling stream that flows through the overgrown thicket.

Finally, the noise comes to an abrupt halt. Once again, the low grumbling of thunder reaches my ears as they adjust to the silence. I watch as Donnie drops the hose, his eyes still fixed on the bottom of the pool.

"Everything all right?" I ask.

"Yeah, everything's fine. Just not sure what to make of this spot here." He points to the area closest to the house. "There's a bunch of concrete blocks all piled up. Hard to tell what it's supposed to be without getting down in there."

"Well, the pool's very old. I can't even remember the last time it was used. There's been tons of vandalism over the years while the place sat empty, so . . . it's hard to say what you might find down there."

"Let me get my waders on and I'll climb on in."

The sound of a car door slamming pulls our attention toward the driveway. Dean appears, juggling his briefcase and coffee mug as he approaches, a scowl etched into his face as he takes in the scene.

"Hi there," Dean says, extending a hand toward Donnie.

"Hello, sir," Donnie replies. "I was just telling your wife I need to get down in there and move some of this junk out so I can inspect the bottom. Shouldn't be much longer."

"Oh please, don't bother. Not in this storm." Dean glances towards the sky, the heavy clouds overhead a clear sign that the rain has no intention of letting up anytime soon. "You could always come back when there's nicer weather. Besides, we'll want to head inside ourselves."

"Ah, I don't mind. What's a little rain?" Donnie shrugs. "I've already got my equipment out, anyway."

Dean glances at me for support, though I'm not completely convinced.

"What? He's the one who has to climb in there. If he's fine with it . . ." I offer with a shrug.

Dean rolls his eyes, lifts his mug in defeat. "Be my guest."

"You don't have to stay out here," I say, noting the sour expression on his face.

"I'm fine." He forces a tight smile, glancing briefly toward the house.

Somehow, I sense his change of tune has more to do with being afraid to be in the house alone than his desire to watch the pool guy work—and who could blame him? But I choose to keep quiet, taking the high road yet again.

Soon, Donnie is wading around in waist-high rubber boots, slinging aluminum cans, bike tires, and tree limbs out of the pit. The rain continues to dump, though the thunder seems to have passed. My clothes are soaked through to my skin, but I won't be the first to call it quits and go inside—I'll leave that up to Dean, and so far, he's holding strong.

"Don't we at least have an umbrella or something?"

"Yeah, of course. It's just inside. You know, in one of those boxes."

Dean sets his jaw. "Which one?"

"Your guess is as good as mine. Why don't you go look? I'll wait out here with Donnie."

I watch a flicker of irritation flash behind his eyes.

"Hey, uh, I think . . . I think you all need to call the police," Donnie says, his voice raised an octave as he scrambles out of the concrete pit.

"Is everything all right?" Dean asks as he reaches out a hand to Donnie, helping to pull him up and out.

"There's something down there."

The tremble in his voice sends goosebumps trailing down my arms as I swallow a lump in my throat.

"Something like what?" Dean casts his gaze from me to Donnie, then down into the pool.

"There—under the cinder block. It's a-a skeleton."

His words set my heart racing as I scramble for a logical explanation. Surely, it's just the unfortunate remains of some animal that managed to get itself trapped under the cover? It couldn't be an actual human . . . could it?

"Dean?" I whisper, the words catching in my throat.

"Stay here," he warns, a protective edge in his voice.

I watch helplessly as he creeps toward the edge, he and Donnie mirroring each other's movements—both looking equally unsure of what to do next.

"I'm calling the police," I say, already dialing.

"Good idea," Donnie mutters, shaking his head. "I've seen a lot of things come out of the bottom of these pools, but never a dead body. No, sir—this is one for the books."

The line rings once before an urgent voice answers.

"911. What is the nature and location of your emergency?"

"Um, hi. My name is Hadley Cunningham. I'm calling from 2458 Duskwood Hollow Lane. We're having an old in-ground pool professionally drained, and the man doing the work believes he's found a body at the bottom."

I can hardly believe the words as they leave my mouth—can hardly imagine how they must sound on the other end of the line.

"Okay, ma'am, I'm dispatching the proper authorities right now."

I close my eyes, take a deep breath, suddenly feeling more panicked than I expected.

"Thank you. Just—hurry. Please."

"The police are on their way, ma'am. Please do not disturb the remains. It's important to preserve the scene until authorities arrive."

"I understand."

The three of us stand outside—waterlogged and shaken—as the echo of sirens rings in the distance. It isn't long before the backyard transforms into a full-scale crime scene: forensics officers snapping photos, coroners wheeling a gurney from the back of a white van, and uniformed officers making their rounds and taking statements. I wince as the sharp bark of a German shepherd cuts through the chaos.

"Is this your house?" an officer asks, approaching Dean and me.

"It is. Dean Freeman." Dean extends a hand. "And this is my wife, Hadley Cunningham."

"Cunningham. You related to the Cunninghams who used to live here? This place has a reputation, you know."

I let out a short, bitter laugh. "Yes, that's right. My family's owned this house for generations. Not sure what reputation you mean, though."

"Ah, nothing serious. Kid stuff, mostly. Stories about the place being haunted. You know how it is with these old places sitting empty. We've had a lot of reports here over the years—break-ins, vandalism, parties—you name it. Anyway, looks like that's what happened here, or at least, that's what we're thinking for now. Someone got too rowdy, snuck under the pool cover for a little fun, got stuck. But of course, we'll need to do a full investigation."

"Of course," Dean says, his tone serious, his shoulders tense. "Is it safe to, you know, stay here, given the circumstances, Officer?"

"Oh, I don't see why not. This guy's been here a long time. I can't see any immediate threat to you or your wife right now. That said, I understand if you want to take some time away. It's a lot to process."

"Mhm. Well, we'll mull it over," Dean says, his eyes dropping to me.

"Looks like we're wrapping up here. We've collected all we need for now, but please hold off on any further work on the pool area until we give the all-clear. If anything else turns up in the meantime—fragments, objects that might be of interest—don't touch them. Call us right away." He reaches into his pocket and pulls out a business card before handing it to Dean. "We'll be in touch."

With that, the officer turns to leave, followed, eventually, by the rest of the brigade, until just Donnie, Dean, and I are left standing on the muddied lawn.

"Well, that's about all the excitement I can handle for one day," Donnie says, wiping his palms across his pants. "I can come back to finish the job, if you're still interested. Just give us a call."

"Thank you, sir," Dean calls after Donnie, who hops into his truck and disappears quickly down the driveway.

"Come on," Dean says, turning toward his own parked car.

"Where are you going?" I ask, crossing my arms against my damp skin.

"Anywhere but here. It's not too late to check in at the hotel down the street. A hot shower and a warm meal sound heavenly right about now. We can pick up some dry clothes on the way."

"Whoa, what are you talking about? Let's go inside."

He ignores me, continuing toward the driveway.

"Dean? Dean! Stop!" I grab his arm just as he reaches for the car door handle.

"Hadley, we cannot stay here. Not tonight, at least. It's nearly dark, and we've just uncovered a dead body in our backyard. This place is filthy. Old. Creepy. And if I'm being honest—" His eyes flick up to the gable, where the tallest singular window looms dark overhead. "Those noises coming from up there, they aren't normal, Hadley. I think we need to take the night to regroup. We can come back in the morning with fresh minds."

The resolve on his face tells me there's little I can do to convince him. I know this face well; I've attempted to reason with it many times before, to no avail.

"All right, all right. You win. But can I at least change out of these wet clothes before we go? There really isn't any reason we can't go in and change. Seriously, Dean. Don't overreact."

"Overreact? Hadley, they just found a *dead person* out here. How aren't you upset about that?"

"I am upset about it, Dean! This is my grandmother's home. Those vandals have taken enough of this place from our family. It's time we take it back. They don't deserve to trash this place any longer. We're here now."

I watch as his hardened expression cracks, his face softening.

"Okay, fine. Long enough to change clothes. But then we're out of here for the night. Deal?"

I nod, solemn but understanding.

The atmosphere in the house is hazy with a familiar sort of tension as we enter the dining room. So many emotions flood through me as I question which one to give in to first. This is the one place I feel so compelled to be, the one place I feel so connected to. And here I am, finally, after so many years of saving, fighting a broken system, and convincing a partner whose dreams don't align. But this is not at all how I envisioned it.

"Let's go, then. I want to get out of here. This place is giving me the creeps."

I turn to face Dean, whose gaze is fixed out the window.

"What are you looking at?"

"Nothing. Just, what if they come back?"

"Who?"

"I don't know . . . the people who liked to come and hang out here while this place was vacant? The people responsible for . . . for that man in the pool." His voice trails off.

"Come here," I say, pulling out a chair at the dining room table.

I take a seat myself, waiting for him to join me.

"What are you doing? You said we would change, then leave. I'm not—"

"Just sit. Please."

"I'm going, Hadley. Whatever this is, it can wait until we get to the hotel." He moves toward the doorway.

"How was work today, Dean? Did you score that *big client*?"

He freezes mid-step. "Hadley—"

"Sit. I want to show you something. Then we can go."

He hesitates, weighing his options. Slowly he makes his way back to the table, lowering himself into a chair beside me.

"Let's get on with it," he huffs.

"Have I ever shown you my grandma's photo album?" I ask, setting the clothbound book down in front of him.

"I-I don't think so. But why do we need to do this—"

"Because. Open it."

He rolls his lips between his teeth in contemplation. Slowly, he opens the album to the first page, though his eyes stay fixed on mine. I raise my brows and gesture toward the page, signaling for him to take a look. Cautiously, he averts his gaze, taking in the old photographs, and I begin to annotate each one for him, one by one, ignoring his sighs and grunts, subtle hints of restlessness.

"Grandma loved hard, Dean. That was who she was. It was how she made a name for herself in this community. People loved her, and she cared for everyone she met. Genuinely cared. That's why this place—this house—matters so much to me, Dean. It stands for love and the quiet everyday sacrifices it takes to keep a family together."

I flip another page, fully invested, my eyes fixed on his. Dean's confusion is growing, palpable now, etched in the furrow of his brow and the stiffness in his shoulders.

"You see, Dean, what I'm trying to say is that none of this would have been possible if it weren't for Grandma. She's the one who single-handedly kept our family together, kept us happy. Even when everything felt too far gone to be fixed, she always found a way. She was resourceful. Quietly so. And I like to think she passed that on."

Dean sits back in his chair, pulling away. "What are you getting at, Hadley?" He tries to sound stern, but I catch the tremble in his voice.

I turn the page for the final time, revealing the photo of Grandpa. Slowly, my gaze trails away from Dean's until I'm locked on to the eyes of my late grandfather.

"Your grandfather?" Dean asks, tapping his fingers lightly on the table.

"That's him."

"You don't talk about him much."

"That's because we don't speak about him in our family, Dean. There's a good reason for that."

I watch his Adam's apple bob as he swallows hard, the lump rising in his throat.

"Are—are you going to tell me why?"

"Because he tore the family apart. Tried to, at least. Broke Grandma's heart."

Silence washes over us. I imagine Dean connecting the dots, replaying in his mind the long, hard day of *work* he's had.

"I'm sorry," he whispers, his voice sheepish.

"So was Grandpa. At least, that was what I heard. Grandma used to love telling me the story. It was our little secret."

"What? Hadley . . . that's messed up. You were just a little girl."

"Maybe. But maybe she thought I'd find the information useful one day."

Dean recoils, mouth gaping open in shock.

"Do you want to know what happened to my grandfather, Dean?"

He clears his throat, pressing so hard against the back of his chair I half expect him to topple backward.

"You said he was killed in a hunting accident."

A sly smile flickers across my lips as I recall the story that I told my husband and so many others—the one Grandma and I rehearsed over and over.

"Hadley?"

Another crash echoes from above, making Dean jump straight up from his chair.

"Sit down." I smirk.

"What the heck is that, Hadley?"

"I don't know. But it hasn't hurt us yet, has it?"

"Do you want to tell me what the hell is happening here? I agreed to come in for a minute! That minute is over—I'm leaving!"

"Sit, Dean. We aren't finished."

We lock eyes across the dusty old table. I hold my expression steady, wearing my calm like a shield. Dean trembles behind a cloak of nerves. His constant glances out the window into the darkness—and toward his phone—reveal everything I need to know.

"Fine. I'll stay. But I'm not leaving this spot. We can talk right here."

I sigh. "You want to know what really happened to my lying, cheating grandfather, Dean? The man who couldn't be bothered to come home to my devoted, loyal grandmother while she raised their children and kept the household running in his absence?"

He says nothing, just stands there, mouth agape.

"Why don't you ask the man at the bottom of that pool, Dean? He ought to know what happens to men like that."

I stand, unblinking, giving him time to digest my words—to understand the meaning behind them.

"Understand this, Dean. Grandma taught me more about life and love, about living and making my way in this world, than anyone else ever has. The most important thing she ever taught me—*never let anyone walk all over you, honey. Know your worth.*"

Dean makes no moves to leave. He just stands there, staring like a blaring idiot. I cringe inwardly at the coward I married.

"If you thought I was going to stand by and allow you and your mistress to carry on like that, well . . . you were right. Because now, Dean, dear, I have this house. I have everything I've ever wanted. A loving husband," I say, my voice saccharine sweet. "My family secrets, safe and sound. And Grandma, here to keep an eye on me."

I glance upward.

The bangs and clatter from above come at the most opportune time, and Dean ducks his head, cowering like a child who's just seen a ghost.

"What's the matter, Dean? Grandma's only here to help."

"What . . . What the—"

"Let me make myself clear. I am your wife. This is our family home. This is where we agreed to spend eternity raising our family—together. As long as we don't have any further *issues*, then I don't foresee Grandma needing to be much help. Have we made ourselves clear?"

A series of bangs from above drives my point home. I remain stone-faced.

"You're mad! You're absolutely—"

"Ah ah ah. Is that any way to speak to your wife, Dean? After your long day at the *office*?"

Time stands still as we face off, staring each other down, each waiting for the other to break. We remain in silence, the rapid rise and fall of his chest the only sign of the storm raging inside him.

"Shall I tell Grandma to pack it in for the night?"

Dean opens his mouth, but no words come. Instead, he raises his hands in a quiet truce and slowly backs toward the staircase.

I slide back into my chair, running my fingers through my damp hair. The patter of rain hitting against the windows carries me back to years ago, sitting in this very room, the smell of roasted chicken hanging in the air, and Grandma's magic words ringing in my ears like it was yesterday.

*"Don't mind that noise, dear. It's only the pigeons in the attic making a ruckus."*

*"Why don't you get rid of them, Grandma?"*

*"Get rid of them? Oh, honey, I don't want to get rid of them. I feed them. Keeps them coming around. You never know when a few hundred hungry pigeons in the attic might come in handy."*

The path to 2458 Duskwood Hollow is lined with moss-covered flagstones, crumbled by lies, and worn thin by deceit. Secrets twist their way up the magnificent stone walls, growing thicker with each generation. A patient executioner, the house shapes those who enter into what they were always meant to become.

Welcome home.

# About the Author

**Cora Laine** enjoys writing psychological thrillers with a touch of romance. She has a deep interest in the shadows people hide behind and is drawn to stories that blur the lines between truth and deception, love and obsession. Her debut novel, *A Familiar Lullaby*, is set to release soon, and her novella, *Unexpected Destinations*, is available in paperback and e-book from Attic Books. When not writing, Cora can usually be found scrolling bookstagram, sipping hot tea, or chasing chickens in the back yard. She's a firm believer in plot twists, quiet mornings spent at home, and the kind of characters that linger long after the last page.

You can find Cora on Instagram, Facebook, TikTok & Bluesky at:
@coralaineauthor

To learn more about Cora, visit her website at:
www.coralaineauthor.com

# Contributors' Library

Please also look for these titles, which were authored by, published by, or feature the authors in this anthology.

*A Beautiful Lily*
Caroline Baccene

*Breathing in the Fog*
Caroline Baccene

*The Charred Grape*
Caroline Baccene

*A Familiar Lullaby*
Cora Laine

*Unexpected Destinations*
Cora Laine

*Emerge 23*
includes "Nagaina"
Jesse Ramon Ferreras

# About the Editor

**Courtney Umphress** has been a copyeditor and proofreader for over ten years. She has edited for authors all over the world, including several *USA Today* best-selling authors. Although her portfolio includes everything from thrillers to horror to self-help books, she specializes in fantasy and romance.

Courtney has worked for various companies, such as EdiPro, Graphic World, and Skye High Publishing, but she has a soft spot for empowering independent and aspiring authors to fulfill their dreams. Courtney lives in the Panhandle of Texas with her husband, three kids, and two calico cats. You can find her in a coffee shop or a library almost any day of the week, but she also loves traveling, hiking, and playing baseball with her kids.

You can find Courtney on:
Instagram @courtneyumphress_editor
Facebook @editorcourtneyumphress

And visit her website at:
www.courtneyumphress.com

# Acknowledgments

Of all the people to thank for the creation of this anthology, I must start with the seventeen talented authors who contributed so much time, attention, and creative energy into their stories. Not only would this anthology not exist without them, but they also made the experience of compiling and editing an entire collection of stories fun and easy.

I am deeply grateful to Nicole Frail, who offered me the opportunity to bring my vision to life. I'm so proud to have worked for Nicole Frail Books and to continue building up a community of publishing professionals.

Thank you to Sydney Ahrberg, who read all the submissions to this anthology and whose valuable insights and opinions helped me select the best ones to include.

Finally, I have to thank my husband and my three kids. They had the utmost patience with me as I read these stories again and again and again. This book exists because of their love and support, and I hope they know just how much they inspire me every day.

# &You

## Another Chance to Get It Right: A New Year's Eve Anthology

9 Stories

## As the Snow Drifts A Cozy Winter Anthology

9 Stories

## Craving You A Spicy Valentine's Day Anthology

12 Stories

# Anthologies

**Recipes for Romance
A Sweet Valentine's Day
Anthology**

19 Stories

**Just One
A Summer Romance
Anthology**

12 Stories

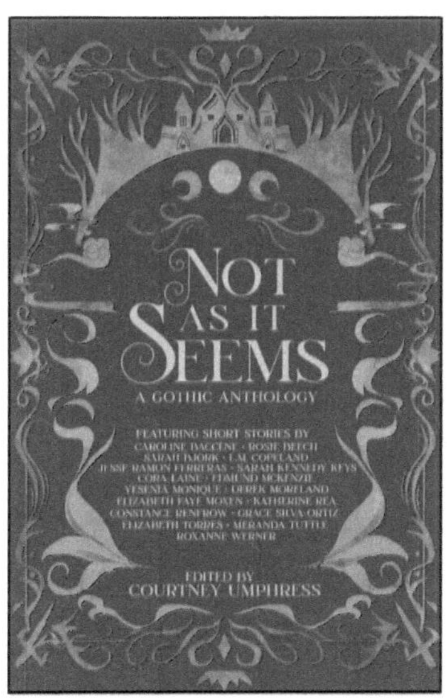

**Not As It Seems
A Gothic Anthology**

17 Stories

And You Press, or &You Press,
is an imprint of Nicole Frail Books, LLC,
an independent ("indie") publishing
company located in Avoca, Pennsylvania.

And You Press was created to release the anthologies built from the short story contests that launched NFB in the fall of 2024. The name reflects the requirement that every book published under this imprint will have multiple collaborators so that every title released brings multiple voices to each project.

These titles may be additional anthologies, novels with two or more authors, author and illustrator teams, or something else entirely. As long as the work has multiple creators who will be credited equally for the work they've put into it or will put into it, it may be appropriate for this imprint.

To learn more about submitting a query to And You Press, visit www.andyoupress.com.

**Readers!**
Join the NFB Street Team for exclusive first reads and swag from And You Press!
www.nicolefrailbooks.com/street

www.ingramcontent.com/pod-product-compliance
Lightning Source LLC
Chambersburg PA
CBHW021040310726
48969CB00006B/1743